KU-514-812

Penguin Books

Whisky Galore

Compton Mackenzie was born in West Hartlepool in
1883, and educated at St Paul's School and Magdalen
College, Oxford. During the First World War he rose
to the rank of Captain and was made Director of the
Aegean Intelligence Service. He wrote more than
ninety books – novels, history and biography, essays
and criticism, children's stories and verse – and
earned the reputation of being one of the outstanding
broadcasters of his time. Two of Mackenzie's
particular interests were gramophones and Siamese
cats – he founded and edited the magazine *The
Gramophone*, and was President of the Siamese Cat
Club. He lived for many years on the Island of Barra
in the Outer Hebrides, and later made his home in
Edinburgh. He was knighted in 1952. Compton
Mackenzie died in 1972.

Compton Mackenzie

Whisky Galore

Penguin Books

In association with Chatto & Windus

PENGUIN BOOKS

Published by the Penguin Group
Penguin Books Ltd, 27 Wrights Lane, London W8 5TZ, England
Penguin Putnam Inc., 375 Hudson Street, New York, New York 10014, USA
Penguin Books Australia Ltd, Ringwood, Victoria, Australia
Penguin Books Canada Ltd, 10 Alcorn Avenue, Toronto, Ontario, Canada M4V 3B2
Penguin Books (NZ) Ltd, Private Bag 102902, NSMC, Auckland, New Zealand

Penguin Books Ltd, Registered Offices: Harmondsworth, Middlesex, England

First published 1947
Published in Penguin Books 1957
5

Copyright 1947 by Compton Mackenzie
All rights reserved

Printed in England by Clays Ltd, St Ives plc

*To all my dear friends in Barra in grateful memory
of much kindness and much laughter through
many happy years*

CONTENTS

AUTHOR'S NOTE

By a strange coincidence the s.s. *Cabinet Minister* was wrecked off Little Todday two years after the s.s. *Politician* with a similar cargo was wrecked off Eriskay; but the coincidence stops there, for the rest is pure fiction.

Chapter 1

THE SERGEANT-MAJOR'S RETURN

FROM the bridge of the *Island Queen*, which three times a week made the voyage between Obaig and the outer islands of the Hebrides, Captain Donald MacKechnie gazed across a smooth expanse of grey sea to where the rugged outline of Great Todday stood out dark against a mass of deepening cloud in which a dull red gash showed that the sun was setting behind it. Captain MacKechnie muttered an order in Gaelic to the steersman, and the mailboat changed her course to round the south-west point of the island that was her next port of call. Presently the low green land and white beaches of Little Todday appeared west of the larger island and the mailboat made a sweep to enter the Coolish, the strait of water two miles wide which separated the two Toddays from each other.

It was a Saturday afternoon toward the end of February in the year 1943, and this was the first time for a week that the mailboat had been able to call at Snorvig, the little harbour in Great Todday which served the two islands.

'And there's some tirty weather coming,' Captain MacKechnie piped in that high-pitched voice of his, with a baleful glance from his bright eyes at the heavy sky louring over the Atlantic Ocean beyond Little Todday.

At this moment the trim soldierly figure of Sergeant-major Alfred Ernest Odd appeared in the doorway of the bridge-house.

'Room in here for a little one?' he asked, with a grin of welcome.

'Well, well,' the skipper exclaimed in astonishment, 'if it isn't Sarchant Odd! Man, where have you been all these months? And where have you been since we left Obaig this morning?'

'I was having a jolly good lay down. What a journey!

9

Stood up in the corridor all the way from Devonshire the day before yesterday. Stood up in the corridor all the way from Euston up to Glasgow the night before last. Stood up in the corridor for the first half of the journey to Fort Augustus where I had to see Colonel Lindsay-Wolseley. He very kindly got me to Obaig in time for the boat and which meant leaving Tummie at three o'clock this morning in the Colonel's car, and as soon as ever I got on board the dear old *Island Queen* I got the steward to find me a bunk and I slept right through the day.'

'You've had a long churney right enough, Sarchant. Teffonshire? That's a place I neffer was in. It's a crate place for cream, I believe.'

'It may have been a great place for cream before this war, but we didn't see much cream where I've been since I got back from Africa,' said the Sergeant-major. 'No, give me good old Scotland before Devonshire any day of the week – except perhaps Sunday,' he added quickly.

'Ah, but the Sabbath's not what it was,' Captain Mac-Kechnie insisted firmly. 'When I was a poy, man, it *wass* a tay. My word, what a tay, too, what a tay! I remember my mother once sat down on the cat, because you'll understand the plinds were pulled down in our house every Sabbath and she didn't chust see where she was sitting. The cat let out a great *sgiamh* and I let out a huge laugh, and did my father take the skin off me next day? Man, I was sitting down on proken glass for a week afterwards. My father was Kilwhillie's head stalker.'

'What, Captain Hugh Cameron of Kilwhillie?'

'Not the present laird. His father. A fine figure of a man with a monster of a peard praking below his nose like a wave on the Skerryvore. Well, well, well, it's nice to see you again, Sarchant. You've been away from us a long while now.'

'Nearly eighteen months,' said the Sergeant-major in disgusted tones. 'But that's the way in the army. As soon as anybody's got a job that suits him and he suits it, shift him. I was getting along to rights as P.S.I. with Colonel Lindsay-Wolseley's...'

'What's P.S.I. at all?' the skipper interjected. 'Man, the alphabet's gone mad like the rest of the world since this war.'

'Permanent Sergeant Instructor with Colonel Lindsay-Wolseley's Home Guard battalion. Yes, I've been away eighteen months too long. However, the Colonel's got me back at last, and he very kindly gave me the week-end to come over and have a look at my young lady in Little Todday. I was reckoning to get married last autumn year, and then biff! Transferred to a special job in Devonshire, and that tore it. The old man kicked up at the idea of her going so far away, and Peggy thought she couldn't leave her dad, and so that was that for the moment.'

'It was pretty annoying for you, I believe.'

'Annoying? It was enough to drive a man off his rocker. But that wasn't the worst of it. Last April instead of getting married as I hoped, biff, again! And it's West Africa, with not enough embarkation leave to risk coming up to the Islands. Then I got back in January only to find myself down in Devonshire again. Did I create? Well, to cut a long rotten story short, I'm back at last, and I'm going to get married as soon as ever it can be managed.'

'You waited a fair time, Sarchant, before you thought about getting married at all,' Captain MacKechnie pointed out, with a shrewd smile. 'Very wise, too.'

'Very wise once upon a time,' the Sergeant-major agreed. 'But I was forty-five last month. And I can't afford to wait much longer. Here, I mustn't talk to the man at the wheel.' He had noticed that the skipper's eyes were turning away from the topic of marriage toward the Snorvig pier thronged as usual with the inhabitants of the two Toddays, though it was already on the edge of dusk. 'Joseph Macroon will probably come over himself for the mail as the weather's so calm.'

'Ay, it's calm enough now, but there's plenty tirty weather away out there in the west. It'll plow as hard as effer by morning.'

'So long for the present, Captain. I dare say I'll be seeing you up at the hotel before we cross over to Kiltod.'

'I don't believe I'll be going up to the hotel this evening at all,' the skipper replied, his usually bright eyes clouded and curiously remote.

'But Joseph will expect to have a crack with you, especially as you have had to miss two runs this week.'

'Ay, it's a pity right enough, but I want to be ketting along up to Nobost. Well, well, I'm glad to see you pack, Sarchant, in what used to be the land of the free before this plutty war.'

Sergeant-major Odd left the bridge and went below to the promenade deck, where he walked up and down the port side looking across to the dimunitive harbour of Kiltod and the small cluster of houses beyond, in one of which the girl he had hoped to marry so many months ago was waiting for him. Oh, well, he was back again now. Not like some of those poor chaps in Africar and Burmar and Indiar and what not who hadn't managed to get married all those months ago and didn't know when they would now.

'Good evening, Sergeant-major.'

He swung round to see the stocky form of the Snorvig bank agent.

'Hullo, Mr Thomson, you're looking well. I am glad to see you,' he declared, shaking Andrew Thomson's hand so fervidly that the bank agent's dark complexion grew darker with embarrassment. He was a man to whom words came with difficulty, and he had been walking behind Sergeant-major Odd twice up and down the length of the deck before he had managed to summon up the necessary resolution to break into speech with a greeting.

'You've been away quite a long while, Sergeant-major,' said the bank agent; but the Sergeant-major knew Andrew Thomson's manner and did not suppose that the scowl which accompanied this observation was meant to convey that it was a pity he had ever come back.

'Yes, but I'm glad to say Colonel Wolseley has got me back again at last.'

'Imphm? Is that so?'

'And how's G Company getting on? I suppose you're all as smart as guardsmen by now.'

The bank agent made a determined effort to smile at this pleasantry and in consequence his scowl became absolutely ferocious.

'Not quite yet,' he gulped. 'As a matter of fact, Captain Waggett has been having a lot of difficulty lately in getting the men together for drill. There were only two at the last parade – that is, there were only Captain Waggett and myself.'

The Sergeant-major clicked his tongue.

'Still, as long as they keep up their shooting ...' he began.

'They're not,' said the bank agent, who was also G Company's sergeant-major. 'The turn-out for shooting practice has been very poor all this month.'

'I expect they'll be more keen as the spring comes along.'

'It's not the weather,' Andrew Thomson observed gloomily. 'There's another reason.' And then to prevent his companion's asking what that was he added hastily, 'I took Mrs Thomson over to Edinburgh on Friday. She's to stay with Mrs Pringle – that's her mother – imphm ...' speech evaporated in a dusky blush.

'And you thought you'd have a little run around on your own, eh? Ah, well, I shall be married myself this spring if all goes according, so I mustn't talk.'

'I intended to return on Tuesday, Sergeant-major,' Andrew Thomson assured him gravely, 'but the weather held the mailboat up on Tuesday and again on Thursday.'

'A good thing I didn't arrange to come over earlier in the week,' said the Sergeant-major. 'I'd have gone bats hanging around at Obaig. Hullo, we're just getting in. I'll see you up at the hotel before I cross over to Kiltod.'

'I'll have to attend to the correspondence, Sergeant-major. There'll be three days' mail, and the head office will be wondering what's happened. I'm afraid you'll find it kind of dull up at the hotel just now.'

'*I* won't find it dull. I'm looking forward to seeing a lot of old friends and having a jolly good Jock and Doris, as you call it, to celebrate getting back to the two tightest little islands in the world.'

The bank agent smiled sardonically.

'They're not very tight just now, Sergeant-major,' he said, and went off quickly to find his bag.

Sergeant-major Odd puzzled for a moment over this remark, and then with a sudden thought that perhaps his beloved Peggy might have come over from Little Todday to welcome him on the pier he hurried off round to starboard. The pier was crowded with familiar figures, among them Peggy's father in his knitted red cap; but Peggy herself was not there.

'You're a proper mug, Fred,' he murmured to himself. 'As if the poor girl would want to see you for the first time after nearly eighteen months with everybody staring at her!'

A minute or two later he was hurrying down the gangplank to greet his future father-in-law.

The movements of the postmaster and leading merchant of Kiltod seemed less quick than he remembered them, and his grey moustache usually so trim was slightly ragged. If Sergeant-major Odd had not been so acutely conscious of the twenty years' difference between his own age and that of his prospective wife he would have said that Joseph Macroon had grown appreciably older during these last eighteen months. There was, too, in the way he shook hands with him a kind of absent-mindedness as if he was hardly aware of the Sergeant-major's presence. And as he wished him '*fàilte do' ndùthaich*' (welcome to the country), he was not looking at the returned wanderer but at Roderick MacRurie, the owner of the hotel, who was working his great bulk up the gang-plank in search of the purser.

'How's Roderick?' the Sergeant-major asked.

'Ach, he's not well at all at all, Sarchant. He's had a terrible time, poor soul.'

'I'm sorry to hear that. And how's ... how's everything on Little Todday?'

'Terrible. Just as bad there as here. Terrible.'

'Nothing wrong with Peggy?'

'What would be wrong with Peggy or Kate Anne?' their father demanded contemptuously. 'Smoking away, the pair of them, like two peats. It's a pity the Government doesn't run out of cigarettes.'

Joseph took a battered clay pipe out of his pocket, lit it with a noise like a rotary pump, drew two deep gurgling puffs at the closely packed twist, removed the pipe from his mouth, spat gloomily between his legs, and replaced the pipe in his pocket.

Several of Sergeant-major Odd's old acquaintances had been greeting him, and one of them, a man with a nose and a chin like a lobster's claw, said something to Joseph in Gaelic.

'I don't know, Airchie, but there's nothing to be seen of Captain MacKechnie, and if they'd brought it he'd have come ashore by now.'

'Ay, I believe he would,' agreed Archie MacRurie, generally known as the Biffer, a fisherman of prowess about fifty years old. 'Ay, he'd have been ashore by now right enough if it had been on board.'

'Look at Roderick now,' Joseph exclaimed. 'You can see it isn't there by the way the man's shoulders have died on him. Ah, *duine bochd*, it's me that's sorry for the poor soul. Ah well, Sarchant, we'll be getting down to the *Morning Star*,' he said, thrusting his hands into the pockets of his greatcoat.

'You'd better come up to the hotel and have a dram with me first while you're waiting for the mails to be sorted,' the Sergeant-major suggested.

His two companions looked at him quickly to see if he was laughing at them. Then, perceiving that the invitation had been given in earnest, their manners forbade them to tell him how futile it was lest he should suppose they had suspected him of a deliberate meanness in giving it. Joseph Macroon sighed deeply.

'What is the use of waiting for the mail? Just a lot of letters for nothing,' he declared. 'We'll be getting them Monday morning.'

Sergeant-major Odd was only too happy not to wait for the sorting of the mail. He had expected to be kept at least another hour or more away from the sight of his Peggy. As Joseph Macroon and he moved across the pier to the steps at the foot of which the *Morning Star* was moored, Roderick MacRurie came down the gang-plank.

'Any news, Roderick?' the postmaster of Little Todday asked.

'Not a single bottle. *A Chruitheir*, this is a terrible war, Iosaiph, right enough. Do you remember that Sunday night the day the war started? Nobody in the islands could mind such a storm of rain. Water? I never saw so much water come down Ben Sticla. My best cow was drowned like a kitten that night. It wass a sign, Iosaiph, it wass a sign right enough of what wass coming to us. Water! Chust nothing but water! My brother Simon said we would have to pay for it by going to war on the Sabbath. I didn't take any notice at the time because an elder has to talk like that, you'll understand. But he was right.'

'But what exactly has happened? How does water come into it?' the Sergeant-major asked.

'Because there hasn't been a trop of whisky in the two islands for twelve days,' Roderick MacRurie replied. 'And I was handing it out for a month before that like my own blood, we were that short.'

'And we'll have Lent on us in a fortnight next Wednesday,' said Joseph Macroon, who as a Catholic of Little Todday was not prepared to allow the Protestants of Great Todday a monopoly of religious emotion. 'Fancy the Government running out of whisky just before Lent. What a Government!'

'Do you think Winston Churchill knows they've run out of whisky?' Roderick asked.

'I don't believe he will,' Joseph replied.

'It's a pity he wouldn't be saying something about it on the wireless,' Roderick observed sagely, for he was a profound admirer of the Prime Minister's oratory. 'You never know what these Governments will be doing next. Before we know where we are there'll be no peer either. We're running terribly low.'

The passage of time since last he had visited Little Todday was brought home to the Sergeant-major by his first sight of Joseph's youngest son, Kenny, who was now a lanky stripling of sixteen in charge of his father's motorboat and always threatening when he was denied anything he wanted for the engine to be off to sea. This evening the *Morning Star* was on her best behaviour and chugged across the Coolish without stopping once. The water was as smooth as a tarnished silver plate and there was still a glimmer of twilight when they reached the tiny harbour on the top of the tide.

'Captain Waggett hasn't managed the perfect black-out at the end of a perfect day yet?' the Sergeant-major observed with a grin when he saw the light from Joseph Macroon's shop streaming across the road leading up from the harbour.

'Ach, they haven't drawn the curtains. Plenty time,' said the Chief Warden of Kiltod. 'Plenty time,' he murmured to himself remotely.

The Sergeant-major felt that he was indeed back in the islands when he heard those two words, and that of course gave him the keenest pleasure. All the same in view of what he hoped to settle about his own future during this precious week-end, he was chary of accepting the dictum too easily.

'Time flies, you know,' he reminded his host. Then in the lighted door of the post-office he saw tall and slim as ever his Peggy, and a moment later he was holding her hands and looking into her deep-blue slanting eyes.

Chapter 2

THE WAKE

===

THE gathering in the bar of the Snorvig Hotel on that February evening was so exceptionally gloomy an occasion for Great or Little Today and the host Roderick MacRurie was so unlike his usual expansive self that it is only fair to give a picture of the islands in happier times and by the kind permission of Mr Hector Hamish Mackay, the well-known topographer of the Hebrides, to quote what he says about the two islands in his book, *Faerie Lands Forlorn*:

And so after sailing for the whole of a fine summer's day along the magical coasts of Tìr nan Òg the gallant *Osprey* reached Snorvig, the picturesque little port of Great Today (Todaidh Mór) where we dropped anchor and soon afterwards went ashore to enjoy the hospitality of the Snorvig Hotel and the tales of 'mine host', Roderick MacRurie, the 'uncrowned king' of the island. After a lordly spread, of which a magnificent lobster was the *pièce de résistance*, we sat outside on a terrace of shingle to pore spellbound over a scene of natural beauty which is nowhere surpassed in all the wondrous West.

Down below we could hear the voices of children playing among the various merchandise lying all over the quay and pier until Iain Dubh, the piermaster, should find time to put it away in the store – sweet Gaelic voices that seemed to reach us like the 'horns of elfland faintly blowing'.

Mr MacRurie, with a grave shake of his impressive head, assured us that the Snorvig children were getting out of hand. Only last week two of them had ridden into the sea a motor-bicycle just arrived from the mainland for the schoolmaster at Bobanish on the other side of the island.

Soon, however, all discussion of modern youth was hushed by the splendour of the sunset beyond Little Today (Todaidh Beag) which was turning the mighty Atlantic to a sheet of molten gold. Kiltod, the diminutive port of Little

Todday, lies opposite Snorvig from which it is separated by a strait of water two miles wide. Little Todday is not so very much inferior in superficial area to its sister island and probably earned its qualifying adjective by the comparative lowness and flatness of the vivid green machair land framed by long white sandy beaches, which contrasts with the more rugged aspect of Great Todday. Here the soil is peaty and the shores are rockbound, while three of its hills, of which Ben Sticla (1400 feet) is the most conspicuous, rise above a thousand feet. The contrast in appearance between the two islands is so remarkable that we are not surprised to learn the inhabitants of both have preserved for hundreds of years an equally remarkable independence of one another, and differ considerably not merely in character but even in religion, Great Todday being Protestant and Little Todday Catholic.

Both of the islands were formerly under the protection of St Tod who is said to have sailed there from Donegal on a log, his monkish habit providing the sail, his arm uplifted in benediction the mast. He built a church at Kiltod the foundations of which beside a holy well are still discernible close to the port. My grief! Nowadays even on Little Todday the old tales of the saint are passing from the memory, and the store of legend has been sadly depleted.

In our time the two islands display no more than a friendly rivalry, but in the old period of clan feuds the MacRuries of Great Todday were always raiding the cattle of their neighbours, and the Macroons of Little Todday were not less adept at making inroads upon the MacRurie sheep. Authorities disagree about the comparative antiquity of the two clans. The Macroons claim to be descended from a seal-woman who loved an exiled son of Clan Donald and bore him seven sons every one of whom brought himself back a mortal bride from the mainland. The MacRuries on the other hand claim to be descended from an exiled Maclean called Ruairidh Ruadh, reputed to have stood seven feet six inches without his brogues. This Ruairidh Ruadh was a noted pirate who stole at least one wife from almost every island in the west. The fact that there is no legend of his having stolen a Macroon wife is held by those who support the claim of the MacRuries to greater antiquity to prove that the Macroons had not yet appeared upon the scene.

We shall not venture an opinion on this vexed question.

The air is too soft and balmy upon this June evening for genealogical controversy. Let us lean back in our deck-chairs and watch the great sun go dipping down into the sea behind Little Todday. Is that St Brendan's floating isle we see upon the Western horizon? Forsooth, on such a night it were easy to conjure up that elusive morsel of geography. And now behind us the full moon clears the craggy summit of Ben Sticla and swims south past Ben Pucka to shed a honey-coloured radiance over the calm water of the Coolish, as the strait between the two Toddays is called. Why, oh why, the lover of Eden's language asks, must the fair Gaelic word Caolas be debased by map-makers to Coolish, so much more suggestive of municipal baths than of these 'perilous seas'? Alas, such sacrilege is all too sadly prevalent throughout Scotland. We turn our gaze once more to rest spellbound upon the beauty of earth and sea and sky and to let our imagination carry us back out of the materialistic present into the haunted past.

We see again Ruairidh Ruadh's dark galley creep out from Snorvig and sweep with measured strokes northward up the Coolish on rapine bent. We see again the seal-beaked galley of the Macroons off Tràigh nam Marbh – the Strand of the Dead – and we hear the voices of the rowers lamenting their own dead Chief as they bear his body to the burial-place of the Macroons on the little neighbouring isle of Poppay. Alas, for these degenerate days, although Poppay is still a breeding ground for the grey Atlantic seals, the Macroons no longer use it as a burial-ground.

But, hark! What is that melodious moaning we hear in the west? It is the singing of the seals on Poppay and Pillay, the twin small isles that guard the extremities of Little Todday, their fantastic shapes standing out dark against the blood-stained western sky. Would that the present scribe possessed the musical genius of Mrs Kennedy Fraser that he might set down in due notation that melodious moaning!

And now in the entrance of the hotel we notice our host beckoning to us. With one last lingering look at the unearthly beauty of this Hebridean twilight we turn to answer the summons. In our host's snuggery the glasses reflect with opalescent gleams the flicker of a welcome fire of peats, and as we raise the *uisge beatha* to our lips with a devout '*slàinte mhath, slàinte mhór*' we feel that we are indeed privileged visitors to Tìr nan Óg, and rejoicing in our own renewed youth we give thanks to the beneficent fortune which has brought us once more to the two lovely Toddays, there to dream away a few enchanted days on the edge of the world.

Tempora mutantur. This evening an almost silent group of elderly or old or very old men sat on the wooden benches round the bar and eyed the glasses of beer on the tables in front of them without relish. Beer does not taste like itself unless it is chasing a dram of neat whisky down the gullet, preferably two drams. To add to the prevailing depression, on account of a shortage of paraffin only two of the six lamps hanging from the ceiling were alight.

'Did you hear any word of Donald in the post, Airchie?' the Biffer was asked by Angus MacCormac, a big crofter with an immense grey moustache who had driven in with the lorry from Garryboo, in the extreme north of the island. Donald was the eldest of Archie MacRurie's four sons now serving their country in the Mercantile Marine.

'Not a word, not a word,' he sighed.

'Och, he'll be a prisoner of war,' put in Sammy Mac-Codrum, another Garryboo crofter, a small man with sparse hair and a nose on him even larger and beakier than the Biffer's own.

'Ay, maybe he will and maybe not,' said the father gloomily. 'His mother's made up her mind the lad's drowned.'

'Where wass his ship sunk?' Sammy asked.

'By what we can reckon it must have been off the Irish coast.'

'Look at that now,' Sammy commented. 'So near and yet so far, as they say.'

'That's the worst of it,' said the father. 'If he'd been torpedoed away out it might have been long enough before we heard if he was safe, but being so near we ought to have heard by now if he's a prisoner of war.'

Heads all round were shaken dejectedly. There was indeed nothing in the atmosphere of the bar that evening to encourage an easy optimism.

It was at this moment that Captain Alec MacPhee, the

patriarch of Snorvig, now in his ninetieth year, rose from his seat and taking his glass to the bar-counter asked his host to fill it up again.

'I'm sorry, Captain MacPhee, but unless the peer comes by Monday's poat the peer will be where the whisky is, and that's nowhere at all,' said the big hotel-keeper.

The ancient mariner, who was sailing the Seven Seas before the Franco-Prussian war, emitted such a tremendous gasp of amazement that his great white beard shivered like a grove of aspens.

'*A Thighearna bheannaichte*,' he exhaled, 'what are you telling me, Roderick?'

'I'm telling you you've had two pints of peer already this evening, Captain MacPhee, and no man can have more.'

The ancient mariner turned on his heels and walked out of the bar without another word. Outside, they heard the shingle of the terrace crunched by his resolute footsteps. There was neither moon nor star to light him on his way home; but an inward blaze of indignation illuminated the road down the hill to his house, which stood back from the main road round the island in a small garden, of which the principal feature was an enormous clam-shell from the Great Barrier Reef, mounted on a small cairn. His own snug sitting-room was a museum of his long adventurous life. The walls were covered with paintings and faded photographs of the ships in which he had sailed, with assegais and clubs and blowpipes, with bits of china and bits of armour, while over the mantelpiece hung a glass case in which two green pigeons from Fernando Po eyed perpetually an emerald bird of paradise from New Guinea.

Into this room the Captain strode upon that dark February evening and struck the Burmese gong with which he was wont to summon his great-grandniece Flora, a pretty, amiable flibbertigibbet of a girl, who at this date was looking after him until she could get to Glasgow and become a tram-conductress.

An hour later Dr Maclaren came into the bar, where by now the frequenters were all sitting in front of empty glasses.

'Did the Captain seem all right when he left here?' Dr Maclaren asked sharply.

He was told what had happened.

'Well, the shock has killed him,' the Doctor announced. 'And I'm not surprised. For the last fifteen years to my knowledge he drank his three drams of whisky and three pints of beer every night of his life and on such a tonic he might have lived to a hundred. He's had not a drop of whisky for twelve days, and before that only one dram a night for nearly a month. And now tonight he wasn't able to get his third pint of beer. Well, it's killed him.'

Dr Maclaren's usually jovial florid face was lined with bad temper. He was a man who liked his dram, and he was beginning to feel the effects of no whisky on himself.

'I've sent Flora along to her mother,' he went on. 'I suppose some of you will be sitting up with the body tonight.'

'Ay, we'll see about the *caithris* right enough,' one of the men in the bar assured him. 'Don't you worry yourself for that, Doctor.'

When the women had laid out the body in the bedroom on the other side of the passage, some seven or eight male representatives of Great Todday gathered in the Captain's sitting-room to watch the night away and keep the dead man company.

Roderick MacRurie sat in the Captain's own armchair, and his presence was a tribute to the sorrow he felt for that failure of his hospitality which had shocked the old mariner out of this world into the next. In the armchair on the other side of the hearth, where a well-laid fire of peats was glowing, sat the Biffer. Round the table were Angus MacCormac, Sammy MacCodrum, Alec Mackinnon, the headmaster of Snorvig School, and two or three more. They were joined presently by Norman Macleod, the attractive young schoolmaster of Watasett, a village at the head of Loch Sleeport near the south-west point of the island.

'I tried to persuade George Campbell to stay with us for a while,' he told the company. 'But he went back in the lorry to Garryboo. He and my sister Catriona fixed things this afternoon and they'll be married at the beginning of the summer holidays.'

'Ah, well, Catriona will make him a good wife,' Roderick MacRurie declared amid general agreement. 'There isn't a better cook in Todaidh Mòr.' He paused. 'Does Mistress Campbell know Chorge is to be marrying himself so soon?'

'George is going to tell his mother tonight,' said Norman. 'Och, I'm glad for Catriona's sake, for I'll be away in the R.A.F. any time now. I've had my papers.'

'Did you have a good dram to drink their health?' Angus MacCormac asked.

'Where would I have a dram in this drought of whisky?' retorted Norman Macleod, with an indignant toss of his long wavy hair.

Sammy MacCodrum shook his head.

'Chorge will neffer be having the courage to tell Mistress Campbell he's going to be married on her. Neffer!' he declared. 'Not unless he'd trunk a tram the size of Loch Sleeport itself, and then I believe it would turn to water inside of his *stamac* when he saw his mother gazing at him.'

Further discussion of the Garryboo schoolmaster's chances of escaping from bachelorhood was interrupted by the entrance of Mrs Farquhar Maclean, the Captain's great-niece and the mother of Flora, with tea, scones, and oatcakes to sustain the watchers. She was a plump bustling woman of about forty whose husband was away at sea.

'Ah, Morag, *eudail*, the Captain went terrible quick,' Big Roderick sighed.

'Och, it was better that way,' said Mrs Maclean. 'He

24

lived a terrible long time before he went at all, and I'm sure himself would have wanted to go quick. The *bodach* was always so quick about everything. Our Flora got as thin as bone the way she would be jumping when he always put his head round the door so quick.' She surveyed the table. 'There's plenty more tea and scones in the kitchen, and you'll just be helping yourselves when I go back home.'

'*Tapadh leat, tapadh leat, a Mhorag,*' said Big Roderick. '*Oidhche mhath.*' The others murmured their thanks and good nights, and when Mrs Maclean had left them to their vigil they started to pour themselves out cups of tea.

'Ah well, well,' Roderick muttered with a deep sigh, 'it's not for us to crumple at what the Lord provides for us.'

'I believe the Captain would have grumbled if he was sitting up here with us this night,' said the Biffer. 'Och, I've often seen him drink a cup of tea right enough, but he would never be looking at it so lovingly before he drank it the way he would be looking at a dram.'

'That's right,' Angus MacCormac agreed. 'It was a pleasure to see the way he would be looking at a dram before he put it to his mouth. You'd almost be thinking you were going to drink it yourself.'

'Ay,' the Biffer agreed in turn, 'there was a relish in the man's eyes which made you warm toward another dram yourself. *A Chruithear*, many's the time I've called for one myself just because the Captain had enjoyed his own so much. When do you think you'll be seeing whisky again, Roderick?'

'How would I know, Archie?' the hotel-keeper replied sombrely. 'Wasn't the Minister's wife asking me that very question this afternoon?'

'The Minister's wife?' exclaimed Alec Mackinnon, his thin body bending over the table like a tall black note of interrogation.

Norman Macleod threw back his head and laughed loudly.

'Ist, ist, Mr Macleod,' the hotel-keeper rebuked, 'don't be laughing, please. Mistress Morrison was wanting some whisky for the Minister's cold. My brother Simon went up to the Manse to see him this evening, and he says the poor soul has no more voice in him than a bit of dead grass in the wind.'

'What kind of a stuffed pird is that at all?' the high-pitched voice of Sammy MacCodrum broke in suddenly to ask. He had been staring for some time at the emerald bird of paradise between the two green pigeons over the mantelpiece. 'I never saw a pird with a tail on him like that.'

'That's a bird of paradise, Sammy,' the Snorvig head-master informed him.

'A pird of baratice,' Sammy echoed in amazement. 'How was the Captain after shooting a pird of baratice and him on earth? You're making a fun and a choke of me, Mr Mackinnon, and this is no time to be making funs and chokes of people whateffer.'

'No, no, Mr Mackinnon's not joking, Sammy,' Norman Macleod assured him earnestly. 'Captain MacPhee shot it in a balloon.'

'Don't you believe him, Sammy,' said Alec Mackinnon. 'The Captain brought it back with him from New Guinea. And those two green pigeons came from West Africa.'

'Ah, well, well, well, fancy a man who's travelled about all over the world like the Captain having to stand before his Creator chust for the want of a pint of peer.'

Sammy MacCodrum shook his head in a bewilderment of ironic and melancholy reflection.

'It wassn't the want of a pint of peer that killed the Captain, a Shomhairle,' said the hotel-keeper. 'Ach, yess, it was a shock right enough when I had to tell him he could not be having his third pint, but if his constitution had not been weakened so powerfully for want of whisky chust at the time of year when a man needs it most, himself would be sitting where I'm sitting now in his own armchair. *A dhuine dhuine*, we are all miserable worrums in the eyes of the Lord. He chust stamps on us when He has a mind to. Did anybody bring the Book? Maybe Mr Mackinnon would read us the death of Moses in sight of the Promised Land flowing with milk and honey.'

'But the poor old Captain never had a glimpse of the Promised Land,' Norman Macleod pointed out. 'There wasn't a drop of whisky in sight.'

'Angus, will you see if the Captain has his Bible there,' said Roderick, with a reproachful glance at the flippant young schoolmaster.

Angus MacCormac searched the Captain's bookshelf. 'The China Pi-lot, the West Africa Pi-lot, the Pacific Pi-lot,' he read out. 'Och, there's nothing but Pi-lots.'

Roderick clicked his tongue. 'The poor Captain! There's only one Pilot for the voyage he's making now. Maybe it's beside his bed.'

'And it's not for us to be taking it from him if it is,' the Biffer declared firmly. 'He was a good man, and he was a very patriotic man. I remember fine when we had no weapons for the Home Guard and we all thought the Germans would be on top of us at any minute, and the Captain brought those assegais hanging up there down to the police-station, ay, and he handed his own shot-gun over to Constable Macrae at the same time.'

'Sarchant Odd wasn't too pleased at all this evening when he heard we hadn't been keeping our shooting up to the mark,' said Angus MacCormac.

'It would be the Panker who wass telling him that. He didn't see Mr Wackett on the pier,' Sammy MacCodrum put in.

'I'll bet Waggett hasn't run out of his whisky,' Norman Macleod chuckled.

'You oughtn't to say a thing like that, Mr Macleod,' the Snorvig schoolmaster urged, 'unless you have positive proof.'

Paul Waggett was the retired stockbroker who had bought Snorvig House and rented the shooting of the two islands from the Department of Agriculture. He commanded the Home Guard Company recruited from the Toddays and in the opinion of the islanders never allowed himself to run out of creature comforts.

And indeed Norman Macleod was right. When the watchers down in the Captain's house were preparing for their long vigil with the support of tea, up at Snorvig House Paul Waggett was pouring himself out a carefully measured dram, which he handed to his wife.

'If you'll add sugar and hot water, old lady, I'll drink it when I'm in bed. I rather think I caught a germ at the Manse this afternoon. Mr Morrison really ought to keep that cold of his to himself.'

'I know, dear, I think it's so selfish the way people scatter colds all over the place. I do hope you've caught it in time.'

'You mean "not caught" it, Dolly,' said her husband with that superior smile which sent his sharp nose up in the air.

'Yes, of course, dear, how silly of me!'

'I think if I drink a double ration of hot grog I may fend it off. That's the beauty of only drinking whisky on rare occasions. One gets the benefit of it when one does drink it.'

Mrs Waggett who had been hearing this observation reiterated over nearly twenty-five years of connubiality tried to look as if she had heard it now for the first time.

'You're worried because there are no lemons,' said her husband kindly. 'Don't worry, old lady. *À la guerre comme à la guerre*, as the French used to say in the last war.' He stressed the word 'last' severely. The French collapse in 1940 was a favourite theme of his for a display of prosy superficiality.

And his wife who knew it hurried off to boil the kettle.

'You go on, dear, and get quickly into bed. I'll bring your whisky up to you.'

When a few minutes later she arrived in the bedroom with a steaming glass of heavily-sugared whisky, Paul Waggett was lying back in pillowed luxury.

'Now sip this, Paul, while I'm getting ready for bed, and then I'll take the glass away. You won't want it left beside you.'

When Mrs Waggett returned in a dressing-gown her husband was leaning back with an expression of profound satisfaction.

'I think that ought to defeat my cold,' he announced with evident admiration of his own cunning. 'Mrs Morrison was complaining this afternoon that she couldn't get any whisky for the Minister.'

'We still have another bottle,' Mrs Waggett reminded him.

'I know, but if every time people run out of whisky we are going to be called upon to supply it we shall be in the same position as them. They must learn not to be improvident. Improvidence is the besetting sin of the Islands. If they had all the whisky in Scotland, do you think they would be able to keep it? No, no, they'd drink it as fast as they could. Just as fast as they could,' he repeated dreamily.

'But poor Mrs Morrison never expected not to be able to get whisky from Roderick MacRurie when it was wanted for medical reasons,' Mrs Waggett ventured to point out. 'The Minister never keeps it in the house.'

'That's exactly what I mean by improvidence,' her husband insisted. 'Look at Captain MacPhee. Maclaren tells me that it was being suddenly cut off from whisky which killed him. Of course, Maclaren always exaggerates. Yet no doubt the old man was inconvenienced. Now, you'd think somebody like him who has had the command of ships would have taken care not to run out of whisky if it was so important to his comfort. But no, he was just as improvident as that silly niece of his who was supposed to be looking after him. It's in the blood. And it's even getting hold of a man like Sergeant-major Odd. I'd no idea he was coming over this evening. I must say I'm rather surprised he didn't come up to Snorvig House before he crossed over to Little Todday.'

'Oh, well, Paul, I expect he was anxious to see Peggy Macroon. He's been away a long time.'

'Yes, that's why it's so strange he didn't come up here as soon as he got off the boat. I noticed before he left us to go to that job in Devonshire that this West Highland casualness was getting hold of him.'

'I wonder if he and Peggy Macroon will be getting married soon,' Mrs Waggett said.

'I'm afraid I'm more anxious to know if he will be able to smarten up my men. They're getting terribly slack.'

'It *is* disheartening for you, Paul, after all the trouble you've taken with them.'

'When duty calls we don't consider our personal feelings, Dolly. Where's the book I was reading? I hope you haven't taken it downstairs.'

'What's it called?'

'*Death in the Jampot*. It's a Crime Club volume.'

'Oh dear, I believe I did take it downstairs. Silly of me. I thought you'd finished it,' said Mrs Waggett.

Her husband shook his head.

'Don't you start going native, old lady.'

She removed the empty glass and went off in search of the book. It was quickly found.

'Is it a good story?' she asked solicitously as she presented it to him.

'Not quite enough action for me, but it's not too bad.'

Mrs Waggett doffed her dressing-gown, got into bed and composed herself for sleep. Her husband read a few pages of *Death in the Jampot*; but the agreeable fumes of the hot grog made him too drowsy to spot even the most obvious clue, and he was not long in following Mrs Waggett's example.

Chapter 3

A QUESTION OF MARRIAGE

THE Sergeant-major found Joseph Macroon in a mood of pessimism about the prospect of marriage. When the two daughters of the household had retired to bed with a paternal reminder that the barrel of paraffin was almost empty, that they must not be late for early Mass, and that the saying of their prayers did not require a lamp, the postmaster took his guest into the little room at the back of the shop and expressed an opinion that there was enough coal on the fire to last as long as they would be wanting to sit up.

'I was hoping we might settle the date when me and Peggy get safely married, Mr Macroon,' the Sergeant-major suggested after he had seated himself in one of the armchairs on either side of the hearth.

'Ah, yes, well, we'll be talking about that when summer's over,' Joseph replied, his eyes wandering round the room, his tone vague. 'Och, that'll be quite time enough,' he added on a firmer note.

'I don't agree with you there, Mr Macroon.'

'We'll see better then the way the war is going. These Chaps are terrible. I believe they're worse than the Chermans,' said Joseph.

'Oh, they're regular bastards. No mistake about that. All the same, I don't see what they've got to do with me and Peggy getting married.'

'No, no,' Joseph murmured ambiguously. 'Will you have a bottle of ginger-ale, Sarchant?'

'No, thanks, I don't think I'll have anything.'

'You won't get anything,' Joseph assured him. 'Do you know when I last had a dram? Twelve days ago, and Lent begins the week after next.'

'Don't you ever drink whisky in Lent?'

'Och, I drink whisky any time of the year. I don't drink so much of it that I must give it up in Lent.'

'Then what difference will Lent make?' the Sergeant-major asked in perplexity.

'Man, we always allow ourselves a few extra drams before Lent begins. You're not a Catholic. You don't understand what a solemn sort of a time Lent is. And it's very long.'

'We have Lent in the Church of England,' said the Sergeant-major.

Joseph Macroon looked doubtful.

'At least, I'm pretty sure I remember having to give up sugar in Lent when I was a nipper.'

'Look at that now,' Joseph exclaimed in astonishment. 'Well, well, well, I never thought that the English ever denied themselves anything. Isn't that strange, now? Ay, ay, you live and learn. That's very true. When do you think this terrible war will be over, Sarchant?'

'Oh, it may go on for another three years with the Jerries, and I daresay you could add another year or more to finish off the Japs. That's why I'm anxious not to waste any more time in getting married. You see, if the war does stop sooner than we expect my job at Fort Augustus will stop too. That'll mean me going to live down in Nottingham to look after my mother's shop. And I want you to have as long as possible to get used to the idear of Peggy living so far away. Fort Augustus is much nearer her old home than what Nottingham will be. And by the time she and me have been living for a couple of years at Fort Augustus you'll hardly notice it if she goes a bit further off. Colonel Lindsay-Wolseley's very kindly offered me a furnished cottage at Tummie for ten bob a week. It's a gift. He's a fine gentleman.'

'Och, he's a fine gentleman right enough,' Joseph agreed. 'We've never had a disagreeable word at the Council meetings. And I believe he'll support us when the question of the new school for Kiltod comes up again at the March meeting.'

'I'm sure he will,' the Sergeant-major declared fervidly.

'The present school is not fit for children at all. It is not fit for chickens. "How many water-closets have you?" one of these wise men from the East as Ben Nevis calls them was asking me at the last meeting? General Mackenzie of Mam. "How many water-closets, General? The whole island is a water-closet," I said. The General was a bit taken aback when I told him that. Och, I believe we'll get our school right enough.'

But Joseph's optimism was all too brief. A moment later he was sighing. 'And yet I don't know so much at all. They want all the rates for themselves in Inverness. They're terribly greedy for themselves on the other side of the county. So many Mackenzies there, and the air just gives them an appetite.'

'But what about me and Peggy getting married?' Sergeant-major Odd pressed. 'Don't you think just before Easter would be a good time?'

'Just before Easter? What are you saying, man?' Joseph exclaimed in horror. 'You have some very peculiar thoughts, Sarchant.'

'Well, just after Easter? Anyway, before April's out?'

'Ah, we'd better talk about it when the summer's over. I don't know at all why you're in such a hurry.'

'If you'd been wanting to marry a girl for nearly two years you'd be in a hurry, Mr Macroon. And I'm getting on, remember.'

'Och, you're not so old as all that, Sarchant. I'm sixty-three myself. Two of my daughters are away married long ago. Peigi Mhór's away married down in Glasgow and Peigi Bhàn's away married in Obaig.'

'I know that,' said the Sergeant-major, trying not to seem impatient.

'And they tell me Peigi Bheag's going with one of the school-teachers in Barra, and talking of getting married to him, Neil MacNeil. Och, he's not a bad fellow, with huge great glasses on him. Ah, well, the fire's going very black. You'll be wanting to be away to your bed, Sarchant,

I believe. You must be pretty tired. You're sure you won't have a bottle of ginger-ale?'

'No, thanks, Mr Macroon.'

'Or a bottle of lemonade?'

The Sergeant-major shook his head.

'I don't blame you,' said the postmaster sadly. 'That's another thing. How can we have a wedding when there's no whisky?'

'There's bound to be plenty of whisky by the end of April,' the Sergeant-major argued.

'It's easy to see you've been out of the country,' Joseph Macroon told his guest. 'There hasn't been plenty whisky for a year and more. It wasn't so bad on Todaidh Beag while that barrel of rum lasted, but it didn't last long at all. There were too many in the secret. We were all hoping for another barrel when the *Jamaica Maid* went down last winter off Barra Head; but if she had any barrels aboard they did not come ashore here or on Todaidh Mór. No, no, nothing but what they call grapefruits, and they were just an amusement for the children.'

'Yes, I expect they enjoyed eating them.'

'Och, they didn't eat them at all. They threw them at one another. Tràigh Swish was alive with them. We never thought they were fruits at all till Mr MacIver the School Inspector came over and told us what they were. But by then what was left of them was all rotten.'

Joseph Macroon rose from his chair, pulled his knitted red cap over his ears, and moved toward the door where he stood listening.

'The wind's getting up again, right enough,' he said. 'You'll find a lamp in your room, Sarchant.'

'And you'll think over what we were talking about,' the Sergeant-major asked.

'I don't think about it at all,' his host replied. 'What's the use of thinking about whisky when there's not a nip to be thinking about?'

'I mean about me and Peggy getting married after Easter?' the Sergeant-major pressed.

'It's too late to be talking about a big subject like that tonight.'

'What about if Peggy's called up?'

'She won't be called up. She's indispensable to the post-office.'

'What about Kate Anne?'

'She's indispensable to the croft. She's an agricultural worker. Hark the way it's blowing. We'll have a dirty night, Sarchant.'

'A very dirty night,' Sergeant-major Odd agreed gloomily.

And as he lay for a long while awake on a mattress that was hard even by the standards of hardness to which many years of military service had accustomed him, the heart of Sergeant-major Odd was weighed down by a heavier depression than that now playing havoc with the Atlantic. The higher the wind rose, the lower his spirits sank. 'The next time I come to Little Todday,' he vowed to himself, 'I'll put a bottle of whisky in my haversack, whatever it costs. That's one sure thing. Whatever it costs! If I'd only have know in time I'd have brought a bottle with me even if I'd have had to pinch one. Her father would have been another man if I'd have been able to produce a dram for him tonight. He'd have taken quite a different view of the matter. That's the worst of these fathers without wives of their own. All they think about is turning their daughters into slaves. Indispensable! Isn't she more indispensable to me than what she is to the post-office? Post-office! With a post three times a week. Why, it's comical.'

Then for a while the mattress seemed to grow softer and the wind to blow more gently as he thought of his Peggy asleep in the room next to him. She'd been a bit shy, of course. Well, any girl would be shy after all those months. Still, she'd been glad to see him. She knew now all right that he loved her. Come to think of it, she'd never kissed him quite so ... well, quite so much as if she liked kissing him. If only this wind would drop they'd be able to walk over to Try Swish tomorrow afternoon, and sit where they'd sat on that Sunday afternoon at the end of April nearly two years ago, that Sunday afternoon when he'd asked her to marry him. She thought then that a man couldn't fall in love with a girl he'd only known for a few days. Well, she knew now all right that a man could. Next April. That's when it had got to be. Whisky or no whisky. All the same, it was going to be hard to persuade Peggy to defy the old man, and insist on getting married whether he liked it or not. They were a bit old-fashioned out here in the Islands. They paid a lot more attention to what their fathers said than what they did anywhere else nowadays. Sergeant-Major Odd's thoughts travelled into the future. 'And quite right too,' he murmured to himself. 'I think a father ought to have a bit of authority at home. Within reason, of course, within reason.' Just then a louder gust than any yet swept round the house, and away to the west the gale was booming. 'Blowing big guns,' the Sergeant-major muttered. How long was the First Army going to be held up in Tunis? Things were going a bit slow there. Of course, the war wouldn't really last another three or four years. Or would it? Well, the war wasn't going to stop him marrying Peggy. Suppose they called her up? Well, she might get directed to work close by.

'I know what I'll do,' the Sergeant-major told himself. 'I'll pop across tomorrow evening and ask Father Mac-alister's advice. Perhaps he'll talk to the old man. And on Monday I'll have to go over to Great Todday and talk to Captain Waggett about G Company. This whisky business is upsetting them over there pretty badly from what I can make out. Well, you can't blame the poor chaps. Fancy coming in to a parade on a night like this all the way from Garryboo or Bobanish and then when you go into the hotel to have one afterwards you can't have one. No wonder they've been slacking off. Wouldn't it be fine if next time I came over from the mainland I could bring a case of whisky along with me! I'll lay there'd be a good turn-out of every blinking section in the two islands.

Don't be soppy, Fred,' he adjured himself scornfully. 'Where are *you* going to find a case of whisky? Be your age, you silly b — r, and go to sleep.'

The foolish body obeyed the wiser mind, and Sergeant-major Alfred Ernest Odd presently fell asleep.

Next day the weather was fiercer than ever. Huge brooms of rain swept the green carpet of Little Todday almost continuously. The huddled sheep were too soggy to browse. The stirks and ponies drooped. The gulls gave up flying and dotted the grass like white stones. No dogs barked. The plan to walk the four miles across to the long white beach of Tràigh Swish on the west coast of the island was beyond the power of the Sergeant-major's romantic determination to carry out on that Sunday afternoon. And when Peggy and he were left alone together in the sitting-room after dinner the wind rattled the door so often that he grew tired of jumping apart from Peggy at every false alarm.

'I think I'll go up and see Father Macalister, Peggy darling,' he said when the wind had interrupted what looked like being the longest kiss she had given him yet.

'I'm sure Father James would like to see you, Fred. Kirstag told me this morning he was asking for you.'

'I'll go right away,' the Sergeant-major declared firmly.

He went to fetch his greatcoat from the porch.

'Coupons!' he exclaimed.

'They're terrible, these coupons,' Peggy grumbled as she helped him into his coat. 'Even if we could be married, Fred, I wouldn't have any coupons for you.'

'Oh, I wasn't wanting your coupons, Peggy darling, I was thinking that if there were coupons for whisky I'd give mine up to your father.'

'You'd do no such thing,' she pouted. 'You'd give them to me for my clothes. Who wants whisky?'

'Your father does. And I'm going to try and get hold of some for him. Don't you want to be married in April?'

He held her to him. She was almost as tall as himself.

'Don't you want to be, Peggy?' he repeated.

'You're holding me awfully tight,' she protested in words.

'I'm always going to hold you tight,' he murmured.

Then a savage gust of wind rattled every door in the house, and they hastily drew apart.

'Ach, be off with you now up to Father James,' she urged him, smoothing her ruffled dark-brown hair.

A couple of minutes later the Sergeant-major was knocking at the door of the Chapel House, which was opened for him by Kirstag MacMaster, Father Macalister's housekeeper, a neat pippin of a woman whose life was devoted to a perpetual struggle to keep the priest's cosy sitting-room as tidy as the rest of the house.

'Will I be disturbing Father Macalister?' the visitor asked.

'Not at all. Not at all. He's just at saying his Office and he'll be very glad to put it aside for a while,' the housekeeper insisted. 'What weather we're having, Sergeant.'

'Dreadful, isn't it! How is his reverence?'

'Och, he's fine and middling, but his wireless isn't working and that fidgets him a bit. He's been very restless for the last few days. He was expecting a new battery yesterday, but it didn't come with the boat. He was very disappointed.'

She opened the door of the priest's room.

'Here's Sergeant Odd to see you, Father,' she announced.

The portly priest shut his breviary with a bang and jumped up with astonishing alacrity for a man of his bulk from the deep armchair in which he had been plunged beside a blazing fire.

'Great sticks alive, Sergeant, I'm glad to see you. Welcome back to Paradise,' he exclaimed in that rich voice whose warm *vibrato* had made so many visitors feel truly welcome to his hearth. 'How are you, my boy?'

'Oh, I'm in the pink. And how are you, Father?'

The bulky priest exhaled a deep sigh.

'Holding on, Sergeant, just holding on. Ach, I'm like my wireless. I've no battery. Ah, well, I suppose you've heard of the rotten condition of the state of Denmark?'

'It's very serious, isn't it?'

'It is very serious,' the priest avowed. 'We were always proud of our hospitality and it touches our noble and beautiful island pride. Look at me now. Here's an old friend back from barbarous places like Africa and Devonshire, and I haven't a sensation to offer him, not so much as a wee snifter. I've nothing but my own chair. Sit down in it, Sergeant.'

'No, really, Father Macalister, I'll take this one,' said the Sergeant-major, turning to the smaller armchair on the other side of the fire.

'You'll do nothing of the kind, my boy,' his host declared sonorously. 'You're in my parish and you'll sit where the parish priest tells you to sit. You may be a heretic in matters of faith, but you'll not be a heretic in matters of behaviour.'

Sergeant-major Odd took the deep armchair but with less assurance of comfort than his host expected.

'Put your backside where your backside ought to be,' he commanded. 'It's not a fence you're sitting on. It's a chair. That's more the style,' he added when his guest was well ensconced. Then he went to a cupboard from which he took a bottle and filled two glasses with what looked like a mixture of port and brown sherry.

'It's not the real Mackay,' he commented, as he offered his guest one glass and took the other for himself. 'A dhuine, dhuine, no, indeed. Still, it's a little better than Joseph's ginger-ale and much better than his lemonade.' The priest raise his glass. 'Ceud mìle fàilte agus slàinte mhór!' Then he drained it in honour of his guest and put it down with a wry face. 'Ah, well,' he sighed deeply, 'we're in a pretty bad way.'

'What wine is it exactly, Father?'

'It's altar wine, my boy. It's the best I can offer. Indeed, it's all I can offer.'

'I think it's very nice,' said the Sergeant-major.

'Ah, well, it's drinkable,' Father Macalister allowed. 'But only just, by Jingo,' he added quickly. 'And when are you going to marry Peigi Ealasaid?'

'I'd marry Peggy Yallasich tomorrow, if I could, but I can't get the old man up to the scratch,' the Sergeant-major replied gloomily. 'And Peggy won't go against her father. Quite rightly, of course. I tried to pin him down to a date last night, but every time he'd try and talk about something else.'

'He's pretty good at that, is Joseph,' the priest observed.

'In the end I held out for Easter week, and he held out for not talking about a wedding till summer was over. That's all very fine, but I was forty-five last month. I'll be getting on for forty-six by autumn. Colonel Lindsay-Wolseley has promised me a lovely little furnished cottage so long as I'm with him as Sergeant-instructor. I've had to wait nearly two years as it is, through me getting sent down to Devonshire like that and then out to West Africa. If the war comes to an end I've got a good home for Peggy in Nottingham. What's your advice, Father Macalister?'

'My advice is to roll right over them and marry her at Easter. She's a lovely beautiful girl. And she's a good girl. Roll right over them, my boy,' said the priest firmly.

'Yes, that's all very fine, Father, but it's jolly difficult to roll over somebody like my future father-in-law to be. He isn't there when you start in rolling. He's as slippery as an eel.'

The priest shook his head in reflective agreement.

'Ay, Joseph can be slippery right enough,' he agreed. 'But don't you worry yourself, Sergeant. I'll speak to him. I'll tell him he's got to have the wedding at Easter. And if he won't agree, by Jove, *I'll* roll right over him myself.'

'I'm awfully grateful, Father Macalister, I am really. You were so kind when it all started. If you remember the idea was to get married in the autumn of '41. Well, that idea went down the drain with me being transferred so sudden. Well, perhaps you'll remember I told you then that of course I'd promise all the children would be brought up as Catholics the same as their mother. Well, I've been thinking over things a bit and – er – I didn't want to say this before I knew you were still in favour of me marrying Peggy, if you know what I mean, and – er ...' The Sergeant-major gulped in embarrassment. Then words deserted him.

'You'd better have another glass of wine,' the priest advised.

'No, really, Father, thank you, it's not that ... I mean to say, what I'm trying to say is a bit awkward. You see, I wouldn't like you to think I was trying to curry favour, if you get my meaning, but the fact is I really have been thinking things over, and my idea was that perhaps if I became a Catholic myself it 'ud make things better at home. I mean to say, anybody doesn't want his kids to look upon him as something different to what they are themselves, and so I thought perhaps. ... I mean to say, well, there it is.'

'Ay, ay, just as you say, Sergeant. There it is. And it's a mighty big It. You'll want instruction. Being a Sergeant-instructor yourself, you'll know what a lot of instruction is required.'

'That's a fact.'

'And so I'll write to Father MacIntyre at Drumsticket and ask him to supply the needful.'

'I'm afraid he'll find me pretty ignorant.'

'Never mind, Sergeant. The less you know the easier for him.'

'And there's another thing, Father Macalister,' the Sergeant-major continued. 'I wonder if it could be kept quiet till it's settled about the wedding? I mean to say, I wouldn't like the old man to think I was trying to get round him by becoming a Catholic. Peggy wouldn't like that. She'd think it was done for the purpose.'

'Don't you worry yourself about that, Sergeant. We'll not say a word.'

41

'What I thought was when the wedding was all fixed up I'd tell Peggy first.'

'That's the spirit, *a bhalaich*. Oh, well, well, it's really a disaster that we can't celebrate the occasion in the glorious traditional way.'

It was at this moment that Kirstag came in to say that Duncan Macroon had called.

'Let him come right in, Kirsty,' Father Macalister told her, and then he added, turning to the Sergeant-major,

'Duncan Bàn is the very man we want. You leave it to me. Duncan is our man.'

Duncan Macroon was the crofter and poet who commanded the Little Todday platoon of G company. Sergeant-major Odd's experience of him in that position made him a little doubtful whether Duncan Bàn was their man, but he had no time to express his doubts, for Duncan Bàn himself with his fair tumbled hair and glowing countenance and eyes as blue as the kingfisher's wing was already in the room as the priest spoke.

'Yes, yes, I'm your man, Father James,' he declared, beaming. 'Hullo, Sarchant. I'm glad to find you here. You didn't give us much of your time after Mass this morning. She's a fine girl though. When is the wedding to be?'

'Just the question we've been discussing, Duncan,' said the priest, 'and we've decided to have it in the week after Easter.'

'Very good,' said Duncan.

'But we must have the *rèiteach* before Lent,' Father Macalister went on, 'and you'll have to speak for the Sergeant, Duncan.'

'What's a rayjack?' Sergeant-major Odd asked nervously.

'The *rèiteach* is the betrothal,' Father Macalister told him. 'It's a great occasion. The future bridegroom's friend tells the future bride's father what a glorious splendid magnificent fellow she is going to marry and the father says what a beautiful lovely capable daughter he is parting with, and everybody drinks the health of the happy couple and the father and the ...'

'Wait a minute, Father James,' Duncan Bàn interrupted. 'How are we going to drink all these healths when there's not a drop of whisky in the whole of Todaidh Beag and Todaidh Mór?'

'There's not a drop today, Duncan, but that doesn't say there won't be a drop next week. The *Island Queen* will be in on Tuesday.'

'Not if it's blowing like this, Father. There's a huge great sea running in on the west just now,' Duncan insisted.

'Quick come, quick go. The wind got up in a moment and it will drop just as suddenly,' the priest declared with the authoritativeness of an archbishop.

'I hope the boat *will* come,' said the Sergeant-major. 'I told the Colonel I'd be back for certain by Wednesday.'

'Suppose the boat comes but the whisky doesn't, Father James?' Duncan asked. 'What *rèiteach* can anybody be having? It's against nature to have a *rèiteach* with tea and ginger-ale and lemonade. Even if there was plenty beer it would still be against nature.'

'The fairies will bring up the whisky, Duncan,' Father James assured him solemnly.

'There's nobody else will bring it nowadays, *a Mhaighstir Seumas,* and that's one sure thing,' Duncan declared.

'*Rèiteach* or no *rèiteach*,' said Father James, 'the Sergeant will marry Peigi Iosaiph on the Wednesday after Easter. That's April 28th. And what you have to do, Duncan, is to tell everybody the date and I'll tell everybody the date, and, by the holy crows, that will *be* the date!'

'Yes, but what if Joseph Macroon refuses?' the Sergeant-major asked.

'He won't refuse,' the priest declared in his profoundest bass.

'Ah, the rascal, he daren't refuse,' said Duncan Bàn. 'Not if Mhaighstir Seumas and I are working hand in glove together....'

'And the fairies,' Father James added.

'Ay, the darling craytures,' Duncan chuckled.

'You'll start composing a good song for the wedding, Duncan,' the priest warned him.

'Don't you worry, Father. I'll compose a beauty – a regular beauty,' the crofter poet promised with enthusiasm. 'But I hope we *shall* soon have a little inspiration. No fiddler can fiddle his best without a bit of resin for his bow.'

Chapter 4

ALSO A QUESTION OF MARRIAGE

SERGEANT-MAJOR ODD was not the only man that week-end who was finding his matrimonial future obscured by the threat of parental opposition. George Campbell was faced by a still more unfavourable prospect. George Campbell was the headmaster of the school at Garryboo, a crofting township some four miles away from Snorvig in the north-west corner of Great Todday.

The low rocky promontory of Garryboo afforded a landing only when the tide was fairly high and the Atlantic absolutely calm, a combination so rare that none of the crofters went in for fishing, preferring to gain their livelihood from the wide and gentle slope of good grazing and arable ground which extended as far as the road that ran round the island, on the other side of which a great stretch of level bog below the rocky bastions of Ben Bustival furnished peat in plenty. Garryboo with its houses dotted about at different angles on the green machair was the only part of Great Todday which resembled the landscape of Little Todday, and the people there were regarded by the rest of the island as only a little less barbaric than the papist inhabitants of Little Todday itself. The people of Garryboo, on the other hand, regarded with contemptuous pity the fierce agricultural struggle of their neighbours in Great Todday with rock and heather and sour peaty soil. They were happy to be considered behind the times so long as their stirks fetched prices at the Obaig sales as high as the well-nourished cattle from Little Todday.

In spite of Garryboo's reputed lag in the matter of progress, in spite of the fact that the girls of Garryboo carried less lipstick than the girls of Snorvig, more impermanent waves than those of Watasett and fewer silk stockings than those of Bobanish, Garryboo possessed the only fairly new school in the two Toddays, a building which claimed to be as modern as any in a Glasgow suburb. No doubt, if it had been erected in a Glasgow suburb, the wind and rain and salty air of the Outer Hebrides would not have made the roughcast walls look like cracked egg-shells only eight years after it had been erected. Jerry-building is a wasteful experiment beside the Atlantic.

The greater part of the school was taken up with two large classrooms, but the main building was extended to include a house for the headmaster, the flimsy shoddiness of which was made more obvious by the heavy mahogany furniture of the headmaster's mother, who presided as heavily as her furniture over the domestic life of her only son. Mrs Campbell, a large majestic old woman, with icy pale blue eyes and a deep husky voice, was the widow of the last factor of Great Todday before the Department of Agriculture acquired the island from Sir Robert Smith-Cockin, a magnate of Victorian industrialism. She had produced her only offspring late in life and still regarded him as a child of ten in spite of the fact that he was thirty-five years old and a headmaster. George Campbell himself was a small shy man who, until the formation of the Home Guard, had scarcely ever been seen in public except when he appeared on the platform of the Snorvig Hall to sing Gaelic songs in an agreeable light tenor at charitable functions patronized by the Minister. In spite of his mother's opposition to his command of the Garryboo section, George Campbell had found his duties in the Home Guard an opportunity to escape some of the maternal vigilance, with the result that he had fallen in love with Catriona Macleod, the sister of the Watasett headmaster, who kept house for him in the cosy old schoolhouse over nine miles away at the south end of the island.

On the afternoon of that Saturday which saw the arrival of Sergeant-Major Odd, but not of the whisky, George Campbell, to his great astonishment, had succeeded in proposing marriage to Catriona and to his much greater astonishment his hand had been accepted. She was pretty. She was a splendid cook. She was for an islander an economical housekeeper. George Campbell was overwhelmed by his success. When he sat down to tea with Catriona and her brother Norman that evening to watch her deft housewifely fingers and to blush in the sparkling warmth of her eyes as she ministered to him with tea and scones and buttered eggs, George Campbell wished that he was on the platform of Snorvig Hall so that he might sing those oft-sung Gaelic love-songs with a fervour he had never dreamed of attempting hitherto.

'Och, it couldn't have happened at a better time,' Norman declared heartily. 'I'll be getting my notice to report for service in the air on the ground any time now, and I was a bit worried what Catriona, would do. She didn't like the idea of looking after the old people on the croft at Knockdown for the rest of the war. Ach, they're reasonable craytures right enough, but the nicest old people can be a bit of a tie. Anyway, at Garryboo she won't be three miles away from them.'

When Norman Macleod made this observation about old people the pancake in George Campbell's hand which had been seeming as light as sea-foam suddenly became as heavy as a dictionary.

'Yes, old people can be a little difficult sometimes,' he agreed.

'I wonder what your mother will say, George, when you tell her you're going to be married,' Catriona speculated. 'I hope she won't be hating the idea too much.'

George gulped down a piece of pancake which felt like swallowing a nutmeg grater.

'Oh, I'm sure she won't,' he muttered.

'I think you'll have a bit of a fight, Georgie boy,' said Norman. 'Mind you, I'm not saying she'll object to Catriona in particular. I think she just won't fancy the notion of your getting married at all. She's had it too much her own way all these years.'

'She doesn't realize that I'm thirty-five,' said George gloomily.

'Boy, boy, she doesn't realize you're weaned,' Norman laughed. 'Perhaps when she sees a baby of your own clinging on to Catriona she'll let *you* go.'

His sister tossed her head.

'What a chick to talk about me like that!' she protested.

'No cheek at all about it,' her brother retorted. 'And I hope you'll ask Captain Waggett to be the godfather. Ah, well, he won't have to worry next summer about my poaching. If I poach as much as an egg in the R.A.F. I'll be lucky.'

George had no heart to laugh even at jokes about Captain Paul Waggett. Within a short while, an all too short while, he would be trying to break the news to his mother that he was going to marry Catriona Macleod. He shuddered.

'I'll tell you what, George,' said Norman, 'if you're going to tackle the old lady tonight you ought to tap the steward first. There should be plenty of whisky tonight. It was expected on Tuesday and this is the first trip the *Island Queen* has been able to make this week. If I'd known you and Catriona were going to get married on me I wouldn't have finished that bottle of Stag's Breath we had for the New Year.'

'You'd have kept anything in a bottle of whisky for two months?' his sister exclaimed. 'Ah, well, it's you that have a nerve to pretend such a thing, Norman.'

'I don't enjoy whisky – really,' George Campbell protested, 'I hardly ever touch it.'

'That's the trouble with you,' his colleague told him. 'If you'd fortified yourself as regularly as I have you'd not be giving twopence about telling your mother you're going to be married. What is it gives me the necessary sagacity to outwit the Inspector? Whisky. What is it that helps me to know just where to put down the net in Loch Sleeport for Waggett's sea-trout? Whisky. What makes me a good shot at a grouse or a snipe? Whisky. What is it makes Maclaren such a hell of a good doctor? Whisky. Love makes the world go round? Not at all. Whisky makes it go round twice as fast. That's why I'm the most revolutionary crayture in the whole of Todaidh Mór.'

'Will you listen to him blowing,' his sister jeered.

'Well, whisky agrees with you,' George argued. 'It wouldn't agree with me.'

'George, you're going to have two powerful drams with me in Snorvig before you go home this evening, and when you come back to dinner with us after church tomorrow you're going to tell us what date you've fixed with Mistress Campbell for the wedding.'

However, when Norman Macleod and George Campbell reached Snorvig, there was no whisky, and they were greeted instead with the news of Captain MacPhee's death from shock.

'Och, well, Doctor dear, we'll all be dead if this drought continues,' Norman Macleod said. 'And don't be looking at me so fierce. You're missing the noble stuff just as much as I am myself.'

'Will you be going down to the *caithris* tonight, Norman?' Doctor Maclaren asked.

'I will indeed. The old man was the finest liar I ever listened to in my life.' Then turning to George Campbell he added, 'You'd better come along with me, George. You'll never face the music tonight.'

George Campbell thought the music might be even more difficult to face if he did not arrive home till morning. The Garryboo lorry was waiting; he climbed up beside the driver.

'I'll be seeing you tomorrow, George,' Norman Macleod called after him. 'Maybe somewhere or other I'll find a dram to celebrate the occasion.'

'You're some optimist, Norman,' the Doctor jeered. 'But I suppose a Red like you has got to be an optimist to believe in his wild dreams for the future. What are you and George Campbell hoping to celebrate?'

'He and my sister Catriona have just come to terms.'

'Good God,' the Doctor exclaimed, 'how on earth did George Campbell muster up the courage to ask her? He's a lucky man, though. She's the best cook in the two islands. You'll miss her.'

'I'll be away in the R.A.F.'

'Ah, yes, I forgot. Don't you go preaching your communism there.' The Doctor took a meditative pinch of snuff. 'So George Campbell is going to marry your sister. I wonder what the old lady will say.'

'I expect George is wondering just that in Donald Ian's lorry,' said Norman Macleod with a grin. 'But see here, Doctor, why don't you join us at dinner after church? Maybe I was a bit optimistic about the dram, but we'll have a good meal and a good crack afterwards.'

'That'll suit me,' said the Doctor.

Norman Macleod was right. George Campbell *was* wondering what the old lady would say, as he sat pensively beside Donald Ian Gillespie in the cab of the lorry, which was roaring up the road below Snorvig House on second speed and provoking a lecture from Captain Waggett to his wife on the bad driving of everybody in Great Todday except himself.

'Very sad about the Captain, Mr Campbell,' said Donald Ian when the lorry was clear of Snorvig and passing the upward sweep of the moorland between Ben Sticla and Ben Bustival.

'Very sad,' the schoolmaster agreed.

'Ay, ay,' Donald Ian sighed, easing himself in his seat and peering forward into the murk, 'we all come to it. First we get born, then we get married, and then we get dead. You'll have to think about getting married yourself soon, Mr Campbell. Your mother must be a tidy bit over seventy now.'

'She's seventy-five.'

'Look at that now. Och, well, she's pretty active right enough. Still, you ought to be getting married.'

If George Campbell had had even one dram he might have told Donald Ian that he was going to marry Catriona Macleod; but without the encouragement of a dram he felt too shy, and they drove on in a silence which was not broken until Donald Ian bade him good night where the road down to the school branched off to the left from the main road.

When the headmaster of Garryboo reached the door of his house he found it locked. He struck a match and looked at his watch before he tapped. It was just a quarter to ten.

'What a time to come back, George!' Mrs Campbell growled when she opened the door. 'Where have you been?'

'The lorry was a little late in leaving Snorvig,' the headmaster of Garryboo muttered as he followed his mother into the sitting-room where she leant down to pick up the bible and spectacles she had deposited on her chair and resumed her seat, the bible and spectacles now upon her knee. 'Why didn't you come back with the six o'clock lorry?' she asked sternly.

'The mails weren't sorted. In fact they weren't ready in time for the nine o'clock lorry. Captain MacPhee died suddenly this evening.'

Mrs Campbell gave a contemptuous grunt which sounded rather like 'Serve him right'. Then she shook her head.

'Well, it's not for us to speak against those who have passed on, and I'm told that he took to reading his bible last year, but what good it could do him after spending every night drinking up at that bar I wouldn't care to say. You haven't been up at the bar tonight, have you, George?' the old lady asked sharply.

'Good gracious me, no, mother. What made you ask that?'

'You're looking guilty, George. You're not looking me straight in the face. George, you've been drinking.'

'I have not been drinking,' he declared with the

51

courageous indignation of unassailable innocence. 'I couldn't have been drinking. There's not a drop of whisky in the whole island.'

'What do you mean, not a drop of whisky in the whole island? It's swimming in it. It always has been swimming in it. Your father spent all his life trying to get the licence taken away from the hotel. He knew it was the only way to get any work out of the people.'

'There's no whisky now,' George insisted. 'There's a shortage on account of the war.'

'The Lord is merciful indeed. What a lesson for us! We go to war on the Sabbath day, but He returns good for evil and leads us out of temptation. Well, if you've not been drinking, what have you been doing all this time, George? Where did you have your tea?'

'I went along to see Norman Macleod at Watasett.'

'Fine company you're keeping. That good-for-nothing Radical! I don't know what the Education authority is thinking of, letting a rascal like that corrupt the minds of children,' said Mrs Campbell wrathfully.

'He's been called up. He's going into the Air Force.'

'The best place for him. He's never had both feet on the ground since he could walk. His mother always spoilt him disgracefully. She spoilt all her children. Was that sister of his – Cairistiona, isn't it? – was she there?'

'Catriona gave us tea,' said George.

'A rattleplate of a girl, just like her mother before her. Permanent wave, indeed! Permanent wickedness more like. I am not one to criticize our Minister, as you know, but he has been sadly weak about all this lipstick and permanent waves and cigarette smoking.'

'Catriona looks after her brother very well,' George ventured to remind the old lady.

'What do you know about being looked after? Don't talk so wildly, George. You've had nobody but your mother to look after you. You'll learn the difference if you're ever so foolish as to marry one of these modern girls.' Mrs Campbell pronounced it 'modderan' as if with the scornful rolling of the 'r' she could drum them out into ignominy.

George tried to conjure up the brightness of Catriona's dark-brown eyes when she had turned to look at him with 'yes' upon her lips, the quick movements of her as she laid the table for tea, and the light touch of her fingers on his hand as she pressed him to have another pancake. Alas, the vision of Catriona eluded him. All he could see was his mother sitting upright in the high-backed mahogany armchair and piercing him with those hard, sharp, light-blue eyes. How could he tell her tonight that this afternoon he had asked Catriona to marry him and that she had said 'yes'?

'Well, it's time we were going to bed,' his mother announced. 'High time, indeed, with the Sahbbath close upon us. I was thinking I'd take advantage of the calmer weather to go to church myself.'

It was accepted in Garryboo that the old lady had the right to commandeer a place in any of the traps driving into Snorvig on Sunday morning, a privilege of which in fine weather she seldom failed to take advantage.

'I'm told the Minister has a terrible cold on him,' said George whose plan to have dinner with Catriona and her brother was threatened by his mother's intention.

'Why would that keep me from worshipping the Lord?' Mrs Campbell demanded.

'You'll get a sermon from Simon MacRurie, and you don't like that at all,' her son pointed out.

The suggestion of opposition made the old lady determined to break it down.

'I'll go to church tomorrow morning, George, sairmon or no sairmon,' she declared.

As the old lady spoke, the first uneasy heralds of the coming gale moaned round the gimcrack house.

'The wind's rising again,' said her son.

And on Sunday morning even Mrs Campbell's resolution was baffled.

'You'd better stay at home yourself, George,' she advised. 'We'll worship the Lord in our own home.'

This meant for George remaining on his knees while his mother indulged herself in long extempore prayers. He preferred to worship in the comparative comfort of church where nobody knelt for fear of being suspected of popery, the interest of presbyterianism once upon a time having been to deprive the kirk itself of any peculiar sanctity.

'I'll walk in to church, mother, if you don't mind. I'm needing the exercise. Miss Ross will come in to you.'

Miss Ross was the assistant schoolteacher at Garryboo – a carroty wisp of a young woman with a nose like a pointer whom Mrs Campbell was considering as a possible daughter-in-law, her influence over Miss Ross being already paramount.

'Dinner will be ready at half past two. Be sure now and be back in good time,' Mrs Campbell warned her son as he bent his head and plunged out into the wind and rain.

On the way up to the main road George stopped at the house of Angus MacCormac where Miss Ross lodged.

'You're never going to walk in to Snorvig on such a morning, Mr Campbell?' exclaimed Mrs MacCormac. 'Himself has just come back from the *caithris* as wet as a dog. I'm just after making him go out and mop his moustache. It was dripping all over my clean tablecloth. Yes, indeed, I'll tell Miss Ross your mother would be glad to see her.'

To his relief George Campbell had no company for most of the long walk to Snorvig in the teeth of the gale. Apart from his shyness he was preoccupied at once with the immediate and the distant future. The engagement to Catriona could not be kept from his mother indefinitely. The tussle between them must take place sooner or later. He would have to confess to Catriona that he had not yet broken the news to his mother. Suppose his cowardice should provoke her into taking back the promise she had made him yesterday? Yet everybody in

Great Todday knew how difficult his mother could be. He would explain to Catriona that he must be the judge of the best moment to make his announcement. He would explain that his long absence yesterday had put her in a bad mood and that he had thought it wiser to postpone the occasion. Perhaps after all it would be tactful to go home to dinner at half past two instead of going on to Watasett after church. But if he was not going to dine with Catriona and her brother he might just as well have stayed at home this morning. The figure of his mother appeared to his fancy as grim and forbidding as Ben Bustival itself when he contemplated turning round; he decided to go on.

The attendance at church was sparse that morning, but that did not persuade Simon MacRurie to shorten his prayers or his sermon. The chief elder, who was also the leading merchant of Snorvig, liked nothing, apart from money, so well as the sound of his own voice. The absence of the Minister was his opportunity, and he took such good advantage of it that it was close on two o'clock when the congregation was released after as tough a couple of hours as any member of it could remember. Even Roderick's loyalty as a brother was strained.

'Och, I was pretty tired after sitting up all night with the poor Captain, and I couldn't get a wink of sleep in church what with the noise of the wind and the way Simon was trying to get the petter of it. And no sooner was Simon quiet than Donald Post must be starting. It was like a couple of pulls pellowing at one another over a fence. And not a tram in the whole of Todaidh Mór, Toctor, chust when I'm feeling chock full of emptiness for want of the smallest sensation as Father Macalister says. Och, poor soul, I'm sure he's feeling the pinch over in Todaidh Beag. He's a man who likes to trink a lot in motteration.'

'Seriously, Roderick, when *do* you think we shall have some more whisky?' Doctor Maclaren asked glumly.

'Toctor, don't be putting rittles to me without any

answer. Hullo, Mr Campbell, so you're going to be married. You've chosen a fine curl. You'll enchoy fine being married to her. Och, with a wife of your own it'll be more cheerful for you at Garryboo. You're a long way from the centre of things out there.'

'Come on, George, get into the car. I'm taking you along to Watasett now,' said the Doctor.

George looked surprised.

'I'm asked to dinner too, and I never lose a chance of eating a dinner cooked by Catriona,' he was told.

Fate had decided at any rate one of the questions which had been perplexing George Campbell's mind during that wind-swept, rain-washed trudge to church. He took his seat beside the Doctor in the Morris Minor, and a quarter of an hour later the dreich aspect of Loch Sleeport was forgotten in the cosy sitting-room of the school-house.

'Well, isn't this splendid?' said Norman, twinkling at his guests with satisfaction. 'And wouldn't it be better still if there were three full glasses in our hands?'

'Don't talk about it,' said the Doctor. 'There aren't. And that's that. I smell something good in the kitchen.'

'Golden plover,' Norman proclaimed. 'We won't be getting so many more now before autumn. Well, George, did Mistress Campbell skelp you last night when you told her the news?'

George Campbell blushed.

'As a matter of fact, Norman, I didn't tell her after all, last night. She was a little annoyed, because she'd expected me back by the earlier lorry. And I don't suppose your people have been told yet,' he added hopefully.

'They have not. The Doctor's going to run Catriona and me up to Knockdown this afternoon. He has to go and see old Hector MacRurie, who's pretty poorly.'

'We'll go round by the west side, and then I can drop you at Garryboo, George.'

'Thanks very much, Doctor,' said George Campbell without enthusiasm. The nine-mile walk from Watasett to Garryboo in this weather would not be pleasant, but at least it would postpone the moment for a full two and a half hours.

'Dinner's ready,' Catriona was calling.

And when they went into the dining-room on the table there was a bottle of claret.

'Oh, well, well, well!' Norman exclaimed. 'Doctor, you're a darling!'

'It's the last,' said Doctor Maclaren. 'And I hope we didn't shake it up too much. I kept it in the inside pocket of my overcoat.'

Presently he raised his glass to Catriona and George:

'I didn't have the pleasure of bringing either of you into the world, but I hope I'll have the pleasure of bringing a few of your children into the world. George, you're a lucky man: you're going to marry one of my favourite lassies in the island. I'm not so sure that she isn't the pick of the whole bunch. Dash it, George, I don't know how you managed to pick her. And I'm not casting reflections on your own worthiness by that remark. No, no, George, I was merely animadverting on your modesty. Well, here's to you both, and may you both be happy and prosperous and, except for an occasional little incident such as I alluded to at the beginning of my speech, may you never see me across the threshold of your house in my professional capacity, though if I'm asked, and I hope I'll be asked pretty often, may I cross it many a time as a friend! And, George, you'll have to learn to be as good a poacher as your future brother-in-law, the MacLenin of MacLenin. First catch your hare, wrote the famous Mrs Beeton in what so far as we know was an unique ebullition of humour. And I repeat her advice to you, George. It's no earthly use marrying a good cook like Catriona if you don't keep her supplied with the necessary material to display her skill, and when, as I've no doubt they will, your neighbours in Garryboo collect the wherewithal for a handsome wedding present, I hope you'll devote a reasonable proportion of it to procuring for yourself a really good gun.'

'Ah, well, Doctor,' Norman Macleod declared, 'it's a pity you were not in the Cabinet before this war started. You have such a fine appreciation of the need to arm for any emergency.'

George Campbell was excused from making a speech in reply to the Doctor's toast, and the company turned their attention to the food.

'Well,' said the Doctor, as he laid down his knife and fork, 'when I eat a grouse I think there's no bird like it and when I eat a woodcock I think there's no bird like it, but dash it, I believe a golden plover cooked to the very moment is the best of the lot.'

'A pheasant's pretty good,' Norman reminded his guest. 'I wish Captain Waggett had a few pheasants on Todaidh Mór. He wouldn't have very many.'

After dinner when the Doctor and Norman Macleod moved to the sitting-room George Campbell remained behind with Catriona for the alleged purpose of helping her clear away.

'I hope you don't despise me, Catriona, for not telling my mother last night about you and me. But, you know, I simply couldn't bring myself to do it.'

She laughed lightly.

'I'm just wondering what she's going to say to me when we meet.'

'I think once she's taken it out of me,' George replied, 'she may be all right with you. After all, she'll have to live with you.'

'Yes, I suppose she will,' Catriona assented, with a hint of a sigh.

'Well, where else could she live? She's too old to live by herself now. Anyway, I'm sure she'll grow to love you as a daughter,' he assured her solemnly.

Catriona's eyes sparkled with mirth.

'Not as a daughter, George. I might find that just a little bit too much like going to school again.'

It was about five o'clock when they dropped George Campbell at the road down to the school at Garryboo and drove on round the north side of the island, past the great aquiline headland of Sròn Ruairidh thrusting itself defiantly into the stormy sea, to Knockdown, the remote little cluster of thatched houses in one of which lived Dr Maclaren's patient, in another John Macleod, generally known as Iain Thormaid, and his wife.

John Macleod was a fine figure of a man with iron-grey hair and a trim dark beard, his wife small and merry with rich brown hair as yet scarcely dusted with grey.

'And so you want to marry George Campbell, Catriona,' said her father. 'Well, well, it's your business, *a nighinn*. And what does Mrs Campbell say to that?'

'George hasn't told her yet. He's telling her now,' Catriona replied.

'Ay, the poor chap is going through it just at this very moment,' said Norman. 'Unless he's run away from the music again,' he chuckled.

'And who would blame the poor *truaghan* if he did run away from it?' Mrs Macleod laughed.

'She's a warrior right enough,' her husband agreed. 'I mind fine when she first came to the island from Mull with the factor, before George was born. They lived where the Doctor lives now. Ay, she went to war the moment she set foot on the pier, and she's been at war ever since.'

'Well, I won't pretend I'm not disappointed you're not coming to live with us when Norman goes to the R.A.F.,' said Mrs Macleod. 'But we want you to be happy.'

'I'll be with you for quite a while, *a mhammi*,' said her daughter. Sitting here in the sunny kitchen of so many childish memories, Catriona felt a sudden dread of the inhospitable newness of the school at Garryboo. She reproached herself for having imagined that she would not be content at home.

'When do you think you will be getting married?' her mother asked.

'We were thinking we'd be married in the summer holidays, if George's mother doesn't make it too difficult.'

And as Catriona said that, Mrs Campbell *was* making it extremely difficult for poor George, who had just reached the schoolhouse and was being greeted by his mother with the information that she knew all.

'I was going to tell you last night,' he stammered, 'but you seemed so anxious to go to bed.'

'The bed I have made for myself and on which I must lie,' Mrs Campbell said in tones that Isaiah himself might have envied. 'This comes of spoiling my only child.'

'Of spoiling me?' George exclaimed in amazement.

'Spare the rod . . .'

'You never did,' he put in.

'And spoil the child,' his mother concluded, ignoring the interruption. 'And now in my old age I am reaping as I have sown. To think that I would be hearing from others that my own son is going to be married!'

'Who told you?'

'Who told me? Jemima Ross told me.'

'It was none of her business.'

'None of her business, indeed? When that great good-for-nothing Angus MacCormac came back this morning from Snorvig with that other rascal Samuel MacCodrum and blared the story all over Garryboo that the factor's son was going to marry Catriona Iain Thormaid?'

George's heart sank. When his mother referred to him as the factor's son he was back in knickerbockers.

'I only knew it myself yesterday afternoon,' he explained apologetically.

'Do you mean to stand there, George, and tell me that you'd not been thinking about that girl until yesterday afternoon?'

'I'd thought about her, yes.'

'Then why was I kept in the dark about your thoughts?' Mrs Campbell demanded sternly.

'What would have been the use of upsetting you until I knew what Catriona's feelings were?' George asked, and realized too late what an opening he had given his mother.

'So you knew it would upset me, and your mother's feelings didn't matter,' she commented bitterly.

'I mean upset you by the uncertainty,' he said, trying to recover the ground he had lost.

But Mrs Campbell was now in too strong a position.

'You knew it would upset me, and yet you went on, thinking only of yourself. You wanted to marry that girl, and if it meant breaking your old mother's heart you were set on having your own way. But you always were set on having your own way, George. How many times as a child did I catch you among the black currants, though you knew I wanted all the black currants there were for my jam? I used to try so hard to make you think less of your own desires, but no, black currants you wanted, and black currants you would have.'

'Catriona is a very nice girl,' George ventured to assert mildly.

'Perhaps you'll allow your mother to know better than you what a nice girl is. Your father had as much trouble with her father, Iain Thormaid, as with any crofter in Great Todday. He was the moving spirit behind the rascals who raided Knockdown and spoilt the best shooting in the island. And when Sir Robert gave orders to burn down the bothies they'd been running up for themselves on land that wasn't theirs, wasn't it John Macleod who loosed the Garryboo bull on your father and the Sheriff's men? No wonder his son grew up to be one of these good-for-nothing socialists who are just a set of thieves breaking the Tenth Commandment every hour of the day.'

'We must move with the times, mother. A lot of good people are socialists nowadays.'

'Sahtan has made you pretty glib, son. Will there be any times to move with in eternity?'

'You're bringing religion into it now, mother,' George protested feebly. 'And I don't see what religion has got to do with my wanting to marry Catriona.'

The old lady stiffened herself in her chair triumphantly.

'That's very true, George. You're just pushing religion right aside for the sake of what some people would call a pretty face. Well, I'm not going to interfere in the matter. I'll go and live in Glasgow with your aunt Ina.'

'But you hate Glasgow, mother,' her son objected.

'Never mind if I do. The Lord chastiseth those whom He loves, and who am I to set myself up against my Lord?'

'Surely you can try the experiment of living here with Catriona? She expects you to be living here.'

'I'm much obliged to her ladyship, but I've never lived anywhere on sufferance yet and I am not going to begin at my age,' Mrs Campbell snapped.

'People will think it so strange if you go away to Glasgow, mother.'

The old lady's cold blue eyes glittered for a moment and then turned again to ice.

'You might have thought more of what other people would think when you started to deceive your mother by going with Catriona Macleod.'

'But, apart from disapproving of her because you think her brother Norman is a socialist, you don't dislike Catriona herself, do you?' he asked anxiously.

'I don't like girls who go gallivanting over to Obaig for these permanent waves. Does she smoke?'

'I believe she smokes a cigarette occasionally.'

'Do you ever see me smoke a cigarette?'

'You don't like smoking. You don't like me to smoke,' George reminded her.

'Did the Apostle Paul smoke?' the old lady demanded.

'There wasn't any tobacco in his day. It hadn't been discovered.'

'If Sahtan had put tobacco in the hands of men, wouldn't the Apostle Paul have preached against smoking as a sin?'

'Well, if I bring Catriona to tea next Saturday will you be nice to her, mother?' George asked, in a desperate effort to get away from that old enemy of his childhood, the Apostle Paul.

Mrs Campbell looked at her son. She scented victory.

'The day you bring Catriona Macleod to this house I leave it and go to Glasgow,' she declared in a triumphant glow of self-righteousness.

George's eyes wavered wretchedly under his mother's icy regard. He longed for the strength of mind to tell her that he intended to bring Catriona to tea on Saturday and that if his mother did not like the idea the boat would be leaving for the mainland that afternoon. It was no use. The strength of mind was not there.

'Well, of course, if that's how you feel about it, I can't bring her,' he said, turning away in dejection.

The consciousness of victory flickered in Mrs Campbell's eyes the way a little blue flame will run across a peat and vanish almost simultaneously.

'That is for you to decide, George. And now you'd better go and feed the hens. I was too much upset by what Jemima Ross told me to feed them myself this afternoon.'

Chapter 5

A RUN ROUND GREAT TODDAY

===

Sergeant-major Odd, fortified by his visit to Father Macalister, did not resume the discussion with Joseph Macroon about the date of his marriage that Sunday evening. Instead, he talked with so much apparently inside information about the length of time the war was likely to last that Joseph was driven to bed in a gloom and left the sitting-room to Peggy and himself.

'It's going to be all right, Peggy darling,' he assured her. 'It's going to be All Sir Garnet as my old dad used to say. Father Macalister is going to tackle your dad. He and Duncan Macroon are going to tell everybody it's all fixed up for the Wednesday after Easter. So you'd better start seeing about your clothes. What I thought was we'd go off next day and take my old mother back to Nottingham....'

'Your mother?' Peggy exclaimed apprehensively.

'Well, I thought she and me would arrive by the boat on Tuesday. Of course we'd have to stay in some other house. I dare say Duncan Macroon would put us up. Then you and me and her might go over to the Snorvig Hotel after the wedding and catch Thursday's boat. We could travel back to Tummie over the week-end and I'd be back on duty by the Tuesday and you'd be lording it over our little cottage.'

'You're very sure of yourself, Fred,' she told him.

'Well, it was going to see Father Macalister. He understood everything so well. What a man, eh?'

'I hope your mother will like me.'

'Like you? She's going to love you. Well, I mean to say her one idea for the last twenty years ever since Dad went has been for me to settle down, and now thanks to you I'm going to at last. No, I'm not worrying about Ma.'

'I wish you weren't a Protestant, Fred,' his Peggy sighed.

The Sergeant-major grinned.

'Well, I am, and there it is.'

She sighed again.

'Yes, there it is, I suppose.'

The Sergeant-major was on the point of revealing his intention, but at that moment Kate Anne put her head round the door and said she was off to bed; the interruption saved his secret.

The wind had abated by morning, but Peggy was busy with the accumulation of the mails from last week; and the Sergeant-major decided it would be tactful to cross over to Snorvig and pay a visit to the company commander.

The prophylactic of hot grog on two successive nights had been effective in defeating the attempt by the Minister's germs to invade Captain Paul Waggett's head.

'No need to ask how you are, sir,' his visitor told him. 'Anyone can see you're in the pink.'

'Yes, I'm very well. Shall we go into my den, Sergeant-major? I think Mrs Waggett wants to do some household chores in the lounge. We've no maid at the moment, but a new one's coming in a day or two.'

'I don't think I was ever in this room before,' said the Sergeant-major when they entered the den, much of the floor-space of which was occupied by Paddy, Captain Waggett's overgrown Irish setter that was more like an auburn-haired St Bernard.

'No, I only made up my mind to have a den last year when Mrs Gorringe, Mrs Waggett's sister, stayed with us all last summer. She had a nervous breakdown.'

'I'm sorry to hear that.'

'Evacuees,' said Captain Waggett simply.

'That's one thing you've been spared, sir, in Great Today.'

'Yes, the people here don't realize how well off they are,' Captain Waggett observed loftily.

'Except for whisky, sir,' the Sergeant-major reminded him.

'Entirely their own fault. They shouldn't drink it all up. I have no sympathy whatever with them. Paddy!'

The huge dog thumped the floor with his tail.

'Get up, old man, and let Sergeant-major Odd get to his chair.'

'I can step over him, sir,' said the Sergeant-major a little too optimistically, for as he stepped Paddy did get up, and for a moment or two Captain Waggett's den had never seemed quite so much like the genuine article. When the confusion had subsided, the owner of the den pointed out its beauties and its conveniences.

'Those photographs are mostly of little shoots friends and I used to take in the days before I bought Snorvig House. That's Hucklebury in Essex.' He pointed to a stubble field across which a party of sportsmen were advancing behind dogs in the September sunshine of 1933. 'Best partridge shoot within reach of London. The tall man on the left of the line is Mr Blundell, the senior partner of the firm of chartered accountants to which I used to belong.' He continued to point out for his visitor's benefit the interesting details of the framed photographs. 'But I always say, Sergeant-major, that I wouldn't exchange any of these places for my own little shooting and fishing in the two Toddays. People in London thought I was mad when I came to live up here, but I've never regretted it. Never once. And I think I can feel that I'm of some use to the Islands. Of course, if the people would listen more to what I tell them, I could be of even more use; but they're very unresponsive to new ideas, except of course the claptrap talked by these Labour fellows. They're responsive enough to that. I see you're looking at my books, Sergeant-major. I have rather a good collection of Crime Club yarns. Did you ever read *Murder on the Escalator*? Or *Death on the Centre Court*? No? Both full of action. I must have plenty of action. You've read *The Garrotted Announcer*? You haven't? Oh, well, when you come over to do a spot of training, I'll lend it to you. It's interesting, quite apart from the story, for the inside view it gives of life in the B.B.C.'

'Talking of training, sir, how's G Company going along?' the Sergeant-major managed to inquire.

'I'm very disappointed,' the company commander admitted sadly. 'The attendance at parades has been growing steadily less for a year now, but just lately it has been appalling. Sergeant-major Thomson has been very conscientious, but then one expects a bank agent to be conscientious. I'm really most disappointed, after all the trouble I've taken to build up the Home Guard in the two Toddays. And then there was the unpleasantness of that Nelson bomber which made a forced landing on Little Todday.'

'What was that, sir? You must remember I've been away nearly eighteen months now.'

'Well, last October a Nelson made a forced landing on the machair about half-way between Tràigh Swish and Kiltod and as requested by R.A.F. Obaig I arranged for the plane to be guarded until the salvage squad arrived. Nobody has ever been able to find out exactly what did happen, but when the salvage squad did arrive there was practically nothing left of the plane.'

The Sergeant-major clicked his tongue.

'How did Lieutenant Macroon account for such a condition?' he asked.

'Fortunately for Lieutenant Macroon he was on the mainland at the time, but when I asked him to make a report he amazed me very much by saying that after inquiring into the matter he had come to the conclusion that the fairies were the culprits. And of course Joseph Macroon made a lot of capital out of it over that new school he's agitating for. He said the schoolchildren must have done all the mischief and that there'd be no keeping them in order until Kiltod had a new school. Why a leaky roof should make children pillage a plane I don't pretend to understand. But what amazed me most of all was to get rather a sharp letter from Colonel

Wolseley to say that it wasn't part of the duties of the Home Guard to assume any responsibility for crashed planes and that he did not want to be involved in a lot of unnecessary correspondence with the R.A.F.'

'I see the Colonel's point of view, sir,' the Sergeant-major said.

'Well, of course I should never dream of criticizing my Commanding Officer, Sergeant-major; but I can't help thinking that Colonel Wolseley is inclined to leave too much to the police just because he's Convener of the Police Committee in the County Council. Constable Macrae actually suggested that I had butted in over his head.'

'And what about the shooting, sir?' put in Sergeant-major Odd, who did not want to find himself committed to any expression of opinion about what had evidently been a lively controversy while it lasted.

'They've been very slack about that too. I offered a cup for competition.'

'I remember that, sir. It was won by the Little Todday platoon in 1941.'

'Well, last year it was won by Snorvig, but the Little Todday people said the markers had altered the targets and they wouldn't give up the cup. It's still on Little Todday. And last week when I put up a notice in the Hall that the cup would be shot for again this August somebody wrote across it, "Will there be plenty whisky in the cup?" It really is rather discouraging, especially when I think what a job I had to get hold of the cup, on which by the way I had to pay luxury tax. I took that up with the Territorial Association, but I got no satisfaction. Still, when one remembers what the Germans have done all over Europe, one mustn't grouse about things like that.'

'That's right, sir. And I'm sure we can work up the keenness again. Of course, I don't know what the Colonel's plans are for me. I understand he wants me to go to Glenbogle on Wednesday for a few days. Major Macdonald of Ben Nevis has got very keen on grenades, and the Colonel made a bit of a point of me going over there before any damage was done, and after I've been to Glenbogle Sir Hubert Bottley wants me up at Cloy for a day or two, but if you was to write to the Colonel right away I'm sure he'd let you have me for a week after that. Say tomorrow fortnight. I think the whisky and beer situation ought to be easier by then.'

Captain Waggett looked at the Sergeant-major in surprise. He hoped that his head had not been affected by the equatorial sun of Africa.

'I meant to say, sir, I think they're all feeling the effect of the shortage. It's bound to make for what they call war weariness. From what I can make out they haven't been without whisky for thousands of years. It's like depriving them of the very air they breathe.'

'They drink far too much whisky when they can get it,' said Captain Waggett austerely.

'And I wouldn't say that, sir, either. Put it this way. A fish doesn't drink water all the time, but you take a fish out of water, and where is the poor animal? Lost. It's the same with the people here. They don't want to drink whisky all the time, but they want to feel it's there.'

'Well, I'll write to Colonel Wolseley and ask for your services here as soon as he can spare you, but I'm afraid, whisky or no whisky, you'll find it a hard job to work up any enthusiasm, Sergeant-major. I'm very fond of the Todday folk, but it's no use shutting one's eyes to the fact that they lack staying-power. Where there was a chance that the Germans would try and invade us they were keen enough; but, now the danger of immediate invasion has faded, all that keenness has vanished. They're not sporting. They don't enjoy doing things just for the sake of doing them. That's where the English are superior to every other nation in the world. They play the game for the sake of the game. Other nations play games just for the sake of winning them. I tried to introduce football on Great Todday. I presented a ball each to the schools at Snorvig, Bobanish, Watasett, and Garryboo. Naturally, I was the referee, and I had to give a foul against one of the Garryboo team. It was more than a foul. It was an assault. What happened? Young Willie Macennan, the captain of Garryboo, deliberately dribbled the ball to the touch-line and kicked it into the sea!'

Sergeant-major Odd turned his head away and coughed.

'Excuse me, sir, something was tickling my throat.'

He did not add that it was a hastily strangled laugh.

'However, Sergeant-major, if you feel that you can pull the men together and get them to take their training seriously, nobody will be happier than I shall be. I'll write to Colonel Wolseley by tomorrow's post.'

'I shall do my best, sir, to buck things up.'

'I'm sure you will, Sergeant-major. Of course, being without a regular P.S.I. all this time has been a great handicap. We've had one or two itinerant Instructors, but they were inclined to bark at the men too much. And that's no use.'

'No use at all in the Islands, sir.'

'By the way, what about your marriage with Joseph Macroon's daughter? When is that to come off?'

'The idear is for us to get married just after Easter, sir, if all goes according. I don't think they can shift me all of a sudden again, touch wood.'

'Well, I'm sure I wish you all happiness, Sergeant-major, but I wish you could persuade your future father-in-law to be a little more strict about the black-out in Little Todday. The whole of Kiltod was a blaze of light one night the week before last. It was better last week.'

'I think there's a shortage of paraffin just now,' said the Sergeant-major. 'And, with all the lighthouses and all the harbour-lights in the Islands going strong, the people can't understand the point of the black-out.'

'Same old story,' Captain Waggett commented sadly. 'No idea of discipline. Can't people understand that the whole point of the black-out is to show the determination of the British people to win the war? And anyway an order is an order surely?'

'Quite, sir, but it is a bit refreshing to find people who think more of what you might call a common-sense order. Perhaps it's having spent all my life in the army makes me feel that. Still, you're undoubtedly right, sir, and I'll say a word in Joseph Macroon's ear.'

Sergeant-major Odd thought it prudent to avoid the slightest appearance of sympathizing too much with the views of Little Todday about the black-out. He was anxious that Captain Waggett should regard him as indispensable to the recovery of discipline.

'I think it would be rather a good idea if I were to run you round the island in the car,' Captain Waggett suggested. 'I'd like them all to see that you're back with us again.'

'Just as you like, sir,' said the Sergeant-major.

'Are you afraid of catching cold?' he was asked.

'We shan't catch cold in your car, sir. And anyway, I think it looks like turning into a really fine day at last.'

'I wasn't thinking about the weather. I was thinking that perhaps it would be a good thing if you called on the Minister, and he's got a very bad cold.'

Captain Waggett himself did not get out of the Austin when they pulled up outside the door of the Manse.

'You'll get away from Mr Morrison more easily if I don't come in,' he explained.

The Sergeant-major found the Reverend Angus Morrison hunched up by a coal fire in the study, a black and yellow Dress Macleod plaid round his shoulders.

'How nice of you to call, Sergeant-major Odd,' said Mrs Morrison, a rather pretty, nervously ladylike young woman from Kelvinside. 'The Minister has a really terrible cold. He can hardly speak, and tomorrow he has to bury poor Captain MacPhee. So sad, wasn't it?'

'Yes, a fine old type. Now don't you get up, Mr Morrison, please,' the Sergeant-major urged, for the little Minister's gallant attempt to welcome his caller had produced a spasm of coughing.

'I can't think where I got this cold,' he gasped when

71

the spasm had exhausted itself. 'I'm sure we're all very glad to welcome you back to Great Todday, Sergeant-major Odd. They've missed you in the Home Guard. I'm afraid they've been inclined to rest upon their laurels too much. You've travelled a long way they tell me since we saw you last, Sergeant-major Odd.'

'I was out in West Africa, sir, yes.'

'You'll have seen something of our missions out there. You've been greatly privileged, Sergeant-major Odd.'

'I'm afraid I was too busy with military duties to see very much of any missions, Mr Morrison. But I know there are a lot of missionaries out there.'

'I would have liked very much to be a chaplain to the Forces,' the little Minister wheezed wistfully. 'A great experience, Sergeant-major Odd. Yes, indeed. A great experience right enough. But with a wife and a baby I did not feel my domestic responsibilities would have justified me in taking such a step. And they tell me you're going to get married yourself. I'm sure I wish you every happiness.'

'Yes, Peggy Macroon and me are hoping to be married just after Easter.'

'I don't know her well,' put in Mrs Morrison, 'but I've always thought she was a very nice girl.'

'You'll be Church of England yourself, Sergeant-major Odd?' the Minister asked.

'That's right, sir.'

'Ah, well, I have a great respect for Father Macalister,' the Minister said. 'He's a great hand at teasing, though. I remember I once said to him, "Ah, well, *a Mhaighstir Seumas*," – for of course we were talking in the Gaelic to one another – "ah, well," I said, "we're all labourers in the same vineyard." And I remember Father Macalister said – I thought it was rather witty, though it was against myself – "Ay," he said, "we're all labourers in the same vineyard, Mr Morrison, but it was we who planted the grapes."'

The little Minister's chuckle was swept away in another spasm of coughing, and the Sergeant-major rose to take his leave.

'I hope to find you quite your active self again when I come back presently for a bit of training. Captain Waggett and me are just having a run round the island this morning. We're going to call on Mr Campbell at Garryboo first.'

'You'll have to congratulate him, Sergeant-major Odd,' said Mrs Morrison. 'He's just become engaged to Norman Macleod's sister Catriona.'

'Well, Captain Waggett was complaining about the falling off in the shooting,' said the Sergeant-major. 'But there doesn't seem much wrong with Cupid's shooting in these parts, that's a fact. He's a proper marksman in the two Toddays.'

The Sergeant-major saluted and withdrew.

'I'm sorry you told him about George Campbell and Catriona Macleod, Janet,' the little Minister said to his wife when their visitor was gone.

'Why, Angus?'

'Old Bean Eachainn Uilleim was in this morning to see me about her pension, and she was telling me that Mistress Campbell is not taking it at all too well. I won't be able to do anything with her until I get my voice back. I'll want all the voice I've got. And then I must try to make her see reason.' The little Minister gave a bronchial sigh and pulled the black and yellow plaid closer round his shoulders.

The Austin was passing Captain MacPhee's trim garden where the giant clam-shell from the Great Barrier Reef in front of the darkened house seemed like Captain MacPhee's coffin.

'I'm sorry I didn't see the old man again,' said the Sergeant-major. 'He had some wonderful yarns about the old windjammer days.'

'But he became absolutely reckless towards the end,' Captain Waggett said. 'I got up a Brains Trust last December, and somehow an argument started about Jonah and the whale. I pointed out that anybody with the most elementary knowledge of natural history knew that a whale couldn't swallow anything larger than a sardine, and Captain MacPhee said I was talking nonsense. So I said, "Surely you're not going to tell me that you were ever swallowed by a whale, Captain MacPhee?" And what d'ye think his answer was?'

'Not that he had been?' the Sergeant-major asked.

'No, he didn't go as far as that, but he said he knew a man who had been. And the audience actually clapped. I said, "Well, Captain MacPhee, the whale may have swallowed your friend, but I'm afraid I can't swallow your story." And, you know, the audience never saw my joke. They just sat like a lot of dummies. Oh, well, the old man's gone now, so one mustn't be too critical, but I confess I was really staggered at the time.'

'I must remember that one next time somebody at Fort Augustus tells me he saw the Loch Ness monster cross the road with a sheep in his mouth.'

'Yes, but what I find so annoying, Sergeant-major, is that people who believe a lot of nonsense about the Loch Ness monster laugh when you tell them that Hitler may still invade us. In my opinion people like that deserve to be invaded.'

Sergeant-major Odd, looking across the Coolish to Little Todday as the car drove northward and wondering whether he would be back in time to walk with Peggy over to Tràigh Swish that afternoon, found it easier for his enjoyment of the drive to agree with everything Captain Waggett said.

George Campbell was in school when his mother admitted them.

'You remember Sergeant-major Odd, Mrs Campbell,' Captain Waggett smirked. 'He's just back from Africa, and we shall have the benefit of his advice again.'

'Advice?' asked Mrs Campbell. 'What about?'

'Our training in the Home Guard.'

The old lady grunted.

'I dare say the Sergeant was better occupied in Africa. I'm sure I hope so.'

'Your hens are looking very well, Mrs Campbell,' said Captain Waggett.

'They *are* very well,' she told him.

'I suppose they've started to lay now?'

'They wouldn't be alive if they hadn't,' Mrs Campbell rapped out.

'We've been rather short of eggs in Snorvig,' Captain Waggett murmured hopefully.

'I quite believe it,' said the old lady.

At this moment George Campbell came in from the school to greet the visitors.

'I've just heard from the Minister that we have to congratulate you, Mr Campbell,' said the Sergeant-major, shaking George warmly by the hand.

'Congratulate him on what?' the old lady demanded.

'On his approaching marriage,' said the Sergeant-major.

'The Minister told you that George was going to be married?'

'Yes, just now.'

'I'll be seeing the Minister in a day or two,' Mrs Campbell said balefully, and with this she walked out of the room.

'And when's the happy day, Mr Campbell?' the Sergeant-major asked.

'I don't quite know yet,' George replied, following his mother's exit with his eyes.

'I suppose you're waiting for the whisky ship to come home the same as everyone else,' the Sergeant-major laughed. 'From what I can make out it isn't lawful wedlock here without there's whisky.'

George Campbell smiled feebly, and Captain Waggett who deprecated so much attention being paid to Venus brought the conversation round to Mars. Five minutes later, the schoolmaster of Garryboo said he really must be getting back into the classroom.

'Any message for your intended, Mr Campbell?' the Sergeant-major asked. 'We shall be calling at Watasett on our way back to Snorvig.'

'No, thank you, there's no message,' said George, looking nervously in the direction of the door, for he heard his mother's footsteps.

'Well, I hope we'll see you over on Little Todday when Peggy Macroon and me get married after Easter,' said Sergeant-major Odd cordially.

'Are you a Roman Catholic, Sergeant Odd?' asked Mrs Campbell, who had re-entered the room in time to hear this invitation.

'No, m'm, I'm not,' he told her.

'And you're proposing to marry a Roman Catholic? A man of your age?' the old lady demanded sternly.

'We must be getting along, Mrs Campbell,' Captain Waggett hastily intervened. 'Sergeant-major Odd and I have to see quite a few people this morning.'

When they were back in the car the Sergeant-major expressed a strong desire to bring his mother to Great Todday in order to give Mrs Campbell an opportunity of hearing what a decent, sensible, and kindly old woman thought of such a fossilized terror.

'And she'd tell her too, sir. Not half she wouldn't. The way that old Tartar glared at me!'

'She's very bigoted of course,' Captain Waggett said. 'I've had a lot of trouble with her. Don't you remember when we had that invasion exercise on a Sunday and she locked Sergeant Campbell up in his room the day before to prevent him from taking part in it?'

'It's hardly credible that there are such people nowadays. Well, it makes anyone feel glad they didn't live once upon a time, and that's a fact. I'd sooner be up against one Hitler than a world full of Mrs Campbells.'

The car drove on past Knockdown and turned south along the east coast of the island, below the steeps of Ben Sticla, until it came to Bobanish, a sizeable village at the head of Loch Bob, the largest of the island's sea lochs. Here they called upon Captain Waggett's second-in-command, Lieutenant John Beaton, the local schoolmaster. Like his colleague at Garryboo John Beaton was in school, but they were warmly welcomed by his wife in the gabled schoolhouse by the door of which the veronica was already in bloom.

'Welcome back to the Islands, Sergeant,' exclaimed trim and dainty little Mrs Beaton, her bright bird's eyes sparkling with pleasure. 'Yes, indeed, I'm sure John has missed you all these months. And so you've found yourself a wife in Little Todday. Bravo, it's you that's a wise man. I'm a Great Todday woman myself, but a Little Todday woman is the next best, and I've no doubt you'll be saying to yourself that she is the best. What a pity we can't offer you a dram!'

'I never drink anything before lunch, Mrs Beaton,' Captain Waggett assured her.

'Ach, it's not you I'm worrying about, Mr Waggett. It's for Sergeant Odd.'

'That's all right, Mrs Beaton,' said the Sergeant-major. 'When there's a spirit like you about there's no other spirit needed.'

'Get along with you, Sergeant. We never had to teach you the blarney. You had enough for yourself, even if you are a Sassunnach. I'm sure it was the way you won Peigi Iosaiph, and a lovely girl she is too. Such lovely eyes. They tell me you're to be married after Easter.'

'Talk about radiolocation,' the Sergeant-major exclaimed. 'It's slow compared with the way news travels on the two Toddays.'

'But, Mr Waggett,' Mrs Beaton went on in a flutter of excitement, 'have you heard the news about George Campbell and Catriona Macleod?'

'We've just come from Garryboo,' said Captain Waggett. 'We found Mrs Campbell in a very gloomy mood. Very gloomy. I don't think she's at all pleased.'

'I'm sure she won't be. Nothing will please her till she finds herself in Heaven and everybody else in the other place. Then she'll be happy. I'm really sorry for poor Catriona, for she's one of the nicest girls on the island, and she'll make George Campbell a splendid wife. And how's Mrs Waggett? I hope the hens are laying well.'

'Not too well, I'm afraid,' said the henwife's husband.

'Ah, well, ours are doing just splendid. But wait you now, I'll go and tell himself you're here.'

Mrs Beaton bustled away to fetch her husband, while the two visitors waited in the sitting room. Scilly White narcissi filled the air with sweetness from pots in the window. The low February sun streamed in through the panes. The door of the cuckoo-clock hanging on the wall beside the fireplace flew open and the wooden bird proclaimed noon.

'This is more like what I call home, sir,' the Sergeant-major observed.

And then John Beaton himself came in, a burly Skye-man in his mid forties with a high complexion and sandy hair.

After the greetings and the congratulations on his approaching marriage, which the Sergeant-major was by now accepting as congratulations on a *fait accompli* in spite of the fact that Joseph Macroon's approval of the date for the wedding had not yet been obtained, the three men came down to the sterner business of war.

'I'm worried about the growing slackness of the Home Guard, Mr Beaton,' said the commander of G Company. 'I'm considering the advisability of prosecuting one or two of the worst shirkers.'

'I don't believe that would do any good at all,' his second-in-command argued. 'Indeed I am sure it would do a great deal of harm. You'll put their backs up, Captain.'

'Well, something must be done to make them realize that they are under military discipline.'

'I'm afraid there's not much anyone can do, Captain,' the schoolmaster insisted. 'You'll never make the people in the Islands do anything they think is a waste of time.'

'They waste a lot of time in talk,' Captain Waggett snapped.

'Ah, well, Captain, they don't think that such a waste of

time. And anyway they'd consider they were wasting their own time. What they dislike is having their time wasted for them by other people.'

'Are the people of the two Toddays going to claim that they know more about what must be done to win the war than the Prime Minister?' Captain Waggett inquired in lofty disgust.

'We would none of us be so presumptuous as that, Captain,' his second-in-command assured him. 'But I think we all of us feel that Home Guard work should not be allowed to interfere too much with really vital jobs. We must remember, Mr Waggett, that both islands have made a great contribution to the war by sending so many of their men to fight the battle of the Atlantic in the Merchant Navy, and indeed, where would the country be now without the Merchant Navy?' John Beaton continued, cracking his finger-joints in the way he did when emotion was rising in his burly frame.

'I'm sure nobody realizes better than Captain Waggett how much the two Toddays have done to keep the Win in Winston and take the Hit out of Hitler,' the Sergeant-major put in, with a lenitive smile.

'Naturally I realize the contribution made by the two Toddays to the Mercantile Marine,' said Paul Waggett huffily. 'But all the food and munitions in the world wouldn't help us if our country was overrun by the Huns.'

'That's true enough, Captain,' John Beaton admitted, 'but the people here feel that, if at this stage of the war the Germans are strong enough to overrun us, there's nothing they can do to stop them.'

'I call that rank defeatism,' Captain Waggett said severely. 'And I must say I'm surprised by your attitude, Mr Beaton. It comes as a painful shock to me.'

Sergeant-major Odd was winking at John Beaton as fast as a heliograph behind Captain Waggett's back; but the choler of the man with a high complexion and sandy hair was beyond the sedative power of winks.

'I take exception to that remark, Mr Waggett. I consider it uncalled for and very injurious to my position. I really don't know what you'll be saying next.'

'I'm sure Captain Waggett wasn't meaning to cast any reflections, Mr Beaton,' said Sergeant-major Odd soothingly. 'Nobody knows better than Captain Waggett what a lot of hard work you've put in over Home Guard correspondence. This is just a little misunderstanding.'

'I am very willing to resign from my position in the Home Guard, Mr Waggett,' the schoolmaster declared, a crimson spot flaming now on both of his cheekbones. 'I had no desire to take on so much responsibility outside my own work. But when you talk about prosecuting men for not attending parades it is my duty to tell you that you would be making a great mistake.'

The last thing that Captain Waggett wanted was to have to deal with the Home Guard correspondence himself, and if John Beaton were to resign there was nobody else in the island to whom he could hand it over. He decided to be propitiatory.

'I'm sorry if I hurt your feelings by that remark about defeatism, Mr Beaton. I didn't intend it to be derogatory. If you think that prosecuting a few shirkers won't effect anything I'm content to abide by your judgement. All I'm anxious about is that Sergeant-major Odd shouldn't take up his duties again only to find that there's nothing for him to do.'

'Sergeant-major Odd was always well liked by the people, Captain, and if he can convince them that they are not wasting their time I'm sure he'll find good support,' said John Beaton.

'Nothing could be fairer than that, could it, sir?' the Sergeant-major urged. 'I'm sure if Colonel Wolseley lets you have my services for a few days presently Lieutenant Beaton and me will fix up a scheme of training for the spring and summer that won't tread on anybody's corns.'

The schoolmaster's choler had subsided under the Sergeant-major's good nature combined with the gratification of having wrung from Captain Waggett the nearest approach to an apology anybody in the Islands had hitherto achieved.

'Well, we must be going on now to see Sergeant Macleod at Watasett,' said the commanding officer.

As they passed out to get into the car Mrs Beaton whispered to him:

'I put half a dozen eggs for Mrs Waggett on the seat at the back. I wish I could have put some butter with them, but our cow's dry just now.'

And while Mrs Beaton was saying this to Captain Waggett her husband was saying to the Sergeant-major:

'I'm really mortified that there is simply not a dram in the house. But you know the state of affairs, Sergeant. It's unprocurable. Nobody in the island can remember anything like it.'

'It may come by tomorrow's boat,' the Sergeant-major said cheerfully.

'It may, it may. But we've been saying that now for a fortnight. And even if it does come I'm sure Roderick will not have a bottle to spare. He'll want every drop for the bar. Ah, well, *beannachd leibh, beannachd leibh.* Good-bye, Sergeant. We'll be seeing you again, soon.'

The car drove on southward, making a wide curve round the base of Ben Pucka, to reach the head of Loch Sleeport.

'Lieutenant Beaton was in a very strange mood,' his Commanding Officer observed to the Sergeant-major.

'He was a bit worried, sir, by your talk of prosecuting men for non-attendance at parades.'

'Well, what am I to do, Sergeant-major? I don't want to prosecute anybody. But something must be done to bring home to these people that there's a war on.'

'I think this drought of whisky has taught them that, sir. And seriously, sir, I don't believe prosecutions would do a bit of good. I don't think they're easy to drive out here, though nobody could wish for a better lot of fellows to lead.'

'I don't want to prosecute, Sergeant-major. It's no pleasure to me. I could have prosecuted a lot of people for poaching, but I never have. Unfortunately, the command of the Home Guard here isn't my private affair. I'm the representative of the country's will to victory, and, however painful it may be to my personal feelings, I may have to ask the Colonel to prosecute. This is total war. We are fighting to preserve England – I mean Britain, and I have to do my bit, as we used to say in the last war. What surprises me is that Lieutenant Beaton didn't seem able to grasp my point of view. He's quite an intelligent man.'

'Ah well, he gets a bit het up sometimes. Anyone with a ginger top always does. Once the fine weather comes on and they get down to shooting I'm sure everything will go well.'

'There's another problem. Who's going to be the section commander at Watasett when Sergeant Macleod goes?'

'I expect Sergeant Macleod will have his eye on somebody, sir.'

'Of course he'll have his eye on somebody, Sergeant-major. But he'll have it on the wrong person. Well, there's one thing, perhaps when he leaves Watasett I shall get an opportunity of catching some of my own sea-trout.'

The car was now in sight of the township of Watasett, the houses of which were clustered along either side of the winding inlet of Loch Sleeport. This had once been the harbourage of a dozen fishing-boats before the destructive activity of trawlers had made fishing profitless.

The discussion between Norman Macleod and the commander of G Company about the best man in Watasett to select for promotion to section commander lasted for about twenty minutes, during which time the class Norman Macleod had temporarily deserted was at work writing a composition on the theme, 'Why I am proud of Great Todday'. Half-way through the examination of the claims of two MacRuries, a Maclean, a Macmillan and a

Fraser to the position Sergeant-major Odd slipped away to have a chat with Catriona.

'Well, Miss Macleod, so you and me are going to take the plunge together,' he said. 'Now see here, I've just come from Garryboo, and your intended isn't looking so happy as any young fellow ought to look when he's just got engaged to a girl like you. And the trouble is your future mar-in-law. Well, when I tell you she actually had the nerve to try and tell me off because I was going to marry a Catholic you'll understand what she'll be capable of saying to her own son.'

'Did she say that to you, Sarchant? What a chick!' exclaimed Catriona.

'It *was* a cheek. If it hadn't been I didn't want to make things worse for your young man I'd have walked into her properly. But what I want to say is this. Peggy and me are going to have what you call a rayjack.'

'A what?'

'Raychack ... rayjack ... what you have before the wedding; I know whisky comes into it. And, of course, that may mean we may have to wait a bit.'

'Ach, a *rèiteach*!'

'That's what I said, didn't I? Only perhaps I forgot the cough at the end. Well, if you have trouble with that old rhinoceros ... asking the poor animal's pardon ... you drag your young man over to our rayjack, and if he doesn't rayjack some common sense into that old Tartar when he gets home that night, well, George Campbell isn't the man I took him for when I heard you and him were going to be married. That's all I wanted to say. I think you're in for a bit of trouble, but don't you worry. I've had a bit of trouble with my future par-in-law, and the only thing to do is what Father Macalister said ... roll right over them.'

The discussion about the future leader of the Watasett section was still undecided when Sergeant-major Odd went back into the sitting-room.

'Well, I'm afraid we'll have to postpone the decision,

Sergeant Macleod. Mrs Waggett will be expecting me back for lunch.'

'Ach, we none of us want to postpone our food, Mr Waggett,' said Norman Macleod. 'But apart from that, I believe postponement is one of the great pleasures of existence.'

'Not of marriage, Mr Macleod,' said the Sergeant-major.

'Ah, well, I've postponed the need of any further postponement in that matter, Sergeant, by postponing the notion altogether,' the young schoolmaster grinned.

'Don't you be too sure of yourself. You don't know what may happen when you get into the R.A.F.'

'I'm not worrying. Cupid rhymes with stupid for me.'

'You're asking for trouble, you are,' the Sergeant-major warned him.

'I'm afraid we really *must* be getting along,' said Captain Waggett, who disliked badinage except on a public platform when he could gently chaff an audience. 'Didn't you tell me Joseph Macroon was going to meet you at the pier at half past twelve? It's twenty to one already.'

Captain Waggett and the Sergeant-major got into the car. Norman Macleod went back to his class.

'Well, let me have a look at what you've been writing,' he told them.

He picked up the first composition by a juvenile MacRurie, and read out:

'I am proud of Great Todday because it is bigger than Little Todday. We have cows and sheeps in Great Todday. The Island Queen comes to Snorvig three times every week but it did not come last week because the wether was too bad. and when there is no wisky we are all very sad.'

Captain Waggett dropped the Sergeant-major by the road down to the pier, but when he reached it there was no sign of the *Morning Star*.

'Are you looking for Joseph Macroon?' Constable Macrae sauntered up to inquire. 'He was asking for you half an hour ago, but he said he had to go back to Kiltod.'

'Well, I've done something I never managed to do yet in these islands, Constable.'

'What was that, Sergeant?'

'I've managed to be late for a boat crossing the Coolish.'

The Constable smiled. He was from the mainland and therefore under the delusion that the islanders were more unpunctual than his own people away in Kintail.

'Ay, it's pretty difficult to be late anywhere in the Toddays,' he agreed. 'Wait a minute, though, Sergeant, there's the *Kittiwake* out there. The Biffer will take you over. He's feeling fine this morning. He's had a letter that his son Donald is safe in Ireland.'

In response to shouts from the pier the Biffer, much to the relief of the Sergeant-major who was seeing his walk with Peggy that afternoon washed out, brought the *Kittiwake* alongside.

'Will you take the Sergeant over to Kiltod, Airchie?' Constable Macrae shouted down to him.

'Sure, I'll take him. Come along, Sergeant,' and when the Sergeant-major was aboard he turned to him, 'I've had some good news, Sergeant. My boy Donald who was torpedoed is all safe and sound. Ay, he came ashore on some island off Donegal, and the weather was so bad they couldn't put him over to the mainland. He got on fine, though. He said they managed to understand one another in the Gaelic very well after a bit.'

'You must be feeling pretty good, Corporal.'

'Och, I'm feeling right on top of the whole world this morning, Sergeant. I was just away to see if my lobster-pots had all been broken to pieces by the terrible weather we've been having. What a morning for a good dram! I believe I'd stay on top of the world for a week if I could have a really good dram. That was a funny way of Joseph to behave going away like a shot out of a gun, and you not there. What kind of hospitality is that at all? Ach, I believe he's in a bit of a stew because you'll be taking Peigi Ealasaid away from him so soon. They tell me the wedding is to be just after Easter. I was asking Joseph, and he was off in the *Morning Star* like a shot out of a gun. Ach, he's feeling the shortage of whisky. We're all feeling it, Sergeant. Never mind. Good things will come again, and we'll have whisky galore. *Uisge beatha gu leòir!*'

While the Biffer was taking the Sergeant-major over to Kiltod, Captain Waggett was occupying the time before his wife brought in lunch by writing to Captain Quiblick, the Security Intelligence Officer responsible for No. 14 Protected Area:

Snorvig House
Great Toddy
Western Isles
February 22nd, 1943

SECRET

Dear Captain Quiblick,

I feel I ought to let you know that there seems to be a wave of defeatism in this island at present. It has affected the Home Guard to some extent, and I think it might be worth your while to investigate the phenomenon which, I confess, baffles me completely. Possibly you might care to notify your opposite number, Captain Lomax-Smith, at Obaig in case he would like to make investigations on Little Todday. I need hardly say that I am entirely at your disposal if you decide to pursue the matter. With kind regards,

Yours sincerely,
Paul Waggett, Capt. H.G.

Captain P. St John Quiblick,
Security Intelligence Corps,
No. 14 Protected Area,
Nobost Lodge,
Nobost, Mid Uist

This letter the commander of G Company enclosed in an envelope marked SECRET in red ink, and the envelope thus inscribed he enclosed in a registered envelope.

'What's the matter, Paul? You look worried,' said his wife.

'Oh, it's nothing much, old lady. But one can't help worrying sometimes over one's responsibilities.'

He sighed patriotically.

Chapter 6

THE TWO TRAVELLERS

━━━━━

A SMALL consignment of whisky did arrive by the boat
on Tuesday; but as John Beaton had foreseen it was all
required by Roderick MacRurie for the bar, and it was in
such short supply that nobody was served with more than
one dram in two days. This naturally led to arguments.
Everybody was convinced that he had had his dram the
day before yesterday, never yesterday. On top of that those
who came in from remoter districts and particularly those
who had crossed over from Little Todday complained
that the people of Snorvig itself were getting preferential
treatment. Finally, although the whisky situation had
been faintly, very faintly, relieved, the beer situation de-
teriorated rapidly, and within a week after Sergeant-
major Odd had gone back to the mainland nobody was
being allowed more than a pint a day.

'And the way things are going,' Big Roderick told his
customers, 'you'll be lucky to have half a pint very soon.'

On Saturday, February 27th, not a barrel of beer
arrived with the *Island Queen*, and that evening
Ruairidh Mór cut the allowance to half a pint a day.

In the corner of the bar on that Saturday night sat a
thin young man with a neo-Caroline moustache. If his
nose had been a little shorter and his chin a little longer
he would not have been bad-looking. He was sporting
plus-fours of the barrage-balloon type, from the umber
convolutions of which his ankles emerged like chicken-
bones. Nobody had paid much attention to him on the
pier that afternoon, and carrying his own bag he had
walked up to the hotel where he had registered as Wil-
liam Anthony Brown, Tweed Merchant. When dark fell
he had proceeded cautiously to Snorvig House, the adverb
meaning that every ten yards he had turned sharply

round and listened for the sound of footsteps following him.

'Can I speak to Captain Waggett?' he inquired when the door was opened by a small girl in a cap and apron.

'Captain Waggett doesn't live here,' said the small girl, panting with shyness. 'This is the Manse.'

'And he turned round just like a flash,' the small girl told Mrs Morrison afterwards.

Mr Brown turned round three times more before he emerged from the drive that led up to the Manse, so fearful was he of being followed. A hundred yards along the road he came to the stone pillars on either side of the gate of the Snorvig House drive. The door was opened to him by another small girl in a cap and apron. It was the first time Kennethina Macdonald had been called upon to answer the front-door bell, for she had only joined the Waggett household on leaving school two days previously.

'Can I speak to Captain Waggett?' Mr Brown inquired again.

'I don't know,' Kennethina whispered, her chubby face shimmering with embarrassment.

'Will you say Mr Brown would like to speak to him?' Kennethina seemed, and indeed was, on the verge of bursting into tears.

'I don't know who you are at all,' she managed to gasp tremulously.

'I'm Mr Brown, and I want to speak to Captain Waggett.'

Luckily Mrs Waggett had heard the bell ring and, doubtful of Kennethina's aplomb yet in dealing with callers, came along to see who it was.

'Is Captain Waggett expecting you?' she asked.

'I think so,' said Mr Brown, in such a mysterious tone of voice that Mrs Waggett's fancy began to race round all sorts of dire possibilities from assassination to blackmail.

'Run and tell the master that a gentleman wants to speak to him,' she said to Kennethina.

Kennethina looked puzzled. Then her face cleared.

'Will I go along to the Manse the way I am now, or will I put my hat and coat on?' she asked.

'Captain Waggett, Ina, not the Minister.'

When Kennethina had gone off to the den, Mrs Waggett decided to assume that Mr Brown had no fell purpose.

'Such a shortage of girls nowadays, Mr Brown. And Captain Waggett and I always encourage them to join up,' she said with a bright smile which covered her face with what stucco experts call hair-cracks.

'Quite,' said Mr Brown sagaciously.

A minute or two later Mr Brown was closeted with Captain Waggett in the den.

'Didn't you get Major Quiblick's letter notifying you of my arrival?' he asked.

'I was just going to open my post when you called.' Paul Waggett looked at the letters and selected a registered one from which he drew a heavily sealed envelope stamped V E R Y S E C R E T He broke the seal and read:

V E R Y S E C R E T   Security Intelligence Corps
No. 14 Protected Area
Nobost Lodge
Nobost, Mid-Uist
25/2/43

Dear Captain Waggett,

I am much obliged for your letter of the 22nd inst. I am taking steps accordingly. Last week No. 13 Protected Area was incorporated with No. 14 P.A. and therefore I am now the S.I.C. officer in charge of both with the rank of Major. This means that it will no longer be necessary to apply for a permit to travel between Great Todday and Little Todday. It also means that I am now responsible for all security intelligence on both islands.

Lieut. W. A. Boggust will arrive at Snorvig on Saturday the 27th inst., to investigate the matter to which you called my attention in your letter of the 22nd inst. He will travel under the name of W. A. Brown, and his apparent object will be to enquire into the tweed industry on both islands. I am sure you will give him any help in your power to fulfil his mission satisfactorily. I have instructed Lieut. Boggust to contact you on his arrival provided that he can do so without calling attention to himself. You can rely absolutely on his discretion.

Yours sincerely,

P. St John Quiblick
Major S.I.C.

'You have a very interesting job, Mr Boggust,' said Captain Waggett.

'Brown, Brown, please, sir. I think it's always best to preserve one's cover all the time.'

'Well, of course, we're quite safe in my den.'

'Oh, I know that, sir. But I'm tremendously thorough. I only think of myself now as Brown. Now, sir, will you put me in the picture here? I understand from Major Quiblick that defeatism in these islands is rampant.'

'I wouldn't go so far as to use the word "rampant". I should prefer to say it was rife.'

'Quite, quite,' the Intelligence officer quacked in comprehension of the nice distinction.

'I'd better call you "Mr Brown", hadn't I? I mean to say if you really were a tweed merchant I shouldn't call you "Brown", should I?'

'Quite, quite. And I shouldn't call you "sir", should I?' Mr Brown suggested.

'No, quite,' Captain Waggett agreed. 'Well, now, what exactly do you want to know, Mr Brown?'

'What can you tell me, Captain Waggett?'

'Well, I think you should form your own impressions.'

'Quite. But what would be the best way of putting myself in the picture?'

'I'd suggest that after your tea – they give you tea up at the hotel – of course, I'd be delighted to give you dinner, but I think that might make you rather conspicuous – yes, after you've had your tea I'd go in the bar if I were you and just listen to the conversation. I think you'll realize then what I mean by this wave of defeatism.'

'Quite. And what about tomorrow, sir? I mean what about tomorrow?'

'What do you mean, what about tomorrow?'

'I mean would it be possible for us to meet somewhere without being too conspicuous?'

'It's not easy. Not at all easy,' said Captain Waggett after a moment's reflection. 'You see it's Sunday tomorrow. If it were Monday you could go round the island looking for lengths of tweed, but you couldn't do that on Sunday.'

'What about Little Todday? That's a Catholic island, isn't it? They wouldn't pay any attention to Sunday there, would they?'

'No, but there's no tweed woven on Little Todday, and anyway unless you'd made arrangements with one of the Little Todday boatmen you wouldn't get across. The people here won't use their boats on Sunday.'

'There seems to be very little intercourse between the two islands,' said Mr Brown. 'I was looking up our card-index of permits issued and I couldn't find that we'd had one application for a permit to travel between the two islands.'

'How long have you been at Nobust?' Captain Waggett asked.

'Only a fortnight, sir. I mean only a fortnight. I was transferred there from Number 22.'

'Number 22 Protected Area? Where's that?'

'No, no, Number 22 is our headquarters in London.'

'Quite, quite,' Captain Waggett quacked hastily. 'Well, you've been out in the Islands such a short time that you probably don't realize the calm way in which the people flaunt every rule and regulation. I did my best when the order was first made over eighteen months ago about permits between the two Toddays to get it enforced. But I had no support from anybody, with the result that it was a dead letter from the start. People just went backwards and forwards over the Coolish as if they were crossing the road.'

'Extraordinary!' Mr Brown exclaimed. 'Don't they realize that there's a war on?'

'That's the question I often ask myself,' Captain Waggett replied sadly. 'You'll be able to answer it for yourself after an evening in the hotel bar. Do you know they actually listen to the news on the Irish wireless?'

'Amazing! Is the reception better?'

'They'd sooner tune in to the atmospherics from Athlone than the best reception from the B.B.C. And mind you that's just as true of Great Todday as it is of a Catholic island like Little Todday. Of course, they listen regularly to the German wireless.'

Lieutenant Boggust stroked his neo-Caroline moustache.

'Staggering!' he murmured. 'Personally I'd make it a penal offence to listen to enemy wireless. I mean to say we can learn a lot from the Germans.'

'Oh, I agree with you every time. I mean to say you've got to hand it to the Germans. They are thorough.'

'Absolutely,' Lieutenant Boggust affirmed enthusiastically. Then he reverted to his cover.

'Well, I'd better be going back to the hotel. And you think it would be much wiser if we didn't meet tomorrow?'

'Much wiser,' said Captain Waggett. 'Come round and see me here on Monday evening, and I'll fill up any gaps in your investigation.'

Mr Brown found his way back to the hotel without meeting anybody. That was satisfactory at any rate. After he had eaten a couple of herrings and drunk the strongest cup of tea he had ever drunk in his life the Security Intelligence officer adjourned to the bar where for some time he sat in a corner listening to the conversation.

'Will you be seeing Donald before he gets another ship?' somebody was asking the Biffer.

'I don't believe we will. Och, he enjoyed himself fine in Ireland. He's in Glasgow now. The *cailleach* had a letter from Johnny yesterday morning. From Liverpool he was writing, and he's away off to Australia again.'

Mr Brown made a note in his pocket-book. This was careless talk. He must find out who this man was.

'You had a tram yesterday, Angus,' the host was saying to Angus MacCormac, who had just moved to the bar to request a whisky.

'I had a dram yesterday?' exclaimed the big crofter, grasping his huge moustache as if it was the only solid thing in a dissolving world. 'How could I have had a dram yesterday when I was working all day at home?'

'You had a tram yesterday,' Ruairidh Mór repeated firmly. Angus MacCormac appealed to his friend Sammy MacCodrum, who himself had just been served.

'Was I working at home yesterday?'

'I believe you were,' Sammy told him.

'I'm not after saying you weren't working at home,' said Roderick. 'What I'm after saying is that you came in with Donald Ian in the lorry and was in the bar till nine o'clock.'

'That was Thurssday.'

'You were in the bar on Thurssday too. And we had the same argument about Wednesday.'

'Ah, well, well, well, well,' Angus declared, apparently overwhelmed by the revelation of the depths to which human nature could sink. 'Did anybody ever hear the like of that now? You've got a bigger imagination than Captain Waggett. He's for ever seeing Germans who aren't there at all and you're seeing whiskies that aren't there at all.'

Mr Brown made another note.

'He's talking very big again about the Home Guard is Wackett,' said one of the Snorvig fishermen. 'Just a lot of nonsense.'

'Ay, it's a nonsense now right enough,' the Biffer agreed. 'But it wasn't such a nonsense when Hitler was almost on top of us.'

'It was nonsense from the start,' the fisherman argued. 'What use would Wackett have been against Hitler? What use would any of you have been if it comes to that? If the Government can't win this war, how would the Home Guard win it?'

'I believe they're doing pretty well in Africa just now,' somebody else said.

'Ay, that's what they say. But who's to believe them?' the fisherman asked.

There was a murmur of agreement from the company in whom half a pint of beer and a dram here and there had induced a sceptical attitude towards the whole of existence.

'I think you can rely on the B.B.C.,' Mr Brown put in from his corner.

'The P.P.C. chust say what the Government tells them to say,' Sammy MacCodrum maintained. 'And efen if it was all true what they were saying who would want to be hearing such foices? Och, I listen to the news in Gaelic when they have it, and you get a bit more sense from them then, but who wants to listen to the news in these days? Chust nothing but war.'

'Well, until the war is over we mustn't think about anything except winning it,' said Mr Brown.

'We can think about winning it without hearing about it all the time,' Sammy MacCodrum argued. 'Here we are with half a pint of peer for the whole evening and a poor kind of tram three times a week if we're lucky. That's what the war has done for us. If we're winning the war, why doesn't the Government give us our own whisky?'

'We're exporting it to America to help pay for our war expenditure,' Mr Brown tried to explain.

'Ay, and when these Americans have drunk all our whisky it'll be they who've won the war not ourselves,' put in the fisherman, who by this time was a suspect in Mr Brown's notebook.

The Security Intelligence officer slept badly that night. The hotel bed was hard. The herrings combined with the strong tea to promote sharp indigestion. He said to himself that Waggett had underestimated the defeatism of the island by calling it rife. It was in fact rampant.

It was pouring with rain on Sunday morning, and

when Mr Brown looked out of the windows of the coffee-room after breakfast he felt that this rampant defeatism if unjustifiable was at least intelligible. The only other guest of the hotel in the hotel was a large elderly commercial traveller with a white walrus moustache from Inverness who was bemoaning the patriotism which had called him forth from retirement to allow a younger man to serve the country in the armed forces.

'I don't know why I did it, Mr Brown ... the name *is* Brown, I believe?'

'Yes, yes, that is my name.'

'Yes, I thought I wasn't mistaken. Well, as I was saying, I really don't know why I did it. I have a nice wee house in Rose Terrace, Inverness ... do you know Inverness at all, Mr Brown?'

'No, I don't know it at all.'

'It's a fine city. Very fine. The air is beautiful. Yes, I made up my mind I was going to do nothing but read a little, and walk along to the library, and play a bit of bowls on a summer evening ... do you play bowls, Mr Brown?'

'No, I don't.'

'It's a wonderful game. You can go on playing it for ever, and you'll never get to the end of it.'

'I can quite believe it,' said Mr Brown.

'However, as they say, man proposes and God disposes. I felt the call of duty, and here I am; but as I tell my firm, what's the use of travelling nowadays when we really have nothing to sell? I could have got any amount of orders for our Dreadnought Sheep Dip. Do you know our Dreadnought Sheep Dip?'

'No, I don't.'

'I'm surprised at that. A tweed merchant like yourself has a stake in our Dreadnought Sheep Dip. I estimate that Duthie's Dreadnought Sheep Dip has saved us tons of wool, yes literally tons. But as I was saying, what's the use of me singing its praises now? If you wanted just a couple of gallons of it I couldn't guarantee delivery in this summer. Yes, it's a wearisome journey up through the Islands in war time. And I find so many of my friends have passed on. Here's my card, Mr Brown.'

Mr Brown accepted it rather ungraciously.

'Ay, Macintosh is my name,' said the traveller, with a touch of complacency.

Mr Brown felt inclined to say that it was a very good name to have on such a morning, but having heard that the Celts lacked humour he decided to refrain.

'I believe I can boast that ten years ago no traveller was better known in the Highlands and Islands than Charlie Macintosh. Oh, and they still remember me, Mr Brown. Oh, yes, I was up in Harris last month. Terrible weather we had.'

'Worse than this?'

'Oh, much worse. This is nothing.'

'Good God!' Mr Brown ejaculated.

'Yes, I was up in Harris ... you know Harris of course?'

'No, I don't.'

'Man, you a tweed merchant, and you don't know Harris!'

'I know the tweed of course,' said Mr Brown irritably. 'But I've never been to Harris itself. This is my first visit to Scotland.'

'Ay, I thought you were from England by the way you talked. It's very noticeable to us in Inverness the queer way the English speak their own language.'

'We might think it equally queer the way you speak our language,' Mr Brown retorted sarcastically.

Mr Macintosh chuckled.

'Ah, that won't do, Mr Brown. Everybody knows that the purest English spoken anywhere is spoken in Inverness.'

'The Americans and the Australians might say the same. That wouldn't make it true.'

'Ah, but everybody admits that the English spoken in Inverness is the purest spoken English,' Mr Macintosh insisted.

'Who's everybody? Everybody in Inverness, I suppose?'
Mr Brown asked indignantly.

'No, no, no, other people too. It's an established fact.
You'll probably find it in the *Encyclopaedia Britannica*.'

'I very much doubt that. Indeed, I'll go so far as to say I
don't believe it.'

'That's a pretty risky thing to say,' Mr Macintosh observed. 'Still, I don't suppose I can have the pleasure of
proving you're wrong. We're not likely to find the
Encyclopaedia Britannica on Great Todday. Unless Mr
Waggett has it. Do you know Mr Waggett?'

Mr Brown hesitated. Had this bore noticed him enter
or leave Snorvig House last night?

'A friend of mine in London told me to look him up if I
found myself on Great Todday,' he answered ambiguously.

'I haven't met the man myself, but the Todday people
seem to consider him a bit of a windbag,' said the
traveller.

'The people here have a lot of extraordinary opinions,'
Mr Brown snapped. 'I was amazed last night in the bar to
hear the freedom with which they were criticizing the
Government. They don't realize what would happen to
them in Germany if they talked like that.'

'But isn't that just what we're fighting for?'

'I don't follow you.'

'To prevent any of us realizing what would happen to
us in Germany if we opened our mouths a bit wide.'

'There is a war on, you know, Mr Macintosh.'

'Indeed, and I do know it. I'd be sitting in front of the
fire in my wee house in Rose Terrace if there wasn't a war
on,' the traveller said. 'You are exempt, I take it?'

'Yes, oh, yes, I was . . . er . . . indispensable.'

How little people appreciated the price paid by a good
Intelligence officer in doing his duty, Mr Brown reflected
in admiration of his own self-restraint in allowing this old
bore to assume that he had escaped uniform.

'I don't believe you'll be able to do much business here,

97

Mr Brown,' said the traveller. 'This rule they've made about giving up coupons for yarn has discouraged the tweed making.'

'As far as I can make out every rule that's made annoys the people here. The only rule they seem to keep is not to do anything at all on Sunday.'

'Ah, well, you'll feel all the fresher for it yourself on Monday morning.'

'After sitting about in this dreary coffee-room looking at that?' asked Mr Brown, pointing to the drench of rain.

'Oh, it is as well for it to rain itself out today when there's nothing doing anyway, and then maybe it'll be a fine day tomorrow. I was thinking we might share the hire of a car round the island. I expect you'll have a list of people you're wanting to call on about these tweeds.'

'As a matter of fact I was thinking of crossing over to Little Todday tomorrow morning,' said Mr Brown quickly, for the prospect of touring the island with this bore of a traveller affected him as unpleasantly as the prospect of being shut up in a room with a bluebottle he was unable to squash.

'You'll find no tweed on Little Todday, Mr Brown.'

'No, I dare say not, but I should like to see what the island is like. I'm making a sort of a holiday of this business trip.'

'Well, I'll be going over to Little Todday on Tuesday morning, and we might share the hire of Archie Mac-Rurie's boat. Do you know him?'

'Isn't he the fellow with two sons at sea?'

'Four sons at sea. Oh, he's a great chap is the Biffer, as they call him.'

'I thought he was talking rather indiscreetly last night about shipping movements. For instance, he let out that one of his sons was sailing for Australia this week from Liverpool. That's exactly what the enemy wants to know.'

'I'm sure the Biffer wouldn't want to say anything to put his own sons' lives in danger,' Mr Macintosh averred warmly.

'That's just it. I'm not saying it's deliberate. It's what we call careless talk.'

'Well, if we take him over to Kiltod on Tuesday, you'll be able to warn him, Mr Brown.'

'Thanks very much, but I think I'll stick to my original timetable. As I say, I'm not expecting to do much business here.'

'Please yourself, Mr Brown. But they're not afraid to charge for motor-boats and cars, you know.'

However, Mr Brown, whose expenses were not his own affair, regarded with equanimity the likelihood of being overcharged.

'I think I'll go for a short walk in spite of the rain,' he told his fellow-guest.

'Well, I wouldn't mind a breath of air myself,' Mr Macintosh admitted.

Mr Brown's skill as Intelligence officer in throwing his pursuers off the trail was useless against the determined adhesiveness of Mr Macintosh, in whose company he had to spend the whole of that wet Sunday besides being given for his evening meal an even stronger cup of tea than yesterday to accompany some tough and desiccated cold mutton.

'I wonder if this is the heel or the sole,' he observed gloomily. 'I think it's too tough for the sole.'

'I think it's the leg,' said Mr Macintosh, apparently oblivious that his fellow-guest had been speaking sardonically.

Mr Brown got up from the table and rang the poached-egg bell beside the fireplace.

'Can I have some whisky, please?' he asked when Annag, one of the two daughters of Roderick who was helping to keep the home fires burning, came in.

'Whisky!' she exclaimed. If he had asked her for arsenic she could not have seemed more shocked. 'You're after having all the whisky you can be having till tomorrow.'

'But I haven't had any today.'

'You had your whisky yesterday evening.'

'There's a shortage, Mr Brown,' the traveller put in. 'We're rationed to one small whisky every other day.'

'Oh, very well,' said Mr Brown, who after the way he had been sticking up for rules and regulations did not feel justified in suggesting that an exception should be made in his favour. 'Very well, bring me half a pint of ale, please.'

'You had your half pint with your dinner, Mr Brown.'

'Do you mean to say I can't have another half pint now?' he asked fretfully.

'No, my father's very sorry, but he can't be serving anybody with more than half a pint for the day,' Annag informed him.

Mr Brown shook his head, and as she went out of the coffee-room shuddered and poured himself out another cup of tea.

When the meal was finished he rose from the table with aching jaws and asked Mr Macintosh if he played cribbage.

'I noticed some of them were playing last night in the bar. It's not a bad game.'

'Oh, I play a good game of cribbage,' the traveller boasted. 'But they wouldn't like at all to see us playing on a Sunday, and indeed, I wouldn't care to do it myself.'

On one thing Mr Brown was determined. He would listen to no more of his fellow-guest's foully boring conversation. He sat down in one of the worn leather armchairs beside the fire and buried his head in the *People's Journal*, which was the only printed fodder he could find except Murray's Railway Guide for June 1939, and even if that had been readable it was much too small to shut out the sight of Mr Macintosh's large face and white walrus moustache and moist pale-blue eyes. Indeed the *People's Journal* was only just wide enough.

'You're sure you won't change your mind, Mr Brown, and make the round of Great Todday with me tomorrow morning?' the traveller inquired after Mr Brown had been reading the *People's Journal* for about twenty minutes.

'I can't. I've asked Mr MacRurie to arrange with the man who owns the boat,' Mr Brown replied, without lowering his paper.

'Oh, well, then, if you'll excuse me, Mr Brown, I think I'll go down to the pier-house for a *céilidh* with my clansman, John Macintosh.'

Mr Brown was suddenly seized by a longing for chocolate. No whisky. No beer. That ghastly tea embittering his inside demanded chocolate to assuage its acrid ferment.

'I wonder if you could get hold of a packet for me?'

'A packet of what, Mr Brown?' the traveller asked in perplexity.

'A packet of Caley's chocolate.'

'I doubt if John Macintosh will have any chocolate. He's the piermaster. Iain Dubh they call him. Black John. He's not a merchant.'

'But you said you were going to get some Caley's from him.'

Light dawned on Mr Macintosh.

'I said I was going for a *céilidh* with him. A *céilidh* is what we call a visit in Gaelic.'

'Oh, well, in that case, please don't let me detain you,' said Mr Brown sombrely.

When he found himself alone the Security Intelligence officer laid down the *People's Journal* with relief. He thought he had never read a paper with such an immense amount of news about nothing. His indigestion grew worse. He had an impression that damp squibs were going off in his inside. He rang the bell again.

'I wonder if you have any Sodamint in the house,' he asked Annag when she answered it.

'I believe we have just one bottle of soda-water left,' she said. 'Will that be what you're wanting?'

'No, not soda-water. Sodamint. Tablets.'

'Tablets? Aspirin?' she asked hopefully.

'No, I'm afraid aspirin would be no use. Never mind,'

he said, and noticing for the first time that Annag was really rather a pretty girl he stroked his neo-Caroline moustache and adjusted the folds of his umber plus-fours.

Annag, however, hurried from the room to avoid any more incomprehensible demands upon her hospitality.

'Extraordinarily primitive people,' Mr Brown murmured to himself. He was thinking of that strange old woman in the shop at Nobust last week who when he had asked her if she kept toilet-paper had replied with a slightly puzzled but equally propitiatory smile, 'No no, I'm afraid we haven't that kind of paper just now, but we have emery paper if that would do as well for you.'

Mr Brown told himself that he really must have something to read.

'If I ring and ask that girl she'll probably bring me in the family Bible,' he muttered to himself.

Then he noticed a small cupboard he had not yet tried. He opened it and found beside two cruets a novel by Annie S. Swan. He settled down to read. An hour later he heard the voice of Mr Macintosh back from his visit. He hurried off to bed, taking the book with him.

Chapter 7

THE CROCK OF GOLD

JUST about the same time as Mr Brown went off to bed in the Snorvig Hotel with that novel by Annie S. Swan, over on Little Todday, Hugh Macroon, a stocky clean-shaven crofter with a bald domed head in which was set a pair of quick shrewd eyes, rose slowly from the long wooden seat at right angles to the range in the kitchen where he had been indulging in an agreeable *céilidh* for an hour.

'Ah, well, *matà. Feumaidh mi falbh*. I'll be going along, Jockey.'

'I believe the rain will have stopped,' said his host, John Stewart, known as Jockey, a round sandy little crofter whose cattle, the best in the island, had been providing an hour of absorbing conversation for the two crofters. 'I'll come along for a bit of the way with you.'

Outside they saw that the machair was now lapped in clouded watery moonlight and that the rain, as Jockey had guessed, had indeed stopped.

'I wonder would we take a bit of a walk up to Bàgh Mhic Roìn,' Hugh Macroon suggested.

'It would give us a bit of air right enough,' Jockey agreed.

Inasmuch as both men had walked three miles each way to Mass in the morning and another three miles to Bene-diction in the late afternoon, it might have been thought that they had had enough air that Sunday.

Bàgh Mhic Roìn or Macroon's Bay was an inlet on the north-west coast of the island, where according to legend the seal-woman had first met the exiled son of Clan Donald who was to make her his bride and become the progenitor of the clan. It was about a mile equidistant from the crofts of both Hugh and Jockey, and opening directly to the Atlantic it provided as rich a store of flotsam as anywhere in Little Todday.

'I was thinking that with the set of the tide and the calm sea we might be taking a look at what's moving,' said Hugh.

'Ay, quite a good idea,' Jockey agreed.

Presently, as the two men trudged northward over the drenched machair, the clouds thinned for the moon to shine through and illuminate the raindrops clinging to the grass. They did not talk. The topic of the cattle had been exhausted at the *céilidh*.

After nearly twenty minutes of silent progress they reached the head of the bay and stood on a sandy bluff scanning the grey water, with their backs still to the moon. Some five hundred yards out to the north-west the fantastic craggy shape of Pillay rose from the sea, the cliffs rising to a couple of hundred feet but seeming higher beside the expanse of Little Todday's gently undulating low land.

'*Seall, Uisdein,*' Jockey exclaimed in sudden excitement, 'what is that black thing floating in?'

'Man, that's the Gobha,' said Hugh.

The Gobha or Blacksmith was a dark rock off the east side of Pillay right opposite the mouth of Macroon's Bay.

'Where are you looking?' Jockey exclaimed, his voice rising almost to a treble in his excitement. 'I don't mean out there. Here man, here, half-way in to the bay, and the tide will be making in another hour.'

'Ay, I see it now,' said Hugh. 'But the tide won't be making for two hours. You're after forgetting about summer time.'

'*A Dhia,*' Jockey expostulated, 'what do they want to jicker about with the clock for? It wass bad enough when we had summer time in summer the way the cows wass putting themselves against it, but summer time in winter is chust laughing at Almighty God. Ay, chust that.'

'Would it be a barrel, Jockey?' Hugh asked in that slow

voice of his, after his gaze had been concentrated on the floating object for a couple of minutes.

'Ach, we can't see yet awhile. I wouldn't say it wassn't a parrel. It might be a parrel from the *Chamaica Maid*.'

'It might be grape-fruits,' said Hugh cautiously.

'*A Dhia, Dhia*, don't be saying that, Hugh. The crape-fruits wass never in poxes. Chust lying on the *traigh*. Crape-fruits *chaca*!'

Hugh Macroon once more contemplated for a while the dark object in the grey water of the little bay.

'That's never a barrel, Jockey,' he decided at last. 'That's a box. The last box I had was lard.'

'*A Dhia*, who wants lart?' Jockey Stewart demanded indignantly.

'The women were pretty pleased about it,' said Hugh. 'It was good lard.'

'Ay, maybe it wass, but who wants to be putting himself out for lart? I like my own putter petter,' Jockey scoffed. 'She's ferry teep in the water,' he said a moment or two later. 'She's not full of emptiness whateffer is in her.'

'Ay, there's something in her right enough,' his companion agreed.

Four hours later the two crofters dragged up the sandy bank a black iron-bound chest on which was painted in white lettering:

> The Manager
> City and Suburban Bank
> Lombard Street
> London, E.C.
> England

'Ah, well, I don't think she will be whisky, Jockey,' said Hugh Macroon.

'No, I don't think she will be,' his partner agreed regretfully.

'It's too heffy for whisky altogether. It's terrible heffy.'

'Look at all the iron that's round it. That would make her heavy enough if she wasn't heavy at all. The Manager,

City and Suburban Bank,' Hugh Macroon read out slowly. 'I wonder if it could be gold,' he added after a long pause pregnant with speculation.

'Cold?' Jockey Stewart exclaimed shrilly.

'*Nach ist thu,*' his partner growled. 'Do you want everybody in the island to hear you screeching about it? If it isn't gold, it must be something pretty valuable, I believe. Who would be sending a box like this to a bank if it was just nothing at all?'

'Ach, it must be cold right enough,' Jockey declared. 'This is petter than that Chinese paper which came ashore by Ard Swish.'

A consignment of Chinese notes printed in England had been lost by enemy action a couple of years back, one of the cases of which had reached Little Todday.

'Now what do we do with it, that's the big question?' Hugh Macroon asked pensively.

'We'll take it back to your place or my place and open it right away,' Jockey told him.

'Ay, and let the whole island know we had something by the noise we'd be making,' Hugh jeered. 'No, no, we'll hide it tonight in your rick and you'll send word tomorrow morning will I come along to give you a hand with your plough because it's broken. Then if there's a lot hammering they'll be thinking it's your plough.'

'Ferry good, ferry good, Hugh,' Jockey applauded. 'Ah, well, it's you that's smart right enough.'

'And now the sooner we get it to your rick the better. It'll be pretty near four o'clock before we get it safely stowed away. I wish it would cloud over again. The moon's as bright as day. She is a bit of a nuisance right enough.'

'Ach, I don't believe anybody will be about at this time of the night.'

'I wouldn't say Willie Munro wouldn't be about. He's always up early enough, seeing what there is moving while other people are still in their beds,' said Hugh.

Willie Munro was the only Protestant in Little Todday and therefore suspected by the rest of the island of an unbridled individualism of thought and action. The fact that he had been appointed a coast-watcher at the beginning of the war only added to the disrepute he enjoyed among his neighbours.

'Och, Willie, who minds about Willie?' John Stewart scoffed.

'I don't care nothing about Willie,' Hugh Macroon affirmed stoutly with the help of two negatives. 'All the same, if there's gold inside this case I'd just as soon that Willie didn't see it at all. So come along.'

Between them the two men lifted the black chest, which had no handles, and proceeded like a couple of crabs for a hundred yards. Then Jockey put his foot in a rabbit-burrow, and fell full length on the wet grass.

'*Ist*, man, you're making more noise than a lorry,' Hugh said crossly, as Jockey gurgled and gasped to recover the breath knocked out of him by the black chest. 'I never heard such a noise in my life.'

'The pox kicked me in the *stamac* like a horse,' Jockey explained. '*A Dhia*, there was no life left in me at all. Never mind. On we go.'

He lifted his end of the box again, and Hugh suggested it might be easier if they took it in turns to walk backwards.

'Ay, and if I wass walking packwards and put my foot in another hole the pox would be more on top of me than effer. No, no, Hugh, we'll carry it chust the way we are.'

Two hundred yards further on Hugh whispered, '*Ist*,' and they stopped.

'Are you after hearing something?' Jockey murmured.

'I thought I saw something move, away there beyond the *sìthein*.'

The *sìthein* was one of the many rounded knolls which broke the level of the machair all over the island, but it had a certain renown as the one in which fairy music had been heard not so long ago.

'What were you seeing?' Jockey whispered.

'Just a kind of quick movement.'

'A rappit?'

'It was a bigger movement than a rabbit.'

The two men peered into the moonshine, listening. A curlew fluted far away. There was no other sound.

'Ach, I don't think it was anybody,' said Hugh, and the black chest was lifted again.

At last they reached Jockey Stewart's croft, which lay due south of Macroon's Bay, and the chest was carried to the rick in a corner of the field behind the little house. Enough hay was pulled out to make a hiding-place for the black chest, which was then carefully covered again.

'Ah, well, I'm sweating,' said Hugh.

'Ay, it's thirsty work right enough,' his partner agreed.

Then both of them sighed for the unattainable.

'Well, well, *matà, oidhche mhath leat,*' Hugh said, turning toward his own croft.

'It's nearer to morning now,' said Jockey. 'I'll send Lachie or Florag along after school to say will you come and help me mend my plough. *A dhuine, dhuine,* if it iss cold that's in it I'll go to Obaig on Tuesday and find two pottles of whisky in this plack market they talk so much about in the papers. It'll have to be pretty plack if I can't see two pottles of whisky in it, ay, and perhaps more, by Chinko,' he added fervidly.

Hugh Macroon walked across to his croft and retired to bed without waking his wife. Jockey on the other hand when he went up to the bedroom felt too much excited by the thought of the gold that might be in the black chest to be able to get quietly into bed. Bean Yockey's vast bulk – she was the largest woman in the island – tranquilly sleeping filled him with a longing to wake her in order to talk about his plans for the future of the croft with the money that was going to be his. He had no intention of revealing the secret of the black chest, but he could talk about his plans without doing that. At the same time he could not quite bring himself to the point of prodding his wife in the back and expatiating forthwith upon his dreams of wealth. He decided to wake her strategically.

To this end, after undressing, he knelt by the head of the bed and began to say his prayers at the top of that high piercing voice of his. Half-way through the *Paternoster* the bed quivered as Bean Yockey stirred in her sleep. At the first *Ave* Bean Yockey moaned faintly. As the second *Ave* finished she turned over. In the middle of the third *Ave* she sat up in bed and gazed about her in affright.

'*A Mhuire mhàthair!* For the love of God, John, what is the matter?' she gasped. 'Have you hurt yourself?'

'*Ist*, woman, I'm at saying my prayers.'

His strategy having been successful, Jockey began the interrupted third *Ave* again and after crossing himself with exaggerated formality rose to his feet. His wife asked what time it was.

'Nearly fife o'clock,' she was told.

'John, have you been drinking?' she asked.

'Trinking?' he echoed indignantly. 'What would I be trinking?'

'God knows,' his wife replied devoutly. 'If you could be drinking that oil you could be drinking anything.'

The oil alluded to was a bottle of the finest vegetable oil used for delicate machinery which her husband had found two or three months ago on the *tràigh*, and which, after he had added some wood alcohol to it, he had defiantly declared to be as good as drambuie.

'Ah, well, *a Chairistiona*, not a trop of anything am I after trinking tonight,' he assured her.

'Where have you been then?'

'Nowhere at all. Chust nowhere at all. I was thinking I would go to Obaig on Tuesday and buy myself two cowss. Apperteen-Angus. Ay, and I wass thinking I would build a punkalow for towrists. We'll be having towrists like flice when the war's ofer. And I wass thinking I would ...'

'It's a pity you weren't thinking you would go to your bed like a man with a little sense,' Bean Yockey interrupted sharply, 'instead of waking people out of their sleep, shouting like a great clown and then pretending it was your prayers you were saying. I'm sure I don't know what's come over you, man. What will the children be thinking if they hear their father talking the way a tinker would be ashamed to talk? Come to bed and stop your nonsense.'

'You titn't let me finish what I was coing to say. I wass thinking I would buy you a new coat. Is that nonsense?' Jockey demanded. Then feeling that he had extinguished his wife he extinguished the lamp as well and got into bed.

It was not one of Jockey's children who came round after school to ask for Hugh Macroon's help with the plough. It was Jockey himself who at nine o'clock was asking Bean Uisdein where her husband was.

'He's still in his bed,' said Mrs Hugh Macroon, a neat prim little woman of fifty, already grey.

'I'll go up if you please, Mrs Macroon,' said the crofter.

'It's not bad news for us?' Bean Uisdein asked in sudden alarm.

'Ay, it's terrible news,' said Jockey.

'It's not about Michael?'

Michael was her eldest son, a corporal in the Clan-ranalds fighting in North Africa.

'No, no, it's worse than that.'

'He's been killed!'

'Not at all. It's worse than that, I'm telling you. Chust let me see Hugh, if you please. It's not a family matter at all. It's a tissaster.'

Bean Uisdein stood aside for Jockey to go up to the bed-room. She longed to follow him lest indeed he should be bringing bad tidings of Michael, or of Anthony, her second boy, who was at sea. However, she had made it a rule of her married life never to be inquisitive about masculine affairs and she held herself in hand.

It was not easy to disconcert Hugh Macroon. Lying back in his bed that morning, he looked as calm as a monk who had long since learned to despise mortal fretfulness. The bald domed head upon the pillow was like a rock against which life's waves must beat in vain.

Yet, when Jockey announced that the black chest had vanished from the rick in which he and Hugh had hidden it hardly four hours ago, Hugh sat up in bed as suddenly as Bean Yockey had sat up at the sound of her husband's third *Ave*.

'Gone? The box is gone?' he repeated.

'Chust nothing but hay,' Jockey groaned.

'You must have looked in the wrong place,' his friend insisted.

'Wrong place? There's no place at all in the rick now, the way I'm after pulling it about. The missus sent Florag helter-skelter to Kiltod to fetch Dr Maclaren with the *Morning Star*.'

'How's the doctor going to find it?'

'She thinks I've gone daft. Och, it's a long story. I'll tell you some other time. The main point for us is to find out which pukkers have taken away our cold.'

'And it'll be pretty difficult,' said Hugh glumly. 'We can't go shouting about the island that we've lost a box of gold. We'd have the constable over in a twinkle. Ay, and before we knew where we were we'd be up before the *siorram* at Loch Fladdy and go to prisson, which wouldn't matter if we had the gold; but while we were in prisson the blaggarsts who've stolen our gold would be laughing at us. No, no, we'll just have to hold our tongues and open our eyes.'

'I opened my ice so wide this morning when I couldn't find our pox they nearly fell out,' said Jockey. 'Och, I wonder who it could have peen.'

'Didn't you hear a sound of anything?'

'I titn't hear a sount of nothing. I was snoring like a pick and talking away in my sleep, the missus said.'

'What were you talking about?' Hugh sternly demanded.

'Ay, I asked her that, and she told me I was talking about the Pearl Harper Hotel.'

'What kind of an hotel is that?'

'Och, how do I know what kind of an hotel one finds in

one's sleep. I was shouting out, "No room in the Pearl Harper Hotel!"'

'No wonder your missus thought you were daft. What else did you talk about?' Hugh asked.

'Otters.'

'Otters? Why would you be talking about otters?'

'How would I know why I would be talking about otters? If I knew why I would be talking about otters in my sleep I wouldn't be talking about otters at all,' Jockey expostulated.

'You didn't say anything about the gold?' Hugh pressed.

'If I did, the *cailleach* never said a word about it.'

'Well, I'll get up and dress myself,' said Hugh. 'And then I think we'll be walking over to Kiltod.'

They reached the port and metropolis of Little Todday just as the Biffer was steering the *Kittiwake* with Mr Brown into the little harbour.

'The *Morning Star*'s not at her moorings,' Hugh observed. 'Joseph must have sent her for the Doctor after all.'

'Get away with you, man, Choseph wouldn't be doing such a thing chust on a word from the missus.'

'Still, it's queer right enough that the *Morning Star*'s away so early on a Monday morning. Joseph will have heard how you were pulling about your rick this morning,' said Hugh, his shrewd eyes glinting under puckered brows. 'Who's yon Rhode Island Red?'

The question referred to Mr Brown, whose plus-fours fluffing out above such thin ankles as he disembarked from the *Kittiwake* made the comparison to that particular breed of fowls a happy one.

'Ach, he will be one of those fellows from the Department of Agriculture. They all wear these bluss-fours,' Jockey replied.

'He might be an exciseman,' said Hugh suspiciously. 'Come to that, I wouldn't say he mightn't be a detective.'

'A detective? *A Dhia*, what's a detective going to be looking for in Todaidh Beag?'

'He might have heard about the gold?'

'How would he know the cold had come ashore here?'

'He might be making inquiries all the way up the islands,' said Hugh Macroon.

Just then Mr Brown approached them from the quay.

'Good morning,' he said, with synthetic geniality. 'It's a fine morning after yesterday's downpour. Do you happen to know anybody in Little Todday by the name of Macroon?'

The two crofters gazed at him in amazement for an instant. They were accustomed to silly questions from visitors, but this was so silly that they could not help believing that it was prompted by an ignorance assumed to cover a cunning purpose directed against the island and its inhabitants.

'Which Macroon would you be wanting?' Hugh asked.

'Mr Joseph Macroon. He has a shop in Kiltod, I believe.'

Hugh Macroon took his pipe out of his mouth and used it as a pointer to the post-office a few yards away.

'I'm interested in tweed,' Mr Brown continued. 'Do either of you know where any tweed is being woven in the islands?'

'Tweet?' Jockey exclaimed at the top of his high voice. 'There's no tweet being made in Little Todday. The Government want coupons for yarn. Who's going to be wearing himself out making tweet when the Government does a stupid thing like that?'

'May I inquire your name?' the visitor asked.

'Perhaps you'd like to have a look at my identity cart?' Jockey suggested.

'No, no, thank you,' said Mr Brown quickly. 'That's none of my business. My name is Brown.'

'Well, my name is Stewart. Chon Stewart,' said Jockey.

'I'm very pleased to meet you, Mr Stewart.' Mr Brown looked inquiringly at Hugh, who did not volunteer his name, but stared hard at the stranger, puffing away at his pipe.

'Chust a Chessie,' Jockey commented when Mr Brown had entered Joseph's shop.

'Ay, he may be just a Jessie,' said Hugh. 'But I believe he's up to no good.'

The two men walked along the quay to greet the Biffer.

'What's that *dreathan-donn* you had perched in your boat, Airchie?' Hugh asked, reducing the Biffer's passenger from a Rhode Island Red to a brown wren.

'*A Chruithear*,' exclaimed the Biffer, spitting over the side of the *Kittiwake*. 'He was preaching me a sairmon about careless talk all the way over the Coolish. I don't know what to make of him at all. He was asking whether he would get any chocolate at Joseph Macroon's shop.'

'Och, he'll be one of these snoobers from the Ministry of Food,' said Jockey. 'We had one of them round last autumn, moaning and croaning that he was starfing and pecking for shooker and tea and putter and cham and when the merchants took pity on the poor *truaghan* and let him have what he wanted without his ration card they wass all threatened to be prosecuted from Inverness. Ach, I don't like such tirty cames at all.'

He spat over one side of the quay. Hugh Macroon spat over the other side. The Biffer spat over the side of his boat.

'Ah, well, he won't get much out of Iosaiph,' said Hugh Macroon. 'Have you had much in along the shore on Todaidh Mór, Airchie, after these gales?'

'Not a great deal at all. I had some tins of what they call sweet corn. *A Chruithear*, I never tasted such stuff. We gave it to the hens. They liked it fine. Hens are queer right enough, what they'll be eating. Ach, it's whisky we're wanting, not sweet corn.'

'*Seadh gu dearbh*. Yes, indeed,' said Hugh, like the sound of a great Amen.

He had been right in supposing that Mr Brown would find it difficult to get anything out of Joseph Macroon. Joseph was in a mood that morning when it was even more difficult to pin him down to anything definite than on the night the Sergeant-major tried to pin him down about the marriage of his daughter. He had noticed Mr

Brown making his way along to the post-office and had immediately decided that he was utterly uninterested in the newcomer's past, present or future.

So when Mr Brown by way of opening the conversation asked if he had any chocolate Joseph repeated the word as if he had never heard it before.

'Chocolate? Ah, chocolate. No, no, there's no chocolate.'

'It's in short supply, is it?'

'No supply at all.'

Mr Brown went on to explain that he was interested in tweed.

'Ah, beautiful stuff,' Joseph sighed in a rapture of his own. 'When will we see it again? You won't find a drop of it in Little Todday.'

'A drop of tweed is a new expression to me,' said Mr Brown.

'Ay,' Joseph murmured remotely.

Then he began to hum to himself, a sure sign of Joseph's intense preoccupation, after which he stopped abruptly and muttered 'Ay, ay, ay,' to that other self with whom he had been communing.

'Brown is my name,' said the visitor, stroking his moustache. Beyond the counter he had caught a glimpse of a most attractive girl in the little room behind.

'Ah, Brown, Brown,' Joseph repeated. 'That will be a well-known name in England?'

'It's fairly common, yes.'

'Ay, Ernest Brown, Secretary for Scotland. I wrote to him the other day about the new school we're wanting in Kiltod. Have you met Father Macalister, Mr Brown?'

'No, this is my first visit to Little Todday.'

'Ah, you'll have to meet him. I'll take you along now. He lives close by.'

Almost before he was aware of it Mr Brown found himself following Joseph Macroon's red knitted cap towards the Chapel House.

'Ay, I told you he wouldn't get nothing out of Iosaiph,' Hugh Macroon observed to John Stewart.

'*A Dhia*, he was pretty quick unloading that cargo,' Jockey exclaimed, when almost as soon as he had entered the priest's house Joseph was hurrying back to his own shop.

Indeed, all that Joseph had said was:

'Here's Mr Brown, Father. And you'll please excuse me, Father, for I'm rather busy this morning.'

Father James Macalister by no means conformed to Mr Brown's conception of what priests looked like, and he conformed still less to his notions of how they behaved.

'Sit right down, Mr Brown,' he was bidden in a profound bass. 'I don't know who you are. But I suppose Joseph wants to get rid of you. *Am bheil Gàidhlig agaibh?*'

Mr Brown looked as bewildered as he felt.

'Ah, well, well, you evidently don't understand our lovely and glorious language. What a pity!' The sigh that followed this ejaculation was so loud and so deep that Mr Brown was on the point of asking the priest if he had rheumatism, when he went on. 'And what brings you to Little Todday, Mr Brown?'

'I thought I'd like to see it.'

'Good shooting!'

'And then I was wondering if I would find any tweed here. I'm a tweed merchant.'

'Are you really now?' the priest exclaimed with such sonority that for a moment Lieutenant Boggust of the Security Intelligence Corps was afraid that he was like a joint of meat from which the cover has been taken.

'Oh, yes,' he said nervously, 'I do quite a lot of business.'

'You won't do much business on Little Todday,' the priest assured him.

'So I understand from Mr Macroon. I suppose the war has affected everything in the island.'

'Och, we're standing up to Hitler in our own way. We've a very fine Home Guard.'

'Men very keen, eh? That's good to hear.'

'Ay, it's a pity we can't send them out to North Africa, and then we might get a move on there.'

'Oh, I think things are moving pretty well out there as they are.'

'Perhaps they are. Perhaps they are. I'm still waiting for a wireless battery. Did Celtic win on Saturday?'

'I'm afraid I don't listen to the football results, padre.'

'Ah well, if you don't speak Gaelic, Mr Brown, you speak Spanish really beautifully.'

'No, I don't speak Spanish either.'

'Don't you really now? Ah well, I thought you did. But then I make these peculiar mistakes sometimes.' The priest exhaled another of those loud and deep sighs. He was finding Mr Brown a little too much of a good thing so soon after his breakfast.

'I'm afraid I'm interrupting your work, padre,' said the visitor.

'Ah well, a parish priest is kept pretty well occupied,' Father Macalister admitted, and when his guest had departed he settled down again in his armchair and went on with the Wild West thriller which Mr Brown's visit had interrupted.

Mr Brown himself found the people of Little Todday extraordinarily stupid. Dullness, not defeatism, seemed their characteristic. At whatever house he called he was received with stares and sheepish monosyllables. He wondered whether to attribute this stupidity to Catholicism or inbreeding, and decided finally that it must be a mixture of both.

'One would almost think that the word had gone round to say nothing to me,' he said to himself.

And indeed that is just what the word had gone round to say. Theories about what his real object was in coming to Little Todday were many and various, but on one thing all were agreed: he was certainly not a tweed merchant. On the other hand if that seems to reflect on the efficiency of the Security Intelligence Corps in disguising itself it must be said at once that nobody suspected he was a

Security Intelligence officer. He was credited with being a snooper from the Ministry of Food, a snooper from the Ministry of Shipping, and generally with being a snooper from the Government. It was speculated whether he was a coastguard in disguise, a deserter from the army, or a detective looking for a deserter from the army. Curiously perhaps, in only one house was he confidently declared to be a German spy. Optimism led some people to believe he was an exciseman because a visit from an exciseman would mean that the Government was expecting spirits to come ashore, and many a man who had been discouraged by grapefruit from beachcombing resolved to be about betimes on the chance that a barrel of rum would be sighted again.

In justice to the usual hospitality of the islanders which was denied to Mr Brown it must be borne in mind that there was hardly a house on Little Todday which did not contain a certain amount of undeclared treasure trove from the sea – turpentine, cheese, lard, tinned asparagus, salt (very salt) butter, tyres, pit props, paper, tomato juice, machine oil, lifebelts, in fact almost everything that could be thought of except spirituous liquors. And besides the treasure trove from the sea there was hardly a house which had not a bit of that Nelson whose forced landing had caused so much anxiety to Captain Waggett. Naturally the people of Little Todday did not want to entertain a guest who might report against them. So when Mr Brown arrived back at the Snorvig Hotel that afternoon he was tired and hungry, and when Mr Macintosh inquired what he had thought of the island he answered crossly that he thought it contained the dullest people he had met since he arrived in Scotland.

'You surprise me, Mr Brown. Did you come across my old friend, Father Macalister?'

'I thought him a most eccentric sort of person. He's not at all my idea of a priest,' Mr Brown snapped. 'And as for that fellow Macroon you made such a point of my seeing I thought him half-witted.'

'You're wrong there, Mr Brown,' the traveller insisted. 'Oh, you're very far out there. Joseph Macroon is as able a merchant as is anywhere in the Islands.'

Mr Brown shrugged his shoulders disdainfully and asked his fellow-guest if he knew what there was for dinner.

'Or rather tea I suppose it should be called,' he added.

'I don't know at all, Mr Brown,' the traveller replied. 'But it'll likely be mutton.'

Lieutenant Boggust was thankful that tomorrow he would be himself again at Nobost, leaving behind him Mr Brown and, he hoped, his indigestion for ever.

'I wonder what's keeping Hugh Macroon and John Stewart hanging about all day in Kiltod,' Joseph Macroon said to Peggy at dusk.

'They were asking where Kenny was a while ago,' she told him.

What exactly was keeping Hugh Macroon and John Stewart hanging about in Kiltod was a strong suspicion (and well Joseph knew it) that wherever the black chest was now it would reach the big shed at the back of Joseph Macroon's house some time in the course of the night. From the start Hugh had made up his mind that the man most likely to have removed the chest from Jockey's rick was the man who lived on the next croft, and that was Willie Munro. If that was so, Hugh argued, Willie Munro as a coast-watcher would be frightened to break open the chest himself. If it had been whisky or rum, as no doubt he had hoped it was when he must have seen them hiding it, that would have been a different matter. He would just have buried it and drunk the contents at his leisure. But if when he saw it he suspected that it contained gold, he would require help if it was to be safely negotiated. The man he would turn to would be Joseph Macroon, who was the only man on the island able to handle such a business. Indeed, Hugh himself had been puzzled to know how he and Jockey were going to deal with the gold when they opened the chest, particularly as Jockey, good man as he was with cattle, was not conspicuously sensible about anything else. His suspicion that the chest would reach Joseph was confirmed when he heard that Willie Munro had come in to Kiltod that morning at eight o'clock and that he had gone off with Kenny in the *Morning Star* shortly before nine, since when neither of them had been seen.

Not long after Joseph made that remark to Peggy, Hugh, who had been worrying himself all day to think out a plan for recovering the chest if he did succeed in tracking it to Joseph, said to Jockey:

'I believe we'll go and see Father James. I didn't like the look of that fellow who was in and out of every house all day. I'd sooner Joseph had it than the Government.'

'Choseph?' Jockey piped. 'I'd rather put it back in the sea than let him or that pukker Willie Munro have as much as one colden pound. But come along, Hugh. We'll see what Father Chames has to say about it all.'

Father Macalister listened to the tale of the night's find with a grave face.

'Ay, ay, you found a crock of gold,' he said, when Hugh had finished, 'and the fairies took it away from you. Isn't that awful? And you think it will be in Joseph's shed by dark? Ah well, I daresay that's not a bad guess. But look here, my boys, if it is gold, it's a pretty serious matter not to declare it. It'll puzzle even Joseph to get away with that one. You leave it to me. I'll tackle Joseph. You go home, and come and see me tomorrow evening and I'll give you the latest intelligence. I wish I could promise you a good dram ...' he exhaled one of his tremendous sighs '... but who knows? We've kept the Faith, and Almighty God won't forget us. No, no, no. The Israelites were in a pretty poor way when the manna fell from Heaven. You remember that peculiar business, Hugh?'

'Ay, Father, though I never understood what kind of stuff it was at all.'

'I don't think anybody does, my boy, but when it falls

on Todaidh Beag I believe it will taste and smell very like *uisge beatha*.'

'The water of life,' Jockey piped. 'It's a pewtiful name right enough, Father Chames.'

'Oh, by Chinko, yes, Chockey, it's really pewtiful,' Father Macalister declared with a magnificent guffaw.

At 1 a.m. Joseph Macroon, wearing his red knitted cap and looking more than ever like a troll at his traditional business, was hammering away at the black chest in the great shed at the back of his house which was heaped high with the lumber of a lifetime. He had already wrenched up all but one of the iron bands when there was a loud knocking on the bolted door.

'*A Thighearna,* who is that?' quaked Willie Munro, a little swarthy man with a yellowish complexion.

'*Co tha'n sud?*' Joseph asked sharply. 'Who is it?'

'Winston Churchill,' a tremendous voice without proclaimed.

'*A Dhia,* it's Father James,' exclaimed Joseph irritably. 'What can he be wanting at this hour of the night? What are you wanting?' he shouted.

'The crock of gold,' Father Macalister boomed in response.

'It's no use trying to deceive that man,' Joseph muttered. 'He has a nose on him like a blind man.' He went across to the door and unbolted it. The parish priest strode in.

'You'd better finish your work,' he said. 'And you'd better be getting back home,' he added, turning to Willie Munro. 'You're not a member of my flock, thank God, so I just won't tell you what I think of a chap who plays a dirty trick on his neighbour like yours.'

Willie Munro hesitated for a moment, and then hurried out into the night.

Joseph wrenched off the final bar and levered up the lid of the black chest with a chisel.

When Father Macalister saw what the contents were he laughed and laughed and laughed until Joseph thought that the lumber of a lifetime would come clattering down upon them. The priest stamped about the shed, slapping his thighs and wheezing and coughing and laughing.

'Ay, it's pretty comical right enough,' Joseph allowed, without a smile on his own face.

This sent Father James off into another spasm of mirth until at last he sat down on a packing-case and mopped his eyes.

'And what will I do with it, Father?'

'Send it to Mr Brown,' the priest replied.

And then he started to laugh again uncontrollably.

On the following afternoon when Mr Brown went into his cabin on the *Island Queen* to return to Nobost he found in the middle of it a black chest tied with rope. He read the address printed in white letters and rang for the Steward.

'This has been put in my cabin my mistake.'

'No, sir, it's for you,' the Steward said. 'You'll see your name on the label.'

And sure enough on the label was written *Mr Brown, Tweed Merchant, c/o S.S. Island Queen.*

'But who brought it on board?' Mr Brown asked.

'I don't really know, sir,' said the Steward.

Lieutenant Boggust was too good an Intelligence officer to betray mystification in the presence of a ship's steward.

'I think I know what it is,' he said. 'It's tweed.'

On the way up to Nobost Mr Brown was tempted to undo the chest and see what was inside, but he was reverting so rapidly now to Lieutenant Boggust that he thought it would be more dignified to refrain. Besides, it would be interesting for Quiblick to be present when the chest was opened. After all it might be anything.

So the black chest reached Nobost Lodge intact so far as Lieutenant Boggust was concerned.

'Hullo, Boggust, had a fruitful journey?' his chief asked. Major Quiblick was in uniform, a lantern-jawed man with the expression of a professional palmist, who had become a major so recently that he was still as proud of his crown as a king.

'I think so, sir. I'll get out a full report for you tomorrow. You'll probably want to strafe one or two people in both islands.'

'What on earth's that black box?' his chief asked. Lieutenant Boggust told him of the way it had arrived.

'We'd better open it,' said the Major. 'What do you suppose it is?'

'I haven't a notion, unless it's tweed.'

'Tweed?'

'My cover, sir.'

'Oh, yes, quite.'

Lieutenant Boggust unroped the black chest and opened the lid.

'Good God, what on earth is it?' the Major exclaimed.

'It looks like some kind of vase, sir.'

'It looks to me more like an urn,' said the Major.

Lieutenant Boggust lifted the vessel out of the heavy box. It *was* a metal urn.

'What's that label round it say?'

Lieutenant Boggust read:

The ashes of Mr H. J. Smith who was cremated at Toronto, December 10th, 1942. Forwarded to the Manager, City and Suburban Bank, Lombard Street, London, Eng., in accordance with instructions received.

'Well, I'm da . . .' but the Major stopped himself in time and saluted the urn with solemn respect. 'Why on earth was this sent to you?' he asked his subaltern.

'I really can't imagine, sir,' Lieutenant Boggust replied.

'Im not in the picture either,' said Major Quiblick. 'Do you think it's a joke?'

'I think it's more likely to be a mistake, sir.'

'We'd better send it on to the consignee,' the Major decided.

'I couldn't agree more, sir,' said his subaltern fervidly.

Chapter 8

THE DROUGHT

═════════

MARCH came in on Monday like a very wet lamb that year, but by the end of the week the two Toddays, except for a begrudged and often acrimoniously contested half-pint of beer a day for the individual drinker, were more dry than they had been yet. Except in a securely locked cupboard in Snorvig House there was not a single drop of whisky in either of the islands, and the only thoroughly happy creature, Catholic or Protestant, was Mrs Campbell. She thrived on the discomfort of her neighbours, the discomfiture of the young woman who had dared to aspire to her son's hand, and the distress of that son himself.

That George was weak nobody denied, but there was not a man in Garryboo or that matter in all Todaidh Mór who was prepared to brag that he would never allow any woman to treat him as Mrs Campbell was treating her son.

'Ach, I don't know at all what we're all coming to, Sammy,' observed Angus MacCormac. 'I'm almost afraid to light up a pipe, the hair on my face is that dry.'

And indeed as he brushed that haycock of a moustache away from his lips it did seem to be shrinking.

'Ay, he ought to put his foot down right enough,' Sammy MacCodrum declared. 'But the Minister himself is afraid to put his foot down to yon woman. She was after coming out of the Manse yesterday with a face on her as fierce as a pollisman. "Och," I said to Macrae, "if you had a face on you like Mrs Campbell, constable, you'd scare all the Snorvig stiffs into law and order chust by looking out of your own door."'

'Ay, I believe he would,' Angus agreed, puffing away at his pipe, which was making noises like a geyser about to erupt.

'And it's time they wass scared,' Sammy went on. 'Did you hear the latest?'

'Breaking into the store and taking away the potatoes the Government sent for us to live on when the invasion comes?' Angus asked.

'Ach, who cares about patatas? No, no, throwing class all over the road and puncturing all the tyres. *A Chruthadair*, as if it wassn't bad enough to be seeing nothing but empty class in the hotel par!'

'I believe the situation will have taken the heart out of Macrae,' Angus MacCormac said gravely.

'It's after taking the heart out of all of us except Hitler and Copples and Mistress Campbell. They're chust enchoying themselfs.'

'Ay, I believe they will be.'

The two friends shook their heads gloomily. In the distance they could hear the voices of their wives summoning them for some domestic task. The low state of their morale made even procrastination savourless. They turned their faces meekly towards tyranny and obeyed the summons.

At Watasett Catriona was inclined to criticize George's feeble surrender to his mother's intransigence.

'It's all very well to say he can't help himself, Norman,' she complained to her brother. 'If he can't help himself, how is he ever going to be able to help me?'

'Ach, it'll be all right when you're married,' Norman argued.

'And if he hasn't the pluck to ask me to tea at his own house, how will he ever find the pluck to marry me?' Catriona asked indignantly. 'I believe I'll just write and tell him it was all a mistake. He can marry Jemima Ross.'

'If I could only get outside a couple of really good drams I'd go along and tackle the old lady myself,' her brother avowed.

'Thank you for nothing,' said his sister tartly. 'It's not me that is going to be married on the strength of my brother's long tongue when he's carrying a big load of whisky.'

'Say that again for God's sake. A big load of whisky! Lassie, you're just speaking the purest poetry.'

'Ach, be done with your nonsense. I've no patience with you,' Catriona exclaimed, and she flounced off to her kitchen. 'Just as soft as dough, that's what men are,' she grumbled to herself as she wielded the rolling-pin.

Not long after this conversation Dr Maclaren called in the Watasett schoolhouse on the way up to have a look at a couple of patients he had in Knockdown.

'Ah, well, I'm sorry for you, Catriona, because George is being so feeble, and I'm sorry for your brother because he can't enjoy a dram with various old friends before he goes into uniform, and I'm sorry for Big Roderick who's being driven nearly off his head by having to say "no" to so many customers, and I'm sorry for all the poor folk on Little Todday facing the grim prospect of Lent without any ammunition, and I'm sorry for John Beaton on whom I simply won't look in nowadays because he suffers so much from an enforced inhospitality, and I'm more than sorry for Father James and myself because both of us really require fortifying; but I'm sorriest of all for old Hector MacRurie who has made up his mind that he will shortly have to face his Maker without a dram inside him to sustain him through the ordeal. It makes me feel I'm no kind of a doctor at all when I visit the old man and can give him nothing better for his rheumatics than some confounded extract of coal tar.'

Hector Macrurie was a white-haired crofter who had fought in the Boer War with the Lovat Scouts and was now looked after by a middle-aged unmarried daughter, his wife having died the previous year. Dr Maclaren found the old man in a more than usually pessimistic mood that afternoon when he went upstairs to his room in the little house at Knockdown. Hector was sitting up in bed, gazing out of the small window at the fog drifting in from the sea and slowly obliterating the rocky moorland between his croft and the cliff's edge eastward.

'No boat today, Hector,' said the doctor. 'There's a lot of fog about. So if there's any whisky on board we shan't see it till Monday at the earliest.'

'Ay, ay, it's the Sabbath tomorrow,' the old man muttered. 'The *Queen* would never be crossing the Minch on the Sabbath. And I believe it will be thicker yet, Doctor.'

'How are you feeling today?'

'Och, I don't feel like anything at all, Doctor. Bones, that's all. Ay, ay, just bones, and most of them aching at that.'

'I've brought you a few ounces of twist, Hector.'

'*Móran taing*, Doctor. It is very kind of you. *Móran taing*. Thank you very much. But my pipe has gone. Just fell to pieces on me. I sent Mairead down to John Mac-Lean's shop. Nothing doing. Not a pipe to be got. And John says he doesn't know when he'll be having another pipe, they're that hard to come by. Och, well, well, I don't believe the world has been in such a terrible mess since the Lord sent the Flood.'

The old man looked across to where on the wall hung a steel engraving, spotted and stained appropriately with damp, of the last pair of animals entering the Ark.

'Come, come, we can't have you cut off smoking as well as everything else,' the doctor exclaimed. 'Here's a pipe of mine. It's what they call a Lovat which is just the shape for you.'

'Och, I couldn't be robbing you of your own pipe, Doctor. You're too kind altogether.'

'Come on, Hector, take this pipe and fill it. Have you never heard of doctor's orders?'

The old man protested for a few moments, but there was no resisting Dr Maclaren's orders. Soon he was rubbing the twist in his furrowed palms, and a minute later he was puffing away at the pipe.

'Ah well, it's yourself, Doctor, that is a doctor right enough,' the old man declared. 'So this is a Lovat pipe, is it? Isn't that beautiful, now? Och, we had some grand times with the Scouts in the old days. The old days, ay, and they are pretty old days,' he sighed. 'Ay, it was South Africa then. Now it's North Africa. I suppose there's no news of Ben Nevis paying us another visit on Todaidh Mór, Doctor?'

'I've not heard of any.'

'I had a fine crack with him about the old days in the Scouts when he came over with the Home Guard. That was before the *cailleach* went ahead of me. He gave me the biggest dram I ever had in all my life that day. Och, I seemed to float in the air all the way back from Snorvig to Knockdown. "My goodness," the *cailleach* said when I got home, "you're looking wild, Eachainn." "Ay, woman," I said, "and I'm feeling pretty wild. I'm after having the biggest dram I ever had in my life with Ben Nevis, and I hadn't seen the man for forty years." Well, I'd like to have one more really good dram, Doctor, before I join the *cailleach*. Glenbogle's Pride, that was what the whisky was called. His butler told me. Ah, well, it was wonderful stuff right enough.'

'I've a good mind to write to Ben Nevis and tell him an old friend is sighing his heart away for another dram of that whisky,' the Doctor declared.

'No, no, Doctor. I wouldn't have you do that for anything. Och, he's a fine gentleman, the finest gentleman in Scotland, is Ben Nevis, but I wouldn't like to be accepting a bottle of his whisky if somebody was asking him for it.'

Dr Maclaren saw that the old man's pride had been wounded by his suggestion and he did not press it.

'Well, Hector, you know best, but I'm sure Ben Nevis would be only too glad to hear he could be of use to an old friend.'

'Och, it's not that I'm dependent on a dram, as you know yourself, Doctor. It's just the idea that you can't have one. We've never been used to that all our lives. And I don't believe I'll be here at all much longer.'

'Nonsense,' the Doctor interjected. 'You've many years to live yet. You'll be about again by early summer.'

'Ah, well, I know better, Doctor, and by that I don't mean any disrespect to yourself as a doctor. Ay, I'm looking at life the way I'm looking at my croft just now and seeing how the fog is creeping in from the sea and covering it up and turning it into just nothing at all.'

The old man gazed out of the window at the view that was gradually being annihilated.

'You're not the only one in Great Todday who's looking at life like that just now, Hector,' the Doctor assured him earnestly. 'No, nor in Little Todday either. We're all watching it fade away from us. But that won't last any more than the fog will last. Whisky will come again and the sun will shine again. And I'll promise you this, Hector. The first bottle of whisky I put my hands on, I'm going to jump straight into my car and I'm coming along with it to Knockdown. And I'm going to sit right where I'm sitting now and Mairead's going to bring up two glasses – not two wee dram glasses ... no, no, I'm telling you ... a couple of tumblers you'd ordinarily see filled up with beer ... and, Hector, I'm going to fill each of them right up with whisky and you and I are going to look each other in the eyes, the two old friends that we are, and I can hear the words chiming in my mind like a noble peal of bells. *Slàinte mhath, slàinte mhór.* And then the two of us are going to drain our glasses to the last golden heart-warming drop.'

'*A Chruithear bheannaichte!*' the old man gasped reverently. 'What a beautiful dream, Doctor!'

Then a twinge of rheumatism made his face contract with pain.

'But it is only a dream,' he added sadly.

'It's a dream that's coming true,' Dr Maclaren averred.

'My goodness, Doctor, if it does, you'll have to be careful not to drive back to Snorvig over the top of Ben Sticla. Ay, you may be floating yourself the way I was when Ben Nevis gave me that great dram yon time, but your car won't be floating and you'll have to be a bit careful. And indeed, I believe you'd be wise to be soon on the road now. It's thickening all the time.'

'Right, I'll be leaving you now. I believe you're feeling better already.'

'Och, I'm feeling the better for seeing you, right enough,' the old man admitted. 'He'd be a queer kind of a crayture who wouldn't be the better for seeing you, Doctor. And thank you again for the pipe and the tobacco. Ay, I'll admit I was feeling pretty far down the drain when my old pipe went to pieces on me. Och, I was just saying to myself, "*Eachainn, a bhalaich*, you may as well go to pieces yourself now." And then you were after coming along.'

The old man held out his gnarled fist. Dr Maclaren grasped it.

'We're going to get that great dram, Hector,' he said. 'I feel it in my bones.'

'Is that so? I wish my bones would be feeling that kind of a feeling instead of what they will be feeling, the rascals,' the old man observed, a twinkle in his eyes as welcome to the Doctor as the sight of the stars to a steersman whose ship was wrapped in such a fog as was now drifting in from the sea.

'Ah, you're laughing at me now,' said Dr Maclaren. 'But you'll be laughing with me when I bring that bottle along.'

'Ach, I believe you'll have to distil it yourself, Doctor, in a *poit dhubh*. Oh, I've had a *poit dhubh* myself and made the stuff. It was a grand sight on a fine summer's morning to see the way the thin blue smoke of it would be stealing into the sky so quiet.'

'Did the exciseman ever catch you out?'

The old man gave a contemptuous ejaculation.

'Not he! He had a long nose on him right enough, but it wasn't long enough to find that wee lochan on Ben Bustival beside which I had my *poit dhubh*. Ay, he was a smart fellow all the same. A *Leodhasach*, he was ... Alec Macaulay was his name, and he was as black as my own *poit dhubh.* Ay, he was that. He went over to Easter Ross when he left the Islands and I never heard what became of him after.'

'We're not much troubled by the present man, Ferguson.'

'I never set eyes on him yet,' said Hector.

'He's from Aberdeen.'

'Ay, they think themselves pretty smart over there,' Hector chuckled. 'But och, what's the good of talking? We're all keeping the law nowadays. Ay, ration cards and coupons and identity cards and filling up forms instead of glasses. Och, I won't be so sorry at all to be leaving it.'

'You'll feel differently when I arrive with that bottle,' Dr Maclaren declared. 'And now I really must be getting back.'

'Ay, indeed you must, Doctor. My goodness, I hope you'll be all right on the road. It's pretty rough between here and Bobanish. I believe the County Council thinks we're just a lot of savages at this end of the island.'

'I'll take the road by the west,' said the Doctor. 'It'll be tricky going along by Loch Bob in this fog, and it may be clearer on the other side. Besides, the surface will be much better once I'm past Garryboo.'

Dr Maclaren's hope of getting out of the fog on the west side was not fulfilled. Indeed, it was thicker there if anything. Not so much as a rooftop in Garryboo itself was visible from the road. Visibility was hardly as much as twenty yards and he drove very slowly, hooting almost continuously to protect himself as far as possible against the recklessness of one or two of the lorry drivers. He was glad when he reached home safely.

'It's about the worst fog I ever remember in the Islands,' he said to Mrs Wishart, his grim but extremely competent middle-aged housekeeper from Fife.

Mrs Wishart pursed her tight lips. She took an equally low view of the weather and the people of the two Toddays, and she was not prepared to accept the worst behaviour by either as anything but an everyday occurrence.

'It's always rain or wind or mist out here,' she commented acidly.

'Ah now, come, Mrs Wishart, we very very seldom get fog. You'll get much more fog in the Kingdom of Fife. Any messages while I was out?'

'Not one.'

'Thank God for that! We'll have no boat this evening. I doubt if we'll get a boat till Tuesday.'

'I'm not worrying about that, Doctor. Indeed, if I was to worry myself every time the boat did not come I'd be in my grave by now.'

At that moment the sound of the *Island Queen*'s siren in the Coolish betrayed Dr Maclaren's prophecy about her non-arrival.

'By Jove, I may get a dram tonight, after all,' he exclaimed. 'Really, Captain MacKechnie's a great seaman. Who'd have expected him in this fog?'

There was a full gathering at the bar that evening in the hope that Roderick's stock would have been replenished; but those who left their firesides to visit the hotel were disappointed. Half a pint of beer a head had to be eked out until closing time.

To make up for the lack of whisky on such a frore foggy night, some of Roderick's customers and Roderick himself had received letters from Major Quiblick which certainly had a warming influence.

'What's this at all?' exclaimed Ruairidh Mór himself, scanning through his spectacles a letter in a buff envelope O.H.M.S. 'Who is this Major Quibalick?'

He began to read it aloud:

'Teer Sir,

I have to notify you that I have received a most unfavourable report about the atmosphere of the Snorvig Hotel. ...'

Roderick broke off in wrath.

'Atmosphere? There was neffer a finer atmosphere in the

whole of the Islands. *Mac an diabhoil*, does he think that
he knows more than the finest ladies and chentlemen in the
country what iss a good atmosphere? Wassn't the Tuke of
Ross himself after shaking me by the hand and conkratu-
lating me on the air in the Snorvig Hotel? "It is petter
than my own castle, Mr MacRurie," says the Tuke to me.

'Let's hear what else my bold major says,' said the
Biffer. 'I'm after having a letter from the man myself.'

Roderick continued:

'I am informed that the conversation there is often unduly
critical of the conduct of the war by those who carry upon
their shoulders a great weight of responsibility. I earnestly
hope that in future you will exercise your influence as landlord to check such criticism to the best of your ability. We
must all remember that we are fighting for our existence
against a skilful and ruthless enemy and that nothing will
encourage him so much as to suppose that the people of Great
Britain are losing confidence in their leaders.

I am sure that you will take whatever steps you consider
appropriate to improve the atmosphere of the Snorvig Hotel
and so avoid putting me under the unpleasant necessity of
taking further action.'

'And he signs himself P. Saint John Quibalick, Major
Sick,' Roderick added.

'Sick?' somebody repeated.

'Ay, S.I.C. And Saint John!' Roderick gasped. 'Look at
that now for a piece of impudence. Joseph Macroon himself would neffer be signing himself Saint John.'

'S.I.C. means Security Intelligence Corpse,' the Biffer
translated. 'It's written the same on his letter to me.'

'No intelligence at all,' Roderick scoffed. 'Chust a lot of
nonsense. What is the clown after saying to you,
Airchie?'

The Biffer began to read his letter:

Dear Sir,
I have to notify you that I have received a report that on at
least three occasions recently you indulged in careless talk
about the movements of shipping viz. . . .'

'What kind of ship is that? Viz?' asked the Snorvig fisherman who on a former occasion questioned Captain Waggett's ability to defeat Hitler on his own. Alan Galbraith was his name, but he was always known as Drooby, a nickname the origin of which none could tell except Drooby himself, and he never would. He was a big, brawny, red-faced man, and his own boat, a Zulu, was called the *Flying Fish*.

'I don't believe it's a ship at all,' said the Biffer. 'It's one of those words these Government fellows write when they want to get anybody in a bit of a muddle about how they have to fill up a form. Where was I? Ay, *the movements of shipping viz. on the 27th ult. ...*'

'What's an ult?' asked Drooby.

'That's another kind of a viz. Och, I'll never be finished reading my letter, Drooby, if you keep on asking so many questions. You ought to belong to the Government yourself. *Viz. on the 27th ult., on the 28th ult., and on the 1st inst.*'

Drooby shook his head.

'Och, it's easy to see he means last Saturday, Sunday, and Monday,' said the Biffer.

'Why can't he say Saturday, Sunday, and Monday, if that's what he means?' Drooby asked.

'Because that's the way these fellows have to write. Ult. means February.'

'You were after saying just now it meant Saturday,' Drooby pointed out sceptically.

'Let the man read his letter, Alan,' said Roderick. 'You and your ult and your viz. It's the right way when you're sending an official communication. You get plenty such letters when you're on the County Council. Och, I don't pay any attention to them. Go on, Airchie.'

The Biffer resumed the reading of his letter from Major Quiblick:

'I realize that you did not intend to do any harm, but in mentioning that your son was sailing from a certain port at a certain time for a certain destination you might have been giving valuable assistance to enemy agents who are always on the ...'

The Biffer hesitated and frowned. 'Do you ever have this one on the Council, Roderick,' he broke off to ask, 'Quy vyve?'

'Quy vyve?' the master of the house repeated. 'No, I never heard that one before. Ay, that's a new one to me, right enough.'

The Biffer continued:

'On the qui vive for information about the movement of shipping which can be communicated to enemy submarines. I hope that in future you will keep a close check on your tongue, and if no further reports are received of indulgence by you in careless talk I shall be spared the unpleasant necessity of taking further action.'

'Oh, well, well, did anybody ever hear the like of such nonsense? But I know who it was. It was that fellow Brown who was staying in the hotel over last week-end. I took him over to Kiltod.'

'The tweed merchant?' asked Roderick.

'Tweed merchant. All the tweed he ever bought he put round his own backside,' the Biffer scoffed. 'Ah, well, they knew better how to deal with that fellow in Todaidh Beag. Not a word could he get out of them, no, and not a bite of food or so much as a glass of milk. Let the rascal come back here again and I'll throw him off the end of the pier. Mr Brown? He'll be all the colours of the rainbow before I've finished with him.'

'Wait a bit now, Airchie,' Roderick advised cautiously. 'You want to go a bit slow with these fellows from the Government.'

'I'll go as slow or as quick as I've a mind to go, Roderick, Government or no Government. Careless talk! Ay, he'll talk a bit careless when I've knocked all his teeth out on him. Aren't you after having a letter, Drooby? You were opening your mouth pretty wide about the Home Guard when this Brown was in the bar last Saturday.'

'I wasn't in at the post-office,' said Drooby. 'But if I'll have a letter on Monday morning I'll throw him off the end of the pier myself.'

At this moment Captain Paul Waggett entered the bar, so unusual an occurrence that a silence fell upon the gathering, and the frequenters in their surprise drank up their glasses of beer nearly an hour before they meant to.

'Good evening, everybody,' said Captain Waggett graciously. 'The fog's still very thick. It looks as if the *Island Queen* will be here over Sunday. I had quite a job to find my way up to the hotel, Roderick. In fact I nearly went to the Manse instead.'

'You would have found chust as much to drink there as you'll find here, Mr Wackett,' said the host.

'Yes, I'm sorry to hear supplies are so short. I'm afraid I can't offer to stand a round.' He smiled his condescending smile to which nobody responded because nobody thought that there was anything to smile at. 'Still,' he went on, 'we must remember that every drop of whisky we don't drink is helping to pay for the war.'

'So is every drop we drink, the way it's taxed,' said Drooby. 'And I'd sooner pay for the war by drinking whisky, tax and all, than by not drinking it.'

This statement evoked a murmur of agreement from the gathering.

'Ah, but the point is that by not drinking whisky the whisky goes to America,' Paul Waggett explained, 'which means that the Americans are helping to pay for the war, whereas if we drink it ourselves they don't.'

'Do they drink our beer too, these Americans?' Drooby asked.

'No, no, that's a question of barley. We have to remember the food situation.'

'Och, we have to remember too much altogether,' Drooby muttered.

'But we must not grumble,' Captain Waggett insisted. 'That's one of the reasons why I've come up to the bar this evening. I've had a letter from Major Quiblick of the Society Intelligence Corps at Nobost to say he's had information that there is a lot of criticism of the country's war effort in the two Toddays.'

'Och, a lot of us are after having letters from Major Quibalick, Mr Wackett,' said Roderick. 'I've had one myself. Ay, some people have nothing petter to do than to write a lot of letters.'

'But it really won't do to let people get an impression that there is any defeatism here,' Captain Waggett urged. 'However, if Major Quiblick has written directly to some of you, I shan't say any more about that. Only, I do hope you realize that the Government have very strong powers in time of war – very strong powers indeed. I mean to say you wouldn't like it if it was decided to evacuate all the people from the two Toddays to the mainland.'

'What are you saying, Captain Waggett?' exclaimed the Biffer.

'I'm not saying that the Government will decide to do that. I'm simply reminding you all that if they did decide to they could. But we'll say no more about that. What really brought me along this evening is to ask if any of you know anything about an urn with ashes of somebody who was cremated in Canada?'

Every man present stared at Paul Waggett in bewilderment. One or two irreverent spirits had already put forward the theory that since he became the commander of the Home Guard on the two Toddays the owner of Snorvig House was showing signs of going off his head. The awkward silence was broken by the entrance of Andrew Thomson, the bank agent, who advanced to the counter and claimed from the host his allotted half-pint.

'You'll be interested in this, Mr Thomson,' said Captain Waggett. 'It appears that an urn with the ashes of somebody who was cremated in Canada and addressed to the Manager of the City and Suburban Bank, Lombard Street, was sent to Major Quiblick at Nobost from Snorvig.'

'I know nothing about any urn, Captain Waggett,' the banker replied, scowling with embarrassment at suddenly finding himself the centre of interest. Luckily for him, Captain MacKechnie now entered the bar and diverted public attention.

'Do you know, Captain MacKechnie, that an urn containing the ashes of somebody who was cremated in Canada was left in a cabin of the *Island Queen* last Tuesday?'

'What?' Captain MacKechnie squeaked. 'Ach, the fock has got into your head, Mr Wackett. Who'd be putting anybody's ashes in my ship?'

'That's just the point,' said Paul Waggett. 'Who did? It's a serious matter. After all, as Major Quiblick points out, it might have been a time-bomb.'

'Major Quiblick is a clown. Ach, he pesters the life out of me at Nobost. He's chust a clown,' Captain MacKechnie declared.

'I don't think you ought to say that, Captain MacKechnie,' said Paul Waggett stiffly. 'You can't call the officer in charge of Security Intelligence for a Protected Area a clown.'

'Ah, but I will,' said Captain MacKechnie. 'What cappin was this firework found in?'

'In the cabin of Mr Brown, a tweed merchant, who spent last week-end at the Snorvig Hotel,' said Captain Waggett.

'Tweet mairchant? Not at all,' the skipper of the *Island Queen* squeaked. 'He's one of those pocket Hitlers at Nobost Lotch. I know him fine. It's a good thing for him there's a fock. He'd have heard the rough site of my tongue if we'd gone on to Nobost tonight.'

'Well, you'll have to settle that with Major Quiblick, himself,' said Captain Waggett, in what he hoped was an impressive tone of voice. 'He asked me to make inquiries this end. Somebody in Snorvig must have put these ashes in Mr Brown's cabin.'

'His real name isn't Brown. His name is Lieutenant Pokkust. Didn't I pring him to Nobost about a month ago, and didn't he come up on the pridge and nearly drive me daft with the questions he was asking?'

Captain Waggett made a mental note to draw Major Quiblick's attention to the indiscretion of his subaltern if an opportunity afforded itself.

'Well,' he said, 'I hope that if anybody here does obtain any information about this urn he will let me know at once so that I can send a report to the appropriate authorities. I mean to say, we don't want unnecessary mysteries. Secrecy, of course, is all-important as you know, but mystery is not. Well, I'll say good night. Do you think you'll get away in time to be back at Snorvig on Tuesday, Captain MacKechnie?'

'I wouldn't care to give you an answer about that in weather like this, Mr Wackett. We were lucky to make the island at all today. It came round us so quick.'

'I only asked because I'm expecting Sergeant-major Odd by Tuesday's boat,' said Captain Waggett. 'I had a telegram from Fort Augustus to say we could have his services for a week. I'm sure you'll all be pleased to hear that,' he added, turning to the Home Guards present.

'Ay, that's good news, Captain,' the Biffer agreed.

'Imphm,' murmured the Banker.

'He's a really fine chap is the Sergeant,' said the Biffer. 'He's no tweed merchant. Och, we'll all be glad to have him with us for a while.'

'Imphm,' murmured the Banker.

When Captain Waggett had withdrawn, the company in the bar began to speculate about the urn.

'What size of a thing would it be at all?' somebody asked.

'Och, it's pretty large,' said somebody else. 'They use then for tea when there's too many people for a teapot.'

'I wouldn't care at all to see my ashes in a teapot,' another said.

'Now I come to think of it,' said the Biffer, 'I saw Kenny Iosaiph and another Kiltod fellow carrying a sort of a black box up the gangway of the *Queen*.'

'If those ashes were after coming from Joseph Macroon,' Captain MacKechnie declared, 'you'll never know where they came from.'

There was a buzz of agreement.

'Ay,' said the Biffer pensively, 'that's right. It might be they were after finding the box and when they found it wasn't what they were hoping it might be ....' He broke off. 'Och, well, well, I'd like to have seen Joseph's face when he found it was ashes instead of whisky. Ach, well, boys, we'll never be knowing. Never. There's not a man on Todaidh Beag will let us have the laugh at him next time we give him a dram.'

'It'll be long enough before we give anybody a dram,' Drooby prophesied sombrely.

And the frequenters of the bar passed out into the clammy darkness of the fog that night like ghosts from a happier age.

Chapter 9

THE *CABINET MINISTER*

'Now where we are I cannot tell
But I wish I could hear the Inchcape Bell.'

THERE is no need to waste sympathy on Sir Ralph the Rover as he paced the deck, because he himself some years earlier had cut the bell from the Inchcape Rock merely to annoy the good old Abbot of Aberbrothock who had placed it there for the benefit of mariners. We can, however, commiserate with Captain Buncher who on that Sabbath morning in March paced the deck of the s.s. *Cabinet Minister*, outward bound to New York, when he expressed a passionate desire to hear the bell which warned mariners against the Skerrydoo, an unpleasant black reef awash at half tide to which ships proceeding down the Minch gave a wide berth. The reason why Captain Buncher could not hear the bell buoy of the Skerrydoo was that he was ten miles away from it and that in his anxiety to avoid it in the dense fog he had taken the *Cabinet Minister* into the Sound of Todday and thus right off his course.

The people coming out of church at Kiltod heard the siren of the *Cabinet Minister* sounding away to the north just as the people going into church at Snorvig heard it sounding to the north-west.

'That's queer right enough,' said Drooby to the Biffer, the expression of piety considered suitable for entering church lost for a moment in an expression of the liveliest curiosity.

'Sounding from the west,' the Biffer observed.

'Some ship's finding herself in trouble,' said Drooby. 'She's no business to be out there at all.'

Then the animation of curiosity which had been

lightening their countenances died away to be succeeded by an expression of severely introverted piety as they turned into church and proceeded toward their accustomed seats.

Over on Little Todday the congregation, gathered in groups outside the towerless church of Our Lady Star of the Sea and St Tod, listened to the sound of the siren with as much attention as they had paid to the brief but eloquent sermon of Father Macalister whose view of Lent's rapid approach had perhaps never seemed quite so profoundly affected by the solemnity of the season.

'He was pretty fierce this morning Alan,' said one of his flock.

'*A Dhia*, what'll he be giving us on Wednesday?'

'Ay, he was fierce right enough,' agreed Alan Macdonald, a long, lean crofter with a trim square beard, as he slowly rolled some twist between his palms preparatory to filling a pipe. 'What do you make of that ship's siren, Hugh?'

Hugh Macroon, who was also preparing his after Mass pipe, stopped to listen more intently.

'I believe she's coming nearer.'

'Och, she's coming nearer all the time,' declared John Stewart positively.

'Will she be in the Coolish?' somebody asked.

'I believe she's more to the north,' said somebody else.

'I believe she'll be pretty near Bàgh Mhic Ròin,' said Hugh Macroon slowly.

A silence fell upon the group, not a man in which did not know the story of the black chest but not a man in which would have considered for one moment alluding to it.

'Ay, I believe you're right, Hugh,' said John Stewart. 'Ah, well, you and me had better be moving along towards home.'

The congregation was dispersing into the fog by the various tracks across the wet machair which led to the houses scattered all over the island. Presently Hugh

Macroon and John Stewart could have fancied themselves
the only people left in all Little Todday as they trudged
northward. Their wives and families had driven on ahead.

'I'm not after hearing her blow for some time,' said
John Stewart presently.

'I didn't hear nothing,' Hugh added in these deliberate
tones of his which seemed to lend such weighty support
of, or offer equally weighty opposition to, other people's
assertions.

'There she goes again,' Jockey exclaimed.

'That's not a ship,' said Hugh. 'That's a stirk or a heefer.'

'Ay, ay, it would be a heefer right enough,' Jockey
agreed as the melancholy mooing sounded somewhere in
the distance of that silver-grey annihilation of figure and
form, of sea and land.

They walked on for half an hour in silence, each preoccupied with the same dream which neither of them
thought it would be decorous to put into words. At last
they came to where the track forked to their respective
crofts.

'I dare say dinner will not be ready for a while yet,'
said Hugh.

'Och, it'll be a long while yet,' Jockey agreed.

'It's pretty quiet,' said Hugh.

'Ay, it's pretty quiet right enough,' Jockey agreed.

'She might have run into clearer weather,' Hugh suggested.

'Ay, she might, but it's kind of queer that she stopped
hooting so sudden,' Jockey commented.

'Ay, it's queer right enough,' Hugh agreed. 'Maybe it
wouldn't be a bad notion to walk on a bit and see if we
could get a sight of her from the head of the *bàgh*.'

'*Ceart gu leoir*. Right you are, Hugh. Ay, we'll walk
along to the head of the *bàgh*, and tinner will be chust
about ready by the time we reach home.'

They had walked on for another twenty minutes when
Hugh suddenly gripped Jockey's wet sleeve.

'*Eisd!*'

Both men stood still. From ahead of them through the viewless air there came thinly, remotely, but unmistakably the sound of someone hallooing at intervals.

'That's never a *Todach* shouting like that,' Hugh declared.

'Neffer!' Jockey agreed. 'Come on, let's hurry. I believe she iss. I was after thinking she wass all the way from church.'

At that moment the figure of a man running toward them along the track materialized from the fog. It was Willie Munro.

'There's a big steamer on the Gobha,' he gasped in excitement. 'I'm away to Kiltod to send word over to Snorvig.'

'What for?' Hugh Macroon asked.

'It's me that's the coast-watcher. The supervisor will want to send word to Nobost for the lifeboat.'

'Man, you're daft,' said Hugh contemptuously. 'What lifeboat could come from Nobost in such a fog? And the sea as smooth as glass. If they want to come ashore they don't want no lifeboat. Wass it you that was shouting just now?'

'I was never shouting.'

'Very well then,' said Hugh, 'I believe some of them will be ashore now. You'd have done better to wait where you were. Come on, Jockey. We'll be getting down to the *bàgh*.'

'Och, well, I'll be getting along to Kiltod,' said Willie Monro. He hurried on his way.

'Ay, he's cunning is Willie,' Hugh observed when he and Jockey had moved on. 'But he's a bit of a fool. Oh well, I don't believe this big steamer will be full of ashes.'

'*A Dhia*, I hope not,' Jockey exclaimed.

'She might be full of nothing,' Hugh suggested. 'If she's outward bound.'

'She would neffer be setting a course through the Sound of Todday if she wass outward bound,' Jockey pointed out. 'No, no, she's homeward bound. *A Dhia*, she might be from Chamaica with plenty rum aboard. Parcels and parcels of it.'

'Stop your dreaming, Jockey,' Hugh Macroon advised. 'We were after dreaming of gold and it turned to ashes. If we go dreaming of rum it'll end up in grapefruits.'

A minute or two later two strangers emerged from the fog.

One of them was tall and lanky with red hair. The other was short and plump and also had red hair.

'Can you tell us where we are, mate?' the short seaman asked in the accent of Clydeside.

'You're on Little Todday,' John Stewart replied.

'Where in hell's that?' asked the lanky seaman in the same accent as his companion.

'I don't know at all where it is in hell,' said Hugh Macroon slowly. 'But I can tell you where it is on earth.' And this he proceeded to do.

'And you don't think she'll float off at high water?' asked the short seaman whose name was Robbie Baird.

'I'm pretty sure she won't,' said Hugh.

'What did I tell you, Robbie?' exclaimed his companion. 'Och ay, the old *Minister* will make a job for the salvage and that's about all she will do. Anyway, Fritz won't get her now.'

'Och, I'm not so sure myself she winna float,' Robbie Baird insisted.

'All richt, all richt. I'm not arguing aboot it,' Sandy Swan replied with a touch of impatience. Then he turned to the crofters.

'Look, will you two fellows come back on board with Robbie Baird and myself? The old man had better get word from strangers what's coming to him. He'll think he's gone plain daft when he hears where he is.'

'What port were you making for?' Jockey asked.

'New York.'

'Outward pound?' Jockey exclaimed in shrill amazement. 'How were you coming round the north end of Little Todday, and you outward pound?'

'Put the blame on the *Cabinet Minister*'s cargo,' Robbie Baird chuckled. 'The old ship was absolutely fou'.'

'There's cargo in her, is there?' Hugh asked. 'There's not much cargo outward bound these days.'

'Cargo in her?' Robbie Baird exclaimed with a wink. 'I'm telling you. There's fifty thousand cases of whisky in the auld *Cabinet Minister*,' he added with a triumphant toss of the head.

'What?' Jockey shrilled like a questing falcon.

Even the imperturbableness of Hugh Macroon was shaken by this news. He gulped twice.

'Fifty sousant cases of whisky?' Jockey lisped. He was never perfectly at ease with 'th' and emotion now deprived him of any power even to attempt the combination of letters. 'She must be a huge crate ship.'

'Four thousand tons. Blue Limpet Line.'

'Fifty sousant! Fifty sousant!' Jockey murmured in awe. 'And twelf pottles in effery case? Oh, well, well, Clory be to Cod and to His Plessed Mother and to All the Holy Saints,' he ejaculated as he crossed himself in a devout rapture of humble human gratitude. '*Uisdein, eudail* wasn't it Mhaighstir Seumas who was saying we'd kept the Faith in Todaidh Beag and Almighty God would not be forketting us?'

The two red-haired Clydesiders grinned at the round sandy-haired Hebridean.

'Here's tae us,' said Robbie Baird, raising an imaginary glass.

The captain's cutter had been made fast to a rock, halfway up Macroon's Bay.

'You were pretty lucky to come in here,' Hugh commented. 'You might have lost yourselves.'

'The fog lifted for a while after we struck. That's why the old man sent us ashore. Then it came down thicker than ever, and we started to shout.'

'Ay, we heard you,' Hugh told them.

Now the fog lifted again, and presently the *Cabinet Minister* was visible.

'*A Dhia*, she's lying terribly crooket,' Jockey exclaimed.

'Och ay, the first big sea's likely to break her back,' Sandy Swan prophesied confidently.

'And there's a big sea running between Pillay and Todday when the tide's making and the wind is easterly,' Hugh observed thoughtfully.

'Ay, and you get a pick sea when the tide iss tropping and the wind is sou-west,' Jockey added.

'Och, you get a big sea whichever way the wind is or the tide either,' said Hugh. 'You'd better not be staying aboard any longer than you have to. You're in luck, too, because the mailboat got into Snorvig yesterday afternoon and couldn't leave again. I don't know if she'll go back to Obaig tonight if the fog clears right away. They're very strict about Sunday over in Great Todday. They're all Protestants there and we're all Catholics here; but still, I believe she will be going back tonight. The coast-watcher must have sighted you when the fog lifted for a bit. We were after meeting him on the way to Kiltod to get word to the Supervisor. But even if they won't send over for you from Snorvig on Sunday we'll get you across the Coolish.'

'Ay, and we'll get some carts over to the head of the pay and you'll be aple to take wiss you what you've a mind to,' Jockey added.

'You'd better tell the skipper all that,' Robbie Baird advised.

'Och, yess, we'll tell him right enough,' Jockey assured the two sailors. 'It wouldn't be ferry nice at all if the wind got up after this fock and you still on the Gobha.'

'Och, aye, it would be a bit gory,' Robbie Baird chuckled.

'It iss not *gobhar*. It iss *gobha*,' said Jockey. '*Gobha* iss a blacksmiss. *Gobhar* is a coat.'

'A coat, eh?' Robbie Baird nodded.

'No, not a coat. A coat.'

'A goat,' Hugh put in to help the seaman.

'Ah, a goat,' Robbie Baird repeated. 'And the name of

this rock we're on is the Blacksmith, eh? Well, it's black all richt. All the same, goat widna hae been a bad name for the b——r the way he butted into us.'

The *Cabinet Minister* had been going dead slow when she struck the Gobha, but she was well on top of the submerged reef which extended for twenty yards on either side of the black fragment of basalt which thrust itself up out of the water. Two hundred yards ahead rose the dark cliffs on the eastern face of Pillay whitened by the droppings of the seafowl that nested upon their ledges.

The steamer was heeling over at enough of an angle to make the Captain's cabin seem as perilous a place in which to remain too long as the two crofters were anxious to persuade him it was.

'So that's where I am, is it?' said Captain Buncher, putting his finger on the chart. 'And you say there's no chance of floating off on the top of the tide?'

Hugh Macroon shook his domed head, and when Hugh did that onlookers were apt to be impressed. Captain Buncher, a small man with a small grizzled beard, a high complexion, and hair as dark as the rock on which his ship had struck, *was* impressed.

'But there's no need for you people to be bringing carts and wagons to this bay. We can row round in the ship's lifeboats to Snorvig. You say the mailboat is there now?'

'Ay, but she might not go back to Obaig till tomorrow morning, being Sunday,' Hugh replied. 'But you'll find good accommodation at the hotel. At least pretty good. There's very little beer just now. And no whisky at all.'

'No whisky, eh?'

'There's not been as much whisky as you'd get in a poorhouse for two months and more.'

'That's bad,' Captain Buncher clicked. He rang the bell, and when the steward came he bade him bring glasses. Then he went to a locker and produced a bottle of Stag's Breath, a brand which had been particularly favoured by the inhabitants of the two Toddays in the good old days of plenty.

'Stack's Press,' murmured Jockey, transfixed by the beauty of the sight before his eyes and under his nose and hardly a couple of feet away from his mouth.

'Help yourselves,' Captain Buncher commanded when the steward had brought the glasses. 'But no, that's not fair. I'll help you.'

'And, poys,' Jockey told them later that famous Sunday before Lent, 'it *wass* a help. It wass reeally powerful. Ay, and the man helped us twice. Neffer plinked an eye. Chust poured it out as if he was a *cailleach* pouring you out a cup o' tay. And mind you, the man's heart must have been sore inside of him, the way his ship was lying there on the Gobha. But he neffer plinked an eye. Chust poured it out.'

When Hugh and Jockey were raising to their lips that second glass Captain Buncher suddenly remarked:

'The glass is high and steady.'

'Ay, it's high right enough,' Jockey agreed. 'But it's not so steady as it wass the first time, Captain.'

Captain Buncher laughed.

'I was thinking, I might leave a couple of my chaps on board till the salvage people took over.'

'You know best, Captain,' Hugh Macroon allowed with grave courtesy. 'But you couldn't have a worse place than you are except when it's calm as it is just now, and when there's anything of a ground swell it's tricky right enough to get ashore at all.'

'Yes, well, I expect you're right, my friend. If she becomes a total loss there'll be no lives lost with her. Well, I'm much obliged to you for your help. Baird and Swan will put you ashore in the cutter, and then I think we'll make for Snorvig in the lifeboats. You don't think the mailboat will leave before evening, that is provided the fog doesn't come back, and she's able to leave at all?'

'Och, she'll never move on a Sunday afternoon,' Hugh assured him. 'Anyway, Jockey and me will go in to Kiltod and send word you'll be round before sunset. And you'll not be forgetting there's not a drop of whisky in Snorvig?'

'I won't forget,' Captain Buncher replied, with a smile. 'And as there isn't a drop of whisky in your island either, perhaps you'd like to take a bottle each with you ashore. Good-bye, and thanks very much for your help.'

When the two red-headed Clydesiders put Hugh and Jockey ashore inside Bàgh Mhic Ròin each pulled out his bottle of Stag's Breath to offer the seamen a dram.

'No, no, mates, we'll not rob you,' said Sandy Swan.

'It is not robbing us at all,' said Hugh in whom the two potent drinks he had had in Captain Buncher's cabin had induced that extreme deliberation of utterance which was the recognized sign that Hugh Macroon had had a hefty one. 'No, it is not robbing us. It is giving us pleasure to be able to offer a dram to a friend. Isn't that right, Jockey?'

'Right? Sure, it's right. It's a pleshure we've not been after having for munce, *a chàirdean*,' Jockey insisted, unfastening the stopper of his bottle.

The seamen saw that the islesmen would be chagrined by their refusal. So each took a short swig from Jockey's bottle, and having wished and been wished good health and good luck they sheered off and pulled back to the *Cabinet Minister*.

The two crofters sat on an outcrop of rock and watched, now the cutter, now the two bottles of Stag's Breath. The sun like a great silver plate was visible again through the ever-lessening fog, and larger patches of pale-blue sky were spreading above them.

'Oh, well, who would have thought when we were walking to Mass this morning that we would be sitting here like this before two o'clock?' said Hugh. 'We'll just have a bite to eat and then we'll get the cart and drive along to Kiltod. I want to give my bottle to Father James.'

'Och, I want to give him my pottle,' Jockey protested.

'We've all had a dram out of yours. Och, one's enough for him just now,' Hugh decided firmly. '*A Dhia*, there's six hundred thousand bottles where this came from.'

'*Tha gu dearbh, Uisdein. Tha gu dearbh*,' Jockey agreed,

in his voice a boundless content. *'Uisge beatha gu leòir, taing a Dhia.* We'll chust be saying three Hail Marys, Hugh.'

'Ay,' the other agreed, 'for favours received.'

The two crofters knelt down, and mingling with the murmur of their prayers was the lapping of the tide along the green banks of Bàgh Mhic Ròin and a rock pipit's frail fluttering song.

Chapter 10

WHISKY GALORE

═══════════

THE strict Sabbatarianism of Scotland has been the target for a good deal of satire. Some have not hesitated to suggest that it encourages among its devotees a Pharisaical observance of the letter of the Divine Law without any corresponding observance of its spirit. Scoffers are invited to contemplate the behaviour of the people of Great Todday on that Sunday in March when the s.s. *Cabinet Minister* became a wreck a few hundred yards from Little Todday.

Not one man was willing to break the Sabbath by crossing the Coolish to investigate that wreck: if cynics demand a lower motive, let it be said that not one man was brave enough to flout public opinion by doing so. The weather was fine. The sea was dead calm. Captain Buncher and the whole of his crew were going off with the *Island Queen* when she left for Obaig at dusk. There was for the moment nobody with authority over the wreck. Excise and salvage had not yet appeared upon the scene. The supervisor of the coast-watchers was John Macintosh the piermaster at Snorvig, known as Iain Dubh, but his only job was to notify the head of the coast-guards at Portrose eighty miles away that a ship had been wrecked or to summon the lifeboat from Nobost if a ship was in danger of being wrecked. After that his responsibility ceased. Constable Macrae was charged with the invigilation of crashed aircraft and with notifying Rear-Admiral, Portrose, if he saw an enemy submarine. Wrecks were not his pigeons.

Captain Paul Waggett was profoundly convinced that the war would not be over until he had been granted authority to deal in the manner he considered appropriate with crashed aircraft, enemy submarines and wrecks, but this authority he had not yet been able to acquire. He was not even allowed to put Home Guards in charge of the stores of food locked up in the now disused old school at Snorvig as emergency rations for the island in the event of invasion. Most of these stores had been removed by what Captain Waggett declared he had no hesitation in calling common thieves, and this was just as well, because the rest of them had gone bad in the course of over two years.

It was obvious to the people of Great Todday that for once in a way there was no time like the present, but the present being the Sabbath their principles would not allow them to take advantage of it. Tribute must be paid to the staunchness of those principles. Mental agony is hardly too strong a term to describe what many of the people of Great Todday went through on that Sabbath evening when they thought of the people of Little Todday not merely breaking the Sabbath but encouraged to do so by the tenets of their religion.

The Biffer was one of those who suffered most acutely. He had seen the lifeboats of the *Cabinet Minister* coming round into the Coolish. He had been down on the pier when they landed. He had been almost the first man in Snorvig to know what cargo the wrecked ship was carrying. For the rest of that afternoon he was jumping up and going to the door of his house built not far from the water's edge on the rocky point that protected the harbour from the north. At last even his large placid wife protested.

'Will you not be sitting quiet for more than one minute, Airchie?'

'I'm keeping a sharp look-out on the weather,' he replied. 'If it came on to blow when the sun goes down she might break in two before morning the way they tell me she will be lying on the Gobha.'

'The weather won't change one way or the other because you're for ever jumping up and running to the door,' his wife observed. 'For goodness' sake be still for a moment. It's the only quiet time I have in all the week.'

'I might take the *Kittiwake* round the north side of Todaidh Beag and have a look at her,' Airchie suggested. 'No one could call that breaking the Sabbath.'

'Couldn't they?' said his wife, shaking her head in compassion for such self-deception. 'You know as well as I do, Airchie, what everybody would say when they saw you out there in the Coolish on a Sabbath afternoon. Indeed, what would yourself be saying if you saw Alan Galbraith out there just now?'

'If I saw Drooby out there I'd be out there myself pretty quick,' the Biffer replied emphatically.

'And a fine sight you'd be giving the neighbours, the pair of you.'

'Och, well, he isn't there.'

'No, indeed, I hope he has more sense, and if he hasn't the sense himself Bean Ailein will have the sense. Goodness me, you're like a child, Airchie. Let the ship bide till Monday.'

'Do you think they'll let the ship bide till Monday on Little Todday? Och, Ealasaid, you're talking very grand about my sense. But where is your own sense, woman?'

'If the poor *papanaich* on Todaidh Beag don't know better than to break the Sabbath, is it you that's wanting them to lead you by that great nose of yours into breaking it with them?'

'I'm not so sure if it would be breaking the Sabbath just to have a bit of a look round,' the Biffer ventured to speculate.

'Are you not? Ah well, I'm not going to argue with you, Airchie. We'll have been married twenty-five years next July, and if I'd argued with you every time you were wrong I don't know where we'd have been today. No, indeed. You'll just go your own way, and if you want to be breaking the Sabbath you'll be breaking it.'

Such recognition of his obstinacy took all the relish out of being obstinate. That had always been Ealasaid's method with him. He felt almost inclined to be aggrieved by her reasonableness.

'I believe I'll go along and see what's doing on the *Queen*. Maybe Captain MacKechnie won't be leaving till tomorrow. He may be afraid of what everybody will say if he goes to Obaig tonight.'

The sarcasm was lost on his wife. She was sitting placidly back in her chair, her hands folded in her lap, her eyes closed.

The Biffer found Drooby standing on the pier in contemplation of the *Island Queen*, aboard which there was no sign of life.

'Is she going tonight?' he asked.

'Ay, six o'clock, the Captain said. They're all up at the hotel now,' Drooby replied. 'They brought a tidy bit of stuff with them in the boats. It's all safe aboard now.'

'What will they do with the boats?' the Biffer asked.

'Och, the salvage men will have them.'

'I was thinking, Alan, I'd go along in the *Kittiwake* after twelve o'clock and see what's doing over yonder.'

'Not a bad idea,' Drooby observed.

'Will you be going along yourself with the *Flying Fish*?'

'I don't believe I will. Two of the crew went home yesterday till tomorrow. I wouldn't be able to get hold of them tonight. And anyway I wouldn't want to take the *Flying Fish* round there. Iain Dubh and me are not very good friends just now. He made a proper mess of that last lot of whitefish I sent over to Obaig.'

'Ay, I heard about that.'

'We lost a lot of money over him being so obstinate the way he was. Ay, and nothing would give him more pleasure than to be reporting me to the Navy up at Portrose if he thought I was doing anything on the side with the *Flying Fish*!'

'Would you like to come along with me tonight in the *Kittiwake*?' the Biffer asked. 'Just you and me, and young Jimmy to stand by while we get aboard?'

'*Ceart gu leoir*. Right you are, I'll come along with you, Airchie.'

'It would be a pity to let them have all that whisky over yonder.'

Drooby shook his head.

'They'll never get it all, Airchie. There's thousands and thousands and thousands of bottles in the *Cabinet Minister*. Some say there are fifty thousand cases. Others say it's fifteen thousand cases. Whichever it is, it's a lot of whisky. And it's wonderful stuff too. Not a drop under proof, they tell me. That's the kind of whisky you and me drank before the last war. And we didn't pay twenty-five shillings a bottle for it in those days.'

'Were you having a crack with some of the crew?'

'Ay, and I had a couple of drams too,' said Drooby.

'Ach, I thought you were looking a bit pleased with yourself, Alan, when I came on the pier.'

'Ay, it's only when you haven't had a good dram for a long while that you're knowing how important it is not to go without it.'

A golden decrescent moon was hanging in a clear blue sky below Ben Sticla and Ben Pucka when Drooby, the Biffer, and the Biffer's youngest boy Jimmy went chugging up the Coolish in the *Kittiwake* soon after midnight. The strait was glassy calm, and even when they rounded the north-easterly point of Little Todday the Atlantic itself was almost without perceptible motion.

'I believe this weather will hold for a few days yet,' said the Biffer.

'Unless it comes on thick again,' Drooby qualified.

'Ay, it might do that.'

The *Kittiwake* was now approaching the entrance of Macroon's Bay, and a minute or two later the 4000-ton steamer loomed before them in the tempered moonshine.

Presently they were hailed by a sizeable fishing-boat.

'Who are you?'

'That's the Dot,' said Drooby.

Donald Macroon, generally known as the Dot, owned the largest of the Little Todday craft; it was called the *St*

Tod, except by Father Macalister who always called it the *St Dot*.

'Hullo, hullo,' the Biffer shouted back. 'This is Airchie MacRurie and Alan Galbraith in the *Kittiwake*.'

He slowed down the engine and presently drew alongside the *St Tod*.

'You've been a very long time coming,' said the Dot, a small, swarthy, and usually taciturn fisherman. Tonight he was, for him, voluble.

'Ay, we had to wait till the Sabbath was over,' the Biffer explained.

The Dot laughed.

'Ay, that's what we were thinking. Never mind, boys, there's enough for everybody from the Butt of Lewis to Barra Head. You'd better have a dram right away now before you get on board. How many crans did you catch last week, Alan?'

'We had nine.'

'Och, well, *a bhalaich*,' said the Dot, 'there's thousands of crans of whisky on board of her. There's more bottles of whisky on board of her than the biggest catch of herring you ever made in your life, Alan. But have a dram with me before you go aboard.'

The Dot thrust a bottle of Islay Dew at the Biffer.

'Don't spare it, *a bhalaich*, you couldn't drink it all if you lived for ever.'

'*Slàinte mhór*,' said the Biffer, and then took a deep swig. '*A Chruithear*,' he commented reverently, 'that's beautiful stuff.' He wiped his mouth and passed the bottle to Drooby.

'Oh, well, well,' said Drooby when he too had drunk deep, 'that stuff would put heart into anybody.'

'When were they saying in Snorvig that the salvage men were coming?' asked the Dot.

'They might be here with Tuesday's boat,' the Biffer told him.

'Och, well, we must do our best to make their job as easy for them as we can,' the Dot chuckled. 'You'd better get on board and help yourselves. We've shifted quite a lot of it. I've been backward and forward loaded with cases a dozen times already, but you wouldn't see what we're after taking, there's so many thousands of cases.'

'You're pretty lucky over here,' said the Biffer. 'It won't be so easy to land it on the other side.'

'You'd better take back a good load with you tonight,' the Dot advised. 'You needn't worry to pick and choose. It's all beautiful stuff. We've rigged a rope-ladder to get down into the hold. It took a bit of doing, too. Still, so long as the weather keeps good for a bit, we ought to get a tidy few cases out of her the way she's lying now. Take another dram before you go, boys. It's pretty hard work coming up with those cases from the hold.'

'Well, I've known the Dot for forty years and more, Drooby,' the Biffer told his friend as they took the *Kittiwake* alongside the wreck. 'But I never heard him say so much in all those years as I heard him say tonight.'

'Nor I either,' said Drooby. 'Mostly it's just "*tha*" or "*chan 'eil*" and a big spit and you've heard all he has to tell you. Islay Dew,' he added reflectively. 'I hope we'll hit on a case of that.'

Many romantic pages have been written about the sunken Spanish galleon in the bay of Tobermory. That 4000-ton steamship on the rocks of Little Todday provided more practical romance in three and a half hours than the Tobermory galleon has provided in three and a half centuries. Doubloons, ducats, and ducatoons, moidores, pieces of eight, sequins, guineas, rose and angel nobles, what are these to vaunt above the liquid gold carried by the *Cabinet Minister*? It may be doubted if such a representative collection of various whiskies has ever been assembled before. In one wooden case of twelve bottles you might have found half a dozen different brands in half a dozen different shapes. Besides the famous names known all over the world by ruthless and persistent advertising for many years, there were many blends of the finest quality, less famous perhaps but not less delicious.

There were Highland Gold and Highland Heart, Tartan Milk and Tartan Perfection, Bluebell, Northern Light, Preston Pans, Queen of the Glens, Chief's Choice, and Prince's Choice, Islay Dew, Silver Whistle, Salmon's Leap, Stag's Breath, Stalker's Joy, Bonnie Doon, Auld Stuarts, King's Own, Trusty Friend, Old Cateran, Scottish Envoy, Norval, Bard's Bounty, Fingal's Cave, Deirdre's Farewell, Lion Rampart, Road to the Isles, Pipe Major, Moorland Gold and Moorland Cream, Thistle Cream, Shinty, Blended Heather, Glen Gloming, Mountain Tarn, Cromag, All the Year Round, Clan MacTavish and Clan MacNab, Annie Laurie, Over the Border, and Cabarféidh. There were spherical bottles and dimpled bottles and square bottles and oblong bottles and flagon-shaped bottles and high-waisted bottles and ordinary bottles, and the glass of every bottle was stamped with a notice which made it clear that whisky like this was intended to be drunk in the United States of America and not by the natives of the land where it was distilled, matured, and blended.

'Ah, well, Jockey,' said Hugh Macroon when he and John Stewart were coming back with the last boat load of the *St Tod*, 'we were after thinking we had found plenty gold last Sunday and it turned to ashes; but it was a sign right enough that a better kind of gold was on its way.'

The grey of dawn was glimmering above the bens of Todaidh Mór, and the high decrescent moon, silver now, was floating merrily upon her back across the deep starry sky toward the west.

'I believe I never worked so hard and enchoyed myself so much in all my life,' Jockey averred.

Over on Great Todday, Drooby and the Biffer were conveying a dozen cases of whisky up the rocky path to the Biffer's house while Jimmy kept watch against any sign of curiosity from the pier house and the police station.

'It's a good beginning, Drooby,' the Biffer said when the cases were stowed away at the back of his shed under a heap of old nets. 'But we mustn't be wasting tomorrow night. There's the weather to think about and the salvage, and I'm sure Ferguson will be along from Nobost, and there's the pollis. Och, you'd better take the *Flying Fish* over and get a big load aboard.'

'I'll do that right enough,' Drooby vowed. 'I'm just wondering where will be the best place to store it.'

'There's the old curing-shed down by your place.'

'Ay, there's that; but, if it got about that the stuff was there, some of my bold fellows who never put foot or hand to bring it across might be helping themselves.'

'That's right enough,' the Biffer agreed. 'How would it be to take the stuff up Loch Sleeport? There's a fine big loft in Watasett School. We used to climb up there when we were children.'

'Not a bad idea, Airchie. And Norman Macleod would likely come along with us tomorrow night. There's bound to be a lot of them over from Todaidh Mór tomorrow. Well, I'll just take half a dozen bottles along with me now.'

'Ay, we'll open a case and I'll take the other half-dozen into the house,' said the Biffer.

'I believe a dram would do us both good just now,' Drooby suggested. 'It'll keep the cold air out of our *stamacs*. Is there any Islay Dew in that case?'

The Biffer looked at the bottles.

'No, this is Lion Rampart and Tartan Perfection. We''ll try Lion Rampart.'

'Well, I don't believe anything could be better than that,' Drooby decided, putting down the bottle with a sigh. 'Still, we might as well try Tartan Perfection. Ah, well, I don't know which is best,' he declared after the second dram. 'I'll take another dram of Lion Rampart just to make sure. And now I'm not sure, after all,' he said.

'And I'm not so sure,' the Biffer echoed. 'We'd better try Tartan Perfection again.'

'Ay, it's a pity not to know which really is the best,' Drooby agreed. 'I don't know what's the matter with me, Airchie, but I'm feeling much better.'

'Ay, I'm feeling much better myself, Alan. Och, I don't believe the war will last for ever at all. *Slàinte mhath!*'

'*Slàinte mhór!*' Drooby wished in return. 'I don't believe anybody could find out which was best. Well,' he went on, 'some people say they're close in Little Today. I wouldn't say that, Airchie.'

'I wouldn't say that myself,' the Biffer agreed. He poured himself out another dram, but whether it was Lion Rampart or Tartan Perfection he was hardly aware. 'I wouldn't say it at all. *Slàinte mhór* to all friends on Little Today.'

'*Slàinte mhór!*' Drooby echoed, with a hiccup like the castanets at the beginning of a cachucha. 'They never grudged us a bottle. "Help yourselves, boys," that was the spirit. I'll never see a Little Today man go without a dram so long as there's whisky in the country. Never.'

'Never,' the Biffer echoed. 'What about a song, Alan?'

Drooby rose to his feet and, swaying to the combined effect of the whisky and the tune, delivered *Mo Nighean Donn* (My Nutbrown Maid) in the very resonant but slightly raucous tenor that hardly suited his bulk, to which a profound bass would have been more appropriate.

'*Glè mhath! Glè mhath.* Very good, Drooby,' the Biffer applauded. 'Let's have another.'

Drooby had started *Mo Run Geal Dìleas* (My Faithful Fair One) even more resonantly when Jimmy appeared in the doorway of the shed.

'*Istibh!*' the boy warned them sharply. 'Are you wanting to wake up everybody in Snorvig?'

'I don't want to wake up nobody,' his father replied with dignity. 'I'm feeling pretty sleepy myself. Is Iain Dubh about?'

'There's nobody about, but it's getting light,' Jimmy pointed out.

'Ay, I'd better be making my way back home,' said Drooby.

'You'd better see that there's nobody about, Jimmy,' his father told him.

The boy went off again.

'Only two of my boys left in the home, Alan,' the Biffer went on sentimentally. 'Four of them serving in the Mairchant Navy.'

Drooby poured out another dram.

'*Slàinte mhór* to the Merchant Navy,' and his toast was followed by a hiccup that rivalled the performance of a xylophone. He then planted bottles in all his pockets and proclaimed his intention of going home immediately in case his wife should be worrying where he was.

'You'd better have a *deoch an doruis* before you go, Alan,' the Biffer advised.

'Ay, I believe you're right, Airchie. I'm just beginning to feel a little tired out. Och, we did a hefty night's work. Up and down, up and down.'

Drooby swallowed the *deoch an doruis*; but it took him no further than the heap of nets on which he was sitting, and leaning back, all his bottles chinking, he fell asleep at the same moment as the Biffer tipped backwards off the lobster-pot on which he was sitting and lay on the cork-strewn floor.

Ten minutes later Jimmy looked in to say that no time was to be lost if Alan Galbraith wanted to get home without being observed. He eyed the two sleepers with a grin. Then he pulled a tarpaulin over them and went off to his own bed.

THE SERGEANT-MAJOR BACK AGAIN

WE have seen that Bean a' Bhiffer was a placid woman. She merely smiled when her youngest son informed her where his father was sleeping.

'You'd better go and tell Bean Ailein or she'll be asking after Drooby.'

'Well, and I was just beginning to wonder what had become of him,' said Bean Ailein, a bright, bustling little woman. 'He's asleep in your father's shed, is he? Och, he'd better stay there till he wakes up. I'm sure he'll be out again tonight,' she laughed.

'There'll be a lot of them out tonight,' said Jimmy.

Just before one o'clock that Monday, Mrs Wishart came in to inform Dr Maclaren that Archie MacRurie and Alan Galbraith wanted to see him.

'Hullo, what's the matter with them?' he exclaimed.

'There's strong smell of liquor in the hall,' Mrs Wishart said severely. 'I noticed it the moment I opened the front door. I asked them why they didn't go round to the surgery and they said they'd come to see you about business.'

'A strong smell of liquor?' the Doctor chuckled. 'Already?'

'Terrible,' his housekeeper sniffed. 'Worse than any bar.'

'You don't mean to tell me you ever frequented bars, Mrs Wishart.'

'I used to accompany Mr Wishart sometimes when we were first married. It was a duty,' she replied mournfully.

'Well, show them in here,' the Doctor told her.

'Don't forget your lunch will be on the table at one sharp,' Mrs Wishart reminded him as she withdrew.

'And what can I do for you both?' Dr Maclaren asked when Drooby and the Biffer were in his sitting-room.

Drooby pulled open his jacket and thrust a huge hand into a pocket. The Biffer did the same.

'Lion Rampant,' said Drooby, putting an oblong bottle on the table.

'Tartan Perfection,' said the Biffer, putting a bottle with shoulders like a Victorian miss beside it.

'Just for a start,' said Drooby.

'You'll be getting a case pretty soon,' the Biffer promised.

'It's really kind of you chaps to think of me,' the Doctor exclaimed. 'I appreciate the thought. You know old Hector MacRurie over at Knockdown?'

'Sure, I know him,' said the Biffer. 'His grandfather and my great-grandfather were second cousins. He was in the Home Guard for the first year, but he had to give it up on account of his legs.'

'As soon as I've had my lunch I'm going to take one of these bottles up to him.' The Doctor picked up Lion Rampant and read the export stamp in the glass.

'Ninety-nine per cent proof,' he ejaculated reverently.

'And Tartan Perfection is the same,' the Biffer assured him.

'Dash it, I've asked a lot of patients to say ninety-nine,' Dr Maclaren laughed. 'But I never expected to say it myself with such relish. Oh, this is the real Mackay!'

'Ay, it's good stuff, right enough,' Drooby said. 'We tried it ourselves when we got back this morning. And, Doctor, there's thousands of bottles in the *Cabinet Minister*. Every kind of whisky anybody could think of. I'm not surprised those Americans have come into the war. I believe we'd have won the war without them by now if they hadn't drunk all our whisky.'

'And the Germans like whisky themselves,' the Biffer added. 'I remember the first time Donald was torpedoed – he's been torpedoed three times – that was in 1940 – the captain of the U-boat asked them if they had any whisky aboard the lifeboat. "Just one bottle," says they. "All right," says he, "hand it over, and take these three bottles of gin instead." That shows you what the Germans think of our whisky.'

'I suppose they're doing well on Little Todday, aren't they?' the Doctor asked.

'They're doing wonderful,' the Biffer replied. 'And I'm glad they are. They couldn't have treated me and Drooby better if we'd been born and bred on the island. "Plenty more where that comes from, boys." That was the slogan.'

'Did you see Father Macalister?'

'No, no. We didn't get across till after twelve o'clock. But they say he was pretty pleased.'

'I hope you'll get plenty of the stuff safely put away before too many officials make things difficult. I hear Mr Waggett is talking of putting the Home Guard on to guard the wreck. That'll cramp your style, Biffer.'

'I joined the Home Guard to keep Hitler out of Todaidh Mór. I'm a sniper, Doctor, not a snooper. Och, Sergeant Odd is coming on Tuesday. I don't believe he'll want to waste his time doing the work of the pollis and the excise-man.'

When Corporal Archie MacRurie was making this observation to Dr Maclaren in Great Todday, over at Tummie the Sergeant-major himself was reading a telegram from Duncan Bàn:

Rèiteach arranged for Tuesday evening everybody very pleased don't worry yourself about the wherewithal all in good order here very strong reinforcements arriving all the time will be on pier looking for you tomorrow tingaloori till then

Duncan

'Did you ever hear of a rayjack, sir?' the Sergeant-major asked his Commanding Officer later on that afternoon.

Colonel Lindsay-Wolseley looked up from the desk where he was wading through the correspondence of his slightly harassed adjutant, George Grant.

'Never. What kind of an instrument is it, Sergeant-major?'

'It's not an instrument, sir. It's a way they have out here of announcing an engagement. It's a kind of party. I know whisky comes into it a good deal.'

'I thought they had no whisky in the Islands.'

'They didn't have, not when I was there a fortnight ago, sir, but I've had a telegram from Lieutenant Macroon which sounds as if the drought had broken. You'll excuse me bothering you with my private affairs, but it's all right is it, sir, about your cottage?'

'I'll be glad for you to have it whenever you want it, Sergeant-major.'

'I'm very much obliged, sir. This rayjack makes it look as if I'll be wanting it in Easter Week. I mean to say it's a rayjack for Peggy Macroon and me tomorrow night.'

The Colonel offered his hand in congratulation.

'That's capital, Sergeant-major. I wish I could come to the – what's it called?'

'Rayjack, sir. I did know how to spell it, but I've forgotten, and you can look through one of these Garlic dictionaries for an hour and not find what you want. Talk about a missing word competition!'

'Well, I'm no hand at the Gaelic myself. Perhaps Captain Grant can tell us. Do you know how to spell "rayjack", George?' he asked the adjutant who had just come into the room.

'I never heard of the place, Colonel.'

'It's not a place, George. It's a ceremony. Sergeant-major Odd is engaged to be married.'

'Oh, really. Congratulations, Sergeant-major. I wish you joy,' said the adjutant.

'I think the excitement must have gone to my head, sir,' said the Sergeant-major. 'I've got the word here in a telegram from Little Todday. R-E-I-T-E-A-C-H.'

'And you think you've got the right pronunciation?' the Colonel asked, with a smile.

'That's what they call it on Little Todday, sir.'

'George, you and I will have to persuade Ben Nevis to give us lessons in Gaelic. By the way, how did you find Major MacDonald, Sergeant-major?'

'Oh, he was very much up and doing, sir. He's anxious to get hold of some more Sten guns for C Company.'

'I dare say he is,' said the Colonel drily. 'But I'm afraid there aren't any to spare.'

A fortnight ago Sergeant-major Odd had slept almost all the way to Snorvig. He was in no mood for sleep when he boarded the *Island Queen* at Obaig on Shrove Tuesday.

'Flat as a pancake, they say,' he murmured to himself as he walked up the gang-plank. 'Well, I don't feel very flat this morning and that's a fact.'

The Sergeant-major took an early opportunity of going up on the bridge to have a chat with Captain MacKechnie.

'Ah, there you are, Sarchant. They told me you were aboard. You're looking petter than when you arrived. Well, what do you think about the *Cappinet Minister*?'

'I think they're all much of a muchness if you ask me. Except Winnie of course.'

'Och, I'm not talking about politics. I'm talking about the ship.'

'What ship?'

'Didn't you hear the news from Little Todday?'

'I didn't hear anything about any ship.'

'Och, fine doings. She struck the Gobha between Pillay and Todday on the morning of the Sabbath in the fock. Ay, high and try with fifteen thousand cases of whisky. We took the crew pack with us to Obaig the same evening. Och, it wass a terrible fock. I thought I was lost myself.'

That phrase about reinforcements in Duncan Macroon's telegram came back to the Sergeant-major's mind. So he had guessed right about the ending of the drought.

'Who's in charge of the wreck?' he asked.

'Och, I believe the *Todaich* from both sides of the Coolish will be in charge chust now. I was expecting to see Ferguson on board at Obaig coming over with the

Island Queen, but not a sign of him. And not a sign of any salvage fellow either. Ah well, we crumple sometimes about the slowness of these officials, but there are times when one's pretty clad that they are so slow.'

'Who's Ferguson? I don't remember him.'

'The Exciseman at Nobost. One of these wise men of the East from Aberdeen. He thinks himself pretty smart. Ay, and he'll have to be pretty smart if he's going to check up on every case in the *Cappinet Minister*. Och, but he's not a bad fellow at all.'

'Was the Captain very much upset?'

'Och, no Captain likes to lose his ship, but if she had to be lost it was petter to lose her like that for the benefit of the *Todaich* than to be sunk in the middle of the Atlantic and let Dafy Chones put all that whisky in his locker. Yess, yess, inteet!'

'I'm very interested in what you're telling me, Captain MacKechnie.'

'Ay, it iss very interesting.'

'It means that my rayjack looks like being a success.'

'What's that at all? Is it some kind of a new weapon?'

'No, it's the party to celebrate two people getting engaged to be married.'

'Ach, a *rèiteach*,' Captain MacKechnie squeaked. 'So you're going to have a *rèiteach*, are you? You and Peigi Iosaiph, eh? You've picked a good one, Sarchant. She's a fine curl. When are you going to be married?'

'Easter Week if all goes according.'

'Ferry good, ferry good inteet. Ach, we'd petter go along to my cappin.'

The skipper of the *Island Queen* led the way out of the wheelhouse and took a look round on the bridge.

'Ah, well, well, who'd have thought last Saturday that we'd be seeing weather like this? It's too fine for the season, Sarchant. We'll pay for it next month, I believe. But come along below and we'll tap the steward.'

In his little cabin Captain MacKechnie took from a locker an almost spherical bottle of whisky.

'King's Own,' he said. 'Captain Puncher gave me a pottle on Sunday evening. In fact he gave me two or three. So don't be afraid of having a good tram. This is good stuff. They send it round the world for a year in a sherry cask before they put it into these queer-looking pottles. Och, I don't suppose the voyage does the whisky any good, but it doesn't seem to do it any harm either.'

Captain MacKechnie poured out drams for himself and the Sergeant-major, and then raised his glass for a toast.

'Here's long life to you, Sarchant, and may you have a full quiffer. *Sonas!* Do you know what *sonas* means?'

The Sergeant-major had to admit that he did not.

'*Sonas* means happiness. It's a much petter word for happiness, don't you think so yourself, Sarchant? *Sonas!* But the Gaelic is a much better lankwitch than Inklish. Do you know this? There's said to be four hundred ways of saying "yess" and "no" in Gaelic. Look at that now. Think of the convenience of such a lankwitch. Have another dram.'

'I don't think I will, thanks very much, Skipper. I've got a bit of an evening in front of me.'

'Ay, you'll have that right enough. And now I'll tell you a pit of a good choke, Sarchant. You know fine what a time they've been having over the shortage of whisky and peer in the two Toodays. Och, I hardly dared bring the *Island Queen* alongside I was so unpopular. Well, now that there's plenty whisky I'm pringing enough whisky and peer with me today to have put everything right. And I'm chust wondering what Big Roderick is going to say about the competition. Joseph Macroon tried many a time to get a licence at Kiltod, but Roderick was always one too many for him. Ach, your future father-in-law knows a thing or two, Sarchant, but Ruairidh Mór knows a thing or three. He won't like the idea of the *Cappinet Minister* as an hotel. It'll be interesting to see chust how he goes to work. Well, well, I'd better go back to the pridge. I'll be seeing you later, eh?'

The pier was crowded with people to welcome the

mailboat on that calm, glittering afternoon which was
more like May than March.

Like a sunbeam himself, Duncan Bàn was dancing about
under the influence of poetry, whisky, and the prospect of
unstinted hospitality.

'How are you, Sarchant? Ah, well, isn't this splendid
now?' he bubbled as he grasped the arrival's hand and
pumped it up and down. 'The *Morning Star* is waiting by
the steps. Will we cross right away and send her back for
the mail, or would you rather wait till they've collected
it?'

'I think I ought to go up and report my arrival to
Captain Waggett,' the Sergeant-major suggested.

'Right you are. I have a few messages I want to take
round. Och, I'll tell you what. I'll get a hold of a car and
bring it up to Snorvig House and then we can invite a few
of your Todaidh Mór friends to the *rèiteach*. I thought
you'd like to have Norman Macleod and his sister
Catriona, and John Beaton and his wife, and George
Campbell ...'

'And his mother?' the Sergeant-major put in with a grin.

'*A Dhia*, no. It's not Ash Wednesday till tomorrow.
Have you heard the story of the ashes yet?'

The Sergeant-major shook his head.

'That's a good one, but you ought to get Father James
to tell you that one. Who else is there we ought to ask?
We ought to have Doctor Maclaren. He's a darling of a
man. Och, we'll think of one or two more. It's a great
occasion. You and I are having something to eat with
Father James first and when it's all over you're coming
back to stay at my place. I thought you'd like to have a
Home Guard parade tomorrow as it's a bit of a melancholy holiday. All right, Sarchant, you go along up and
see Captain Waggett. I've got to fetch a bag up from the
steps. Do you want to ask Captain Waggett and Mrs Waggett to the *rèiteach*?'

'I suppose it would be polite,' the Sergeant-major replied without enthusiasm.

'Ay, it might be a little bit too polite,' Duncan Bàn commented.

'Do you think I ought to ask them?'

'Well, you'll just see how you feel when you see him.'

'Yes, we'll leave it open,' said Sergeant-major Odd.

As he turned round to look back at the view of the harbour from the steps of Snorvig House he saw Duncan Bàn disappearing into the bank with a large and apparently very heavy kitbag.

'How are you, Sergeant-major? Very glad to see you back to Snorvig,' said Captain Waggett, who was in one of those graciously languorous moods in which he seemed to bask in the warmth of his own effortless superiority. 'Come into my den. I forget if I showed you my den the last time you were here.'

'Yes, sir, you did ask me in. Very snug, too.'

'Of course I intend to put in electric light after the war. I'd do it now, but I don't think it's fair to the country to take people away from the war effort. Well, what are your plans for this week you're spending with G Company?' the commanding officer inquired when they were settled down in the den.

'Well, sir, tonight if you don't mind I think I'd like to cross over to Little Todday, and then tomorrow being Ash Wednesday, and which is more or less of a holiday for them there . . .'

'They're always having holidays on Little Todday,' Captain Waggett interrupted with austere disapproval. 'However, it's part of their religion, so I suppose we mustn't criticize. What were you going to say about Ash Wednesday?'

'Well, I though it would be a good opportunity to give the Little Todday platoon a bit of an exercise with some shooting practice. But it's just what you say, sir?'

'You'd get back here by Thursday morning?'

'That was my notion, sir.'

'Approved,' said Captain Waggett loftily. The War

Office itself seemed to be speaking. 'Where are you going to stay in Snorvig?'

'Miss MacRurie – Miss Flora MacRurie is going to put me up. I was always very comfortable there,' said the Sergeant-major. 'Er – do you know what a rayjack is, sir?'

'Something to do with radiolocation, I suppose.'

'No, sir, it's a Gaelic word. It's when you announce your engagement. Well, there's going to be a rayjack tonight for me and Peggy – Peggy Macroon. It's to be in her father's house.'

'I hope you'll see that Joseph doesn't forget he's the warden for Kiltod, Sergeant-major. It's very discouraging when I look across the Coolish and see a blaze of light coming from the post-office.'

'I was wondering if you and Mrs Waggett would care to come to the party, sir?'

'It's very kind of you, Sergeant-major. I don't know whether Mrs. Waggett will feel up to it. She's at the Manse just now. She and Mrs Morrison are getting up a jumble sale for the Red Cross. May we leave it open? Transport may be a problem. I suppose you've heard about this wreck off Pillay?'

'Captain MacKechnie was telling me about it on the way across, sir. Quite a goldmine, according to him.'

'It's a heavy responsibility for me, Sergeant-major,' said Captain Waggett, with a deep sigh.

'For you, sir?'

'You see, I feel I ought to arrange for the wreck to be guarded by the Home Guard until the salvage men arrive. But I ask myself whether I can trust my own men. That's a fearful thing for an officer to have to ask himself after nearly three years in command of a company.'

'If you'll excuse me, sir, I don't see what responsibility you have for this wreck. I mean to say a wreck is right outside our beat. Why, Major MacDonald of Ben Nevis might as well assume the responsibility of guarding the Loch Ness monster. And in fact that's what he did want to do, only Colonel Wolseley put his foot down and said the Loch Ness monster wasn't the Home Guard's pigeon.'

'Well, I can't accept any comparison between the Loch Ness monster and this ship wrecked off Pillay. The Loch Ness monster isn't full of whisky.'

'You'd think it was, sir, if you believed some of the tales they tell about it round Fort Augustus.'

Captain Waggett frowned slightly. He hoped Sergeant-major Odd was not trying to be flippant.

'The point is, Sergeant-major, that unless this wreck is properly guarded some of the cargo may be tampered with.'

'I wouldn't be at all surprised if it was, sir. You could hardly blame the people here if they did do a spot of tampering.'

'Which, don't forget, is robbing the Revenue.'

'Yes, I suppose it is, sir, if you put it that way. All the same, if I was you I'd wait for instructions first before I started in to protect the Revenue. The authorities know that the *Cabinet Minister* has been wrecked and it's up to them to call on your services if they require them.'

'Oh, of course, I shall get no thanks,' said Captain Waggett virtuously. 'But I'm not looking for gratitude. I'm thinking solely of what is right. And it can't be right to put temptation in the way of the people here by leaving that wreck without a soul in charge of it. We had a very curious incident last week which the Security Intelligence wallahs at Nobost took up with me. An urn with the ashes of somebody who had been cremated in Canada came ashore apparently on Little Todday, and the box was put in the cabin of Lieutenant Boggust who was conducting an investigation here.'

'What was he investigating, sir?'

'A report of the defeatist atmosphere in the two Toddays which reached them at Nobost.'

'Defeatist atmosphere?' the Sergeant-major exclaimed. 'Who do they think is going to defeat them?'

'The Germans, I suppose.'

'That was just the shortage of whisky, sir. There was a
good deal of grumbling about that when I was over a fortnight back. These chaps in Security Intelligence must have
something to investigate. It's what they're for, in a manner
of speaking.'

'They were very much upset about this urn. In fact
Major Quiblick wrote me a personal letter about it. He
also said that Lieutenant Boggust had reported a lot of
careless talk. If they were talking carelessly when there
wasn't a drop of whisky in the island what kind of talk
will they indulge in if they get hold of any of that
whisky?'

'Well, sir, if you'll pardon my plain speaking, I think if
they mean to get hold of any whisky it won't make any
difference who's in charge, and I don't believe the Home
Guard or anybody else will stop them. In fact it would be
putting temptation in the way of the Home Guard.'

'That's why I'm feeling so depressed, Sergeant-major.
After all my work to make G Company a crack unit, I
feel I can't really trust my own men.'

'I wouldn't trust the Brigade of Guards to look after
that ship, sir. No, not if the old Duke of Wellington himself was in command of 'em. Well, sir, I mustn't keep
you any longer. If you and Mrs Waggett look in on us this
evening we shall be very proud to welcome you.'

'Thank you, Sergeant-major. We shall come if it can be
managed.'

When the Sergeant-major reached the road he found
Duncan Bàn waiting for him in the most disreputable of
the island cars. It looked not unlike a dustbin on wheels
and belonged to a Watasett man, Calum MacKillop, more
familiarly known as the Gooch – why, not even the
Gooch himself was able to say.

'We must be back at the pier by six o'clock,' said
Duncan Bàn. 'So I got hold of the Gooch because he's a
fast driver.'

'Ay,' the Gooch admitted with a complacent grin, 'I
can drive pretty fast.'

As the car shot northward by the west side Sergeant-major Odd reflected with gratitude that all the island lorries and cars were probably in Snorvig at this hour of the afternoon.

'What have you got in that kitbag?' the Sergeant-major asked.

'That's a pretty easy conundrum to answer,' Duncan replied. He pulled open the bag and showed it half full of bottles. 'It's not as heavy as it was. I unloaded half the contents on old friends in Snorvig.'

Just then the Gooch jammed on the brake to avoid a dozen black-face sheep which had decided to cross the road in front of them. The bottles in the kitbag clinked at the narrow escape, but Duncan went on imperturbably.

'Ay, I gave three bottles of Moorland Cream to Iain Dubh. Nothing like a bit of bribery and corruption for these rasscals. Oh yes, he's an accessory after the fact now, right enough.'

'Captain Waggett passed the remark to me that he thought the Home Guard should be put in charge of the wreck,' said the Sergeant-major.

'There'd be a big turn-out for that parade,' said Duncan. 'And we could practise our shooting with the empty bottles afterwards. Did you ask Waggett to the *rèiteach*?'

'I asked him and his missus, and he said they might come. He seemed doubtful about transport.'

'What a pity. If we'd known in time we could have sent for the royal barge. Did you ever try crossing the Coolish in this Rolls-Royce of yours, Calum?'

The driver looked round in amazement.

'What are you saying, man? She never would be able to cross the Coolish.'

'Why don't you offer to take Mr and Mrs Waggett over this evening?' Duncan pressed gravely.

'Och, I wouldn't be trying such a thing, Mr Macroon. This car was never built for going on the water. Och; you're after making a fun,' said the Gooch, suddenly aware of the twinkle in Duncan Bàn's kingfisher-blue eyes. 'I might have known it was a fun,' he added, as he accelerated to restore the dignity of himself and the car.

At Garryboo, while Duncan Bàn visited one or two houses with bottles of whisky, Sergeant-major Odd went along to the schoolhouse.

'Didn't you see my son in Snorvig?' Mrs Campbell asked suspiciously.'He went in with the lorry immediately after school.'

'I must have missed him, mum,' said the Sergeant-major. 'I came to ask him if he would come to our rayjack tonight at Kiltod?'

'If that's some nonsense with the Home Guard, George won't be able to come,' said his mother.

'No, it's a rayjack.'

'I don't know what you're talking about, Sergeant. But whatever it is George can't come,' the old lady answered emphatically.

'It's the announcement of my engagement to Peggy Macroon,' the Sergeant-major explained.

'A rèiteach? A rèiteach in Little Today, with all that liquor they're talking about? Certainly not. George won't be able to come.'

'I'm not going to argue the point, Mrs Campbell ...'

'I wouldn't think so indeed,' she broke in sternly.

'I say I'm not going to argue the point, but it'll be a bit of a jollification and I thought ...'

'Jollification? Did the Lord send us into the world for jollification as you call it? No, no, Sergeant, my son will not be at any jollification tonight,' the old lady declared confidently.

Mrs Campbell was too confident. When Duncan Bàn and Sergeant-major Odd reached the schoolhouse at Watasett, Duncan't kitbag empty by now except for a bottle of Heather Blend and two bottles of Cabarféidh, they found George Campbell there. He had been having a difficult half-hour with Catriona who had told him that he must choose between her and his mother. She could not continue any longer in the ridiculous position of being engaged to somebody who was afraid to let her meet his mother. It was idle for George to say that his mother would have behaved in the same way to any girl he intended to marry. If that was true, George looked likely to remain a bachelor for the rest of his life.

'I'm sorry, George, but if you don't love me enough to stop your mother from interfering between us it's better for us to break it off. When Norman goes into the R.A.F., I'll volunteer for the A.T.S.'

This was the ultimatum she had just delivered when Sergeant-major Odd and Duncan Bàn arrived at the schoolhouse.

'Come to your *rèiteach*, Sergeant Odd?' Catriona exclaimed. 'Why, surely we will.'

It was perhaps less a tribute to the Sergeant-major's Gaelic pronunciation than to Catriona's state of mind that she understood him immediately.

'Drooby was along yesterday. He's bringing the *Flying Fish* up Loch Sleeport tonight,' Norman Macleod murmured, a twinkle in his eyes.

'I was hoping you'd come too, Mr Campbell,' the Sergeant-major said, turning to George, 'but Mrs Campbell didn't seem to think you'd be able to manage it.'

Catriona looked sharply at George.

'Oh, you went to see my mother, did you?' George asked.

'Yes, I called in special to give you the invite.'

'And she said I wouldn't come?' George repeated.

'That's right.'

'Well, I will come,' George gulped.

'Come along, Sergeant,' said Duncan Bàn, 'we must be getting down to the pier.'

'You'll have a dram first,' said Norman. 'Man, you can't give a fellow three bottles of the real Mackay and then refuse to take a dram with him.'

But the Sergeant-major was firm.

'No, we mustn't keep the boat waiting. Peggy will be

wondering where I am. We've got a long evening before us, and we'll be seeing you all on the other side.'

When they were going across the Coolish in the *Morning Star* Duncan asked his companion if he'd noticed anything at the Schoolhouse in Watasett.

'Nothing particular, no.'

'It's my opinion that perhaps we changed the whole course of a man's life by calling in there when we did,' said Duncan.

'What d'ye mean?'

'Did you not notice the look Catriona gave George Campbell when you said that about the old lady's not thinking George would be able to come tonight? If George had listened to the echo of his mother's voice at that moment he was finished. Ay, just completely on the scrapheap. Ah, well, poor George, he saved himself in the nick of time.'

Duncan Macroon went on up to Father Macalister's house to announce their arrival while the Sergeant-major turned into the post-office to greet Peggy. He found she had already gone up to her room to start the preparations for her toilet, but her father was about.

'This was a very pleasant surprise you gave me, Mr Macroon.'

Joseph was just turning over in his mind the problem of the best place to store twenty-five cases of 'Minnie' as the *Cabinet Minister*'s cargo was now called affectionately by everybody on Little Todday. That pet name would become famous far beyond Little Todday. Indeed, although 'all too rarely com'st thou, spirit of delight', you may still be offered a dram of the famous Minnie as far away from Little Todday as Glasgow.

For the present, Joseph was saying to himself, they would have to go in the shed, but his fancy was playing with the idea of burying them on Poppay, Pillay's companion isle on the south side of Little Todday. One advantage of Poppay was its reputation as a rendezvous for ghosts or *bòcain* on account of its having been the burial place of the Macroons in ancient days. On the other hand, tourists enjoyed digging about in Poppay for relics.

'How are you, Sarchant? Glad to see you. Are you staying with us in Kiltod?' he inquired vaguely, his mind still on the cases of Minnie.

'I'm staying with Duncan Macroon tonight. Yes, it was a very pleasant surprise.'

'What was that?'

'The rayjack.'

'*A Dhia*, I was forgetting about the business,' Joseph exclaimed. 'What else could I do? Father James and Duncan Bàn between them arranged it on me over my head. Ach, well, never mind; we'll be able to offer people a decent dram. That reminds me, Sergeant. Did you say anything to Colonel Wolseley about the new school in Kiltod?'

'I didn't as a matter of fact. I thought he might think I was butting into what didn't concern me.'

'I'm very glad you didn't. I don't believe we want a new school so much just now. I believe we want a new road. Ay, I think we ought to have a road running from Bàgh Mhic Ròin right across the island to Tràigh nam Marbh.' The latter was the sandy beach at the south end of Little Todday on which once upon a time the bodies of dead Macroons were embarked to be ferried over to Poppay. 'Yes, I believe we want a road more than we want a school. I'll bring it up at the Council meeting later on this month. Ay, ay, we want a road on which a lorry can run.'

'But you used to have a lorry on the road to Try Swish, didn't you, and found it didn't pay?'

'Ay, but if we had the two roads the situation would be easier altogether.'

'You know best, Mr Macroon, but I should have thought the traffic just now was a bit exceptional, and by the time you get a road surely it'll have quietened down for a long while. Well, I'll be getting along to Father James. I'll be seeing you presently, eh?'

Joseph gave a gesture of vague agreement and went out

to the shed in order to choose the best corner for those
twenty-five cases of Minnie pending their ultimate con-
cealment elsewhere.

Peggy who had laid the foundations of her toilet came
downstairs to greet him.

'Peggy darling,' he told her as he held her to him, 'this
is the biggest day in my life. No, and that's not right. The
day I met you first was just as big, and the biggest day of
all will be when we're married.'

'We're not married yet, Fred. You'll see if my father
doesn't make it just as difficult as he can.'

'Well, I'm feeling right on top of the world today, and
something tells me we're going to be married on the
Wednesday in Easter Week.'

'I know fine who told you,' she murmured. 'It was just
Minnie who told you?'

The Sergeant-major chuckled.

'I did have a dram with Captain MacKechnie coming
over, and I had another with Lieutenant Beaton and Lieutenant Macroon when we looked in at Bobanish to invite
him and Mrs Beaton over to the rayjack.'

'*Rèiteach*,' she corrected.

'Raychack, I mean. And we asked Sergeant Macleod and
Catriona and Sergeant Campbell and Sergeant Thomson
and Mr Mackinnon, the Snorvig schoolmaster, and Captain and Mrs Waggett.'

'*A Mhuire mhàthair*,' she exclaimed. 'What made you
be asking them for? They're so snop.'

'I daresay they won't come.'

'So stiff and stuck up,' she pouted.

'Still, it was only tactful, Peggy darling. I mean to say
it wouldn't do for Captain Waggett to think I was making
a convenience of him just to get over here and see you.'

'Indeed, it's a queer kind of a *rèiteach* anyway,' Peggy
said. 'Father James and Duncan Bàn going all over the
island inviting people, and my father never inviting a soul.
I'm sure I hope everything will be all right.'

'All right? It's going to be super. Give me a kiss, Peggy

180

Machree. That's a good one, isn't it?' he beamed. 'I got that one off a gramophone record.'

'I suppose you mean *mo chridhe*.'

'Peg o' my heart, eh?'

And he held her so close that she began to fear for the foundations of her toilet and sent him off to Father Macalister.

'Come in, Sergeant. Come in, my boy. Oh well, this is really a glorious moment,' the burly priest declared in his most hospitable bass. 'Sit right down. You're going to have a snifter before Kirsty tells us the food is on the table. Now then, which will it be?'

Father Macalister pointed to the ten bottles of Minnie, each a different brand, upon the top of one of his bookcases.

'I leave it to you, Father.'

'Then it's going to be Prince's Choice. Oh, a real beauty.'

The drams were poured out and drunk with genuine reverence.

'Oh well, Sergeant, I've really suffered lately because I could not offer my friends even the most minute sensation. Och, indeed, yes. Never mind. Almighty God has been very good to us. You'll have seen Father MacIntyre by now, Sergeant?'

'Yes, Father.'

'Good enough, my boy. And Duncan has written a great song for tonight. Oh, really good. It's a pity you can't follow our noble and glorious language.'

'I was a bit rushed with it, Father,' Duncan Bàn explained apologetically.

'Ay, but the Pierian spring was in full spate, my boy. The fountain did not fail. *Gradus ad Parnassum!*'

'They were pretty erratic steps, Father,' Duncan laughed. 'I was walking up and down the Tràigh, and it was a pretty curly kind of a track.'

Kirsty came in to say that the food was on the table.

'Come along, boys, and eat as much as you can,' said Father James. 'We've a hefty evening before us.'

Chapter 12
THE RÈITEACH

━━━━━━

THE lavishness with which Father Macalister and Duncan Bàn had flung out invitations to the *rèiteach* of Sergeant-major Odd and Peggy Macroon had made the host's house too small for the entertainment of the guests, and so it was held in the parish hall, one of those erections of corrugated iron and matchboarding with a platform at one end which are familiar objects of the countryside from Caithness to Cornwall. The food problem caused by the war made anything like a feast out of the question at such short notice, but the knowledge that there was whisky galore more than compensated for the absence of the muscular fowls which were usually the main dish of such an occasion. There was a lack of young men in the prime of life, for the great majority of the young men of the island were sailing the seven seas in ships of the Mercantile Marine. The question of winding up with a dance had been mooted, but Peggy and Kate Anne had declared that this would mean abandoning the evening to boys and girls in their 'teens, while the rest of the company sat on the hard bench which ran right round the hall against the walls and allowed the very young to take control of the proceedings. Speeches, songs and piping were declared likely to make the evening more enjoyable for everybody than dancing.

A trestle table had been set on the platform, at which Joseph Macroon presided patriarchally over a few relations and special friends. On his right was Father Macalister. On his left was Peggy, the convention being that he was not allowing her to be betrothed to her suitor until he had been persuaded by the eloquence of the suitor's advocate. Duncan Bàn, the advocate appointed, sat at the other end of the table with Sergeant-major Odd, the suitor, on his right. On Duncan Bàn's left was Dr Maclaren who had come over with Catriona and Norman Macleod, George Campbell, Andrew Thomson, and Alec Mackinnon in the *Flying Fish*, which after depositing them at Kiltod had proceeded round to Bàgh Mhic Roin on business that was itself a pleasure. Others at the special table were the headmaster of the Kiltod school, Andrew Chisholm and his wife, Michael Macroon, a schoolmaster from the west side of the island and a nephew of the host, two or three girl friends and contemporaries of Peggy and Kate Anne, and two or three middle-aged aunts and elderly great-aunts.

The company had just settled down to the scones, bannocks, girdle-cakes, pancakes, and oatcakes which mixed with tea would provide a solid basis for the whisky, when Captain and Mrs Paul Waggett entered the hall. Mrs Waggett had by no means welcomed the prospect of crossing the Coolish in the Biffer's *Kittiwake* even upon so calm and clear an evening, but her husband had stressed the importance which everybody would attach to their patronage and she had, as always, surrendered. She was looking a little more like a battered nursery doll than usual because she had just discovered that the *Kittiwake's* engine had deposited a large patch of oil on her squirrel coat.

'*A Dhia*,' muttered Joseph, 'here's Wackett! What's brought him over?' Then he rose from his chair and stepped down into the body of the hall to welcome the newcomers almost effusively. '*Thig a stigh*, Mr Waggett. Come right in please. Very glad to see you, Mrs Waggett.'

'Come right in to the body of the kirk, Colonel,' Father Macalister boomed.

If there was one thing Captain Wagget disliked it was being called 'Colonel' by Father Macalister. He disliked it so much that he never hesitated to attribute what he considered a breach of good manners to the fact that the priest of Little Todday must have had a drop too much.

Mrs Waggett, who now heard her husband greeted as 'Colonel' for the first time, looked anxious.

'It's quite all right, Dolly, he's just being funny in his own rather primitive way,' he whispered reassuringly. 'Good evening, Mr Macroon. Good evening, everybody,' he went on, smiling his *haut ton* smile.

'Come up to the table, Mrs Waggett,' Joseph invited. 'Will you give Mrs Waggett your chair, Mairead, and you'll give Mr Waggett yours, Morag.' The two contemporaries of Peggy and Kate Anne to the annoyance of their friends and themselves were banished from the special table to make room for these two unwelcome guests. Nor was Captain Waggett himself pleased because he thought that by taking the places of Morag and Mairead he and his wife were not being treated with so much ceremony as they were entitled to.

For a time the evening was heavy going; but presently the whisky began to go round, and it was wonderful to see the effect of even one dram, particularly on the old ladies, who all looked at the glasses as if they had not the least idea what was in them and who on being told to drink up turned to their neighbours, giggling and waving away temptation until they felt they had protested enough, when they took their drams like seasoned warriors and immediately afterwards all began to talk at once, interspersing the chatter with jocund squeals and much laughter.

It was now time for Duncan Bàn to make his speech on behalf of Sergeant-major Odd. He opened with a few conventional compliments in English about the soldier who had come back from the wars to the girl with whom he had fallen in love and extolled the military virtues of his friend in whom, when he was married to her, Peggy Iosaiph would find domestic virtues not less notable.

The orator stopped abruptly at this point.

'Ach, ladies and gentlemen,' he resumed, 'it's no use at all for me to be talking to you in a language which isn't my own language at all.'

'Hear, hear!' Father Macalister declaimed sonorously.

'I'm just making a ringmarole of it,' Duncan apologized.

'Ay, ay, going round and round in a ringmarole,' the priest gurgled. 'You'd better speak in the language of Eden, my boy.'

So Duncan Bàn addressed the company in Gaelic and to judge by the shrieks of merriment he was making a good job of it. The Sergeant-major wondered what on earth Duncan Bàn was saying about him when people kept turning round to gaze at him and grin. He tried asking Dr Maclaren once or twice, but all the Doctor would say was what a pity he couldn't understand what Duncan was saying because it was so good, and English would only spoil the flavour of it anyway. Then suddenly everybody began to look at Peggy, who was blushing hotly, and the Sergeant-major had to sit and look vacant, though he was sure he ought to be looking knowing.

At last Duncan Bàn's speech came to an end amid loud applause led by Father James, and Joseph rose to make his reply.

'Reverend father, ladies and gentlemen,' he began, 'it is a great occasion for me to offer the hospitality for which our island is so famous. I have always tried as the representative of Little Todday on the Inverness County Council to keep the flag flying. We want a new school.'

'Hear, hear!' ejaculated Andrew Chisholm, who was a very dark little man with burning eyes.

'My friend the Sgoileir Dubh says "hear, hear!" He can feel sure that I will take every opportunity to bring the question of a new school for Kiltod before the Council. But a school is not all that we want. No, indeed. We want a new road running from the north to the south of the island like the road I was able to persuade the Council to make from east to west. I'm sure you'll all agree with me that a road from Bàgh Mhic Ròin to Tràigh nam Marbh would be a benefit to the whole community. Well, I don't believe I have anything more to say, except to make you all welcome and wish you ...'

At this moment Peggy pulled her father's coat, and looking round to see what she wanted suddenly remembered why she was sitting by him.

'Carried away by the great enthusiasm which always takes a hold of me when I begin to speak of the island we all love I never said a word about my own daughter. My friend and fellow clansman, Duncan Macroon, has spoken about our friend Sarchant Odd, and we all agree that if a stranger is to come and take away one of our island beauties – and she is a beauty right enough, she's very like her father – why, then we'd as soon that a fine fellow like the Sarchant would do it as anyone. Well, ladies and gentlemen, Peigi Ealasaid is a good girl and I ought to know, for I have had five girls to teach me. And she's a good daughter. But daughters are not wives. I'm sure there isn't a man here who would want to be giving his wife away and keeping his daughter. Well, seeing that wives are so much better than daughters I don't believe I ought to stand in the way of letting my own daughter become a wife.'

There was loud applause at this.

'And so I'm not going to stand in the way of the pair of them coming to an understanding about the future and we'll drink their health in this beautiful whisky which arrived in the very nick of time.'

After the health of the engaged couple had been drunk Father Macalister rose to his feet.

'I'll just say in that unfamiliar tongue for the benefit of the Sergeant, who has the misfortune not to speak or even to understand our glorious language, that we welcome him to the finest island in the world. He has chosen a lovely and beautiful girl and he has been lucky enough to find that she chose him. Sergeant Odd is not a Macroon himself, but I'm not a Macroon myself either, and so he need not feel too much cast down by the failure of his ancestors. And I'm going to remind all Macroons present tonight that they wouldn't be here at all if once upon a time a stranger had not come to Todaidh Beag and chosen a seal-woman for his bride, and we are told that the seven

THE *RÈITEACH*

sons of this stranger who came to Todaidh Beag once upon a time went off to the mainland when they grew up and came back, each of them, with a bride from there, which goes to show that there were Macroons on Todaidh Beag before ever there were MacRuries on Todaidh Mòr, because nobody would go to the mainland for a bride if he could find one in an island close at hand.'

After the applause evoked by this triumphant demonstration of the greater antiquity of the Macroons the priest went on more gravely for a few moments.

'And now I'm going to reveal a secret. Some of you may be wondering why I am such a keen supporter of a mixed marriage. I'll tell you why. It's because Sergeant Odd confided in me his desire to become a Catholic, and by the time he and Peigi Ealasaid Nic Ròin kneel at the altar to be made man and wife on the Wednesday in Easter Week ...'

'Och, you're galloping ahead too fast, Father James,' Joseph broke in to protest. 'The date of the wedding is not settled yet.'

'But it is settled, Joseph. I settled it myself,' declared the parish priest amid rapturous applause.

'As I was going to say, when the County Councillor for Todaidh Beag interrupted me, when I marry them on the Wednesday in Easter Week it will not be a mixed marriage at all. And now if you poor unfortunate people who can only speak the tongue of the Sassunnach will excuse me I'll say the rest of what I have to say in a more impressive way.'

When Father Macalister sat down after what was evidently an extremely lively discourse in Gaelic the Sergeant-major was called upon for a speech.

'Father Macalister and all friends, I thank you very much for the kind way in which you have drunk the health of Peggy and – er – myself. I took a fancy to Little Todday the moment I set foot on it nearly two years ago and I think I must have realized I was going to find here the girl who I'd been looking for all my life. You'll hear a

lot of people say there's no such a thing as love at first
sight. Isn't there? I know there is. Owing to circumstances
over which I had no control I was away from you all for a
long time, but here I am again. I'm a lucky man if ever
there was one. I don't think there's anything more to say
except thank you very much one and all for your kindness to yours truly.'

The Sergeant-major was about to sit down when Father
Macalister ejaculated in a reproachful tone.

'Great sticks alive, Sergeant, you've forgotten all we
arranged.'

'You've forgotten the ring,' Duncan reminded him.

The Sergeant-major wrung his hand.

'Tut-tut,' he clicked. 'Nice example to show the Home
Guard, I don't think.'

And then he began to search the pockets of his battledress, innumerable as the laughters of the sea, for the
engagement ring he had bought for Peggy – the two small
sapphires on a gold circlet with which he intended to
symbolize her eyes. The bridegroom searching frantically
for the wedding-ring at the altar steps is a spavined hack
of humour. The Sergeant-major's behaviour was essen-
tially the same except that instead of the whispered
advice of the best man to try this or that pocket he received advice from all the people at the table on the
platform except Peggy, who tried to look as if she
didn't know what all the fuss was about. In the end
the ring was found, appropriately in the pocket over his
heart.

'Put it on her finger, Sergeant,' advised Father Macalister, who after three or four drams of a whisky called
All the Year Round was sitting like old Saturn himself
exhaling wisdom and benignity upon the air of the
Golden Age.

The Sergeant-major placed the sapphire ring on the
third finger of Peggy's left hand and leaning over kissed
her upon the lips to the accompaniment of tremendous
applause. He then led her away from the seat next to her

father and brought her to sit by himself at the other end of the table.

'Now what about a *pìobaireachd*?' Father Macalister asked. 'Come along, Andrew, and give us a real rouser.'

The Sgoileir Dubh was about to obey these orders when Captain Waggett rose to his feet.

'Excuse me, Father Macalister, but before Mr Chisholm gives us a tune on the pipes I should like to say just a few words.'

'Certainly, Colonel, as many as you like,' the priest assured him, with deep dithyrambic emphasis.

'I don't know why Father Macalister gives me a rank to which I'm not entitled,' Captain Waggett began with a hint of peevishness in his voice. 'I am a simple captain.'

'Simple Simon met a pieman,' the priest intoned.

'Father Macalister will have his little joke,' said the speechmaker.

'He will indeed,' the priest asserted with an almost portentious nod, followed by a profound sigh.

Mrs Waggett, who felt that her husband was being treated with a deplorable lack of courtesy, tapped the table to admonish everybody.

'Well, ladies and gentlemen, it is my pleasant duty to propose the health of my friend Mr Joseph Macroon, the father of the young lady whose engagement to our good friend Sergeant-major Odd we are celebrating this evening. He has entertained us lavishly and I am sure we all wish to express our grateful thanks for such hospitality. And now I hope you'll none of you take it amiss if I utter a word of warning, and in doing so I am not going to beat about the bush. I don't like beating about the bush, and ever since I came to live among you at Snorvig "far from the maddening crowd" as they say ...' Father Macalister breathed out an immense sigh at this misquotation but refrained from comment, '... I've always tried to avoid beating about the bush.'

'Quite right, Mr Waggett,' said the priest, 'there's usually very little in a bush when you have beaten it.'

'Every man here knows that a steamer of the Blue Limpet Line called the *Cabinet Minister* has been wrecked off the island of Pillay and that the greater part of the cargo of the *Cabinet Minister* consists of whisky.'

A burst of loud applause greeted this statement.

'I want to ask you to beware of considering that this cargo belongs to you. No, it belongs to the Government. This whisky was being exported to America in order to do its bit towards lightening the grievous burden of the war against aggression. The war is now costing us about fourteen million pounds a day....'

Father Macalister rose.

'Really now, Mr Waggett, I don't think this is the suitable occasion for a political speech.'

'I'm not making a political speech, Father Macalister. I'm only trying in my own humble way to show the other side of the picture. I want the people of the two Toddays to realize that the cargo of the *Cabinet Minister* is the property of the Government and that if they help themselves to Government property the penalties are very heavy. Major Quiblick of the Security Intelligence Corps at Nobost has already reported most unfavourably on the general attitude in these islands towards the war, and I expect most stringent measures will be taken if the people here give the Authorities the least excuse for action.'

Captain Waggett sat down in a puzzled silence, and Dr Maclaren jumped up.

'I think myself it's time we all paid a little attention to the business before us, and the business before us tonight is to enjoy ourselves. If the Government are concerned about what happens to the cargo of the *Cabinet Minister* it's up to them to take the necessary steps accordingly. I think we can safely leave it to them, my friends.'

'I don't agree with you at all, Doctor Maclaren,' said Captain Waggett.

'Well, Mr Waggett, you and I have disagreed so often on so many different questions that I don't think the world will come to an end if we disagree once more. Anyway, in spite of the Government, I'm raising my glass to Sergeant-major Odd and Peggy Macroon, and I hope I'll be invited to the wedding, and now I'm not going to stand in the way of the piper any longer. *Suas am pìobaire!*'

Andrew Chisholm was given a great ovation when he tucked the bag of his pipe under his arm and began the fearsome process of tuning up. Feeling that the gathering required a tune to set their feet tapping he began with *The Road to the Isles,* and as the little dark man marched up and down the middle of the hall he was not unlike a black cock displaying his virtuosity for the admiration of the grey-hen he was wooing. *The Road to the Isles* was followed by a reel and a strathspey. Then old Michael Stewart, an uncle of Jockey, sang a *port a beul,* which means literally mouth music and is usually a comic narrative delivered at some speed, with a lilt to it that used to serve dancers for a pipe or a fiddle once upon a time. It is a dying art and only to be heard in perfection from old men and old women. Michael Stewart was wildly applauded, and after he had put away another dram he sang another *port a beul* with such verve that four old ladies took the floor and executed a Scots reel to the loud delight of the onlookers.

'Now, Duncan, you'll give us your song,' Father Macalister proclaimed. 'Och, it's a great pity you won't be able to follow this, Sergeant. It's really a beauty.'

By this time Duncan Bàn's fair hair was tousled, his face vividly flushed, his blue eyes bright as ever but faintly out of focus for his immediate listeners and concentrated upon some vision beyond the hall. The song, delivered in a nasal tenor, was evidently full of personal allusions, the Sergeant-major decided, because the people were continually looking at him and Peggy; and once or twice when she clutched his arm and murmured, 'Oh well, what a chick!' or '*A Mhuire Mhuire,* what will he be saying next?' he tried to get a translation from her, but every time she merely said *'Ist, ist,'* and waggled a forefinger to rebuke his interruption. The Sergeant-major promised himself that when he and Duncan Bàn got home after the rayjack he would make him translate the song for him right through before he went to bed.

And so the evening went on its way with songs and piping, occasional reels, much chatter, and an ever-increasing volume of laughter, which reached its maximum when the Banker who had been sitting monosyllabic for three hours suddenly rose from his chair and going down into the hall solemnly began a Highland fling, for which the company in an ecstasy of appreciation provided the music with a *port a beul* in unison.

'And now Captain Waggett will sing *The British Grenadiers*,' Father James announced.

'No, no, Father Macalister, I never sing.'

'There's no such word as "never" in your language or ours on a beautiful occasion like this. Come along, my boy, and sing *The British Grenadiers*.'

'No, really, Father Macalister, I'm afraid I have no parlour tricks.'

'Parlour tricks?' the priest repeated in a richly wrathful bass. 'Music and love will come from the West until the day of the seven whirlwinds,' he quoted sonorously. 'And he calls them parlour tricks. You'll give us *The British Grenadiers*, or by all the holy crows I'll disband the Home Guard. Come along now, we respect your modesty and we honour you for it, but you can't indulge in your modesty to the detriment of a glorious and beautiful occasion like this. We *must* have *The British Grenadiers*.'

'But my husband doesn't sing,' Mrs Waggett tried to explain, growing pink with indignation.

'Then the sooner he starts the better, Mrs Waggett.'

Luckily – for Mrs Waggett was beginning to get really angry – Drooby and the Biffer appeared in the entrance of the hall just then to say that the boats were waiting.

'Thig a stigh, a Dhrooby. Thig a stigh, a Bhiffer,' the

parish priest bombilated like a great bee, 'you've got to drink the health of the happy couple. And then I'll be leaving you. It's not yet midnight by Almighty God's time, but I think Lent is close enough at hand to make it advisable to break up the party.'

So, after Drooby and the Biffer had drunk the health of the Sergeant-major and his Peggy, the guests from Great Todday gathered to make their way down to the quay and the guests from Little Todday gathered to take their various tracks across the machair under a moonless sky full of stars. Duncan Bàn expressed a firm resolve to see the Great Todday guests safely aboard before going home himself, and thus gave the Sergeant-major an opportunity to nave a few words with Peggy before he went home with Duncan. Her father had gone off to have a look at his shed and make sure that nobody had taken advantage of the merry evening to carry off any of the cases of Minnie stored away there until a more secure hiding-place could be found.

'Do you like your ring?' he asked when she was looking at it by the glow of the peat fire in the little room at the back of the shop.

'Who wouldn't be liking such a lovely ring?' She turned to him suddenly. 'Fred, you never told me you were going to be a Catholic.'

'I didn't want you to think I was just doing it to make your dad agree to us getting married. Are you pleased, sweetheart?'

'Och, Fred, I am really happy.'

'I'm getting instruction from Father MacIntyre at Drumsticket which is about ten miles this side of Fort Augustus. I run over on my motor-bike two evenings a week. And there isn't half a lot to learn.'

'We'll go to Mass tomorrow,' she said.

'Rather! Funny thing, isn't it? If anybody had have told me two years ago that I'd be buzzing in and out of church like a bluebottle and sitting down learning a catechism like a kid in a Sunday school I'd have said "sez you".

And talk about soppy reading! You know, a book can't be too soppy for me nowadays. Did you notice George Campbell tonight?'

'He was looking all the while at Catriona.'

'Goggling at her, I know. And he had quite a few drams. So did Norman Macleod. I hope they won't fall into the harbour when they're going aboard. There's one sure thing; if they do, Lieutenant Macroon won't be able to do much about hauling them out. In fact he was so top heavy I don't think I ought to have let him go down to the harbour with them. I wouldn't have, only I did want a few minutes with you, Peggy darling.'

'Och, it's Duncan Bàn you're talking about,' she exclaimed, her brow clearing suddenly. 'For goodness' sake don't be calling him Lieutenant Macroon. He hates anybody to laugh at him.'

'I'm not laughing at him. That's what I've got to call him so long as I'm a Sergeant-instructor.'

'You're talking like Mr Waggett. *A Mhuire, Mhuire*, what nonsense he was talking, poor soul! I felt quite sorry for him, and Father James was just encouraging him and then putting his hand up to his mouth and laughing away to himself. And then trying to make him sing! It was really too bad.'

'Well, we owe a lot to Father James, you and me do, ducks. Think of it. Next month we're going to be married. Next month!'

'Don't be too sure. My father can be terribly thrawn when he likes.'

'Thrawn! Do you remember when you told me I was thrawn, and I thought it was Garlic and asked you what it meant? And do you remember when you thought I didn't know the Garlic for kiss and I did and I kissed you for the first time? That was the end of April 1941, and at the end of April 1943 we shall be married. No wonder I've gone in for soppy reading! Lovely weather it was too, if you remember. I hope we'll have lovely weather like that at the end of next month.'

'Was your mother angry when she heard you were going to be a Catholic?'

'Angry? Not she! I tell you, she's been trying to get me to settle down for over twenty-five years, and now I've done it properly. No, Ma's highly delighted, Mar is. She's going to think no end of you, Peggy.'

'I'll be terribly shy when I see her.'

'No, you won't. Not a bit, you won't. I mean to say, she's so homely and jolly. I wish she could have been with us tonight. Here, I wonder what's happened to Lieutenant Macroon.'

'Goodness me, Fred, you can't be calling him that. You're making a fool of the man when you call him that.'

'I hope he hasn't fallen into the harbour.'

'Are you getting so tired of being with me?' she asked demurely.

He caught her to him.

'All the soppy reading in the world won't tell me what I'd like to say to you, Peg of my heart. I loved you the first moment I saw you and I'll go on loving you till the end.'

'*A ghràidh,*' she murmured, raising her lips to his.

'Gry? That's a new one on me. What's it mean?'

'That's a secret for me,' she trilled.

The voice of Duncan Bàn was heard without.

'Hullo, hullo, where are you all?'

His flushed face appeared in the doorway.

'Oh, *eudail,* what a set out at the quay. Everybody holding up everybody else. And the *Kittiwake* has hardly a couple of inches of freeboard she's that loaded up with Minnie. I tried to persuade Drooby to take the Waggetts. Nothing doing. "I wouldn't take him, Duncan," he says to me, "not if the *Flying Fish* was Noah's Ark herself." Oh well, I had to laugh. So the Captain and his missus are sitting up each of 'em on a couple of cases of Minnie in the stern of the *Kittiwake* and I don't believe the tiller will move twelve inches to port or starboard. It's a real comedy. "You'll have to steer her with your nose, Airchie,"

I said to the Biffer. Poor old Waggett, he was looking a bit nervous. "Och," I said, "You'll be all right, Captain. You won't drift farther than Mid Uist on a night like this unless you might be drifting to West Uist or East Uist." "Ay, he'll be able to see the Security Intelligence Corpse," says the Biffer, who you'll understand had had a hefty one, and didn't mind what he said at all. Anyway, away they went and God knows if they'll ever reach Snorvig to-night.'

'Why wouldn't Alan Galbraith take them?' the Sergeant-major asked.

'Och, he had a huge load of Minnie in the *Flying Fish*, and he was taking her to Loch Sleeport. I believe he and Norman Macleod will have found a safe place in Watasett to hide the stuff away. He wouldn't want Waggett to know about that. And indeed, it's as well he wouldn't be knowing after that sermon we had from him this evening. He'll be up to mischief. Och, he doesn't really mean any harm. Somebody must have told him once that he was a clever boy and he's grown up on the strength of it. Dr Maclaren's the one for Waggett. Did you hear what he said to me when Waggett was preaching that sermon? Och, well, he made me laugh right enough. "Duncan," he says, "if yon *pitheid* yatters much longer I'll tell him to stick out his tongue and have a look at it."

'He put away a tidy few drams did the Doctor. He said to me, "Duncan," he said, "if Waggett's figures are right, this evening we must have drunk what would pay the cost of the war for about one thousandth part of a second." Oh well, the Doctor enjoyed himself right enough. Ay, ay, he was as red as a geranium in a pot. And the Banker! I don't know what Mrs Thomson will be saying to him when he gets home. He was telling Alec Mackinnon a really long story about the first job he ever had at Corstorphine, and Alec Mackinnon sat looking at him the way anybody would look if a statue of St Joseph started talking to him. And did you see George Campbell? There's breakers ahead for him when he gets back to

Garryboo tonight and has to tell his mother where he's been. Yon woman's a pure terror. She got me a fierce skelping once when she was the factor's wife and caught me at her currants when my grandmother sent me down to Snorvig to pay the feu of the croft.'

'Do you think he and Catriona Macleod will ever be married?' Peggy asked.

'I wouldn't care to give an opinion,' Duncan replied. 'Norman was telling me that George has been pretty feeble. Still, George was asking me if I knew where you got that ring for Peggy, and you'd do the man a kindness if you let him know.'

'I hope he won't be giving Catriona one just like mine,' said Peggy apprehensively.

'That's all right,' her affianced told her. 'There wasn't another one like it in the shop in Inverness where I bought it.'

'Catriona has brown eyes. I think rubies would suit her better,' Peggy decided. 'But look, you and Duncan ought to be going along, Fred. The second Mass is at ten.'

It was about three miles to Duncan Bàn's croft, almost due west from Kiltod but a little to the north of the metalled road which Joseph Macroon had secured from the County Council about a couple of years before the outbreak of war. It ran right across the island to the long sandy beach called Tràigh Swish, of which Hector Hamish Mackay has written in *Faerie Lands Forlorn*:

Many and fair are the long white beaches that stretch beside the western shores of the islands at the edge of the mighty Atlantic, but none is fairer than lovely Tràigh Swish of Little Todday. Philologists differ about the origin of the name. So let us fly backwards out of the prosaic present upon 'the viewless wings of poesy' and accept the derivation from Suis, a Norse princess of long ago who, legend relates, flung herself into the ocean from that grey rock which marks the southern boundary of the strand. Alas, her love for a young bard of Todaidh Beag, as Little Todday is called in the old sweet speech of the Gael, was foredoomed.

And while we are back in the faerie days of yester year let us ponder awhile that grey rock which marks the northern boundary of Tràigh Swish. Does it seem to resemble the outline of a great seal and justify its name – Carraig an Ròin? Some relate indeed that it is no mere likeness of a seal but the petrified shape of the seal-woman herself from whom the Macroons sprang. Who shall say? Upon this magical morning of spring when the short sweet turf of the machair is starred with multitudinous primroses, the morning-stars of the Hebridean flora as they have been called, we yield our imagination to the influence of the season and are willing to believe anything. We stand entranced midway along Tràigh Swish and watch the placid ocean break gently upon the sand to dabble it with tender kisses. We listen to the sea-birds calling to one another as they wing their way to their nesting grounds on the two guardian isles of Poppay and Pillay. We gaze at the calm expanse of the Atlantic and try to forget its winter fury of which the heaped-up tangle along the base of the dunes reminds us. We are at one with nature. We have the freedom of Tìr nan Óg – the Land of Youth.

It was on the green turf above this beach that Sergeant-major Odd had first declared his love to Peggy just on two years ago, and it was on this beach that Duncan Bàn found his chief source of poetic inspiration. Duncan had not been at all grateful to Joseph for his metalled road, particularly when he put a lorry on it. Nobody liked that lorry. It frightened the ponies in the carts and disturbed the cattle, and everybody on the island had been pleased when Joseph sold the noisy monster to Simon MacRurie in Snorvig.

'We'll have to put a stop to this notion Joseph has taken for a road from Bàgh Mhic Ròin to Tràigh nam Marbh. Does the man think we will be spending the rest of our lives unloading cases of whisky and carting them away to a safe place? I never knew a crayture like Joseph for getting an idea into his head and keeping it there till it goes bad on him. Poor old Andy Chisholm saw his new school fading from him like a morning dream.'

The starry walk back to Duncan's croft had given him

a fresh thirst by the time they reached this thatched house,
one of the few left on the island. It was built in a hollow
of the machair sheltered from the worst of the Atlantic
blasts by a grassy ridge which ran between two knolls.
Here Duncan Bàn had lived alone since his grandmother's death, his mother having died when he was a
baby and his father having been drowned at sea when he
was a small boy. He had been a student at Glasgow University, and a promising student too. However, when a
girl jilted him and almost at the same time he had found
himself the owner of the croft he had left the University
without taking a degree and chosen this solitary life with
a particularly intelligent dog called Luath, a couple of
cows, some fowls, and a good Gaelic library. He had inherited some £2,000, the income from which allowed him
to indulge from time to time in bouts of deep drinking,
when one neighbour or another would look after his cows
and his fowls until he had recovered. He wrote good
Gaelic poetry, of which a collection had been going to be
published for some ten years but was always being postponed because Duncan was dissatisfied with what he had
written and thought that if another year was allowed to
pass the collection would be a better one.

'Welcome to Tigh nam Bàrd, Sarchant,' he said as he
lighted the lamp and pointed to an armchair in the little
room off the kitchen. 'I'll soon have the fire in good order,
and we'd better have a dram before we take ourselves to
bed.'

'A very small one for me,' said the Sergeant-major.

'This is one I don't think you've tried yet. Bard's
Bounty. And you're going to drink it in Tigh nam Bàrd –
the House of the Bard. The word has gone round that
every bottle of Minnie with that name on it rolls right
along here. It's not often that a bard gets his due in these
days, but by Jingo, he is going to get it from the good ship
Cabinet Minister.'

Duncan Bàn poured out a hefty dram for his guest and
a hefty one for himself.

'Here, you've given me too much,' the Sergeant-major protested.

'Not at all. Not at all. Free and easy, my boy. That's the way when there's whisky galore. Ah well, *slàinte mhath, slàinte mhór.*'

He raised his glass.

'Slahnjervah, slahnjervaw,' said the Sergeant-major, raising his.

'Ay, it was a grand evening right enough,' said Duncan. 'I've never enjoyed myself better. And the Great Todday contingent enjoyed themselves fine.'

'I wish you'd do something for me, Lieutenant Macroon,' Sergeant-major Odd began.

'I'll give you such a terrible bang on the head with this bottle if you call me that, you won't know which island you're on. My name is Duncan, and Duncan is what you'll call me or the end of the evening won't be as enjoyable as the beginning, and that's a fair warning. A man toils hard to write a song for your *rèiteach* and you call him Lieutenant Macroon for his trouble.'

'It was about that song I wanted you to do something for me, Duncan.'

'That's more like it.'

'I want you to translate it into English for me,' said the Sergeant-major earnestly.

'Och, it sounds like nothing at all in English,' the author protested.

'Never mind, I'll get the general sense of it.'

'*Ceart gu leoir.* I'll do my best for you when I've had another dram. And you'd better have another yourself.'

'No, no, I won't really. I'm full up.'

'You may be full up, but you're not overflowing, and when Almighty God sends His bounty to the bard He expects his gratitude to be overflowing. So you'll just drink up another, or not a word will I be translating for you.'

'But look here – isn't it tomorrow now?'

'And if it is just tomorrow now, what does it matter? Och, I don't think very much at all of Father MacIntyre at Drumsticket if he's afer instructing you that you can't drink a dram in Lent. We deny ourselves voluntarily. Voluntarily. And that's a pretty long word for me to be saying in English by now. I'm not going to Communion tomorrow. We'll go along quietly to the ten o'clock Mass and we'll get a cross of ashes on our foreheads. "Dust thou art," the priest will be saying, "and to dust thou shalt return." And, man, it's myself that will be feeling I really am dust, with the mouth on me I'll have by tomorrow morning, because I have a date with a fairy woman on the Tràigh when you'll be in your bed and she and I will be drinking Bard's Bounty together till the bens of Todaidh Mór are dark against the dawn. Now come along, fill up your glass and I'll try to give you an idea of my song, though it'll be a pretty poor idea.'

The Sergeant-major, seeing that he would get nothing out of the bard unless he accepted his bounty, allowed his glass to be replenished.

Duncan found the piece of paper on which the Gaelic version was written out and began:

'From over the sea a warrior came to our green and sunny island as long ago there came a son of Donald who was banished ...' he broke off. 'Och, that's just all about an old tale of this MacDonald who came here and found the seal-woman and she put love upon him and they had quite a family. It goes on for two or three verses, but it all happened a long time ago, and I'm sure you won't want to be hearing all that ringmarole tonight. And then I sing about a girl with lips like the rowan and a neck like a swan and eyes as blue as the sea and then I say how she's like a seal-woman....'

'That's Peggy, of course?' said the Sergeant-major, who was wondering if it was being compared to a seal-woman which had made Peggy exclaim at Duncan's cheekiness.

'Yes, yes, that's Peigi. And then I say that she must have seven sons like the seal-woman because seven is an *odd* number. Och, there's a whole lot more, but you want to hear it in the Gaelic.'

'I wonder you never married yourself, Duncan,' said the Sergeant-major, who was so happy that he wanted the rest of the world to be as happy as himself.

'Ah, well, the *cailin* I wanted to marry married somebody else,' said Duncan. 'And that was that.'

'Don't you ever feel lonelified?'

'Ay, I was feeling pretty lonely when Minnie came along in the nick of time to cheer me up. But, my word, she's a good companion. And now you ought to be going to your bed, Sarchant.'

'What's Fred done, Lieutenant Macroon?'

Duncan laughed.

'That's one to you, *a Fhred*.'

'A red?' the Sergeant-major exclaimed.

'I'm giving it to you in the Gaelic. You always aspirate in the vocative, and the F becomes mute; but if you want to speak to Peggy, you'd say "*a Pheigi*".'

'That's what it is, is it? I thought Fecky was some sort of a nickname she had. I really must get down to it after I've mugged up this catechism and learn a lot of Gaelic, even if I sprain my jore in doing it. Are you coming up to bed yourself?'

'No, I'm going to take Minnie for a walk on the Tràigh.'

'You are? Hadn't you better come to bed? Don't forget we arranged we'd have a parade tomorrow and a bit of shooting practice.'

'Don't you be worrying about me, boy. I will be quite all right tomorrow.'

'Well, I suppose you know best what you can do,' said the Sergeant-major, 'but I'd have said bed was what you wanted.'

However, he realized it would be useless to argue with Duncan Bàn, who after seeing that his guest had all he wanted vanished into the starshine with the bottle of Bard's Bounty.

Duncan arrived at Mass next morning in a state of such confused piety that when he knelt to receive the ashen cross upon his brow he put out his tongue under the impression that he was going to be given the Host.

'Dust thou art and to dust thou shalt return,' said the parish priest in Latin. Duncan, his eyes closed, kept his tongue out.

'And when I put some ashes on his tongue to bring him round to his senses,' said Father Macalister afterwards, 'I don't believe Duncan was aware of it at all, his mouth was so much like the inside of an ashbin itself.'

Nevertheless, when it came to shooting that afternoon, Duncan Bàn Macroon scored more bull's-eyes than any man in the Little Todday platoon.

Chapter 13

MRS CAMPBELL'S DEFEAT

'I REALLY don't know what's going to happen to the two islands,' Captain Waggett in the *Kittiwake* said sadly to his wife as across the Coolish came the sound of a ragged but extremely hearty chorus from the deck of the *Flying Fish*. The raggedness was due to the fact that half the singers were singing *An t'eilean Muileach* – the Island of Mull, and the other half *Maighdeanan na h' airidh* – Maids of the Shieling.

Captain Waggett had taken advantage of the Biffer's being occupied with the engine to make this observation.

'I think the warning you gave them tonight ought to do good,' Mrs Waggett assured him hopefully.

'I don't think any of them will pay the slightest attention to it,' her husband replied. 'There's nobody with the faintest sense of responsibility, and the non-Toddayites are just as bad as the Toddayites. I must say when Thomson the Banker started making a fool of himself by dancing that fling I was shocked.'

'I'm afraid it's going to be rather a shock for poor Mrs Thomson when her husband gets home tonight,' said Mrs Waggett.

'I've never seen him give a sign of being the worse for drink,' her husband went on. 'If there was one man in Snorvig I would have said would always know how to keep himself in hand it would have been Thomson. Before we know where we are we shall hear that the Minister has been tippling.'

'Oh, Paul, what a frightful idea!'

'Well, it hasn't happened yet; but something will have to be done to stop this stuff being handed about like water. Here we are fighting a war for our very existence as a nation, and the one idea of the people here is to get hold of whisky which doesn't belong to them. And I hear that the *Island Queen's* brought a plentiful supply of whisky and beer this afternoon. I'm going to talk to Roderick MacRurie about it tomorrow. He may see things in a reasonable light if he thinks his pocket will be touched.'

'I thought Sergeant-major Odd behaved very well, this evening,' said Mrs Waggett.

'I've no complaint to make against him. Of course, he was flattered by our turning up. That's what annoys me. You and I take the trouble to cross the Coolish in order to enter into the spirit of the island life, and all the thanks we get from Father Macalister is to call me "Colonel", which he knows I dislike, and then badger me to sing, which he knows I never do. These Roman priests have far too much power. Of course, he'd had too much to drink tonight. Something will have to be done about this wreck. I'm going to telegraph to Ferguson the Exciseman at Nobost tomorrow and say I think his presence here is urgently required.'

'Wouldn't the people resent that, dear?'

'I don't care if they do. I'm not going to sacrifice duty to cheap popularity.'

'No, of course you wouldn't, Paul. But you could send Mr Ferguson a letter. It would be less conspicuous.'

'A letter wouldn't reach him till Friday morning, and the matter is urgent. Do you know that at this very moment we're sitting on cases of whisky taken off this wreck? Look what a position that puts me in. The officer commanding the Home Guard in the two Toddays sitting on cases of whisky rifled from a wreck. It would be funny if it weren't so serious.'

At this moment the owner of the *Kittiwake* looked up from his argument with the engine.

'Keep her a bit more to starboard, Captain. The tide's running northerly and we don't want to find ourselves the other side of Snorvig. I don't know what's wrong with the engine. She's not putting her back into it at all. I believe somebody's been putting Minnie in my petrol tank.'

'I can't keep as much to starboard as I should,' Captain Waggett explained, 'because the tiller has not enough play between these cases, which I suppose contain whisky,' he added severely.

'Ay, that's Minnie right enough,' the Biffer said. 'We're loaded pretty deep. I wouldn't move about too much. We've hardly three inches of freeboard.'

'I hope there's no danger,' Mrs Waggett said tremulously.

'Oh, you're safe enough if you sit quiet, Mistress Waggett,' the Biffer assured her. 'The only thing is if the tide takes us past Snorvig we may have to go in to Garryboo. There'll be a bit of a ground swell, but we'll get ashore quite easily.'

'Go on to Garryboo?' Captain Waggett gasped. 'But how will Mrs Waggett and I get home from there?'

'You'll have to ring up for a car to come out and fetch you. You can telephone from the schoolhouse. It's awkward for you right enough, but och, these things happen and it's no use worrying yourself beforehand. Keep her as much to starboard as you can, and maybe we'll not miss the harbour at all.'

'You know, Dolly, sometimes the people here make me feel as if I was in a lunatic asylum,' Captain Waggett ejaculated in exasperation. He could give vent to his feelings because the Biffer was absorbed again by the behaviour of the engine. 'Snorvig? Garryboo? What does it matter where we go? And I suppose if we fail to make the point at Garryboo it won't worry Archie MacRurie. We'll get somewhere.

'It'll be rather awkward for you with all this whisky on board if we find ourselves at Nobost,' he told the Biffer when he left off messing with the engine for a moment.

'Och, that wouldn't worry me. There were two boats from Mid Uist taking the stuff away tonight. They'll be coming over from all the islands, perhaps over from

Obaig and Mallan and Portrose before the week's out. The fiery cross has gone round everywhere.'

'Complete demoralization, that's what it is,' Captain Waggett said to his wife. 'Utter and complete demoralization!'

The *Flying Fish* with her choral passengers had steered southward for Loch Sleeport, and her powerful engine had soon taken them out of earshot of the little *Kittiwake*.

During the singing the Banker had been inclined to dance another fling, but the rest of the party were sufficiently sober to insist that the deck of a zulu under way was not the safest of platforms, and he had seated himself on a coil of rope to conduct the singing, the Gaelic words being beyond him. The crew of the *Flying Fish* had taken enough refreshment in the course of loading her with cases of Minnie to join in the choruses themselves. Drooby himself was at the wheel. Presently the impulse to sing exhausted itself, and the passengers sat about the deck in the starshine.

'I'll drive you back to Garryboo, George, if you like,' Dr Maclaren volunteered. 'My car's at Watasett!'

'Thank you, Doctor. That's very kind of you,' said George Campbell who in his mind accepted the Doctor's offer as a sign that the resolve he had made at the *rèiteach* would be accomplished. He turned to Catriona, who was sitting by him on a case of Minnie. 'I'm going to have it out with my mother once and for all tonight,' he told her.

'You've promised me that before, George,' she reminded him.

'Yes, but I feel much more sure of myself tonight. I suppose it was seeing other people so happy at the prospect of being married soon.'

'And a few drams to make yourself believe you're a brave man after all,' Catriona added.

'I may have had too much to drink,' said George gravely. 'I don't really know. I've never had too much to drink in my life.'

'Ask Norman,' Catriona advised. 'He knows the symptoms well. Norman,' she called across to her brother. 'George wants to know if he's tipsy.'

'You're after having had quite a few drams, George,' said Norman.

'I had four.'

'Is that all? Man, I believe I had a dozen, and hefty ones at that.'

'Yes, but you're used to whisky. I'm not.'

'How do you feel? Is your head swimming?'

'I feel grand. I felt when we came out of the hall that I was swimming down to the harbour instead of walking, but that feeling has gone away. I feel more clear-headed than usual and better able to express myself,' George declared.

'I certainly never heard you talk so free and easy in all the years I've known you,' Norman assured him.

'I was just telling Catriona that I intended to have it out with my mother once and for all tonight.'

'Good enough, *a bhalaich*. But won't the old lady be in her bed?'

'If she is I will get her out of it,' George proclaimed with real resolution in his tone.

'You'll want to be sure, my bold George, that this furious condition you're in will last as far as Garryboo,' Norman warned him. 'Speaking as one with a considerable amount of experience in these matters, I'm telling you you'll have to beware of the reaction. You may be feeling as bold as a lion just now, but by the time you get home your courage may have evaporated and you'll be as timid as a mouse when you face up to Mistress Campbell.'

'Of course he will be,' said Catriona scornfully.

'There's a saying, you know, pot-valiant,' Norman went on. 'You'll have to beware the pot isn't empty by the time you reach home.'

'Doctor Maclaren has very kindly offered to drive me back to Garryboo from Watasett.'

'Then I'll tell you what we'll do. We'll prime you with another dram and that ought to bring you into the ring in the pink of condition. Stand up a minute, George, and let's see how you hold yourself.'

George Campbell did so.

'Ay, you're standing steady enough on your pins,' Norman admitted. 'Not a doubt of it. He's standing pretty steady, eh, Mr Mackinnon?'

'He certainly is,' said the tall thin headmaster of Snorvig school. 'Did you enjoy yourself this evening, Mr Campbell?'

'Oh, I enjoyed myself very much indeed. Very much indeed I enjoyed myself,' said George earnestly.

'I think we all did. Was Mr Chisholm telling you about the tooth-paste, Mr Macleod?'

Extreme formality was always a sign that Alec Mackinnon was carrying a good load.

'No, I heard nothing about tooth-paste. Sit down, George. You don't have to be standing all the way back.'

'Well, it would appear that there's a certain amount of mixed cargo in the *Cabinet Minister*, and among other things some boxes of toothe-paste in tubes, and Mr Chisholm was saying the children were using them as squirts. He said the Kiltod school smelt like a chemist's shop, tooth-paste everywhere.'

'If any of the little devils start squirting tooth-paste at Watasett I'll spread it between a couple of pieces of bread and make them eat it,' Norman Macleod vowed.

The two schoolmasters moved to another part of the wreck, leaving Catriona and George to themselves.

'I know you think I won't have it out with my mother tonight,' he said to her. 'But I'm absolutely determined. I realize that my whole future happiness is at stake. You've every right to jeer at me, Catriona, but you won't have to jeer at me any more. I'm going to tell my mother, that you and I are going to be married at Easter. . . .'

'At Easter?' Catriona exclaimed. '*A Thighearna*, how will I have enough coupons to be marrying at Easter?'

'I thought we'd go and get married in Glasgow,' said

George. 'I know Sergeant-major and Peggy Macroon are going to be married in Little Todday, but the Sergeant-major doesn't belong to the place and he's an older man and they wouldn't be playing the tricks on him they might be playing on me. So if you don't mind, Catriona, I'd rather we were married in Glasgow.'

'Och, I'd rather be married in Glasgow myself,' said Catriona quickly, 'but I'll want just as many coupons in Glasgow as here, and we'll have to wait till the summer holidays.'

'No, we're going to be married at Easter,' George declared firmly. 'I've made up my mind.'

Catriona could not withhold a glance of admiration for this new and resolute George Campbell.

'Och, it's just the whisky that's talking,' she said.

'I admit that I probably wouldn't have been able to talk like this without the drams I had this evening, but when the effect of them passes off I'm not going back to being my mother's slave. If I find I'm in any danger I will take a few more drams.'

'You'll not become a drinker if you're going to marry me,' Catriona told him.

'I may have to until we're safely married,' George replied. 'So that's another reason for us to be married at Easter. Then I'll settle down.'

'Did anyone ever hear the like of the way you're talking, George?'

'Would you rather I just went on havering?' he asked.

'No, I don't believe I would,' she said softly.

'You could stay with your mother's sister in Glasgow before the wedding,' George went on. 'And I'll stay at an hotel. I've never stayed at an hotel by myself. It'll be quite an adventure.'

The *Flying Fish* was rounding Ard Slee, and even the trifling motion of her progress against the tide in the Coolish vanished as she glided up Loch Sleeport to Watasett.

'Not too much noise, boys,' Norman Macleod warned.

'We don't want everybody in the place to know there's quite so much of the stuff.'

Dr Maclaren's car was pretty full, with George Campbell, Alec Mackinnon, Andrew Thomson, and four cases of Minnie. Just before they started Norman Macleod came along to the door with a bottle of Annie Laurie and some glasses.

'A *deoch an doruis*,' he said.

'Not for me, Norman,' Dr Maclaren replied. 'I have to drive these chaps home.'

'Not for me, thank you very much, Mr Macleod,' said Alec Mackinnon. 'I'm just exactly right.'

'Not for me, Mr Macleod,' said the Banker, who did not feel that his forthcoming encounter with Mrs Thomson would be sweetened by the breath of Annie Laurie. He put a peppermint in his mouth instead.

'George?' Norman Macleod asked.

'Thank you, yes, I'll have just one more.'

'You've nine miles to drive,' said Norman pensively. 'You'll be home in about half an hour. I think this is about the right dose.'

He poured three fingers of Annie Laurie and handed the glass to George, who drank it down with the aplomb of young Lochinvar, waved to Catriona and settled down in the seat beside Dr Maclaren with a look on his face of what was known in Wardour Street English as derring-do.

The Banker and Alec Mackinnon were dropped in Snorvig, Each with his case of Minnie, and the Doctor drove on towards Garryboo with George.

'I feel I'm imposing on your kindness, Doctor,' the latter said.

'Not at all. You wouldn't expect me to leave a man to walk the better part of four miles at past one in the morning with a case of whisky after such a party as we've just been enjoying.'

'All the same I'm very grateful, Doctor, I really am,' said George earnestly. 'I wonder if Captain Waggett is back yet.'

'They'll have been home half an hour ago,' the Doctor replied.

'I did enjoy myself at the *rèiteach*. Usually I feel terribly shy when I go to a party like that, but it was all so homely. I think Father Macalister is a wonderful man.'

'He is a wonderful man. I never met a better.'

'Catriona and I decided tonight to get married at Easter ourselves,' George went on.

'You did, did you? What's the old lady going to say to that?'

'I don't care what she says. She can say what she likes. It won't have the slightest effect on me one way or the other. One way or the other,' George repeated firmly.

'Is that so? George, I think you're more than a little tight.'

'I may be. I don't care. I thought that drink made me muddled. Well, I never felt less muddled in my life. I see quite clearly that the time has come for me to put my foot down, and I am going to put my foot down tonight, Doctor. Mind you, I knew I was treating Catriona badly by not insisting on my mother's inviting her to tea as soon as she heard we were engaged, but I just hadn't the strength of mind to assert myself. And then suddenly tonight at the *rèiteach* I saw that I was risking the whole of my future happiness and I made up my mind that I must do something about it. Either my mother is going to behave sensibly and decently to Catriona or I'm going to turn her out of the schoolhouse.'

'George, I think you must really be very tight.'

'I may be. I don't know. I've never been tight before.'

'The test will come when you're sober again.'

'If I find that being sober means being shy and feeble and unable to stand up to my mother I shall get tight again, Doctor. I've got this case of whisky that Alan Galbraith gave me.'

'You'll have to watch out you don't become the slave of drink, George. I very nearly let that happen to me, and I only just pulled myself out of it. Indeed, a lot of people don't think I've pulled myself out of it yet.'

'If Catriona and I are married at Easter, I won't need drink to give me confidence in myself. I'll have her.'

'Yes,' said the Doctor, with half a sigh. 'You're lucky, George Campbell. Yes, yes, you're a very lucky chap.'

'I know fine I am,' George agreed solemnly.

They drove on in silence after that, and soon enough the car approached the point where the road to Garryboo branched off from the main road.

'Don't you bother to take me right down to the house, Doctor. I'll walk from here. The road's very rough.'

'You can't lug that case of whisky all that way. Besides, I rather want to wake up your mother.'

'Don't you worry, Doctor. She won't be asleep. She'll know where I've been because the Sergeant was along this afternoon and she told him I wouldn't be at the *rèiteach*. It was when I heard she'd said that that I suddenly made up my mind I'd go. I had a feeling that the whole of my future life depended upon what answer I gave him.'

'I wouldn't say you were wrong, George.'

The car turned off to go bumping over the quarter of a mile or so of road for which the people of Garryboo held Roderick MacRurie personally responsible. They had even gone so far as to threaten to put up a rival candidate for the County Council at the next election, and by appealing to regional passions they stood a good chance of putting him in by making it a fight between Snorvig and the rest of the island.

Outside the schoolhouse Dr Maclaren sounded his horn several times.

'Just in case the old lady isn't awake,' he said to George. 'I think you're in the right mood to tackle her tonight. *Oidhche mhath*. Good night.'

He swung the car round on the grassy stretch in front of the school, and with one loud final blast such as knights used to give outside castles Dr Maclaren shot off back up the bumpy road on his way home.

Norman Macleod had timed the effect of that *deoch an doruis* to a nicety. While George Campbell waited outside the schoolhouse for his mother to come and open the door, which, as he expected, he found locked, he felt absolutely calm, absolutely determined, absolutely certain that what he intended to say (and if necessary do) was right. The sound of his mother's padded tread advancing along the passage on the other side of the gimcrack door had once upon a time made him gulp with nervousness and mop his forehead with a handkerchief. Once the sound of that padded tread would have made a man-eating tiger's tread seem as harmless in comparison as the pitterpat of childish footsteps. Once the sight of that black quilted dressing-gown had been as awe-inspiring as the last Empress of China at the height of her ruthless power. Now thanks to two drams of Pipe Major, two drams of Fingal's Cave, and three fingers of Annie Laurie the padded tread and the black quilted dressing-gown were like childish fears and fantasies which have been outlived.

'And what have you to say for yourself?' demanded the old lady when she opened the door.

'I have a great deal to say when I come in,' her son replied. 'But I'm not going to start a conversation out here. And will you please go back into the sitting-room, mother, while I take this case of whisky along to the dining-room? I don't want you to tear your dressing-gown on it, and if you stand there that's what may happen.'

'Case of whisky?' Mrs Campbell exclaimed. 'Did you say case of whisky?'

'Yes, yes,' said George impatiently. 'Don't pretend you're getting deaf.'

'George, you're drunk.'

'It's possible I am,' he admitted. 'If I am, it's nobody's business except my own. Anyway, will you make a cup of tea? There are a few things I want to talk over with you and we'll both be the better for a cup of tea.'

'I will certainly not start making tea at this hour of the night,' Mrs Campbell replied. 'Do you know what the time is?'

'It must be after half-past one.'

'It is a quarter to two,' Mrs Campbell answered in a doomsday voice.

'Yes, I daresay it will be,' her son said with an almost elaborate casualness. 'You'd better go in the sitting-room. I want to open a bottle of whisky and get myself a dram.'

'You'll do no such thing, George,' the old lady declared grimly.

'Won't I? Ah, but I will. If you're not going to make a cup of tea, I must have a dram.'

'If I make a cup of tea, George, will you not open a bottle of the liquor?'

'As long as I have something to drink I don't mind,' he answered, and almost chuckled aloud, for this was the first time his mother had ever bargained with him. He knew now that she was beaten before the battle began.

When Mrs Campbell came into the sitting-room with tea George noticed that she had brought a cup for herself. This he regarded as fresh evidence that she was losing her self-confidence.

The peat-fire in the sitting-room had been smoored, but it was soon stirred into life, and the mother and son sat down opposite one another on either side of it, she straight as a statue in her high-backed mahogany chair; he lolling as far as it was possible to loll in the old leather armchair of his father the factor. He lolled purposely because ever since he had inherited the right to sit in that armchair his mother had been accustomed to bid him sharply not to loll, and he was anxious now to disregard her injunction by lolling more defiantly. Perhaps instinct warned her not to risk a rebuff. At any rate, she said nothing about lolling.

'I'm waiting, George, for an explanation of your behaviour in coming home at a quarter to two,' she said, after they had sipped their tea for a while in silence.

'It's a very simple explanation, mother,' he replied. 'I've been to the *rèiteach* of Sergeant Odd and Peggy Macroon at Kiltod.'

'After I told Sergeant Odd that you couldn't possibly go?' she demanded.

'You were answering for yourself, mother. You weren't answering for me. I saw the Sergeant-major myself at Watasett, and he told me you'd said I couldn't be going which ...' George paused. 'Which,' he repeated with emphasis, 'made me absolutely determined to go.'

'And I suppose Catriona Macleod went with you?' Mrs Campbell asked bitterly.

'Surely. We were quite a party. Her brother, Doctor Maclaren ...'

'Was there any chance of getting liquor that *he* ever missed?' she exclaimed scornfully.

'Now don't be talking against Doctor Maclaren, mother. He drove me home tonight.'

'So that was he, was it, blaring away outside the house. The man's without any shame at all.'

'If you mean to stay on the island, you'd better keep the right side of him, mother. You never know when you won't be needing his services,' said her son.

'If I stay on in the island? Is there any question of my not staying on?'

'That's for you to choose. Catriona and I are going to be married next month, and she's not terribly impressed with the notion of yourself as her mother-in-law. And indeed I don't blame her. I think you'd be wise to make yourself as agreeable as you can.'

'Have you gone mad, George?' the old lady gasped.

'Not at all,' her son replied. 'I've gone sane. I think I may have been a bit mad all these years, the way I've let you order me around and treat me as if I was still a child, but that's over now. Yes, I think I must have been a bit mad,' he went on reflectively. 'When I think of the time when we had that Home Guard exercise on a Sunday and you locked me up in my bedroom and I was actually soft enough to let you do it!'

'So the Sahbbath has become Sunday has it since you took to visiting your papist friends on Little Todday?'

'Oh, for goodness' sake, mother, don't be talking such nonsense. Are you really so ignorant as to suppose that only Roman Catholics say Sunday?'

'I think we'd better resume this talk tomorrow when you're sober.'

'We'll resume it all right,' her son told her, 'because I'm going to give you a night to think over what I have to tell you before you go up to bed. All my life it's been you who've ruled it. When I was small you terrorized me, and my father who had a kindly side to him hadn't the pluck to interfere. I suppose you'd terrorized him from the moment you married him ... no, don't interrupt. You've talked enough. I'm doing the talking now.'

Mrs Campbell passed a hand across her brow as if she was testing it for an escape of brains which had left her incapable of grasping what was going on around her.

'Don't worry yourself,' said her son, 'this is real. This is not a bad dream. This is George Campbell, your son, speaking his mind.'

'And forgetting the Fifth Commandment,' the old lady reminded him, mustering her voice to repeat it.

'I don't want to hear thát Commandment again,' said George, holding up his hand. 'You've dinned it into my ears since I was three years old.'

'Blasphemy now!'

'Och, please don't be stupid, mother. You don't help your case by being stupid. I'm not going to give you a catalogue of all the miseries you made me suffer as a child, and I am not going to give you a catalogue of what you've made me put up with, first of all when I was an assistant-teacher at Snorvig school and even more since you came here to keep house for me. You wouldn't be in bed before dawn once I started. All I want you to get into your head tonight is that it won't ever happen again. I don't want to turn you out of the house, but that's what I will do unless in future you do what I say in all matters that affect me.'

'I must wait for my own son to speak to me as I've never been spoken to in all my life,' Mrs Campbell bemoaned.

'It would have been much better for you if I'd spoken earlier. I wish I had. Unfortunately your pride has never been curbed, and you've reached an age now, mother, when pride's the worst ticket to take for the next world. You've read your Bible an awful lot, but I wonder if you've ever read a verse of it with an eye on yourself instead of on other people. Now, don't look so angry. It's only that pride of yours which is making you angry. It was your pride which made you think you could break up matters between Catriona and me. You said to me when I first told you I was going to marry her that if I did you'd go and live with Aunt Ina in Glasgow, and I like a fool thought I had to appease you. You were Hitler. I was Chamberlain. What I ought to have told you was to go off right away and live in Glasgow because Catriona and I would be much happier here without you. All the same, you are my mother, and I feel I ought to give you a chance to pull yourself together and end your days where you've lived so long. So if you write a note to Catriona to invite her to come back with me after church on Sunday and spend the rest of the day here, and if when she comes you welcome her as a daughter, and if you give her all your coupons, I'll try to persuade Catriona that when we get married next month and she comes to live at Garryboo you'll keep your own place in the house and won't attempt to take hers. But if you'd rather not put your pride in your pocket, why, then, I think you'd better telegraph to Aunt Ina that you'll be crossing to Obaig by Saturday's boat and will arrive in Glasgow that night.'

'Have you forgotten that the furniture in this house is all mine?' Mrs Campbell demanded in what she fancied was a menacing tone of voice, but which was in fact not much more than a croak.

'All but two or three pieces of my own,' said George. 'No, I've not forgotten that, and I'll have all your furniture sent down to the pier. I don't know when it will reach Glasgow, but I would think that when it does it won't look very much like furniture at all.'

'And where will you get furniture?' Mrs Campbell asked. 'Furniture is an expensive business these days.'

'I know that, but Norman Macleod will be leaving Watasett for some time when he goes into the R.A.F. and he'll be able to lend us enough to get on with for the present. Don't count on our being unable to manage. We shall manage all right, somehow. I believe I'll find people pretty anxious to help. I've had to make a good many excuses for you, mother, in Great Todday, and I know how nearly everybody in the island feels about you. You won't get any sympathy – even from Jemima Ross.'

'If you bring that Macleod girl to this house,' Mrs Campbell was beginning when her son rose from his chair and cut her short.

'I told you to go to bed and think it over. If you want to make your choice now, make it, but don't turn round and say I never gave you a chance to stay where you are,' her son said firmly. 'And I'll tell you this,' he went on. 'I wouldn't give you that chance if I didn't blame myself a bit.'

'Ah!' his mother put in.

'For not having told you before what a proud domineering old *cailleach* you are.'

Mrs Campbell was searching for a piece of scripture to cite for her own purpose, which was to annihilate this rebellious son of hers, when a knock on the front door made both him and her momentarily oblivious of what had passed between them in their astonishment at such a sound at such an hour.

'Who on earth can that be?' George exclaimed.

The knocking was repeated.

'You'd better go to the door and see who it is,' his mother told him.

'It may be survivors from a torpedoed ship,' he speculated.

In the first two years of the war a good many survivors had reached Great Todday and knocked in the night on the doors of houses near the sea. None had arrived for more than a twelve-month now, which to the islanders was the surest sign of victory in the Battle of the Atlantic.

'It's to be hoped it isn't more whisky,' said Mrs Campbell in gloomy disgust.

Chapter 14

CAPTAIN WAGGETT'S ADVENTURE

═══

WHEN what can now be called the master of the house opened the door he began to think that a second stage of drunkenness had succeeded the phase of truth and resolution, that phase of imaginary visions such as pink mice of which he had read in teetotal tracts handed to him by his mother.

'Mr and Mrs Waggett!' he exclaimed, half expecting to see both dissolve into nothingness as he spoke.

'I'm sorry to get you out of bed at this time, Sergeant Campbell, but I wanted to ask if you would let me use your telephone. Mrs Waggett and I have had rather an unpleasant adventure.'

'Come in, Mr Waggett – er – Captain Waggett. My mother and I were just having a cup of tea. I'm sure you'd like a cup of tea, Mrs Waggett.'

'Oh, I'd love a cup of tea,' she gushed gratefully. George Campbell led the way to the sitting-room.

'Here's Mr and Mrs Waggett, mother. And Mrs Waggett would like a cup of tea.'

The old lady rose from her mahogany chair, looking slightly dazed, as much by her son's inviting a visitor to have a cup of tea without wating for her to give the invitation as by the unexpected arrival of Mr and Mrs Waggett in Garryboo after two o'clock in the morning.

'Would you prefer a dram, Captain?' George asked.

Captain Waggett would greatly have preferred a dram at that moment, but in his present mood of waging war against the cargo of the *Cabinet Minister* he felt he ought not to accept this offer and said he would prefer tea.

'Quite right, Mr Waggett, I'm glad to hear it,' Mrs Campbell applauded sombrely.

'All right, mother,' said her son. 'But don't keep Mr and Mrs Waggett waiting.'

The old lady went off to the kitchen, looking not unlike Lady Macbeth in the sleep-walking scene.

'I'd better telephone before I tell you what happened,' said Captain Waggett.

'I hope you get an answer at this time of night, Captain.'

'They're on duty all night at the post-office,' Captain Waggett reminded him loftily. 'I spoke to Donald MacRurie about that. I explained to him that the whole point of having a telephone is that it must be answered at any hour. Any hour,' he repeated.

After he had been ringing for ten minutes a sleepy small voice at the other end asked:

'Who is it?'

'This is Captain Waggett speaking.'

'Who is it, please?'

'Captain Waggett. I'm at the schoolhouse in Garryboo.'

'Do you want the Doctor's house, Mr Campbell?'

'This isn't Mr Campbell. This is Captain Waggett.'

'Who?'

'Captain Waggett of Snorvig House.'

'This is the post-office.'

'I know it's the post-office. Who is it speaking? Is that you, Mrs MacRurie?'

'Mrs MacRurie's in her bed.'

'Where's Mr MacRurie?'

'Is it Mr MacRurie at the hotel you're wanting? Or is it Mr Simon MacRurie the merchant.'

'No, no, no. Mr Donald MacRurie the postmaster.'

'He's in his bed too. Who is it speaking, please?'

'Captain Waggett. W for what . . .'

'I want to know who's speaking, please?'

'Captain Waggett. W for Wind. A for Accident. G for George. G for George again. E for Empty. T for Tommy, and then T for Tommy again.'

'Will I wake Mr MacRurie?'

'There's no need to wake Mr MacRurie. Have you understood who I am?'

'We can't be sending any telegrams till the morning.'

'I don't want to send a telegram. I want a car. Do you know who's speaking?'

'No.'

'But I spelt my name.'

'I'm sorry, I thought it was a telegram you were sending.'

'No, no, no. This is Captain Waggett. Mr Waggett.'

'Oh, it's Mr Waggett?'

'Yes, I'm at the schoolhouse in Garryboo. And I want you to ring up Donald Ian ...'

'Donald Ian's lorry is at the pier. It's broken down.'

'Yes, but I want him to come for me in a car.'

'They were after carrying him home to bed two hours back or more.'

'Did he have an accident?'

There was a faint giggle at the other end of the telephone.

'No, he was asleep in the telephone kiosk. I think it was Minnie.'

'Who's she?'

Again there was a faint giggle.

'You're just laughing at me, Mr Waggett.'

'I'm not laughing at all. Mrs Waggett and I are stranded at Garryboo, and I must get hold of a car.'

'I'm sure I don't know where you'll get a car now.'

'Is Calum MacKillop on the phone?'

'Who?'

'Calum MacKillop. The Gooch.'

'No, he hasn't the telephone at all.'

'Is John MacPhail on the phone?'

'He has the telephone, yes.'

'Well, please put me through to him.'

Five minutes passed.

'I can't get any reply.'

'Who else on the phone has a car?'

'I really don't know.'

Captain Waggett put his hand on the receiver and called on George Campbell for help.

'Who is this stupid girl they have on night duty at the post-office now?' he asked irritably.

'I expect it will be Mrs Donald MacRurie's niece, Murdina Galbraith,' said George.

'I wish you'd speak to her and try to find out where I can get hold of a car.'

George Campbell took the receiver from Captain Waggett, but by the time he announced himself the telephone had been cut off.

'I wonder what would happen if the Germans had landed in Garryboo,' Captain Waggett sighed. 'I do wish I could implant the most elementary rudiments of responsibility in the people here,' he added fretfully.

'Will I speak to her, Captain Waggett?' George Campbell asked when Garryboo was again in communication with Snorvig.

'She may be a little more intelligent in Gaelic,' said Captain Waggett. 'Apparently Donald Ian is drunk and the Gooch isn't on the phone and John MacPhail isn't answering.'

Sergeant Campbell was no more successful than his company commander.

'I'm sorry, Captain Waggett, but I'm afraid there's no chance of getting a car for you,' he said at last. 'The only thing to do is to get hold of Angus MacCormac or somebody who has a pony and trap and see if he'll drive you and Mrs Waggett into Snorvig. There's Murdo MacCodrum's lorry of course, but Murdo's apt to be a bit difficult. He's never really got over that time when we had the Home Guard exercise for putting all the motor vehicles on the island out of action.'

'Very petty,' Captain Waggett commented with disapproval. 'Very petty indeed. I wonder what Murdo MacCodrum would have done if the Germans had taken his car. A lot of compensation he would have got from them.'

'And we also queried his charges for transport once or twice. In fact, he says we still owe him two pounds. He was over at Bobanish only the other day seeing Mr Beaton about it.'

'Hopelessly unpatriotic of course,' Captain Waggett commented scathingly. 'Well, I suppose a pony and trap is the only solution. Will you go along to Angus Mac-Cormac, or shall I?'

'It might be as well for me to go. Mother, will you look after Mr and Mrs Waggett while I go along and wake Angus MacCormac?' said George. 'What actually did happen, Captain?'

'Well, it seems that while Archie MacRurie was down in the hold of the *Cabinet Minister* somebody put whisky in his petrol tank with the result that the engine of the *Kittiwake* was running very badly.'

'I would think so indeed,' Mrs Campbell interposed. 'The engine just as drunk as its owner! Disgraceful!'

'Of course that may merely have been an excuse for being unable to manage his boat properly,' Captain Waggett went on.

'Yes, indeed,' Mrs Campbell agreed. 'Sahtan will always find an excuse for those who serve him well.'

'I was at the tiller,' Captain Waggett resumed, 'but there was no room to give it full play, and with the tide taking us up the Coolish all the while we couldn't keep the bow of the boat enough to starboard. The reason why I was so cramped at the tiller was that Corporal Mac-Rurie had loaded up the *Kittiwake* with cases of whisky. Well, to cut a long story short, we failed to make Snorvig harbour and had to steer close inshore up to Garryboo Head.'

'And where's Airchie MacRurie now, Captain?' George Campbell asked.

'I suppose he's down at the landing-place. I was so angry that I left him. If it comes on to blow he'll lose his boat, cargo and all, and I'm bound to say it would serve him right if he did.'

'Don't worry yourself, Mr Waggett. He'll lose nothing,' said Mrs Campbell. 'Sahtan looks after his own.'

'It was really rather nerve-racking,' Mrs Waggett put in.

'I'm sure it was,' Mrs Campbell agreed. 'But that set of MacRuries were always a disgrace to the whole island. Donald Angus MacRurie, Airchie's father, was always brawling and bragging about the place. The old minister used to say he was a thorn in his side. And Airchie himself was the most mischievous boy in Snorvig. A regular young rascal if ever there was one. Just one of Sahtan's favourites.'

'You might remember, mother, that Airchie MacRurie has four sons in the Merchant Navy,' George said in rebuke of his mother. 'And I don't know how you'd be drinking that tea you're drinking now without the Merchant Navy.'

Captain Waggett looked at the headmaster of Garryboo in astonishment. He had never heard him, or indeed anyone else, speak like that to Mrs Campbell. He ascribed such self-confidence to the gradual effect of the training he himself had given George in the Home Guard and the authority he had acquired as sergeant in command of the Garryboo section.

'Well, I'd better be getting along to Angus MacCormac, Captain,' said the rebel. 'I'm sure you'll be anxious to get back home after your unpleasant experience. My mother will look after you while I'm away.'

When George Campbell reached Angus MacCormac's house the sitting-room was lighted up, and on being admitted by Angus he found Sammy MacCodrum and the Biffer in the sitting-room with a bottle of the favourite Stag's Breath on the table.

'Very glad to see you, Mr Campbell,' said the Biffer cordially. 'Angus and Sammy and myself are just having a little refreshment. You'll join us in a dram?'

George swallowed like a veteran the dram offered to him.

'By Chinko, Mr Campbell, you put that tram away ferry well,' Sammy MacCodrum exclaimed in admiration. 'I neffer knew you could put a tram away so well.'

'Slàinte,' said Angus, putting away a dram himself with equal dexterity, afterwards wringing out a few drops from his big moustache with his hand and absorbing them noisily.

'Mr Waggett was wondering if you would drive him and Mrs Waggett to Snorvig,' said George Campbell. 'He can't get a car anywhere.'

'Och, I'll take him back in the *Kittiwake*,' said the Biffer. 'Sammy here is going to get some petrol from his brother Murdo. I'm leaving most of the Minnie here. That was my idea in coming to Garryboo. Captain Waggett was plaguing the life out of me to take him over to Kiltod this evening.'

'And you meant to come here all the time?' George asked with a smile.

'I had a big cargo to deliver at Garryboo. Fifteen cases at £2 a case,' said the Biffer. 'Three of them going along to Knockdown. The Doctor bought a case for old Eachann Shimidh.' This was Hector MacRurie, the son of Simon.

'He's a grand fellow is the Doctor,' George declared.

'Och, he's a darling of a man,' the Biffer agreed.

'There never wass a petter man,' Sammy echoed. 'Slàinte to the Doctor.' He drained his glass.

'Ay, and he's a good man at his job,' Angus MacCormac added. 'I don't believe anybody would find a better man not if he went to Glasgow.'

'You wouldn't find as good a man,' the Biffer asseverated. 'Is Waggett at your place now?' he asked, turning to George Campbell.

'Yes, my mother's giving them tea.'

'Is Mistress Campbell up and doing at this time of night?' exclaimed Angus MacCormac.

'She is. I was telling her that Catriona Macleod and I were going to be married next month,' said George with an elaborate nonchalance.

The two Garryboo crofters stared at him in amazement.

'By Chinko,' exclaimed Sammy, 'we must have another round on that.'

The glasses were filled again; the health and happiness of George and his future wife were drunk with enthusiasm.

'That'll be a bit of a shock for somebody in this house,' observed Angus, looking up at the ceiling.

'Does the teacher sleep chust over head?' Sammy asked.

'Ay, that's where she sleeps,' said the owner of the house.

'Och, well, I hope the news will give her a nasty sort of a tream,' said Sammy with enthusiasm. 'I wasn't after complaining to you, Mr Campbell, but she's really fishus. She strapped Annag last week till the child's hand was plack and plue. Ay, and she shook her like a tuster for no reason at all.'

'Well, I ought to be going back to let Mr Waggett know where he stands,' said George who was not anxious to be involved in a discussion of Jemima Ross's demerits as a teacher. 'What time will I say you'll be ready for him, Airchie?'

'If he gets down to the boat by three o'clock I won't be keeping him very long at all,' the Biffer replied.

'You don't think you could take him in your trap, Angus?' George asked.

'No, no, no. We have to get all this Minnie stowed away. That'll keep Sammy and me busy for another two hours.'

'Tell him he'll be back in Snorvig in no time,' said the Biffer. 'The tide will have turned by the time we start.'

So George Campbell went back to the schoolhouse to break the news to Captain Waggett that he would have to return, as he had arrived, by sea.

'Well, well, well, well, well,' Angus MacCormac ejaculated when he was gone, 'what's after happening to George Campbell? I never saw such a change in any man.

Did you see the way he took his dram? Just a real warrior. And mind you, he's going right back to herself.'

'Ay, it's a pity the factor isn't alive,' said Sammy. 'I believe he't have been proud of Chorge in his heart, though he would neffer have had the pluck to say so to herself.'

'It's wonderful right enough what a woman can make of a man,' the Biffer observed.

'I'm not so sure it was Catriona Iain Thormaid,' Angus opined, stroking his moustache as if it was a judge's wig. 'There was plenty talk about him and Catriona getting married next summer, but if anybody was saying a word about it to the factor's wife she came down like a hammer on such talk. And Miss Ross up there was telling the missus that Mistress Campbell refused to have Catriona in the house. It was something stronger than Catriona which changed George Campbell. Did you ever see him take two drams the way he took those two drams just now, Sammy?'

'Neffer.'

'There you are now.'

'Ay, ay, it wass Minnie right enough,' Sammy declared.

'There was plenty Minnie at Peigi Iosaiph's rèiteach,' the Biffer said. 'Boys, they were swimming in it. "*Thig a stigh, a Bhiffer*," says Father James to me, and he gave me a huge dram with his own hands. "That'll keep the *Kittiwake* afloat, Airchie," he says. No, no, I reckon Mistress Campbell found she wasn't able to sink George tonight, though he may be a bit unseaworthy by tomorrow morning Well, if I'm going to take the Captain and his missus back to Snorvig we'd better be getting the rest of the Minnie up, and if you can get that petrol from Murdo, Sammy, I'll be much obliged to you.'

It was exactly a quarter to four when the Waggetts embarked again in the *Kittiwake* after waiting three-quarters of an hour for the owner.

'It was rather a pity you didn't arrange to call for us at the schoolhouse on your way down,' said Captain Waggett in dudgeon.

'Ay, it would have been better right enough,' the Biffer agreed cheerfully. 'But Sammy MacCodrum had to get some petrol from his brother. Never mind, Captain, we won't be long now. The tide's running strongly with us, and you'll have more room for yourselves now the cargo has been unloaded.'

'Have you left all that whisky at Garryboo?' Captain Waggett asked sternly.

'Ay, I left most of the cases there, but we've still some left.'

'Look here, Archie, I do think you're playing rather a dangerous game,' Captain Waggett told him.

'In what way, dangerous, Captain?'

'I don't pose as an authority on the law, but I feel pretty sure that the sheriff could put you in prison for what you've been doing tonight.'

'If the *siorram* put me to prison he'd be sending plenty others to prison with me.'

'Yes, but you ought to set an example,' Captain Waggett pointed out in a tone of kindly patronage. 'After all you are a Corporal in the Home Guard, and as such you have a special responsibility.'

'But, if we didn't unload the whisky here ourselves, there'd be plenty more from all about would be unloading it,' the Biffer argued. 'They're round the ship already like flies on a sunny window. If the Government are so much worried about what happens to the wreck, why don't they put somebody in charge? We've had a spell of fine weather since she went on the Gobha in that fog on the Sabbath, but the fine weather won't last for ever, and if there came a heavy sea she might break in half the way she's lying now. We'd all feel pretty foolish if we left all that whisky for the fishes.'

'That's not the point, Archie. A burglar doesn't get off more lightly if the house he breaks into is empty.'

'I don't see why anybody would want to break into an empty house.'

'I mean empty of people,' said Captain Waggett.

'And anyway I don't know why you're worrying your head about what happens,' the Biffer went on. 'You're not in charge of the *Cabinet Minister.*'

Captain Waggett was silent. Feeling as he did that he ought to be in charge of the *Cabinet Minister* he did not like being reminded that he was not.

It was well after five o'clock when the Waggetts reached Snorvig House. The thin decrescent moon was floating clear of Ben Pucka.

'Oh look, Paul dear,' said Mrs Waggett wearily, 'there's the new moon. I must turn my money over.'

'That's not the new moon, old lady. We only see the new moon just before it's setting. That moon is nearly a month old.'

Mrs Waggett was only too glad to be relieved of the ceremonial of superstition, and she smiled gratefully.

'Shall I make you some hot grog, Paul?' she suggested.

'Thank you. I would like one,' he told her.

'Or would you rather go straight to bed?' she added hopefully. 'You must be frightfully tired.'

'I am tired, Dolly, but I'm going to write one or two letters before I go to bed.'

'Paul!'

'I must get them off my mind. I should only lie awake worrying about my responsibility. You must have realized tonight that both islands are on the verge of a complete moral collapse.'

'Yes, but surely there's nothing you can do about it at this hour,' she protested. 'Won't the letters wait till tomorrow? The post doesn't go till Thursday.'

Captain Waggett smiled compassionately at his wife's weakness.

'You know my rule, Dolly. Do it now. I'll be in the den. You'd better make yourself some grog too.'

When Mrs Waggett brought him the whisky, sugar, lemon, and hot water her husband looked at it reverently.

'I suppose this is the only whisky in the island on which

duty has been paid,' he said. 'And now you go off to bed, old lady. I shan't be long over these letters.'

The first letter was to the Security Intelligence Corps in Nobost:

March 10th, 1943

Dear Major Quiblick,

You have probably been informed by now of the wreck of the s.s. Cabinet Minister (Blue Limpet Line) on the rock called the Gobha (pronounced Gaw) off Pillay, but you may not have been informed that up till now nobody has been put in charge of it with the result that the people of both Great and Little Todday are 'recovering' as much as they can of the cargo, which I hear is anything between fifteen and fifty thousand cases of whisky consigned to New York.

I should be quite willing to make arrangements to put the Home Guard here in charge of the wreck, but I do not want a repetition of the unpleasantness caused by my attempt to prevent a Nelson bomber which made a forced landing on Little Todday last year from being looted, and I can take no steps about this ship without being expressly authorized to do so.

I don't have to point out to you how much the danger of careless talk about which you were so rightly concerned will be increased by what amounts to a flood of 'free for all' whisky let loose in the two Toddays. Of course, I'm not in a position to know just how dangerous careless talk here can be and so I hope you will not think I am trying to butt in. I thought that it was my duty to let you know that I was at a gathering to-night in Little Todday at which approximately nobody except my wife and myself was absolutely sober.

Yours sincerely,

Paul Waggett

The second letter was to Mr Thomas Ferguson the Exciseman at Nobost:

Dear Mr Ferguson,

I am far from wishing to intrude, but I think it is my duty to inform you that the s.s. Cabinet Minister is without a guard of any kind and that everybody is helping themselves to whisky from the cargo. I am credibly informed that yesterday evening two large fishing boats from Loch Stew – probably from Nobost itself – and another from West Uist went off loaded. As Commanding Officer of the Home Guard on the two Toddays I shall be glad to offer my co-operation if there is anything I can do to help you. Of course you may be arriving here by the Thursday boat as also may the salvage party. Meanwhile, hundreds of bottles of whisky on which no duty has been paid are already in circulation. As a taxpayer I feel some resentment at seeing the country's revenue being poured down the drain like this.

Yours truly,

Paul Waggett, Capt.

O.C. G Company

8th Bn. Inv. H.G.

The last letter was to his own commanding officer:

Lt.-Colonel A. Lindsay-Wolseley, D.S.O.,
H.Q. 8th Bn. Inv. H.G.,
Fort Augustus.   March 10th, 1943
Dear Colonel,

You may not have heard that the s.s. Cabinet Minister (Blue Limpet Line) with a cargo of 50,000 cases of whisky consigned to New York has been wrecked off Little Todday. Nobody is in charge and the cargo has been steadily pillaged since the ship struck last Sunday. Do you wish me to assume control of a situation which is rapidly deteriorating all the time? Please telegraph instructions.

Yours sincerely,

Paul Waggett

O.C. G. Co.

8th Bn. Inv. H.G.

With the steady tread of the village blacksmith Captain Waggett left his den for a well-earned night's repose.

Chapter 15

NOBOST LODGE

═══════

IT is beyond the scope of this simple tale to make any attempt to clarify the obscure motives which animate the business of salvage. They present a problem which might puzzle the most expert psychologist. The four representatives of the salvage company were preoccupied with the best method to save the ship itself: the cargo was apparently in theory already lost. Therefore the first thing which had to be done was to dump the cargo of the *Cabinet Minister* into the sea together with the coal out of her bunkers and the ship's furniture. If a curious observer asked why the coal could not be sold to anybody prepared to carry it away the answer was that such a transaction would complicate matters too much from the point of view of the insurance. If the same curious observer asked why the cases of whisky could not be transferred to a salvage ship and sold in due course to a thirsty public on the mainland, the answer was that the whole matter was such a complicacy of insurance, Inland Revenue, Board of Trade regulations, and Lease-Lend, that it was far more simple to dump the whisky in the sea.

So the four representatives of the salvage company were boarded and lodged in various houses in Little Todday and worked steadily every day at emptying the *Cabinet Minister*. They could hardly be expected to watch by night to see that nobody continued their job. For about a fortnight the cargo of the *Cabinet Minister* went into the sea by day and over the sea by night. Boats came from every island in the Outer and Inner Hebrides to help in lightening the task of the salvage men. A few came from ports on the mainland. Then the weather broke, and after a series of gales the *Cabinet Minister* broke in half which spared the salvage men the wearisome job of emptying the coal into the sea. It was then decided to postpone further operations until May, when an attempt was to be made to tow to a mainland harbour the half of the *Cabinet Minister* that was left. The cases of whisky in that half were much more difficult to reach in the changed condition of the wreck, but that did not worry the people of the two Toddays who by now had hidden away as much as they could safely hide.

Captain Waggett's letters had not been successful in stirring up authority in any shape to take action. Major Quiblick wrote to say that a wreck was not the pigeon of the Security Intelligence Corps. Tom Ferguson the Exciseman had merely acknowledged the receipt of Captain Waggett's letter of the 10th inst., and Colonel Lindsay-Wolseley had telegraphed that the Home Guard must avoid meddling in matters which did not concern it.

'Well, I've done what I can,' Captain Waggettt told Sergeant-major Odd when the latter came up to the den to report his imminent return to the mainland after his week in the Islands. 'If Colonel Wolseley says anything to you you'd better try to put him in the picture here. What was the shooting like at Garryboo yesterday?'

'Very encouraging, sir. Very encouraging indeed. Sergeant Campbell was in particularly good form. They'll be strong candidates for your cup next August.'

'Of course, the Home Guard has made a new man of Sergeant Campbell. It seems to have given him real self-confidence at last.'

'Yes, sir,' the Sergeant-major assented, a slightly remote expression in his eye. 'And in fact he's getting married next month.'

'So are you, aren't you?'

'Yes, sir. The date we're hoping for is Wednesday, April 28th; but Mr Macroon is being a bit hard to pin down to it, if you know what I mean.'

'It's very difficult to pin Joseph Macroon down to anything.'

'He hasn't actually said "no" to Easter Week, but he keeps on talking as if it was to be in October, and which of course is a bit annoying for Peggy and I, especially after the raychack. The trouble is she's too useful to him just now. Oh, I think he'll come round all right. I'll take a run in to Inverness when he comes over for the Council Meeting, and try and get it all firmly fixed. He'd counted on putting up the salvage chaps, but they're lodging with people nearer to where the wreck is, and I think that was a bit of a disappointment.'

'When do you expect you'll be able to get over to us again, Sergeant-major?'

'That depends on what the Colonel says, sir. If I'm to get a week's leave for my marriage at the end of April, I expect he won't want me to spend any more time over here for the present. And I really think you'll find the men'll be more keen now. There's a very different spirit now to what there was when I first came back.'

'I hope you're right, Sergeant-major,' said Captain Waggett with obvious pessimism.

'Might I pass a remark, sir?'

'By all means,' the Sergeant-major was told graciously.

'It's none of my business, sir, in one way, and yet in another way it is, being naturally keen to get the best out of the men. I think there's a feeling that you're against them getting the stuff out of the wreck, and as it's now been laid down that the Home Guard has no responsibility for wrecks, I think it might be as well, sir, if you closed your eyes to anything they might be doing. Their point is that if it's all going to be dumped overboard, they have a right to it.'

'I'm afraid I can't accept that view, Sergeant-major. The people here have no right at all to suppose that they know better than the Authorities what ought to be done with this whisky. And I'm rather surprised to find you defending such a deplorable lack of discipline.'

'I'm not saying that the people here are right, sir. I'm simply trying to give you their point of view.'

'Which is another word for anarchy,' Captain Waggett commented sternly. 'Complete anarchy!'

The Sergeant-major was silent. He felt he had given the officer commanding some good advice about the handling of his company. If he did not choose to heed it he himself was not prepared to say any more about the matter.

'I ought to be going down to the boat soon, sir. Are there any orders or messages? I won't forget to speak to Captain Grant about the Sten guns, but they're being a bit close with them at Fort Augustus.'

'Keeping them all for the Loch Ness monster, I suppose,' Captain Waggett commented, with what he hoped was withering sarcasm. 'However, if they go on drinking whisky here at the rate they're drinking it now we shall have a Loch Sleeport monster presently.'

'Funny you should say that, sir. As a matter of fact one of the Bobanish chaps was telling me only yesterday that what they call a Yak Ooshker had been seen in Loch Skinny.'

'A Yak Ooshker? What on earth's that?'

'A sort of long-haired horse that lives in lochs, and by what I can make out a very fierce animal too. I was in calling on old Hector MacRurie at Knockdown later on that evening and he wouldn't have it at all that there's no such thing as a water-horse. He said his father Simon often talked about one of these Yak Ooshkers which chased a man his grandfather knew half-way up to the top of Ben Bustival, and if he hadn't have hid in that cave where you arranged to store ammunition for the gorilla fighting he'd have been eaten alive.'

'I'm afraid old Hector's famous for tall stories,' Captain Waggett sniffed. 'By the way, how is he? I heard he was very ill.'

'He seems to have got much better all of a sudden just recently, sir. You wouldn't have said there was anything the matter with him last night. He told me some rare good yarns about the South African War.'

'You mustn't miss the boat, Sergeant-major,' Captain

Waggett reminded him. He was bored by other people's stories.

'No, sir, I'll be getting along.'

The Sergeant-major saluted and retired.

Captain Waggett's own strict sense of discipline might have been tried to the point of criticizing the conduct of his Commanding Officer, twenty-four hours later, if he had seen Sergeant-major Odd lay on the Adjutant's desk at Fort Augustus two almost spherical dark-green bottles labelled King's Own.

'The Little Todday platoon was anxious for you and the Colonel to accept these, sir.'

'I say that's a very sporting effort, Sergeant-major,' Captain Grant exclaimed.

'I don't know this brand,' Colonel Wolseley said, stroking one of the bottles almost affectionately.

'I think you'll find it to your liking, sir,' the Sergeant-major declared confidently.

'I'm really very much obliged to the good folk in Little Todday,' the Colonel said. 'I take it that this ... er ...'

'Yes, sir.'

'Quite,' said the Colonel quickly.

'Quite,' the Adjutant echoed.

'Thank you, sir,' said the Sergeant-major. 'Excuse me, sir, but if you liked the idea I think I could get both you and Captain Grant a case next time I go over. They're charging two pounds a case for them now, but I wouldn't say the price wouldn't go up to three pounds presently. And that's not unreasonable.'

'Not unreasonable at all,' the Colonel agreed. 'What do you say, George?'

'Not much black market about that, sir,' he laughed.

'We can manage that, I think, Sergeant-major,' the Colonel decided.

'I won't guarantee it'll be King's Own, but it's all top-notch stuff, sir. There's nothing below ninety-eight or ninety-nine under proof.'

'Good God,' the Colonel ejaculated.

'Marvellous,' the Adjutant murmured dreamily.

The Sergeant-major withdrew.

'What a capital chap he is,' said the Colonel. 'And a first-class Instructor.'

'Oh, absolutely,' the Adjutant agreed. 'I must get him to tell us the whole story of this wreck.'

'If Ben Nevis hears about it, he'll be wanting to invade the two Toddays again,' the Colonel chuckled. 'Still, I think we'd better keep quiet about this whisky, George.'

'Oh, every time, sir.'

'I don't fancy poor Waggett would approve at all. I wonder why some fellahs go looking for trouble.'

'I think it makes them feel important, sir,' said the Adjutant.

'I suppose so. Some fellahs feel important when they've got a toothache,' Colonel Wolseley observed.

It was nearly three weeks after the Sergeant-major had left the Islands that Roderick MacRurie paid a visit to Captain Waggett on his return from the County Council meetings.

'Come into my den, Roderick.'

'Your ten, Mr Wackett? What's that at all?'

'Haven't you been into my den yet? I found I wanted a place where I could get together with myself and do a spot of reading and a bit of quiet thinking.'

'Och, well, well, it's snock right enough,' Roderick declared when he had been greeted by Paddy and taken the comfortable armchair offered him.

'A man wants a place he can call his own,' said Captain Waggett, the full weight of philosophy in his tone.

'*Seadh gu dearbh*. Ay, a man wants that right enough. Look at me, Mr Wackett. Chust at the peck and call of efferypotty. And no thanks at all from anypotty. Och, I don't believe I'll stand for the Council next time. Crumple crumple, crumple, that's chust all it iss. I believe I'll sell the hotel and go and live in Glaschu.'

'That sounds rather a revolutionary step.'

'I'm chust about fed up with it all. You know what a

commotion they keep on with at Garryboo to put their road in order for them? Well, on the way across in the boat I said to Choseph, "Look, Choseph," I said, "if I give you good support for the new school you're wanting at Kiltod will you be giving me good support for the Garryboo road?" And what do you think he was after saying? "Och," he says, "*a Ruairidh*, I don't believe we want the new school at all chust now. I think we want a road from Bàgh Mhic Ròin to Tràigh nam Marbh." I was really stackered for the moment. And then I got a bit angry. "If you think the rates will give you a road chust to be selling whisky at three pounds a case you'll find yourself in trupple," I said to him. He gave me a rather peculiar look, but he knew fine I wasn't chust speaking to hear myself talking, and we heard nothing more about that road. He wass back to his school when the meetings began. But he was so annoyed with me for what I said that he stood up and opposed a grant for the Garryboo road.'

'Did you oppose a grant for the new school?' Captain Waggett asked.

'I certainly did after the way Choseph spoke against the Garryboo road. And so the road and the school are both put back till Chune. Well, the way I look at it, Mr Wackett, is thiss. We can't afford to be quarrelling among ourselfs in the Islands, and so long as there's whisky it means quarrels. Would you believe me, Mr Wackett, I've not sold hardly a drop in the bar since this Minnie was going around efferywhere. No, they chust fill themselfs up with whisky outside and then come to the par for peer to chase it down. And, mind you, I've plenty whisky now.'

'I can assure you, Roderick, I did my best to get the Authorities to take action, but they've paid no attention to me whatever.'

'Ay, I know you were trying to wake them up at Nobost. That's why I thought I'd come around and have a quiet talk with you. Something really must be done. Ach, it wasn't too bad at first when they were chust helping themselfs to what they could trink, but now it hass become a reckular business. Ay, selling it at three pounds a case already, and before long it will be at five pounds and perhaps more. I know if I wass to try and buy a few cases myself they'd be asking me five pounds at the ferry least.'

'What do you suggest should be done?' Captain Waggett asked.

'There's only one thing we can do. Ferguson must come over here and make an example of one or two. I don't know at all what Macrae's thinking about.'

'Oh, as usual he shuts his eyes,' said Captain Waggett bitterly.

'Ay, he shuts his ice all right, but he doesn't shut his mouth,' Roderick complained. 'That's open pretty wide all the time chust now. No, no, Macrae won't do a thing unless he's made to.'

'Colonel Lindsay-Wolseley is Convener of the Police Committee. I might get him to speak to the Chief Constable,' Captain Waggett suggested.

'Ach, I don't believe the Colonel would say a word. He had a bottle of Minnie himself.'

'Coloenel Wolseley had a bottle of contraband whisky?' Captain Waggett gasped. 'Where on earth did he get it?'

'Why, I suppose Sarchant Odd would be taking him back one.'

'Most extraordinary,' Captain Waggett exclaimed. 'I simply don't know where I am nowadays.'

'Well, to come back to what we were saying, Mr Wackett. Couldn't you be writing a letter to this Major Quibalick? He seems a pretty interfering kind of a chap.'

'I've already written one.'

'Ay, I know you have.'

'How did you know?'

'Somebody was after telling me. Donald MacRurie himself likely enough.'

'A postmaster has no right to tell people who are sending letters to whom,' said Captain Waggett indignantly.

'Och, we don't pother about little things like that in

Snorvig. We leave that sort of thing to folk on the main-land to pother their heads about. Couldn't you be writing Major Quibalick another letter? He wrote me a pretty fierce letter about the atmosphere in the hotel.'

'I'll write to him again, but I haven't much hope that he'll be paying any attention. Anyway, I think Ferguson would be more effective.'

'I'll write to Ferguson myself. He'd be over quick enough if I wass to start selling Minnie in the bar. But perhaps you'll write again yourself to Ferguson. If he hears from the pair of us that they're selling the stuff he may do something about it.'

'And now that the salvage people have gone away till May.' Captain Waggett added, 'what is left of the ship is not guarded at all. Of course, this is exactly the moment when I should be asked to arrange for the Home Guard to take over, but apparently that's frowned upon. Well, I don't suppose it will do any good, but I'll write.'

However, Captain Waggett's pessimism was not justi-fied, although it must be added that it was not entirely his second letter to Major Quiblick which set in motion the machinery of Security Intelligence. The day before it reached Nobost Lodge, Major Quiblick, Lieutenant Bog-gust, two staff-sergeants, four stenographers, and one of the two corporals attached to the headquarters of the Security Intelligence Corps for what was now Number 14 Protected Area incorporating Number 13 Protected Area had been perturbed by the disappearance of Ruskin, the other corporal, a sturdy burly rosy-cheeked young warrior of the East Anglia Light Infantry whose indispensable services Major Quiblick had managed to retain for over three years in spite of the most vicious and determined efforts to transfer Corporal Ruskin to various centres of Intelligence overseas.

'I'm worried about Corporal Ruskin,' Major Quiblick had said to his subaltern. 'We must have the Island combed.'

So Mid Uist had been combed, but by late afternoon

not a tooth had emerged with Corporal Ruskin himself impaled upon it, or even with any news of Corporal Ruskin.

At dusk, when Major Quiblick and Lieutenant Boggust were walking along the road beside Loch Stew to discuss with the police-sergeant in Nobost the mysterious business, they saw vanishing round the corner of a large byre four men carrying with solemn tread a khaki-clad body.

'My God,' Boggust exclaimed, 'that must have been Corporal Ruskin, sir.'

'Steady, Boggust,' Major Quiblick hissed, 'don't make a sound. Have you got your pistol with you?'

'No, sir; but my stick is loaded.'

'That's all right. You know where to hit a man?'

'On the head, I take it.'

'No, no, behind the knees. Then jump on him and sit on his head.'

'I see, sir.'

Lieutenant Boggust's heart was beating fast not with nervousness but with the exhilaration of at last tackling a real secret service job in the traditional style. So far he had been rather disappointed by the whole business of hush-hush, so much inferior was it to what he had been led to expect by the writers of spy stories. Only the face and figure and manner of his own chief had come up to that standard set by his reading.

As they crept round the corner of the byre nobody was in sight, but when they drew near to the entrance they could hear the murmur of voices within.

'They're speaking in Gaelic,' the Subaltern whispered.

'By Jove, if we were as thorough as the Huns we shouldn't allow Gaelic to be spoken,' Major Quiblick muttered. 'However, they'll speak English fast enough when they see me.'

With this the lantern-jawed Chief Security Intelligence Officer of Number 14 Protected Area sprang forward like a black panther into the dark byre and, landing in the middle of an archipelago of cowpats, demanded to know what all this was about.

The four men who were looking at the body of Corporal Ruskin lying motionless upon the straw where they had just laid it turned their eyes on the two Intelligence officers.

'Och, he'll sleep it off where he is,' one of them said.

'Ay, he'll be quite comfortable like that till the morning,' observed another.

'Minnie was a bit too much for him,' chuckled a third, with a sympathetic grin.

'Minnie?' Major Quiblick repeated. Under his breath he bade his subaltern make a note of that name.

'He was pretty lively last night,' said the first man who had spoken. 'But he started again when he woke up and Bean Phadruig Ruaidh was after saying he could not be sleeping on her kitchen table no more, and so we brought him in here.'

'Whose house was he in?' the Major asked sharply.

'Mrs Macdonald's.'

As there were quite five hundred Mrs Macdonalds in the three Uists, this did not go far towards elucidating where Corporal Ruskin had spent the night.

'Mrs Patrick Macdonald. Her husband's away out in India with the Clanranalds. Padruig Ruadh we call him.'

'Make a note of that name, too,' Major Quiblick told his subaltern. Then he went across to where Corporal Ruskin was lying on his back, the top button of the blouse of his battledress undone, his rosy cheeks a vivid aniline cerise, snoring in a steady ground bass mostly but from time to time in a sudden burst of mounting arpeggios.

'Corporal Ruskin!' his Commanding Officer barked.

The Corporal went on snoring.

'Shake him, Boggust,' the Major ordered.

The Subaltern bent over and prodded Corporal Ruskin several times.

'Minnie,' the Corporal muttered, and then suddenly emitted such a terrific arpeggio of snores that Lieutenant

Boggust involuntarily jumped back as if the prostrate form was on the point of exploding.

'I'm afraid he's right out, sir,' he said to his chief. 'What do you think we'd better do about it?'

'He'd better stay where he is for the present,' Major Quiblick decided. 'I don't think he's capable of careless talk in his present condition, but I'm wondering what he said to this woman Minnie Macdonald before he passed out. Who does this place belong to?' he asked the bearers of the corpse.

'It belongs to me,' said a small-red-haired crofter.

'What's your name?'

'Patrick Macdonald.'

'I thought you said Patrick Macdonald was out in India with the Clanranalds,' Major Quiblick checked him sternly.

'That's my brother.'

'Look here, my man, don't try to be funny with me,' Major Quiblick snapped.

'He iss my brother,' the small red-haired crofter insisted.

'That's right enough,' another of the crofters put in. 'This is Padruig Og, and his brother is Padruig Ruadh.'

'We'll have to go into the whole matter when we get back to the Lodge,' the Major told his Subaltern. 'We can settle then what to do with Ruskin. All right,' he said to the bearers, 'you can leave the – er – you can leave the Corporal here. I'll probably send somebody to fetch him.'

'You'd better be sending more than one,' the owner of the byre advised. 'He weighs very heavy.'

'Well, I'm much obliged to you. Good evening,' said Major Quiblick, and then he and Lieutenant Boggust steered their way through the archipelago of cowpats out of the byre.

'You'd better clean your right boot on the grass, sir,' Lieutenant Boggust advised his chief when they were outside.

'What? Oh yes, I see. Thanks. You know, I'm worried

about this business, Boggust,' said Major Quiblick. 'Anyway, I'm glad we've found out who Minnie is. I wonder if we ever gave her a Milperm.'

Milperm, it should be explained, had nothing to do with hairdressing. It was an affectionate abbreviation of Military Permit, the talisman with which the inhabitants of a protected area were able to move into it, out of it, and about it. It was also the telegraphic address of the Military Permit Offices in various parts of Scotland, England, Wales, and Northern Ireland, whose grand objective was to immobilize as much of the population as possible.

Back at the Lodge, Major Quiblick sent first of all for the other corporal.

'Sir?'

'Corporal Beard, I have discovered where Corporal Ruskin is.'

Corporal Beard looked a little worried. He had been to Mrs Patrick Macdonald's house during the comb-out and made an unsuccessful attempt to get Corporal Ruskin back to the Lodge.

'He is in a byre on the left of the road half-way between here and Nobost.'

'Is that so, sir?'

'So when it's dark I want you take the car along, get Corporal Ruskin round somehow and put him to bed. I will see him tomorrow morning.'

'Is he under the influence, sir?' Corporal Beard asked, assuming hopefully an expression of cherubic innocence.

'He's utterly drunk and incapable,' the Commanding Officer replied.

'Tut-tut. I'm sorry to hear that, sir. It's not like Corporal Ruskin at all.'

'You have your orders, Corporal,' his Commanding Officer rapped out to cut the testimonial short.

Corporal Beard clicked his heels.

'Ask Miss Pippit to come to my room.'

Corporal Beard retired.

Presently an earnest-looking young woman wearing

spectacles wrought out of one of the more exotic forms of plastics came in.

'I'm so sorry, Major Quiblick,' she said breathlessly, 'but Miss Pippit has just gone for a walk with Miss Aynhoe. I wondered if I could do anything.'

'I want you to look through the card index, Miss Cuffins, and see if we have issued a Milperm to a Mrs Patrick Macdonald whose Christian name is probably Minnie.'

'You'd like her card if I can find it, Major Quiblick?'

'Certainly.'

Ten minutes later Miss Cuffins returned.

'I have three Mrs Patrick Macdonalds here, but none of them seems to be called Minnie,' she informed her Chief. 'One living in West Uist to whom we have issued three Milperms to travel to Mid Uist is called Flora,' Miss Cuffins tittered romantically. 'Another living in Mid Uist to whom we issued a Milperm in October last year to travel to Glasgow via Mallan. Her Christian name is Measag.'

'What?'

Miss Cuffins had pronounced it 'Meesag,' but even if she had pronounced it properly as 'Mesac' Major Quiblick would probably had said 'what'? He regarded all Gaelic Christian names as a threat to Security Intelligence.

'Do you think Meesag could be a mistake for Minnie?' she asked hopefully.

Major Quiblick shook his head.

'Who's the third?'

'Another Mrs Patrick Macdonald in Mid Uist who had a Milperm to go to East Uist last July. Her Christian names are Mary Angustina. Do you think they could have been run together into ... oh, but isn't "Minnie" short for "Mary"?' she gulped in the excitement of the chase.

'No,' Major Quiblick said firmly. He was always inclined to be restive under Miss Cuffins' eager helpfulness.

'I'll look through all the Macdonalds in the card index if you like, Major Quiblick, in case we have the husband's name wrong,' she suggested.

'No, no, no. You'll be up till midnight if you're going

to look through all the Macdonalds in our card index. Don't bother any more. Will you ask Lieutenant Boggust to come along to my room? Good night, Miss Cuffins, and thank you.'

When Miss Cuffins was gone Major Quiblick picked up the telephone receiver and asked to be put through to the police-station.

'Is that you, Sergeant Macfarlane? Oh, I wonder if you can help me. I want to trace a Mid Uist woman whose Christian name is Minnie and whose surname may be Macdonald ... the only Minnie you know is what? ... whisky? ... Oh, I see, it's what they call this contraband stuff ... why? ... oh, short for *Cabinet Minister*? ... I don't know why they didn't call it "Cabby" – ha-ha! ... Well, I think we shall have to do something about it, Sergeant. ... I knew they were relaxing the rules about Military Permits for people travelling from one island to another much too soon ... you think it was about time? ... well, I suppose it's always the same when we're at war ... the police think the military authorities are trespassing on their preserves ... all right, thank you, Sergeant. Good night.'

'My opinion of the police in the Highlands and Islands gets lower and lower, Boggust,' Major Quiblick told his subaltern, who had come into the room while he was talking to Sergeant Macfarlane on the telephone.

'Well, they're bound to be rather primitive out here, sir,' said Lieutenant Boggust who had taken a dislike to the Gael on his native heath since that week-end he spent at the Snorvig Hotel.

'It appears that Minnie is the name given to the whisky in that Ship which was wrecked off Little Todday.'

'The one Waggett was worrying us about?'

'That's it. I'm beginning to wonder if Waggett wasn't right after all. You remember he was stressing the likelihood of careless talk if the people's tongues were loosened by whisky? Well, as you know, I didn't really think we could interfere merely on the grounds that it *might* lead to careless talk. And anyway, although in principle these fellows with relations at sea and in the army have no business to be saying where their ships and units are, still, I didn't think it was a serious menace to Security. But now this whisky is reaching Nobost, and if Ruskin succumbs today it may be Beard tomorrow, and who's to say it won't be Briggs or Pershore the next day?' Briggs and Pershore were the two staff-sergeants. 'I can't run the risk of careless talk by our own people. Now, I don't want to interfere in anything which isn't our pigeon. Those Navy fellows at Portrose are as touchy as a lot of schoolgirls. Nor do I want to give those Home Guard dug-outs an inflated idea of their own importance. I think I'll get Ferguson the Excise fellow to come round and see me and suggest that he and I pay a surprise visit to Snorvig in MacWilliam's motor-boat. Then if he reports that the whisky situation is as serious as it sounds I'll establish an S.I.C. control on Snorvig and Kiltod and get Milperm to make permits again necessary for travelling to and from the Toddays.'

'Will that mean my going to Snorvig?' Lieutenant Boggust asked in a depressed voice.

'I expect it will until the situation is restored.'

It was on the next morning that Captain Waggett's letter reached Nobost Lodge.

'I say, things do sound pretty sticky in those two confounded Islands,' Major Quiblick commented gravely. 'Apparently they're selling these cases of whisky at three pounds.'

'Three pounds a dozen for whisky?' his subaltern gulped. 'It must be most frightful hooch.'

'No, according to Waggett it's first-class stuff. They were selling it for two pounds a case up to last week.'

'My God, sir, no wonder Ruskin took the dressing-down you gave him so calmly. Really good whisky at three and six a bottle. It's the kind of thing my old grandfather talks about. And when I was in Snorvig a month ago I could only get one small whisky every other day.'

'If you did go over to Snorvig, you'd have to be very careful, Boggust,' the Major said in a meaning voice.

'I might have a case put in my cabin, sir, like that urn. Or how would it be if I took a black box with me? They'd think it was a regular part of my luggage. Two pounds a dozen,' he murmured to himself.

'It's three pounds a dozen now,' his chief reminded him.

'Well, that's six bottles for you, sir, and six bottles for me at the price of what we're paying now for one.'

'I wonder if you could get hold of two cases.'

'I'll have a jolly good try, sir,' the Subaltern promised with enthusiasm.

When Tom Ferguson the Exciseman came along from Nobost to the Lodge that morning, Major Quiblick told him how much worried he was by the evidence he had just received that illicit whisky was being smuggled into Mid Uist.

'Well, I'll be perfectly frank with you, Major, and admit that I'm beginning to be more than a bitty worried myself,' said Tom Ferguson, a sharp-nosed little man in a suit of Glenurquhart tweed, with the sing-song accent of Aberdeen. 'I thought at first it would be wiser to leave things to the salvage people, but it seems the ship has broken in half and they've all gone away till the fine weather. And now I hear they're selling the stuff. Well, of course, that's something I've just got to inquire into, even if it means a few prosecutions.'

'A few prosecutions won't do any harm,' said Major Quiblick sternly.

'Ay, but I've been treated very well since I was in Nobost, and the last thing I want is to bring the police into it and the sheriff and perhaps get a few old friends of mine heavily fined, ay, or perhaps even sent to prison. If they'd only keep off selling the stuff. Do you know this chap Waggett?'

'I've met him,' said the Major.

'Well, he's an interfering bumptious kind of a chap, and

I don't at all like giving him the pleasure of thinking he's cock of the roost. However, I've had a letter from big Roderick MacRurie at the Snorvig Hotel and I can see I've just got to do something.'

'What about you and I paying a surprise visit in Mac-William's boat?' Major Quiblick asked.

'That's all right in summer, Major. I'm not so fond of a twenty-mile trip round these waters in the *Pearl* at this time of the year.'

'We'll pick our day, and it'll be convenient to have our own boat. The Todday boats would probably warn the people there.'

'And do you think John MacWilliam won't be warning them? John must have made half a dozen trips to the wreck and come back with the *Pearl* loaded every time.'

'You surprise me. I should have thought he was a thoroughly reliable fellow.'

'So he is,' said the Exciseman. 'Could I catch a single bottle? Not one. Well, well, I suppose we'd better take John. We might make it Monday, weather permitting.'

'That's all right for me,' the Major said. 'By the way, Mr Ferguson, what kind of a woman is Mrs Patrick Mac-donald?'

'Which one? The wife of Padruig Ruadh or Padruig Og? They're brothers.'

'The one whose husband is serving in India with the Clanranalds.'

'Oh, that's Measag.'

'Is she all right? One of my men seems to have struck up a friendship with her. I mean to say is she a chatter-box?'

'She'd talk the head off a donkey, but there's no harm in her otherwise. She likes to have lots of laddies sitting around in her kitchen, and they get up to all sorts of larks, but I don't think you need worry at all about your men.'

'You heard, I suppose, that they're selling this stuff at three pounds a case, Mr Ferguson?' the Major asked.

'Ay, and they'll be selling it at twice that presently.'

'You don't think it would be better if you and Major Quiblick went down with MacWilliam tomorrow?' Lieutenant Boggust put in.

'No, no, I can't get away before Monday,' the Exciseman said quickly.

'All right, then, Mr Ferguson, we'll make it Monday,' Major Quiblick decided.

Chapter 16

ALARMS AND EXCURSIONS

━━━━

T HE Sergeant-major's visit to Joseph Macroon when the latter was in Inverness for the meetings of the County Council had not been successful in pinning him down to a definite acceptance of the proposed date for his daughter's marriage.

'Ah well, we'll see about it later, Sergeant,' he had procrastinated.

'Yes, but it's already the end of March,' the Sergeant-major had argued. 'Peggy must know as soon as possible when it's to be because of her clothes.'

'Ah, clothes,' Joseph had groaned. 'That's all they think about. Clothes.'

'Women have got to think about clothes. And once Peggy is married you won't have to bother about her clothes any more. That'll be my job.'

However, no arrangements the Sergeant-major could produce had been strong enough to extract from Joseph a clear-cut answer about the date of the wedding, and he wrote to her:

My darling Peggy,
 I've just come back from a run over to see your Dad in Inverness, and I can't get him to give the O.K. to us being married on April 28th. He doesn't say no but he doesn't seem able to bring himself to say yes. I believe he can't think of anything just now except Minnie. From what I can make out he and Roderick MacRurie had a bit of a row. Your Dad's going down to Edinburgh now to see the Department of Agriculture about getting their support for his application for a licence to sell spirits in Kiltod. I think he sees a profit of something like 600 per cent. And very nice too if it doesn't land him in gaol and which in my opinion it will. I do hope when he gets back you'll tell him your mind is made up and if

he doesn't want you to be married from your own home you
can easily be married from your sister's home in Glasgow.
Father MacIntyre reckons I'l be ready for you know what in
about a fortnight. I wish you could be there. Do I think about
you all the time, my darling Peggy? Yes, all the time, and the
more I think about you the more I know you're the only girl
in the world. If love was whisky I wouldn't half be one over
the eight. With love and kisses.

I am for ever your fond and loving

Fred

P.S. Mind you get onto your Dad to hurry up and fix the
day. I think Father James would say a word if you asked him.
He told me once the raichach had been held the wedding had
got to come off pretty soon afterwards. Anyway I've told my
old Ma she's got to travel Bank Holiday and cross with me on
the Tuesday.

After Joseph Macroon's dilly-dallying it is satisfactory
to be able to record that George Campbell had stood no
more nonsense from his mother after the night of the
rèiteach. When Catriona went to tea with her future
mother-in-law, Mrs Campbell was as nearly pleasant as she
had ever been in her life. There was no more talk of re-
moving her furniture or herself, and she gave Catriona
thirty coupons.

At the end of March Norman Macleod had received his
summons to report for service.

'So you'll be off into the blue tomorrow,' Dr Maclaren
had said, lifting his glass of Over the Border to pledge the
schoolmaster.

'That's right, Doctor. Off into the Air Force blue,' Norman had laughed.

'Well, it's satisfactory to know that Catriona will be
married next month.'

'Yes, yes. George broke the old lady's spirit that night
right enough.'

'She'll probably make a good grandmother,' the Doctor
had prophesied. 'It's often the way. Good luck to you,
Norman, and I hope you'll not be away too long. By the

way, what's happening to all that whisky stored away in the loft of the schoolhouse.'

'Och, it's been most of it distributed,' Norman had replied. 'I've hidden my own particular nest-egg in a safe place.'

'Well, I'll miss you a lot, Norman,' the Doctor had assured him warmly. Then they had shaken hands and Norman had gone down to the pier, where his sister and George Campbell were waiting to see him aboard.

'If I can get leave so soon,' he had promised Catriona, 'I'll come and give you away to George in Glasgow.'

When Major Quiblick and Tom Ferguson the Exciseman reached Snorvig from Nobost on that Monday in the front of April the first person they called on was the landlord of the hotel.

'Och, I'm glad you've come, Mr Ferguson,' said Roderick. 'You won't find any of the stuff, but maybe the sight of you will serve as a pit of a warning, and it would be a good thing if you said a word to Macrae the constaple. He's taking it all chust a bit too easy. I have plenty whisky chust now and it's ferry annoying to hear of the stuff being bought and sold.'

'Who are the chief culprits?' Major Quiblick asked.

'Och, I'll name no names. They're all culprits if it comes to that. Are you from the Excise yourself?'

'No, no, Mr MacRurie,' Ferguson put in. 'This is Major Quiblick, the head of the Security Intelligence Corps at Nobost.'

'Ach, you're the man who wrote me a letter complaining of the atmosphere in my hotel! Do you know the Tuke of Ross, Major Quibalick?'

'Quiblick.'

'I said Quibalick. It's a name I won't be forgetting in a hurry. I wass neffer after having such a letter before. Do you know the Tuke of Ross?'

'I know who you mean,' the Major replied. 'I don't know the Duke personally.'

'Well, there's no finer chentleman in the whole of the

country, and the Tuke himself said to me that the air in the Snorvig Hotel was better than the air in his own castle. I took a good deal of offence at what you were writing to me, Major Quibalick.'

'I'm afraid there's a war on, Mr MacRurie, and some of us haven't the time to think about whether we hurt people's feelings. We're fighting for our existence as a nation.'

'Aren't we fighting as hard in Snorvig as you are?' Roderick demanded.

'I should like to think so.'

'And you can think so as much as you like. Are you here about the whisky yourself?'

'Major Quiblick is worried about careless talk,' said Ferguson, with a touch of malice.

'Ay, and so he may be. He was talking pretty careless himself when he was crumpling about the atmosphere in my hotel.'

'I don't think we shall get much help in that quarter, Mr Ferguson,' the Major observed to the Exciseman as they made their way down from the hotel to the police-station.

'Roderick just wants to give them a wee fright,' said Tom Ferguson. 'He wouldn't like to get any of them into trouble.'

'Oh no, of course not,' the Major commented bitterly. 'Like everybody else in these islands he simply doesn't realize there's a war on.'

By Major Quiblick's standards neither did Constable Macrae appear to realize that there was a war on. Instead of welcoming the opportunity to display the majestic authority of the Law and in doing so perhaps earn promotion for himself, he seemed to resent what he called work that didn't properly come under the police at all.

'I have quite enough to do, Major, without making myself responsible for ships. If the Navy aren't interested and the Salvage people aren't interested and . . .'

'The Excise *is* interested now,' Ferguson put in.

'Ay, now, when all the damage is done,' the Constable complained. 'The *Cabinet Minister* was wrecked just a month ago, and this is the first time we've had a sight of you down here, Mr Ferguson.'

'Yes, yes, Constable, I know, I know. We've been very busy. Very busy indeed. Yes, yes, short-handed and all that,' said the Exciseman. 'I'm not criticizing the police at all. No, no, no. But perhaps you'd come across with us to Little Todday and just take a wee walk round. I'll do the same myself. And that's about all we can do. I'm a wee bitty worried about this selling of the stuff.'

'I'm sure you will be, Mr Ferguson,' said the Constable. 'But what can you expect? There must be hundreds of cases hidden away by now all over the two islands. Whisky's so plentiful that some of them are using it to wash their hands.'

'To wash their hands?' Major Quiblick gasped.

'Och, soap's pretty difficult to get just now,' the Constable told him. 'And it takes off grease fine.'

The Major shook his head.

'They'll be using it for cleaning their windows and floors next.'

'Och, the women do that now,' said the Constable.

'It was certainly high time we intervened,' Major Quiblick observed to the Exciseman. 'I wonder if we should ask Waggett to come along with us?'

'Captain Waggett?' the Constable exclaimed. 'What has he to do with it at all?'

'I don't think we want him, Major,' said Ferguson.

'Indeed, and we do not, Mr Ferguson,' the Constable declared. 'I wouldn't want General Montgomery himself on a job like this, and I certainly don't want a man who thinks he's General Montgomery and isn't him at all.'

'I agree with Constable Macrae,' said Ferguson.

'Oh, I don't press for him,' said the Major. 'This is no job for amateurs.'

So when MacWilliam's motor-boat the *Pearl* set out for Little Todday Captain Waggett was left behind.

'Extraordinary,' he commented to his wife, when in battledress he stood watching through a pair of glasses the progress of the *Pearl* across the Coolish. 'Quite extraordinary. It's entirely through my initiative that action is being taken at last, and nobody comes near me. It would be comic if it weren't really rather tragic.' He sighed. 'Well, I suppose if one does a good job one must expect jealousy. It was the same in the last war. The professional soldiers couldn't bear me always being right then. You remember when I . . .'

'Yes, dear,' Mrs Waggett replied automatically.

Captain Waggett turned upon his wife those light-grey eyes of his which had been watching the *Pearl*.

'Look here, Dolly, you mustn't let this war get you down. I hadn't said what I was going to say, so how can you possibly remember?'

'I'm sorry, Paul,' she apologized tactfully. 'So stupid of me.'

Her husband continued relentlessly.

'I was going to say you remember when I told the Brigadier that the Germans would make their main thrust against us at Haut Camembert and not at Petits Fours?'

'Yes, of course, dear.'

'Well, when I was right, as I always was, not one of the fellows at G.H.Q. had the generosity to admit that if it hadn't been for my foresight we might have had a repetition of what happened to the Fifth Army in March 1918. Of course, I'm not comparing this whisky business to France and Flanders in the last war, but *plus ce change,* as the French say, *plus ce le même chose.*'

One of the few facts of her education which had remained in Mrs Waggett's memory was the gender of '*chose*', but in all the years of her married life she had never summoned up the courage to impart that fact to her husband. His glasses were turned again upon the *Pearl*.

'Tch!' he ejaculated.

'Oh dear, what is it now, Paul?'

'They're going round to the wreck first. Of course, if I'd

been with them I should have pointed out that by the time they landed on Little Todday every case would be safely hidden.'

And in justice to Captain Waggett it has to be admitted that he was right – perfectly right.

Peat-stacks became a little larger than they usually were at this time of the year. Ricks suggested that the cattle had eaten less hay than usual this winter. Loose floorboards were nailed down. Corks bobbed about in waters where hitherto none had bobbed. Turf recently disturbed was trodden level again as carefully as on a golf-course. In one household only was there anything in the nature of a panic. This was at the post-office where Joseph Macroon would not be back from Edinburgh until the *Island Queen* brought him over from Obaig next day. The news that a strange motor-boat with the Exciseman, the Constable, and an officer in uniform was headed for Kiltod from Snorvig struck Peggy and Kate Anne with dismay.

'*A Mhuire, Mhuire*, what will we do if they come here?' Peggy asked tremulously. 'They'll put my father in prison if they find all that whisky in the shed.'

'Don't be saying such a thing, *a Pheigi*,' her sister adjured her. 'They mustn't be finding it. Where's Kenny?'

'Och, Kenny!' Peggy scoffed. 'It would just be a fine excitement for Kenny if his father was taken away to prison.'

'What will we do then?' Kate Anne asked in much agitation.

Peggy took her father's decrepit spy-glass and went outside the shop to watch the hostile boat.

'He's looking terribly fierce,' she said to her sister.

'Who is?'

'The Constable. *A Mhuire mhàthair*, just as black as a crow. And there's a soldier with him right enough. The other will be the Exciseman from Nobost. They're just coming straight for us.'

'There's Kenny down by the quay,' said Kate Anne. 'Kenny!' she cried. '*A Choinnich!*'

But their young brother paid no attention. He was absorbed in watching the approach of the *Pearl*.

'Will they be taking us away with them if they find all that whisky?' Kate Anne asked.

'Och, I don't know what they'll be doing,' said Peggy almost in despair.

'Will I run up to the Chapel House and ask Father James what we'd better do?' Kate Anne suggested as a last hope.

'Father James will be thinking about his own whisky,' her sister replied. 'He'll just be laughing at us. Och, there's only one thing we can do. We must just empty it all away.'

'What will himself be saying when he comes back from Edinburgh and finds all his whisky gone?' Kate Anne asked.

'Don't be daft, Kate Anne. If he comes back from Edinburgh and finds us gone and his whisky too, what will he be saying then at all?'

'Where would we be gone to?'

'To prison. Where else?'

'To prison? Us?' Kate Anne gasped. '*A Dhia*, Peggy, come on and pour it all away before they get here.'

At this moment the decrepit spy-glass, which only Joseph Macroon himself knew how to nurse, collapsed in Peggy's hands, and without waiting to see which direction the hostile boat was taking, she led the way at a run toward her father's big shed at the back in which the lumber of years was stored.

'We'll never get all these bottles out before they catch us,' Kate Anne declared when they pulled away the tarpaulin from the pile of cases.

'We'll try anyway,' said Peggy resolutely. 'Maybe they won't be coming here first. Get a hammer and a chisel and don't be standing there like a dummy. I'm sure it's me that will be glad when I'm married. Going off to Edinburgh like that and leaving us here with all this whisky! Wait you till my father comes back tomorrow and see what I'll be telling him.'

As fast as the girls could pull them out of the cases they opened the bottles and poured out the liquid gold on the floor of the shed. Highland Hope and Highland Heart, Tartan Milk and Tartan Perfection, Stag's Breath and Stalker's Joy, yes, even Stalker's Joy, which Joseph had finally decided was the brand he liked best of all and of which he had collected a dozen bottles for his own consumption, all were blended ruthlessly upon the earthen floor of the big shed for only the air to taste.

'A Mhuire, Mhuire, I feel quite funny, Kate Anne,' said Peggy when nothing remained of the contents of at least a couple of hundred bottles of whisky except the heady fumes.

'I'm just going round inside my head like a top,' her sister declared.

The two girls emerged from the shed to recover themselves, as their brother appeared in front of the post-office.

'Where's the Constable?' Peggy asked.

'Och, the boat went round to the bay,' Kenny told them. 'They'll be taking a look at the wreck.'

'Did they not come here at all?' Peggy asked.

'No, but maybe they will later. The Exciseman from Nobost will be looking for Minnie. Mac an diabhoil, he won't be finding much of it ashore.'

'He won't be finding any here,' Peggy announced proudly.

'Och, he won't be looking here,' her brother asserted scornfully. 'He and the old man are too good friends.'

'Even if he did look he wouldn't be finding any,' Peggy said. 'Kate Anne and me have emptied it all away.'

'You're after emptying away all the Minnie in the shed?' Kenny exclaimed. 'A Dhia, the old man will be wild when he comes back tomorrow. Oh boy, will he be wild? He has plenty Minnie put away safe on Poppay, but that won't make him any less wild to be losing the stuff here.'

Kenny had been perspicacious when he was sure that Tom Ferguson would not put an old friend to the inconvenience of raiding his premises for contraband.

When the Exciseman, the Constable, and the Major reached Kiltod late in the afternoon after calling at some twenty houses in the island, they did not even look in at the post-office but went straight down to the quay and boarded the *Pearl* which had come back from Macroon's Bay to wait for them in the harbour.

'Well, they've been warned now,' said Ferguson.

'Ay, they've been warned right enough,' the Constable agreed, with a hint of cynicism in his tone.

'Yes, I'm sure our visit has done a lot of good,' Major Quiblick decided. 'I don't think it will be necessary for me to put back permits to travel between Great and Little Todday. I was thinking of sending my subaltern down for a week or two to establish an S.I.C. Control, but I *don't* think that should be necessary after our visit.'

Did John MacWilliam blink at the westering sun as he made his way aft to take the helm or did he wink at Major Quiblick?

'I'll have a wee walk round Snorvig tomorrow morning,' said the Exciseman, 'and then I expect you'll be wanting to get back to Loch Stew, John.'

'I'd like to start back by about eleven o'clock if that suits you, Mr Ferguson.'

'Is that all right for you, Major?'

'That'll suit me,' said Major Quiblick in whose attitude there was discernible a serene good-will toward his fellow men of which he had hitherto shown not a sign. 'I suppose we ought to look in on Waggett,' he added, as the *Pearl* cleared the diminutive harbour of Kiltod and set out for Snorvig.

'I don't think I'll be bothered with him, Major,' said the Exciseman. 'We've had an amusing day trying to catch muckle whales with wee sprats, and I'd rather have a crack with Roderick.'

Captain Waggett was inclined to stand on his dignity with Major Quiblick when the latter arrived at Snorvig House, but his visitor made himself so agreeable that finally he was invited into the den.

'I could have told you before you started, Quiblick, that you would find nothing if you gave them time to cover up their traces.'

'The idea was to warn them, Waggett.'

'When you've lived in these islands as long as I have, you'll know that warnings are no use at all. No use at all,' Captain Waggett repeated firmly. 'I've warned them about almost everything under the sun without the slightest effect. They think they know best. They're very pleasant to you on the surface and at first you think they are paying attention to what you say; but underneath they simply go their own way. Bilingual and double-faced, that's what the people are here. Can I offer you a glass of whisky on which duty has been paid?'

'Oh, thanks very much,' said the Major. 'I'd like a peg. It's thirsty work tramping about over Little Todday.'

'Do you know what they're selling it at now?' Captain Waggett asked as he unlocked his tantalus.

'Three pounds a case,' said the Major quickly.

'Five pounds,' Captain Waggett corrected. 'Soda?'

'Thank you, just a spot. Five pounds, eh? Really? I – er – heard it was three pounds.'

'Five or three,' Captain Waggett observed, 'it's equally disgraceful.'

'Oh, quite, quite. Most disgraceful,' the Major agreed, without a vestige in his tone of wounded morality. 'Five pounds,' he repeated pensively. 'Is that the price on Great Todday?'

'A corporal in the Snorvig section of my company offered me a case for five pounds this afternoon, I gave him a rare wigging. No use, of course. I don't delude myself. However, he saw that I was angry.'

'I should be deuced angry if one of my corporals offered me a case for five pounds,' Major Quiblick declared.

The Major spoke sincerely. Thanks to John MacWilliam's skill he had secured two cases at three pounds that afternoon. They travelled back with him and the Exciseman to Nobost the following morning.

'You know, Boggust,' he said to his subaltern, 'I had great difficulty in resisting the temptation to tell that fellow Waggett I'd only paid three pounds a case. He was so damn cocksure he knew more about it than I did.'

'That *would* have been careless talk, sir,' said the Subaltern.

Then they pledged one another in glasses of Trusty Friend.

'This is wizard stuff,' the Subaltern sighed.

'Tophole,' his Commanding Officer agreed.

'It was a jolly sporting effort of yours, sir, to bring the stuff back, with Ferguson aboard.'

Major Quiblick smiled.

'That's an old Intelligence trick,' he said complacently.

The return of Joseph Macroon from Edinburgh, where he had not succeeded in persuading the Department of Agriculture to support his notion of applying for a licence to sell spirituous liquor at Kiltod, was less happy that Tuesday than the return of Major Quiblick to Nobost.

As soon as the *Morning Star* brought him across from the *Island Queen* he went to his shed, having heard on the pier of the activity on Little Todday the previous day. He opened the door. He sniffed the air. He muttered something under his breath. He darted forward and pulled away the tarpaulin. He gazed at the hillock of empty bottles. He groaned. He took from his head the ceremonious bowler he had been wearing to keep his end up in Edinburgh. He flung it down on the whisky-soaked earthen floor, and hurried away to his own room at the back of the shop.

'*A Pheigi! A Chatriona! A Choinnich!*' he cried. '*Cà bheil sibh? Thigibh an so! Thigibh! Thigibh! A Dhia nan Gràs, cà bheil sibh?*'

'What's the matter, father?' Peggy asked coming in from the post-office. 'Kenny's away back to Snorvig for the mail. And Kate Anne's away with him.'

'My whisky! Who's after throwing away all my whisky?'

'Kate Anne and I were afraid the Constable was coming

here. They were all over the island yesterday and every-body was hiding away their Minnie as hard as they could be.'

'*A Dhia*, then why weren't the two of you hiding it?' the stricken father moaned.

'How could we be hiding all those cases?' Peggy asked indignantly. 'Kate Anne and me nearly killed ourselves opening them and emptying out the bottles. I don't know how many there were.'

'Eighteen cases,' Joseph groaned. 'Two hundred and six-teen bottles, and twelve of them Stalker's Joy, the best of all. Daughters? *Ochòin mo thruaighe!* They're just a misery and a burden to a man.'

King Lear himself was speaking.

'I'm sure Kate Anne and me did it for the best,' said Peggy.

'Your mother would never have done such a fool of a thing for the best,' Joseph reproached her. 'Never. She had more sense in her. Daughters? Clothes and cigarettes and all this sticklips.'

'I'm sure it's not me that wants to be a burden to you,' Peggy avowed. 'I don't want to be a man's daughter at all. I want to be a man's wife. And it's just yourself that's keeping me back. If you'll say the word now Father James can be giving it out in church next Sunday, and Fred and me can be married in Easter Week.'

'Indeed, and I'd sooner see you married than pouring away any more of my Stalker's Joy on me,' her father affirmed. 'There never was such a whisky.'

So on April 11th the banns of marriage between Alfred Ernest Odd and Peigi Ealasaid Nic Ròin were read for the first time without any objection from Iosaiph Mac Ròin. Two days later Peggy left Little Todday on a visit to her sister in Glasgow where she would assemble a hasty trous-seau.

When she went on board the *Island Queen* her luggage was larger than it usually was by two wooden boxes wrapped in brown paper and addressed to Lt-Colonel

A. Lindsay-Wolseley, D.S.O., Tummie House, Fort Augustus S.O., and Captain G. F. Grant, M.C., H.Q., 8th Bn. Inv. H.G., Fort Augustus, the explanation of which may be found in the following letter:

Ness Cottage
Tummie
Fort Augustus S.O.
7/4/43

My darling Peggy,

Your telegram this morning made me go all of a doodah with excitement. Please read above address carefully because it is where you and me will be living like two lovebirds in a nest this very month as ever is. It's a treat. There's a quite a lot of flowers blooming now and I'm getting the garden to rights already for the veges and which you'll be cooking with your own dear hands by summer. I'm to be received into the Church next Saturday and on Sunday I'm making my first Communion and which will make me feel like when I first paraded as a drummer boy in the sweet bye and bye. So if you're at early Mass in dear old Kiltod think of your loving Fred going through it in Drumsticket. I would have liked to have got over to do this with you but the Colonel has been so good about this cottage which is furnished a treat that as he's giving me ten days' leave for the honeymoon and which means we could take my old Ma back to Nottingham and you could see what it's like there, I didn't like to ask to come over to the islands just now. There's a night attack on against C Company at Glenbogle Castle with Captain Cameron of Kilwhillie and D Company in support of Major MacDonald of Ben Nevis, and the Colonel's rather anxious to knock sparks out of them with the attacking force. And that brings me to something I want to ask. Can you get hold of two cases of Minnie for the Colonel and the Adjutant? I believe £3 is the price per case, and I enclose notes with addressed labels to stick on. If you leave them at the St Ninian's Hotel, Obaig, the Colonel will send and call for them. I'm sorry to cause you this trouble when you go to Glasgow next Tuesday but I'd like to do something for the Colonel and Captain Grant because they've both been very kind to me. Of course I'm not paying for the Minnie only just getting it for them. Don't find somebody in Glasgow you like better than me. I've scrounged 23 coupons for you and which I enclose. I can't hardly believe that you and me will be aboard the good ship 'Darby and Joan' 21 days from now. Do you remember when you said I was 21 years older than you and I knew you'd worked it out for yourself? *If* you were the only girl in the world? You *are* the only girl in the world for

Your ever most loving and devoted

Fred

Chapter 17

MRS ODD

═══════

ON the afternoon of Easter Sunday Sergeant-major Odd went down to Glasgow to meet his mother who was arriving at St Enoch's station next day from Nottingham in time to catch the last train to Obaig and go on board the *Island Queen* that night. Mrs Odd was now seventy-one, a hale old woman, small and plump, with white hair, a fresh complexion, and a wonderfully quick step. Nobody who saw her alight from that train would have given her a day more than sixty.

'Ah, here you are, Mar. Have you had a good journey up?' her son asked.

'I've had a lovely journey. Couldn't have been more comfortable if I'd been in my own chair.' She turned back to address a private of the Highland Light Infantry who had been in the compartment with her. 'Good-bye, Harry Lauder the Second,' she said. 'And don't forget if you're ever in Nottingham again to look in and have a cup of tea and plenty of cigarettes. You've got my address. Now, mind you don't forget.' She turned back to her son. 'I didn't introjuice you. He's a bit shy, poor lad, and as Scotch as a good bottle of whisky. "What's your name?" I said after he'd put my bag up on the rack for me, and you could have knocked me down with a feather when he said "my name's Lauder". "Not Harry Lauder for goodness' sake?" I said, and he said, "No, Jimmy Lauder," and I said, "Oh, well, you'll be Harry Lauder the Second to me," and after that we got on a treat, though I couldn't understand more than three words in ten of what he was mumbling. Well, how do you feel, Fred, now you're almost on the brink. Shiverified? And how did you get on with your religious business?'

'It was quite all right, Ma.'

'I always remember your poor old Dad saying to me once, when you was blaring round the house with a tin trumpet and he was trying to get his Sunday afternoon snooze, "That blessed kid'll join the Salvation Army the way he's going," and I said, "Army, if you like, Ernest, but there won't be much salvation about it, if I know the young Turk." That was when we were living in Graves Road, Fulham. Oh, I'd properly sized you up already. And now you're going to be married. Well, I never expected to be a grandmother on the right side of the blanket, as they say, and when you went off to Africa, "Yes," I said to myself, "that's the last we'll hear of poor Peggy." Well, I respeck that girl, Fred. A girl who can hold a man like you for two years and turn him religious at the end of it must have a lot in her.'

'She has, Ma. She's a jewel.'

'I never thought there was much in a jool,' said Mrs Odd. 'Expensive glass that's what I call joolery.'

'Well, you know what I mean.'

'That's all right, Fred. Your Ma Knows. She's a girl in a thousand, eh?'

'She's a girl in a million,' Sergeant-major Odd declared fervidly.

'Good job everybody isn't so dainty as you, Fred. There'd be marriage queues on top of all the others. What they won't queue up for nowadays! I won't do it myself. I said to Mr Dumpleton the other day – that's my butcher – I said, "I haven't gone one over the allotted span, Mr Dumpleton, to spend the rest of what I've got left in the tail-end of a kite."'

'You won't find any queuing up in Little Todday, Mar. I hope we get a fine day tomorrow for the crossing.'

When Mrs Odd was shown the berth in her cabin on the *Island Queen* she asked what it was.

'That's where you sleep, Ma,' her son told her.

'Yes, if I was a canary-bird,' she declared, 'it'ud make a comfortable perch. Or if I was Blondin I mightn't fall off it. But being what I am, that's no bed for me.'

'You're in the lower berth,' said the stewardess, 'and you'll have the cabin to yourself.'

'I should hope so,' Mrs Odd commented. 'You don't mean to tell me you ever try and pack two into this what-not? That would be a concentration camp and no mistake.'

However, next morning when the Sergeant-major came along to inquire if his mother was ready for breakfast he found she had slept well.

'Except for some Nosey Parker who put his head round the door to ask for my permit. "I thought this was a free country, Ribbingtrop," I said.'

'But you have got a permit,' her son pointed out.

'That doesn't say anybody's got to be woken up before sunrise to wave it about like a flag, does it?' the old lady demanded. 'I told him to clear out and come back at a Christian hour.'

'What did he say?'

'I don't know what he said or didn't say. I turned over – well, squeezed over – and went to sleep again.'

Later on the Sergeant-major took his mother up to the wheel-house to introduce her to Captain MacKechnie.

'Well, this is a life on the ocean wave and no mistake,' she exclaimed as they came to the top of the companion. 'What a pity your dear old Dad isn't here to enjoy it with us. He was such a one for the sea. Get him aboard the *Margate Belle* and he was in his element. And he was always seasick. Never mind, he'd just go to the side looking as green as a gooseberry on Whit-sunday and then come back humming *Nancy Lee* as cheerful as a cricket until he went green again.'

'This is my mother, Captain MacKechnie,' said the Sergeant-major. 'I thought you wouldn't mind me bringing her up to meet you.'

'Ferry glad you did, Sarchant. Ferry glad to meet you, Mistress Ott,' the Captain squeaked cordially as he shook her hand. 'You'll be pretty excited about the wetting, Mrs Ott? He picked a fine curl for himself. Oh yess, chust a real pewty.'

'And I'll lay you know what a fine girl is, Captain Mac-
Kechnie,' Mrs Odd told him.

The skipper of the *Island Queen* laughed high with delight at this.

'Look at that now, Sarchant,' he chuckled, shaking with
self-congratulatory mirth. 'Wait you till I tell my missus
that. Ah, well, we're all very proud that the Sarchant has
chosen an Island curl for himself. He's ferry much liked is
the Sarchant. I neffer heard anything but praise for him.
Has he introduced you to Minnie yet, Mistress Ott?'

'Minnie?' the old lady repeated. 'You don't mean to say
you've got another girl up here, Fred?'

'Ferry good. Ferry good,' the Skipper chuckled, slapping
his leg. 'Yess, yess, that's a good one right enough.'

'Minnie is what they call that whisky ship I was telling
you about, Ma,' the Sergeant-major explained.

'You'll please come along to my cappin and tap the
steward before you go ashore,' Captain MacKechnie invited them. 'I'd like to trink to your happiness, Sarchant,
as I can't be at the wetting myself.'

The bens of Great Todday were in sight when Mrs Odd
and her son went along to tap the steward.

'Well, here's to you, Sarchant, and here's to you, Mistress Ott, and may all your trupples be little ones!' Captain MacKechnie wished, raising his glass.

'That's a big lot of whisky for an old woman,' Mrs Odd
said, eyeing her own.

'Och, you won't notice it, Mistress Ott,' the Skipper
assured her. 'It's Caberfèidh. The antlers of the stack. Ay,
it's a grand whisky. Mackenzie and Mackenzie of Inverness.

'Well, seeing I've waited twenty years and more for my
son to turn sensible,' said Mrs Odd, 'here goes.'

And she drained her dram with a verve that the Biffer
himself might have envied.

'By Chinko, that's the right way to put down a tram,
Mistress Ott,' her host declared enthusiastically. 'I don't
like to see a woman pecking at it like a hen. Not at all.'

'A nice reputation I'll have presently,' said Mrs Odd.

'It's a good thing you're getting married tomorrow, Fred.'

Once the date of the wedding had been definitely fixed Joseph Macroon had stinted nothing to make it a memorable occasion. A hoard of sugar, the existence of which had been unsuspected by his family, was drawn upon for the cake. He had allowed Peggy a generous sum for her trousseau. Now he was on the pier waiting to welcome the Sergeant-major and Mrs Odd.

'That's him,' said the former, from where they were standing on the upper deck.

'That's who?' asked his mother.

'My future par-in-lore in the red knitted cap.'

'Now who does he remind me of?' Mrs Odd exclaimed. 'I know. Will Atkins.'

'Will Atkins? Who's he?'

'The feller who had it in for Robinson Crusoe in the panto. Oh, he's the spitting image of Will Atkins. And who's that big dark feller?'

'That's Roderick MacRurie who has the hotel here in Snorvig.'

'Yes, and he'd need an hotel to live in. What a whopper, eh? And who's Boatrace Bill?'

The Sergeant-major guessed that this name was inspired by Captain Waggett's light-blue tweed suit latticed with dark blue.

'That's Captain Waggett who commands the Todday company of the Home Guard.'

'Thinks quite a lot of himself, doesn't he?' Mrs Odd commented.

A few minutes later she was being greeted by Joseph Macroon on the pier.

'I'm proud to welcome you, Mistress Odd,' he told her. 'You've come a long way, I believe.'

'Nottingham. Was you ever in Nottingham?'

'No, I was never there. It'll be a fine city, I daresay.'

'Not so bad. It's not dear old London of course, but what place is?'

'I was never there either.'

'You was never in London?' Mrs Odd gasped. 'Well, if that hasn't torn it!'

Joseph looked round apprehensively to see what had been torn, and at that moment Duncan Bàn came hurrying up.

'I never heard her blowing,' he explained. 'I was away up the hill having a crack with Alec Mackinnon, and when I looked round there she was.'

'This is Mr Duncan Macroon with who you and me are staying tonight,' said the Sergeant-major.

'*Fàilte do'n dùthaich,*' Duncan bubbled as he warmly wrung the old lady's hand. 'Do you know what that means, Mistress Odd?'

'I can't say I do,' she told him, beaming. 'But I suppose it's a bit of this Garlic you all gabble among yourselves.'

'Welcome to the country. And I never welcomed anybody more heartily,' Duncan declared. 'My goodness, I can see where Fred got that twinkle in his eye. Well now, Joseph, will we go right across, or will we wait for the mails?'

'You'd better be going across right away with Mistress Odd, and the *Morning Star* can come back for me,' Joseph replied.

Kenny was inclined to be a bit shy with Mrs Odd at first, but it was not long before she had him laughing and by the time they reached Kiltod he was suggesting taking her round tomorrow morning early to have a look at the *Cabinet Minister*.

'You let me go in and see Peggy by myself for a moment, Fred,' his mother said when they reached the post-office.

She found Peggy in the little room behind the shop.

'My goodness, you're taller than I expected, my dear. You must be nearly as tall as Fred,' she said as she pulled Peggy down to kiss her after the first formal handshake.

'Well, you've made Fred happy and I see you're going to make his old mother just as happy. He's a lucky man and I'm a lucky old woman.'

'You're being terribly kind, Mrs Odd,' Peggy murmured.

'And what a pleasure to be able to see a girl blush again,' Mrs Odd exclaimed. 'I'd almost forgotten what it looked like.'

'I hope you don't mind Fred becoming a Catholic, Mrs Odd,' Peggy almost whispered.

'I wouldn't mind not if he'd become a Weslean. I'm good old Church of England myself, and I haven't missed a harvest festival in donkey's years, but I don't think Fred has been inside any kind of a church since he was a nipper before he met you. Yes, you've done something I wouldn't have believed anybody could do with Fred, and now what you've got to do is make me a granny as soon as poss. There you go blushing again. Well, really, it's a treat to see it. All these Ats and Whats and Wrens and Whens and Waafs, and those saucy little hussies with their lipstick and powder. Well, I'm not going to make a nuisance of myself now. I'm sure you'll have lots to do, with the wedding tomorrow, and we'll have a good talk when we go away together on Thursday. I'm glad you'll be able to see the place which will be your own one day. It's nothing grand, mind you, but it's cosy. And there's a lovely big room at the back for a nursery.'

Mrs Odd took the two hands of her future daughter-in-law in her own.

'Yes, Fred's waited a long while, but you was worth waiting for.'

One more house Mrs Odd had to visit before she got into the trap in which she was to drive to Tigh nam Bàrd and that was Father Macalister's.

'Well, really, you know, Sergeant, your mother's a wonderful woman,' the parish priest avowed. 'Fancy travelling all the way from that peculiar place where she lives just to see you married. Oh, by Jingo, good shooting! And now you'll take a small refreshment, Mrs Odd.'

'I don't know as I ought, Father Macalister. I had some Caperfay as he called it with Captain MacKechnie, and I thought "Yes, you'll be cutting capers yourself, Elizar Odd, if you do this sort of thing."'

'Ah well, I think you'll manage a small sensation with me. Thanks be to God, we're in a position to offer it these days.'

'Minnie, eh?'

'Ay, Saint Minnie we call her now.'

The parish priest went to his cupboard, and pondered the choice.

'All the Year Round,' he decided. 'Just the smallest sensation, Mrs Odd. Oh, really beautiful stuff. You'll just think you're sipping cream. Really a baby in arms would hardly know it was whisky. *Uisge beatha*. Water of Life!'

'That's Garlic I suppose?'

'Ay, Gaelic it is. What a pity you don't know our glorious language.'

'Say that again, will you, Father Macalister.'

'*Uisge beatha*.'

'I see. Something like a sneeze and then a yawn,' said Mrs Odd.

'Ay, ay, that's just what it is. Something between a sneeze and a yawn. Did you hear that, Duncan? Ah well, really now, I never heard a better description of it. Something between a sneeze and a yawn. I won't forget that, Duncan. And you won't forget it either, my boy.'

'I won't forget it, Father,' the poet assured him.

'You'll enjoy Duncan's company, Mrs Odd,' the priest went on. 'And tomorrow my friend here is to marry a lovely and beautiful girl.' He raised his glass. 'Ah well, Sergeant, you know I wish you everything you can wish for yourself,' he said in his richest bass.

'I know you do, Father. And if I might take advantage of this opportunity I'd like to say on behalf of Peggy and myself how much we owe to you and my friend Duncan here. The course of true love never does run smooth, they say, and certainly the course of true love for Peggy and I ran very wonky for a time — very wonky. However, thanks to Father Macalister here ...'

'And St Minnie,' the priest interposed.

'All is now going according.'

The Sergeant-major drained his glass.

'Well, I suppose we ought to be going along,' he said. 'You've got quite a bit of a drive yet, Mar, and I expect you're feeling a bit tired. You've had two long days, and you'll have a long journey back Thursday.'

'Oh, I'm feeling quite bobbish,' said his mother. 'Or if I'm not, the whisky is.'

'It'll do you no harm, Mrs Odd,' Father Macalister assured her sonorously. 'In fact it'll do you a power of good.'

Although the clock said half past six, double summer time made it still golden afternoon, and the myriad daisies on the machair were only just beginning to close their petals. Wheat-ears flashed their white rumps as they dipped in flight ahead of the trap. Stonechats with ebon heads and chestnut breasts clicked beside the track. Oyster-catchers, Bride's pages, were whistling gleefully to welcome the ebb of the tide on Tràigh Swish.

'Lovely, isn't it, Ma?' the Sergeant-major exclaimed contentedly.

'Oh, it's beautiful,' his mother agreed.

'Are you riding comfortable, Mistress Odd?' asked Duncan.

'Very comfortable, thank you. And what a treat to look at the back of a horse for a change instead of the back of a taxi-driver. Not but what me and taxi-drivers don't get on. You hear a lot of people say they're disobliging. That's not my experience of 'em at all. I went down to see Aunt Lou last August Bank, Fred, and when I got to St Pancras there wasn't a taxi to be seen.

' "Where do you want to go, mum?" the porter asked, and when I said "Peckham," he said, "You'll never get no taxi to take you to Peckham, never. There's a war on." Oh, what a dismal Jimmy! "Yes," I said, "you won't blow up Hitler if they drop you over Berlin, will you?" Well, just as I was thinking I'd have to get that South London Tube, a taxi drove up and deposited an elderly party in trousers.

"Hi," I said, "are you engaged?" "Where do you want to go, mum?" he asked. I looked him straight in the eyes and "Peckham," I said. "All right, jump in, Mar," he said, and I reely couldn't help but smile the way that porter stood staring after us when we drove off. He couldn't have stared more if I'd have been the Queen.'

'Duncan doesn't know where Peckham is,' the Sergeant-major reminded his mother.

'Doesn't he? Oh well, you go to the South Pole and take the first turning to the right,' Mrs Odd told him.

'I was never in London at all,' Duncan told her.

'Goodness gracious me, that's the second one who's said that to me inside an hour. What do you do with your-selves up here? Don't you want to go to London, Mr Macroon?'

'No, I don't believe I do at all.'

'Well, I suppose there's no accounting for tastes,' the old lady decided. 'And mind you, I don't say it isn't beau-tiful here. It is beautiful. Very beautiful. All the same, there's something about dear old London if you're a Cock-ney born and bred like what I am that makes you think London's the best place in all the world. And London done well in the war, mind you. Yes, London can take it, but Hitler can't take London. What a man, eh? Well, it's really not fair to other men to call him a man at all. A freak, that's what he is. I remember going to Barnum's freaks at Olympia in '99 – not so long after you was born, Fred, and very glad I was you had come into the world or you might have been in the freak business yourself – where was I? Oh yes, well, I sore a freak there called Jo-jo, the Dog-faced man from Siberia, and believe me, he was a human being beside Hitler. Goodness, am I letting my tongue wag? That's this Minnie as you call it. Well, I mean to say, first caperfaying with Captain MacKechnie and then All the Year Round with Father Macalister, and if I'd have had any more of it I'd have been going round with the year, that's one sure thing. What's the matter with that cow?'

An Ayrshire cow was prancing about the machair ahead of the trap.

'She's after having a dram herself,' said Duncan.

'Go on. You don't mean to say you give your cows whisky?' Mrs Odd exclaimed.

'He's pulling your leg, Ma,' said the Sergeant-major.

'I knew he must be. But, seriously, is it all right? It won't come prancing into us, will it, Mr Macroon?'

'No, no, don't you be worrying yourself, Mistress Odd,' her host reassured her.

'That reminds me, what relation exactly are you to my Fred's Peggy?'

'Och, we're pretty far away from one another.'

'But you are cousins?'

'Ay, we're distant sort of cousins.'

'So when Fred and Peggy are married, you'll be a sort of relative of mine. Oh, I'm going to call you "Duncan". I'll tell you what it is. It's always on the tip of my tongue to say Macaroon instead of Macroon. That's Fred's hand-writing, that is. When he wrote first and told me he was engaged to a girl called Peggy Macroon, I read it Mac-aroon, and in fact I told all my friends she was called Macaroon. I remember Mr Hewitson, my greengrocer, who likes a joke, and which is unusual for a greengrocer because most of the greengrocers I've known never make jokes – I think they're always worried whether they'll sell out whatever it is before it goes rotten – well, this Mr Hewitson said to me, "I suppose your son's getting married on his sweet ration, Mrs Odd?"

'"I'm sure I hope not," I said, "I know Fred's style, and he won't want something he can put in his waistcoat pocket and forget she's there." So I'll call you "Duncan" if you don't mind.'

'I'll be very pleased if you'll be calling me Duncan, Mistress Odd. I don't care at all for Mr Macroon, and if anybody calls me Lieutenant Macroon I just feel in a mind to give him a slosh in the jaw. Did you see Captain Waggett on the pier?'

'Wasn't that the feller that looked like the Boatrace, Fred? Yes, I sore him.'

'Then you've seen our aristocracy,' Duncan chuckled.

'I'll tell you somebody who I did like,' Mrs Odd said. 'And that was Father Macalister.'

'There's no better man anywhere,' Duncan declared.

'I'll add "hear, hear" to that,' said the Sergeant-major.

'Oh, I could see that the moment I set eyes on him,' Mrs Odd said. 'And what a voice! I never heard anything like it since I sat close to the double-bass in the orchestra at some play Mr and Mrs Hewitson and me went to. Mrs H. kept nudging me to look at the stage, but I couldn't take my eyes off this double-bass. A very old man he was, with a beard as big as a doormat, but what a rumble he got out of that instrument of his! You know it sort of tickled my tummy the way a toothcomb and tissue-paper used to tickle your lips when you was a kiddie. And Father Macalister's voice had the same kind of a rumble.'

'You can see my house now,' said Duncan pointing to Tigh nam Bàrd. 'The House of the Bard.'

'What's it barred against?'

'No, no, Ma. Bard means poyt,' the Sergeant-major put in.

'Are you a poyt then?' Mrs Odd asked.

'Och, yes, I'm a poet.'

'You mean you write songs and things in rhyme?' she pressed.

'In Garlic, Ma,' her son explained.

'I only knew one feller who wrote rhymes,' said Mrs Odd. 'Jack Bewick his name was. He lived in the same street where I lived when I was a girl. Off the London Road. Islington way. And I remember he frightened the life out of us once, writing a rhyme about Jack the Ripper. There was something about "sliver" and "liver". I know he got all us girls screaming before he was done.'

'Ay, Jack the Ripper,' said Duncan. 'I remember my grandmother used to talk about him. They were always afraid he would come out to the Islands and start his games here. There was a fellow called Stewart, a big joker he was – ach – you heard him give a *port a beul* at your *rèiteach*, Sergeant. Well, Michael was coming back from Kiltod one night, and he thought he'd play a joke on two chaps he saw coming along. So he put his coat up round his face and stopped them and asked where he could have a night's lodging. He could put on any kind of a voice he liked, and they didn't know who he was from Adam himself. Well, they said they didn't know where he could find a lodging at all, and he pointed to Joseph's house – it was his father's then – old John Macroon – and they said he'd never find a lodging there, because you'll understand, Fred, Peggy's grandfather was a bit of a tough nut altogether. Well, Michael drew himself up as tall as he could and he had a voice as big as Father Macalister's when he liked. "I can find a lodging anywhere," he says. "Do you know who I am? I'm Jack the Ripper." *A Dhia nan gràs*, one of them called out and fell down on his back in the ditch saying Hail Marys as fast as he could and crossing himself nineteen to the dozen but the other took to his heels, and by Jingo, he roused the whole island and Michael saw them coming along for him with pitchforks and scythes and guns and he had to take to his heels himself.'

This tale about Jack the Ripper brought them to Tigh nam Bàrd.

'Make yourself at home, Mistress Odd,' said the host. 'Do you like lobster, please?'

'Do I like lobster?' Mrs Odd exclaimed. 'I never finished eating lobster yet but what I could have eaten another clore.'

Duncan Bàn exhibited the lobsters he had secured for his guests.

'What a pair of mammoths!' she gasped in admiration. 'Look at 'em, Fred. Well, I mean, you'd only have to put them two in sentry-boxes outside Buckingham Palace and the Household Brigade could go home to bed.'

Chapter 18

THE WEDDING

———

THE wedding was timed for five o'clock in the afternoon because everybody in Little Todday, including Father Macalister himself, had a deep antipathy to what was still known in the Islands as Lloyd George's time, from the head of the Government which introduced the novelty during the First World War. The bridegroom-to-be walked in to Kiltod to make his Communion with his bride-to-be beside him, and then he parted from her until they would meet, never to part again he hoped, for the marriage ceremony.

Later on that morning Duncan drove his two guests to the head of Bàgh Mhic Ròin where Kenny met them with the *Morning Star* and took them out to see the half of the *Cabinet Minister* that was left lying on the Gobha, with the other half almost completely submerged.

'And that's where it all comes from, is it?' said Mrs Odd. 'Well, I never thought I'd live to see a proper shipwreck after seeing so many in panto.'

'Would you like to come down into the hold, Mrs Odd?' Kenny asked. 'I'll take you down if you like. You have to go down a rope.'

'I think that's a bit beyond my mother, Kenny,' said the Sergeant-major. 'No, it's not that you couldn't do it, Ma,' he added quickly. 'But you'd get covered with a sort of black oil, and don't forget I'm getting married this afternoon.'

'Och, I wouldn't be spoiling an adventure for anything,' Duncan urged in support. 'But you'd come out looking like a Hottentot, Mistress Odd, and your clothes would be in a terrible mess.'

So the old lady allowed herself to be dissuaded from descending into the hold of the *Cabinet Minister*, once she had made it clear that it was not her lack of physical capacity which was in question. As the *Morning Star* chugged slowly round the wrecked ship she was much delighted by the hundreds of puffins swimming in the water all round them.

'I never saw such comical-looking objecks,' she declared. 'They're a bit like a bookie I used to know – Sam Orgles. He died of heart failure coming home from Hurst Park. A nice feller he was too. Never owed nobody a farthing. What is it you call these birds? Puffins? Yes, that's right. Well, funny thing, but this Sam Orgles used to puff a lot.'

Anything more that might have transpired about Sam Orgles was interrupted by the sudden appearance from the water of the head of an Atlantic seal, just in front of the *Morning Star*.

'Whatever was that?' Mrs Odd exclaimed as the animal dived again and was lost to view. 'A seal? Well, talk about likenesses! I said these puffins reminded me of Sam Orgles, but that *was* Mr Dumpleton.'

'Who's Mr Dumpleton?' Duncan Bàn asked.

'My butcher in Nottingham. Yes, that seal was Mr Dumpleton to the life. Same pop eyes and thick neck and bulging forehead. I won't half pull his leg when I get back. "You've started early this year with your bathing," I'll say to him. I only wish Mr Hewitson looked like a seal – he's my greengrocer – because Mr H. is more one for a good laugh than what Mr D. is. But really that likeness! It was uncanny. If he'd stayed up above water for another minute I'd have been asking him for a nice undercut.'

When Mrs Odd returned from her marine excursion, her son took her for a walk to Tràigh Swish.

'What sands, Fred!' she exclaimed. 'I mean to say sands like that put Margate off the map. Margate's nowhere. Nowhere at all. Or Ramsgate either. A pity they aren't full of people.'

'I don't know so much about that, Mar. I think crowds of people'ud spoil them,' he objected.

'Well, I like to see people enjoying theirselves. This'ud be a proper paradise for kids, and there isn't a soul in sight from one end of it to the other. It's wasted, away up here.'

'It wasn't wasted for me,' said the Sergeant-major. 'Two years ago all but a day I told Peggy I loved her just about where you and me are sitting on the grass now. It was on a Sunday actually, and the date was April 27th. It was a lovely day the same as what it is now, and the macker was covered with daisies the same as what it is now.'

'Macker? What's that?'

'Macker's what they call all this grassy land. Garlic. And I remember Peggy was making herself a bracelet out of daisies while I was telling her the old old story, and I took the bracelet from her and stuck it in this pocket.' He pointed to the pocket over his heart. 'And I've got that withered daisy-bracelet put away in my blotter, and where it'll remain till death do us part.'

'She wouldn't have you at first, would she, Fred?'

'Well, she wouldn't say "yes"; but mark you, she didn't say "no" either. Oh, I firmly believe that if I hadn't have been sent off to Devonshire and then to Africar in the autumn of '41 you'd have been Granny Odd today. Still, there you are, war's war, and human beings get pushed about like luggage in time of war.'

'That's quite right, Fred, pushed about and bumped about a good deal in the pushing. Well, I'm glad I'm not Hitler. Fancy going to bed every night and knowing that millions of people all over the world were wishing you'd never wake up. Oh well, you've had to wait two years, Fred; but as I told Peggy yesterday afternoon when I went in and had those few words with her alone, she was worth waiting for.'

Mother and son sat silent for a minute or two, gazing at the pale-blue ocean breaking placidly upon the lonely expanse of long white beach.

'What's that bird I can hear singing as sweet as a canary?' Mrs Odd asked presently.

'That's a lark, Ma.'

'Yes, he sounds as if he was enjoying himself, the pretty dear,' she said. 'Well, you may grumble at having had to wait so long for Peggy, but you're a lucky feller, Fred. Most men when they reach forty-five have forgotten what it was to be in love, and here are you as soppy as a kid in a Sunday school making goo-goo eyes at the girl who lives round the corner. Well, when you're lying snug with Peggy in your arms tonight, do you know where I shall be?'

'In bed too I should hope.'

'Oh no, I shall be out here.'

'Out here?' the Sergeant-major exclaimed.

'Yes, Duncan's invited me out here to see the fairies by the light of the moon.'

'He's apt to come out here and drink a lot,' the Sergeant-major warned his mother.

'Never mind. If he shows me fairies whether he's two-pence on the can or as sober and la-di-da as one of them B.B.C. announcers, I'll go back to Nottingham very pleased with myself. Did he ever tell you about that fairy who came in regular three winters ago and washed all his clothes for him?'

'I have heard him talk about her, yes,' the Sergeant-major admitted cautiously.

'Well, what a godsend for the man! I mean to say, if there's one thing that's gone to pieces more than anything in this blessed war it's laundries. I still do most of my own washing, as you know. But three weeks ago I sent a sheet to the laundry, and really when it came back Peggy could have worn it for a bridal veil it was so full of holes.'

'I think Duncan was imagining this fairy washerwoman, Ma,' her son argued. 'I don't think you ought to take him quite seriously. He's a good chap. I wouldn't want a better for a best man. But he does put away the whisky sometimes.'

'You mean to say his fairies are just the D.T.s?'

'No, I wouldn't go so far as that. I think it's more his fanciful nature. And which *is* very fanciful.'

'Well, you never know. I'm not going to feel sure of anything I mightn't see after that seal who came up and had a squint at us. I mean, look at the story about this seal-woman who was the mother of all these Macroons. Well, I wouldn't have believed that if I hadn't seen with my own orbs that seal who was the living double of my butcher in Nottingham. And after all Macroon, by what Duncan Bang tells me, means "son of the seal" in Garlic. There must have been something in it for them to get their name in the first place. You don't go calling anybody the son of a seal for nothing,' Mrs Odd declared firmly.

'Yes, but it was all a long time ago,' her son pointed out.

'So was Adam and Eve, and if a big snake started off talking to Eve and edging her on to eat fruit strickly forbidden for her to eat, don't tell me a seal couldn't have been half-human once upon a time.'

'Yes, but this fairy of Duncan's was supposed to have done his washing for him in the first winter of this war,' said the Sergeant-major. 'That's not very long ago.'

'Well, perhaps I won't meet her. Or again perhaps I will. Anyway, this beach'll look like a transformation scene by moonlight and I'm going to make the most of my holiday. We may not see fairies in Nottingham any more, or even in dear old London, but that doesn't say we mightn't see them here. And if a fairy had have looked over your shoulder when you was courting Peggy here two years ago, would you have been as surprised as all that?'

The Sergeant-major tossed his head.

'Perhaps I shouldn't,' he agreed with a smile.

Mrs Odd had been invited down to Kiltod to join in a small family dinner before the ceremony in church. The bridegroom and his best man were bidden to present themselves at the bride's house to lead the procession to the wedding sharp at a quarter to five. Neither of Peggy's two married sisters had been able to leave the cares of wartime households to be present, and John, her elder brother, was away at sea; but Peigi Bheag, the schoolteacher at Barra, was at home, and determined to follow her younger sister's example by marrying Neil MacNeil in the summer holidays. The rest of the company was made up of aunts and uncles and cousins living in Little Todday.

'*A Dhia*, your mother's a very fine woman,' Joseph Macroon said to his all but son-in-law when the Sergeant-major supported by Duncan Macroon arrived at the house of the bride's father. 'Full of stories. She took my mind off that catastrophe.'

'What catastrophe?' the Sergeant-major asked.

'The whisky catastrophe. I was thinking about those two hundred and sixteen bottles when I was putting out the bottles for this evening.'

The procession for church was lined up ready for to start. First went the bridegroom, who had so far broken with the professional etiquette of years of soldiering as to stick a nosegay of daisies in his uniform, with his bride upon his arm, she in a bridal dress of real white silk made up from that of her eldest sister, Peigi Mhòr, who was as tall as herself. Then came Duncan Bàn Macroon with Kate Anne, the bridesmaid, in white artificial silk, obtained it must be confessed through the kindly offices of a case of Minnie. Joseph Macroon, his ceremonial bowler bearing the scars of that whisky catastrophe, went next with Mrs Odd upon his arm, the old lady beaming with delight. Other couples of relations followed, and on either side of the procession Kenny and a young friend of his fired off shot-guns into the air all the way up to the church.

After the ceremony a much longer procession formed up to walk round and be greeted by as many families as possible before it was time to gather at the tables that had been spread in the parish hall. Many friends had come over from Great Todday in the *Flying Fish* and the *Kittiwake*, all of whom took part in the procession. Over the green machair in the golden light of that afternoon at April's end the long line of couples walked laughing and chatting, with not so much firing as Kenny and his friends would have liked owing to the famine of cartridges. Even the few that were fired made Captain Waggett shake his head censoriously.

'They've no business to be wasting ammunition like that,' he told his wife who was on his arm. 'I'm surprised Sergeant-major Odd doesn't stop it. They simply will not remember there's a war on.'

'Oh well, Paul, people only get married once,' she pleaded. 'That is, I mean, nice people.'

'I'm glad we're going to be married in Glasgow,' George Campbell was saying to Catriona Macleod.

'Would you be ashamed, then, to be walking with me in front just now?' she asked.

'No, darling, of course not, but it is very public. And I feel relieved to think that when we go off tomorrow the Sergeant-major and Peggy will get all the attention. They may forget we're going to be married at all,' he added hopefully.

'Don't you be thinking that, George,' she told him, and with justice, considering the number of her girl friends in Great Todday with whom Catriona had discussed that going away.

The houses at which the bride and bridegroom stopped to be greeted were all flying small flags, including at two the Japanese flag the nationality of which was unknown to those who flew it. Anyway, what did it matter? The flags were not flown to celebrate an international event but to express in colour the pleasure of the people of Little Todday that Peigi Ealasaid was married to the Sarchant.

'Och, they're good people, right enough,' the Biffer declared to Bean a'Bhiffer who was moving along upon his arm with her usual placidity. 'I'll never forget the way they welcomed us that night when Drooby and I went over to fetch the first case of Minnie we ever had.'

And to Bean Ailein on his arm Drooby was expressing the same sentiments.

Dr Maclaren had taken for his partner Roderick Mac-Rurie's daughter Annag, who was representing her father at the wedding.

'And when are you going to be walking at the head of a procession like this?' he asked.

'Och, indeed, I don't know, Doctor,' she replied sadly. 'I believe I'll soon be on the shelf.'

'Ay, you'll soon be twenty-one, Annag,' he chuckled. 'Never mind, I believe the war will be over before you're an old *cailleach*, and he'll be home again.'

'I don't know at all what you're talking about, Doctor.'

'Oh no, you don't know, do you?'

'It's pity George Campbell and Catriona aren't being married in Snorvig,' she said, changing the subject. 'We could have had some fine fun.'

'George wasn't taking any risks,' the Doctor laughed. 'George didn't see himself being undressed by half a dozen of his friends at the end of the evening and bedded with the bride.'

'Och, really, Doctor, what terrible things you say!'

'Now, don't be a humbug, Annag. You know perfectly well you'd have been in the lead yourself at undressing the bride.'

'What you think about!'

'What I think about at this moment is what a foolish old bachelor I feel.'

He looked round at the merry procession following the bride and bridegroom over the green machair on that golden afternoon – Alec Mackinnon and the teacher from a small school on the other side of Little Todday, Andrew Thomson and Mrs Thomson, Andrew Chisholm and Mrs Chisholm, John Beaton and Mrs Beaton, Angus Mac-Cormac and Bean Aonghais, Sammy MacCodrum and Bean Shomhairle, Hugh Macroon and Bean Uisdein, Jockey Stewart and Bean Yockey, old Michael Macroon the joker with his plump grand-niece Peigi Bheag whose

heart was in Barra with her own young man and wasn't
bothering about a young partner as Neil himself was not
there, couple after couple of them, and twenty couples
more. Good wishes from every house they passed and
shrill cheers from the children. Flags waving in the gentle
breeze. The daisies already crimson with sleep. The whim-
brels in the distance crying that May was almost here.
Larks and wheatears and stonechats everywhere.

'Peggy, darling Peggy,' the bridegroom turned to mu-
mur to his bride. 'I never thought anybody *could* be as
happy as what I am.'

'*Mo ghràidh*,' she murmured back, her deep-blue slanting eyes alive.

'What *does* that mean? I've wanted to ask a lot of
people, but I never would.'

'It means "my love",' she told him tenderly. 'It means
my love, *a ghràidh mo chridhe*.'

'Mar isn't half enjoying herself with your dad,' exclaimed the bridegroom, too much overcome by emotion
to say a word in reply to the exquisitely welcome words
from his Peggy.

'I think she's just a beautiful *cailleach*, Fred. She's been
so sweet to me.'

'She's going out on Tràigh Swish with Duncan tonight,
looking for fairies.'

'I'm sure if anybody would be seeing them, it's herself
would be seeing them,' Peggy replied.

When the procession reached the parish hall, the feast
had been spread by Kate Anne with the help of her
friends Flora, Morag, and Mairead and some of the older
women. Muscular fowls and cold mutton were in abund-
ance. Bottles of beer, tactfully ordered in quantity from
Big Roderick, were waiting to prepare the way for the
whisky, half a dozen bottles of which had also been tactfully ordered from Roderick. Pre-war pickles had been
unearthed. Synthetic fruit juices were there to sustain
those who did not drink beer or whisky until tea was
served. There were heaps of chalk-white Glasgow bread

interspersed with healthier home-made scones and bannocks. The wedding-cake owing to a mishap in the baking
rose like the leaning tower of Pisa in the middle of the
table.

Father Macalister sat on the bride's right, Mrs Odd sat
on his other side. Duncan Bàn was next. Old Bean Sheu-
mais Mhìceil, the senior matriarch of the Macroons, sat
next the bridegroom, and on the other side was her
nephew Joseph.

'*A bhòbh bhòbh*,' Joseph had muttered to himself when
he found that Mrs Waggett was to be on his other side.

Before the speeches Duncan Bàn was called upon to
read out the sheaf of telegrams which had arrived during
the morning, half of them in Gaelic half in English and at
least a dozen of them expressing a hope that all the
troubles of the married pair might be little ones.

'Ah well, Mrs Odd,' said the parish priest with a deep
sigh, 'original eloquence is pretty rare. Thank God, he's
nearly come to the end of them.'

There were many speeches, but the substance of most of
them has already been heard at the *rèiteach*. On this occasion Joseph Macroon, under the influence of the whisky
catastrophe and the failure to obtain any support for his
proposed licence to sell spirituous liquors in Little Todday,
made no allusion either to a new road or a new school. He
was content to be the father of the bride. Captain Waggett, too, kept himself strictly to the utterance of the
conventional speech made at weddings. He made no
allusion to the *Cabinet Minister*.

The only really new contribution to the convivial
oratory of Kiltod was the speech made by Mrs Odd in rising to reply to the toast proposed to her both by Duncan
Bàn and Joseph Macroon.

'Well, I can't very well say I'm not accustomed to talking
because it's a well-known fact that I can talk the hind-
legs off a donkey, as the saying goes. All the same, ladies
and gentlemen, this is the first time in all my life as I've
got up on my tootsies and made a regular speech. Well,

first of all I must say what a joy it has been to an old woman to find her only son making such a sensible choice as what Fred has made in marrying my daughter-in-lore Peggy. You'll often hear that mothers-in-lore are a nuisance, and which in fact I think they very often are. Well, my son will tell you I've never tried to interfere with him ever since he was on his own. Mind you, I don't say there weren't times when I wanted to interfere, yes, and when I felt I ought to interfere. But I never did, and I'm certainly not going to start in trying to interfere now. If he doesn't know his own mind at his age, nobody else is going to know it for him, that's one sure thing.

'And I'll tell you this, ladies and gentlemen, apart from falling in love with my daughter-in-lore, he fell in love with Little Today itself.'

'Good shooting!' ejaculated Father Macalister.

'And I don't blame him,' the old lady went on. 'I've fallen in love with Little Today myself.' (*Loud applause.*) 'Unfortunately my stay here this time will be all too short, but, make no mistake about it, I'm coming back to spend a real holiday here as soon as ever I can. Let 'em try and ask at the railway station if my journey is really necessary and see what answer they get from me. Protected Area? This isn't the only area that needs a bit of protection these days. There's plenty of areas where I live in Nottingham wants a bit of police protection. Bu then I always was a bit of a Radical. My old man often used to say to me, "Eliza," he used to say, "you're a proper Radical." So you haven't seen the last of me. I don't know whether Duncan Bang here will invite me back to stay with him ...'

'Don't you be afraid of that, Mistress Odd,' Duncan bubbled.

'And I hope my son's father-in-lore'll ask me.'

'You'll have the freedom of Little Today, Mrs Odd,' the parish priest proclaimed in his most sonorous bass.

'Well, for once in my life I don't know as I've anything much more to say except to thank you one and all for your kindness to me and my son. I can't hardly believe that I only landed here yesterday afternoon, for I never felt so much at home since I left dear old London. And the only time I ever saw fairyland before was the other side of the footlights.'

'*A Dhia*, what kind of lights are they at all?' Joseph muttered.

'The lighting at a theatre,' Mrs Waggett whispered to him.

'But now here I am right in the middle of fairyland. God bless you all!'

The old lady sat down amid a tumult of applause.

'That was really beautiful, Mrs Odd,' Father Macalister assured her. 'You'll need a small sensation after that. What have you there, Duncan?'

'White Label, Father. Duty paid.'

'Ay, the white label of a blameless life, Mr Waggett. The duty on this has been paid,' said the parish priest, with a profound sigh.

'I'm very glad to hear it, Father Macalister.'

'I'm sure you will be, Mr Waggett. I'm sure you will be.'

'Did you get this from Ruairidh Mór, Joseph?' he asked, turning to his host.

'I did, Father.'

'Ay, you're a great diplomat, Joseph,' the priest assured him gravely.

When the bridal feast was eaten and the speeches all made, the hall was cleared for a dance. The absence of so many of the island's young men made this less of a jollification than usual, and there were more songs than dances. Duncan Bàn, of course, had composed a special one, and his epithalamium was received with rapturous applause. Joseph Macroon delivered one of the *sgeulachdan* or tales for which he was famous. Her inability to follow the Gaelic was a grief to Mrs Odd, for she was sure by the expression on her host's face and the laughter of the audience that the tale he was telling was a really saucy one. Father Macalister, who sang seldom nowadays, gave them two songs which put the audience into an ecstasy.

At last the time came for the bridal reel which was danced only by the bride, the bridegroom, the bridesmaid, and the *fleasgach* or best man. Neither the Sergeant-major nor Duncan Bàn was a first-class performer at a reel, but any awkwardness they displayed was more than made up for by the grace and beauty of the dancing of the two girls, whose white forms in a shower of pre-war confetti unearthed for the occasion like the pickles made by Mrs Odd declare that they could knock sparks off anybody she'd seen in the panto for donkey's years.

'But Fred's very clumsy,' she declared. 'Very clumsy indeed. He gets that from his father. I was always very quick on my tootsies.'

More songs followed, and then about ten o'clock came the last reel.

'Now you're going to see something very peculiar, Mrs Odd,' Father Macalister told her. 'After they've been dancing for a while you'll see a couple of the girls come in and steal away the bride and another girl will take her place. That's to cheat the fairies in case they took it into their heads to steal away the bride themselves. They'll think the bride is still dancing.'

'So there *are* fairies about?' Mrs Odd asked, looking at the priest very seriously.

'That's the idea. Then in a minute you'll see the bridegroom look round and find that the bride has vanished, and two or three friends of his will come along and lead him away to where she is, and somebody else will take his place to cheat the fairies again.'

The parish priest did not add that these friends would then proceed to undress the bridegroom and bring him along to the room of the bride who would already have been undressed by her guardians.

As a matter of fact, owing to the Sergeant-major's comparative seniority and his not being a native, he escaped the further attentions of those who led him away from the hall after the mischief of the fairies had been foiled by the stealing away of the bride by Flora, Morag, and Mairead.

They were joined, when the last reel had been danced, by Kate Anne and Peigi Bheag, who had taken her sister's place in the reel. If the bridegroom escaped, the bride was spared nothing, and the shrieks of mirth coming from the bridal chamber made the bridegroom wonder what on earth was happening.

Back in the hall the party still went on.

'Unfortunately, you'll be leaving us tomorrow, Mrs Odd,' Father Macalister told her, 'but if you lived here there would have been a gathering in your house tomorrow night. That's what we call the *bainis tighe* or house wedding.'

'You don't mean to let anyone forget they've been married on Little Todday,' Mrs Odd observed. 'But I'm sorry I haven't got a house here. We'd have made a proper night of it again tomorrow.'

At about eleven the guests from over the water gathered to make their way down to the harbour, and the wedding party broke up, although at Joseph's house the uproarious friends of the bride were still making as much noise as ever, and the Sergeant-major in his pyjamas kept coming out of his dressing-room and then dodging back into it again as another peal of mirth came from the bridal chamber.

'Aren't you glad we're being married quietly in Glasgow, Catriona?' George Campbell asked when they heard the laughter coming from the post-office on their way down to the harbour.

'I don't know. It would have been fun here right enough,' Catriona said a little wistfully. 'Still, it wouldn't have been much fun with Norman away,' she added. 'I hope he'll get leave to come to Glasgow for us on Saturday.'

'Well, well,' said Dr Maclaren, overtaking them at that moment, 'if I weren't the only doctor in the two islands I'd come to Glasgow and give you away myself, Catriona. And how's your mother bearing up, George?'

'She's fine, thank you, Doctor.'

'Well, see and ask me up to have a meal with you, Catriona, when you and George get back.'

'We surely will, Doctor.'

'I'll be glad when Norman gets back. You know, I miss that brother of yours a lot. That's quite a nice wee lassie they've put in charge of Watasett school.'

'Effie MacNaughton,' said Catriona. 'Yes, she's very nice. She'd make you a good wife, Doctor.'

'Ach, get away with you. I'm too old a hand to be caught now. Duncan Bàn and I were born to be bachelors.'

'You never know. I'm sure George never thought he'd be anything but a bachelor for the rest of his days,' Catriona laughed.

'And he would have been if it hadn't been for what Father Macalister calls St Minnie,' the Doctor chuckled. 'There wasn't quite so much of it this evening as there was at the *rèiteach*. Joseph's not going to take any risks. It's fetching five pounds a case now. And I hear the Excise people are likely to make an example of one or two presently. Ah well, all good things come to an end,' he sighed.

While the Great Todday guests were making their way down to the harbour, Duncan Macroon was harnessing up his pony preparatory to driving Mrs Odd back to Tigh nam Bàrd. Soon she was seated beside him and jogging homeward along the metalled track that ran westward over the machair from Kiltod, a humpbacked moon in full silver shining to the south. After a couple of miles they turned off to take the grassy track that led to Duncan's house, driving now in the moon's eye. Now that the rattle of the heels and the clip-clop of the pony's hooves were muffled the long sigh of the Atlantic was audible.

'Just like when you hold a shell to your ears,' Mrs Odd commented. 'Well, I must say I think it's a much nicer way of winding up a wedding than flinging a lot of rice and old shoes at a hired motor-car. But *did* these fairies ever steal away a bride?'

'Och, I believe they will have once upon a time,' Duncan replied. 'Otherwise why should we still be taking such precautions?'

'Um, that's quite right,' the old lady agreed pensively. 'As you say there'd be no sense in carrying on like that, would there? Still, these fairies would have had a tricky job carrying off Peggy. She's no wurzit.'

'Wurzit? What's that at all?' Duncan asked.

'Well, I suppose it's short for "where is it?" It's what we used to call anybody who was a bit smallified. And you wouldn't call my daughter-in-law small, would you?'

'That wouldn't trouble the fairies,' Duncan assured her.

'It wouldn't? But I always thought fairies were such teeny-weenies. Of course at the panto they're usually a lot of whopping fat kids, but the County Council would create if they employed tiny tots.'

'Ay, they're wee right enough, the fairies, but they're terrible strong,' Duncan declared. 'Look at the *sluagh* and what it can do.'

'The slewer. Whatever on earth's that?' she exclaimed.

'It isn't on earth at all, Mistress Odd ...'

'Here, I don't want to interrupt, but I meant to say this before. I like being called Mistress Odd. But go on about this slewer.'

'The *sluagh* is the fairy host, thousands and thousands and thousands of small glittering craytures. My grandfather saw them once.'

'He did?'

'Ay, just about where we are now.'

'Good gracious! What did they do?'

'They didn't do anything at all. They just swept past him like a wind of gold at sunrise on a summer morning. He was lucky, though. There was a cousin of my grandfather's living in Little Todday then, and the *sluagh* would never be leaving him alone at all. Michael Macroon was his name. He'd be sitting in his room and he would hear the *sluagh* coming for him. "Hold the door, friends," he used to call out, and they'd be holding the door as hard as they could. But it was no use at all. In the door would come, and there'd be a great rushing like a wind and Michael would be gone.'

'Gone?' Mrs Odd ejaculated.

'And the next thing would be that Michael would turn up again from where the *sluagh* took him. They took him to Islay once, and they took him to the top of the Clisham ... that's a big hill in Harris. And once they took him over to Ireland....'

'To Ireland?' she interjected in amazement. 'Go on, you're kidding, Duncan.'

'No, no, it's as true as I'm standing here. It was nearly three weeks before he got back to Little Todday.'

'And your grandfather saw these slewers just about where we're standing now?'

'Just about here.'

'Well, I wouldn't mind if they took me to Nottingham, even if they do sound a bit bloodthirsty. It'ud save a lot of messing about in trains. It wouldn't half give Mr Dumpleton a shock if he saw me arriving like a golden blitz. It's a pity these slewers can't get hold of Hitler and drop him inside one of these volcanoes. That'ud be well on the way to where he's going one day. Well, I'm glad they didn't cop Fred tonight. He'd have felt a bit chilly on top of a mounting.' She chuckled to herself. 'You know, it's wicked of me to say it, but I reely should have had to laugh. Poor Fred! What a disappointment!'

'Well, maybe we'll see the *sluagh* when we go on the Tràigh presently,' said Duncan.

'I'd sooner see this fairy washerwoman of yours. But wait a moment, Duncan, what size was she? I mean to say, if she wasn't bigger than half a dot how did she manage your washing?'

'She was about the size of a large midget. Och, she'd be all of two foot tall. We used to have great talks together.'

'In Garlic I take it?'

'Och yes, she'd never be talking the English.'

'What sort of clothes did she wear?'

'She had a green dress and a green cloak, and when she was washing for me she would put her cloak over a chair and lay her hat on it. A tall hat it was with a point to it. And when she'd finished the washing she'd climb up and sit in my grandmother's chair. Och, she was the sweetest wee crayture you ever saw, with a voice as soft as the falling dew. I remember fine the last night she came. It was a clear warm night in June, and when she was after finishing my washing she climbed up into the chair and she said, "O Duncan Bàn,' she said, "O Duncan Bàn, you'll never be seeing me again, and who's going to be washing your clothes for you next winter I'm sure I don't know." And when I was going to speak back to her the kind wee crayture was gone.'

'And you've never seen her since?' Mrs Odd asked in awe.

'Never a glimpse of her since the month of June 1940.'

They drove on in silence till they reached Tigh nam Bàrd, and after Duncan had fed the pony he came back to ask his guest if she still felt inclined to come on the Tràigh.

'I wouldn't miss that treat for anything,' she declared.

So they walked down to the long stretch of sand gleaming with the silver of the moon. Presently they sat down upon a tussock of grass and listened to the melodious lapping of the tide all the length of the beach, and to the vast whisper of the ocean upon that tranquil midnight.

Duncan produced a bottle of Bard's Bounty and poured out a dram for his guest and himself.

'Here's to when we meet again, Mrs Odd. And don't be forgetting that there's always a room for you in Tigh nam Bàrd.'

'And we will meet again,' she declared. 'I've been making plans, I have. How about if I was to build myself a little house on Little Today? And then when Fred and Peggy come down to Nottingham after the war and take over the shop I could make myself scarce, and they could come up here for their holidays while I looked after the business in Nottingham.'

'You needn't build yourself a house, Mistress Odd. In fact, the way the rascals are carrying on, you wouldn't be able to build yourself a house just now, I believe. But there's a house just about half a mile away from my own, which I'm sure you could get for a reasonable price. I'll show it to you tomorrow morning before you go away.'

'That would be grand.'

'Ay, it would be grand right enough. I believe you really have fallen in love with Little Todday, Mistress Odd.'

'Except for dear old London I never like a place so much in all my life,' she affirmed.

'Mind you, it was pretty glum before St Minnie arrived,' he told her. 'And it may be pretty glum again when St Minnie is gone. Och, but it won't be glum when the war is over and the boys are home from the sea.'

'Duncan, why didn't you ever marry?' she asked suddenly.

'Och, that's a sad story. And she didn't leave me with a kind word like my dear fairy. No, no, just rang me up on the telephone when I went back to the University after my grandmother died and said she was going to marry quite another chap altogether.'

'Well, all I've got to say is she was a very silly girl,' Mrs Odd declared vigorously. 'Very silly indeed.'

'Have another dram of Bard's Bounty, Mistress Odd.'

'One more, and one more for yourself, Duncan Bang, and then I'm going to toddle back and get to bed.'

They pledged one another again.

'Well, I've talked a lot and laughed a lot and shed one or two quiet tears in Little Todday,' Mrs Odd said. 'Still, I've done as much in other places. But I've never drunk so much anywhere as what I've drunk in Little Todday. And I don't suppose I ever will again. Well, thank goodness, we haven't got an early start. I'm going to have a jolly good lay in bed tomorrow morning. Do you know what time they got me up on Monday so as to get here for the wedding? Four o'clock. What a game, eh? It was the first time I've felt my age since years ago they let our rooms over our head in Margate and me and my late husband had to sleep on the beach and it come on to pour about four o'clock in the morning. Fred was warm enough. He was in Indiar at the time, and I wished I was. It was a year after he became a drummer-boy. Well, if I stay jabbering much longer I'll be sleeping on the beach here, and, not being a fairy myself, I'd get a nice go of the rheumatics.'

Mrs Odd rose and they walked back to Duncan Bàn's house. In the doorway she paused to look back for a moment at the silver rim of the Atlantic beyond the moon-drenched machair. A curlew fluted somewhere by the tide's edge.

'Tootle-oo to you,' she said. 'But you'll be seeing me again.'

And the curlew fluted once more.

GLOSSARY OF
THE GAELIC EXPRESSIONS

*The pronunciation indicated in brackets is
only roughly approximate*

CHAPTER 1

CHAPTER 2

CHAPTER 3

page

42 *a bhalaich* (a vahlich) O boy
42 *rèiteach* (raytchach) betrothal
43 *a Mhaighstir Seumas* (a vysh-chir shamus) O Mr James

CHAPTER 4

59 *a nighinn* (a neein) O daughter
59 *truaghan* (trooaghan) poor creature
59 *a mhammi* (a vammy) O mammy

CHAPTER 5

81 *beannachd leibh* (byannak leev) good-bye with you
86 *Uisge beatha gu leòir* (ooshki beh-ha gul-yor) Whisky galore. *Gu leòir* is almost the only Gaelic phrase which has passed into English so nearly like the original

CHAPTER 6

87 *Ruairidh Mór* (rooary mor) Big Roderick
101 *Céilidh* (cayley) literally visit, but used for any entertainment

CHAPTER 7

103 *matà* (matah) then
103 *Feumaidh mi falbh* (faym-ey me falav) I must be going
104 *Seall, Uisdein* (shoul, ooshdjin) Look, Hugh
105 *chaca* (hahca) dirt
106 *Nach ist thu* (nach isht oo) Will you not be quiet
107 *sìthein* (shee-in) fairy hill
109 *bean* (ben) literally woman. Used for wife. I do not know how to write the genitive of Jockey in Gaelic, but the effect is of 'Y' in English
109 *A Mhuire mhàthair* (a voorye vahair) O Mary Mother. *Mhuire* is reserved in Gaelic for the Blessed Virgin *Màiri* is used as a Christian name
109 *a Chairistiona* (a haristcheeona) O Christina
111 *siorram* (shirra) sheriff
112 *cailleach* (calyach) old woman

GLOSSARY

114   *dreathan-donn* (dreean down) brown wren

114   *Seadh gu dearbh* (shay gu jerrav) Yes indeed

116   *Am bheil Gàidhlig agaibh?* ('m vail ga-ylic acav) Have
      you Gaelic?

121   *Co tha'n sud?* (co hah'n shüt) Who is there?

CHAPTER 8

125   *A Chruthadair* (a chrooatir) O Creator. A variant of
      Cruithear which is also spelt *Cruithfhear*

127   *Móran taing* (moran tang) Many thanks

130   *poit dhubh* (poytch goo) black pot

130   *Leodhasach* (lyosach) Lewisman

133   *Mac an diabhoil* (mac an jeeol) son of the devil

CHAPTER 9

143   *Ceart gu leoir* (carst gul-yor) right in plenty

143   *Eisd* (eeshd) listen

144   *Todach* a Toddayman

150   *a chàirdean* (a haarshtjan) O friends

CHAPTER 10

158   *tha* (hah) it is

158   *chan 'eil* (hahn-yale) it is not

161   *Glè mhath* (clay vah) very good

162   *deoch an doruis* (joch an doris) drink at the door

CHAPTER 11

181   *mo chridhe* (mo chree) my heart

CHAPTER 12

183   *Thig a stigh* (hick a sty) Come in

185   *Sgoileir Dubh* (skolir dooh) dark scholar, literally black.
      Dubh, bàn (fair) and *ruadh* (red-haired) with more rarely
      donn (brown) are common additions to names and
      occupations

187   *Peigi Ealasaid Nic Ròin i.e.* Peggy Elizabeth Macroon.